Bellerophon's Champion

Pennywhistle at Trafalgar

BELLEROPHON'S CHAMPION

PENNYWHISTLE AT TRAFALGAR

BY

JOHN M. DANIELSKI

www.penmorepress.com

ISBN-13: 978-1-946409-86-7 (Paperback)
ISBN :-978-1-946409-87-4(e-book)

BISAC Subject Headings:
FIC014000FICTION / Historical
FIC032000FICTION / War & Military

Editor: Chris Wozney

Cover Illustration by
The Book Cover Whisperer:
ProfessionalBookCoverDesign.com

Please send all correspondence to:

Penmore Press LLC
920 N Javelina Pl
Tucson AZ 85748

Dramatis Personae on HMS *Bellerophon*

1st Lieutenant Thomas Pennywhistle, Royal Marines
2nd Lieutenant Luke Higgins, Royal Marines
2nd Lieutenant Peter Wilson, Royal Marines
Captain James Wemyss, Royal Marines
Sergeant Andrew Dale, Royal Marines
Private Martin Combs, Royal Marines
Private James Warwick, Royal Marines
Private Jonathan Edmonds, Royal Marines
Captain John Cooke, Royal Navy
Lieutenant William Cumby, Royal Navy
Lieutenant David Scott, Royal Navy
Lieutenant Edward Thomas, Royal Navy
Lieutenant James Douglas, Royal Navy
Lieutenant George Saunders, Royal Navy
Midshipman James Jewell, Royal Navy
Midshipman James Barron, Royal Navy
Midshipman Thomas Barron, Royal Navy
Midshipman Charles Barrow, Royal Navy
Midshipman James Fairbrother, Royal Navy
Midshipman Thomas Walker, Royal Navy
Able Seaman Peter MacFarlane, Royal Navy
Able Seaman James Parker, Royal Navy
Able Seaman, Roger Perry, Royal Navy
Able Seaman Colin Ferguson, Royal Navy
Quartermaster Geordie Ferguson, Royal Navy
Landsman George Jepson, Royal Navy
Landsman Piers Jansen, Royal Navy
Edward Overton, Sailing Master
Russell Mart, Carpenter
Thomas Robinson, Boatswain
Thomas Jewell, Purser

John Stevenson, Gunner
Alexander Whyte, Surgeon
Roger Godwin, Schoolmaster
Jonathan Hazard, Captain's Secretary
Mary Stevenson, Gunner's Wife
Nancy Overton, Master's Wife

Animals

Screwloose, Ship's Cat
Mau, Mr. Pennywhistle's Cat
Archer, Mr. Douglas's Dog
Mrs. Taffy, Wardroom Goat
Jobu, Midshipman Jewell's Monkey

1/80 Scale Model of HMS *Bellerophon*.
(The lateen sail on the mizzen mast was replaced shortly
after commissioning with a spanker sail.)

DEDICATION

This book is dedicated to Joe H. who assisted in a hundred great and subtle ways; and to the memory of David Sadler whose tart tongue and generous heart will be greatly missed.

Special acknowledgment to Chris Wozney, who showed me the right path when I lost my way.

PRELUDE

Edinburgh, Scotland: 21ˢᵗ July, 1802

The only thing worse than finding out that a woman you love has committed suicide is being the first to discover the body. Thomas Pennywhistle had just exited the front door of the townhouse when he heard the gunshot.

"No, no! Please God, let it not be!" he muttered as he raced back through the foyer to the library door. It was locked from the inside. He pounded it hard in fear and frustration. "Caroline! Caroline!" he shouted frantically even as he knew there would likely be no answer.

He regarded Caroline Murray as more a sister than a second cousin because they had spent so much time together as children. Since being cruelly deserted by her fiancé the week before, she had cried incessantly, eaten little and slept less. Her father had requested that he speak with her in the desperate hope that his warm, kind words would call her out of a deep melancholy that seemed to worsen with each passing day.

"It was my father's fault," she tearfully proclaimed. "He only consented to the match because I pitched so many fits. Boots—that is my pet name for my dear heart—broke the engagement because he was afraid of my father."

Pennywhistle formed a mental picture of a handsome gentleman of polished manners with no discernible source of income: the classic fortune hunter who had fixed his sights upon a well provided, naïve heiress. As with all cads of that caste, the gentleman had no doubt listened to her carefully, treated her every concern as if of supreme importance, and made her feel the center of his universe.

Through a series of gentle questions, he had carefully guided her toward the realization that such a man was not a good prospect for a happy married life. She had acknowledged that none of her friends trusted him, and agreed that no doubt her father had her best interests in mind. She had suddenly grown calm, and Pennywhistle had patted her hand reassuringly. She had been smiling serenely when he left. He'd believed that she had finally accepted what was both logical and good for her future. He had agreed to return for tea the following afternoon to see how she was faring.

He kicked hard at the box lock. On the third kick, the lock yielded and the door flew open. He walked through slowly, like a man on his way to the gallows, hoping against hope that he would not see a sight that told him he had utterly failed someone he held dear.

She lay with her head on her writing desk, a river of red streaming from a wound over her left breast. The ruined bottle green dress was a mass of blood and gore; a .60 caliber ball at six inches' range was terribly unkind to flesh, yet her beautiful face was surprisingly peaceful. There was no note on the desk and the whiskey decanter next to her right hand was unopened. The air reeked of brimstone, and when he picked up the dueling pistol that lay at her feet, its barrel was still hot.

Tears started to his eyes, but he reminded himself that as a second year medical student, it was his professional duty to make certain that no spark of life still resided within the body. He detached himself from his feelings and clinically examined the wreckage of his cousin; no pulse and no respiration, as expected. He reminded himself that this was not Caroline, but merely the suit of clothes that her soul had worn. She had not been seeking attention by inflicting a cosmetic wound but had made absolutely certain the shot was fatal.

The next hour passed in a blur. He put his feelings in a mental lock box; summoned the servants, cleaned up the body, and laid it with the utmost care on her bed. He dispatched the butler with an urgent message for her father at his club. He would have gone himself but he felt a strange compulsion to honor her memory by staying at her side until another loved one could take up the duty.

Her father was so stunned that he refused to believe she was dead. Even after Pennywhistle showed him the body, he talked as if she were just visiting relatives and would shortly return. "She'll be back tomorrow, I am certain of it," a vacant smile on his wan face. His brain would simply not accept the verdict of his eyes.

Since there was no reasoning with a man living in a comforting fantasy. Pennywhistle sedated him with laudanum balls that he carried in his medical bag. He waited until Caroline's father was sound asleep before leaving. There was nothing more to be done until tomorrow. He needed a long walk to still his badly riled emotions.

As he slowly trod George Street in the fading sunlight, his grief turned to anger and finally to rage. A beautiful life had been snuffed out because of the actions of a scoundrel; so many undreamed of possibilities turned to dust. Words did not exist to describe how wrong it was. If only he had been smarter or more understanding, she might still be alive. Had he missed something important? Had he accidentally spoken words that pushed her over the edge?

He was angry at Caroline, too. How dare she deprive her father and himself of her grace and kindness! She had no right to do that! Her absence dimmed the light of the world and made it a much poorer place.

"Help! Help!" The screams of a woman jolted him out of his morbid reflections. A quarter of a block away, a small crowd had gathered around a dandified gentleman who was beating a woman of quality with a riding crop. Her face was a mass of welts, while his was a manic combination of rage and glee.

"Please, God, no more, no more!" she pleaded.

"You have acted the part of the whore, now you will pay the price!" shouted the swell in a voice that indicated he was well into his cups.

Pennywhistle's emotions burst forth like hornets from a nest on fire, and he broke into a run. It was monstrous that thirty men were passively watching an atrocity unfold. Another woman would not die on his watch!

"Let her go! Let her go, damn you!" he shouted angrily as he ran. The crowd heard his words, the dandy did not. He continued pummeling the woman, who was now close to losing consciousness.

The swell had his riding crop raised above his head for another strike when Pennywhistle grabbed his wrist. "By God, that's enough!" Pennywhistle locked the man's wrist with his right hand. He used his left to snap the swell's fingertips backwards at an unnatural angle. He did it so violently that the blackguard was knocked off his feet.

Pennywhistle stood over the stunned swell, breathing heavily.

The swell rose uncertainly to his feet and shook his head several times. "So you wish to play the hero, sir? I will make you sorry that you were ever born!" He drew a stiletto from the inside pocket of his cranberry colored coat and flourished it about boldly, clearly intending to sow fear before he caused harm.

The swell's attack was predictable. When the thrust at his stomach came, Pennywhistle's knowledge of *savate* kicked in. His wrists shot downwards in an x block, imprisoning the swell's wrist a foot from his stomach; squeezing his own wrists tightly locked the swell's arm. With a quick, clockwise

4

motion he forced the arm back toward the swell as he raised it to eye level. The fingers of his right hand ripped the knife loose by deep pressure on the finger joints. The blade clattered to the pavement as he swiftly retracted his left and jabbed the swell sharply in the nose, then raked the man's chin with his right elbow. The swell staggered, then collapsed like an old pillow suddenly emptied of feathers.

The crowd started clapping, which further angered Pennywhistle. There were no lions in a crowd; not a one of them had the courage to take action himself. He bent down and helped the woman to her feet with all the tenderness he could manage.

"I won't ask if you are well, but can you walk?"

She breathed deeply. When she spoke, she sounded lucid. "I...am not sure. I only live a block from here. Can you see me home?" She began to wobble.

"Of course, of course!" Pennywhistle decided the most sensible course was to simply pick her up and carry her. She weighed under a hundred pounds; no great burden to his rangy six foot, two inch frame.

"You are my savior, sir. I shall be forever in your debt."

In the five minutes that it took to reach her home, she told him her tale. It was a conventional one of a naïve girl of good family seduced by a man of great charm, quick wit, and low morals: not unlike Caroline's story. When she had tried to leave him, he had turned violent. Pennywhistle was surprised when he learned the name of the swell: Sir Atholl Campbell, Scotland's most notorious duelist.

Her parents thanked him profusely, but he did not tarry long. His eagerness to atone for his failure with Caroline had just landed him in some very hot water. He fully expected to be called out on the morrow.

He was handy with a pistol but had only killed targets, never a person. Campbell was known to have slain fifteen men. Some men developed a taste for dueling, in the manner of a rogue tiger that no longer stalked animals after its first taste of human flesh. Men such as Campbell viewed their deadly assignations as a hobby that not only provided constant proof of one's manhood but also gifted the practitioner with a certain dark fame.

Pennywhistle's odds of survival were poor, unless he could out-think his opponent. Hence, the avalanche of tears for his cousin that he expected never materialized, because grief was a luxury that he could ill afford. Grief would exact its portion, just not tonight. He slept little and paced his bedroom as the moon rose and set. As the first rays of dawn lightened the horizon, he hit upon a way to even the odds.

Campbell's Second, Sir John Peel, called at precisely one clock that afternoon with a formal summons to the field of honor.

Pennywhistle understood the unwritten rules of the Code Duello. A Second usually offered the challenged man the opportunity to give satisfaction in the form of a written or verbal apology, but Campbell's public humiliation had made that untenable. "I accept Sir Atholl's challenge, Sir John," he told Peel. "I wish to resolve the matter as soon as possible. Rather than wait until dawn tomorrow, I propose that we settle it at sundown today. I and my Second will meet you and your Principal at the usual spot at eight o'clock, if that would be convenient?" The usual spot was an isolated field three miles south of town; since duels were illegal, every city had dueling grounds far away from the eyes of authority.

"It would indeed, sir," replied Peel. "My Principal will supply the pistols, if that is acceptable."

"It is, sir, though the choice of weapons should be mine as the challenged party. As the challenged party, I will assert my right to control the conditions of the duel. I propose that it be fought at three feet distance."

Sir John blinked in astonishment. "But, but, but," he stammered. "That is extraordinary, sir; unprecedented:

almost certain death for both parties. It is the act of a madman, yet you appear quite sane. Are you certain?"

Pennywhistle looked him sternly in the eye. "It is my right and I am certain.'

Peel stood speechless. His confusion was evident, but in the end he gave the only response that the Code admitted."My Principal accepts your condition."

The hours until the duel passed slowly. Pennywhistle called upon Mr. Murray and found that he was no better. Shock had utterly unmanned his reason. Pennywhistle took charge and spent the rest of the day making the funeral arrangements.

There was another problem. As an Edinburgh University medical student, he had taken the Oath of Hippocrates which enjoined him to "Do no harm." What lay ahead was a direct betrayal of that sacred vow, though it was the proper fulfillment of his personal honor. He could legitimately bow out by using the Oath as his justification.

Nevertheless, he would not back down. He hated bullies, particularly men who abused women. The term "lady killer" had an entirely different meaning in Campbell's case.

Suicide and the violation of an oath were both wrong, but then, so was dueling. He stiffened his resolve by repeating to himself, "Two wrongs don't make a right, but three do."

At twilight, Pennywhistle watched Campbell and Peel approach in the dying warmth of a bleak day. Peel looked steady, but Campbell was lurching slightly and his nose was literally out of joint from Pennywhistle's jab. Pennywhistle had turned the contest into one of nerves rather than skill, and Campbell's resolve apparently could not bear it without a stiff dose of whiskey.

"Are you sure you want to do this, Tom?" asked Steven Gordon, his cousin and Second. "We can still end this without bloodshed. Speak a few careful words and let him gloat. In the end, those words mean nothing, and you walk away with your life."

"No, Steven. I am damned if I will apologize for saving a woman's life."

Gordon sighed in exasperation. "I wish you were not so pig-headed about principle, Tom. I would be more than willing to speak a few soothing phrases on your behalf, but I see in your eyes that I am wasting my breath."

Campbell was dressed, as was Pennywhistle, in white silk shirt and white woolen trousers. White was the color of choice as it made it easier to see blood and so determine a round's point of impact. Since most wounds were in the torso, silk was preferred because it carried the least risk of infection when driven into a wound.

Pennywhistle recognized Professor James Ogilvie at Campbell's side. It was standard to bring a doctor along to immediately attend to the injured, and Campbell had chosen the best.

Gordon advanced to meet Peel. The two Seconds shook hands and spoke briefly. "Is there not some way to compose this quarrel, sir?" said Peel, as if he were reading from a legal form. "No, sir. There is not," replied Gordon with utmost formality. "Let us proceed and load the pistols. You may have the honor of giving the signal to open fire, Sir John."

The Seconds withdrew the pistols from an exquisite mahogany case, and each loaded one in clear view of the other, to ensure that each pistol carried the same charge and ball. Each pistol featured a beautiful Ebony stock and was of 13 inches length and .50 caliber. Each was supremely well balanced and would come instantly to the point.

Pennywhistle looked at his gun hand. It was as firm and steady as his stomach was not. His face flushed crimson as his body signaled its resolve to fight. He breathed deeply three times to calm himself and focused his mind on what he must do.

He carefully examined his opponent and was surprised by what he saw. Campbell's aristocratic face wore none of its usual arrogance. His cold grey eyes looked uncertain and watery; as if he had just rubbed them with vinegar. He was trying to stand tall and firm, but a marked twitching in his right knee would not permit it. Yet all that really mattered was the slightest hint of a tremor in his gun hand.

The Seconds were ready and beckoned their Principals forward.

"One final time," said Peel, "is there no way that you gentlemen may be reconciled?"

Campbell and Pennywhistle both shook their heads.

"Very well then, gentlemen. Take your positions. Fire the moment I drop the red handkerchief and not a second before. Understood?"

Both men took up their assigned positions three feet apart. Campbell's stance was less steady than Pennywhistle's. Each stood sideways to lessen the size of the target, although at this trifling distance the gesture was more instinctive than effectual.

Each Second handed a loaded pistol to the opponent of his own Principal.

Pennywhistle looked Campbell deep in the eye. He was probably going to die, but he wanted his opponent to know that it would be with defiance, and that Campbell would be joining him on a journey to Hell.

Campbell's eyes wilted before Pennywhistle's. "You bastard," he slurred.

Both men looked at Sir John's upraised hand. He dropped the red handkerchief, and in the eternity that it took to flutter an inch from his grip, Pennywhistle's will steeled and his concentration became that of a monk in meditation.

Campbell fired first, but his shaking hand sent his ball an inch wide of Pennywhistle's left ribs. Pennywhistle glanced down at his unmarred shirtfront and knew that he could end the matter in a civilized fashion: fire his pistol into the ground, honor satisfied, and harm no one. It would be reckoned a gallant gesture and would preserve his fidelity to the Hippocratic Oath. Campbell was also the grandson and heir of the enormously powerful Duke of Argyll: a vindictive old misanthrope whom it would be unwise to offend.

Nevertheless, an older, primitive part of Pennywhistle seized control, concerned only with rough justice. Campbell was a bad man who liked to hurt people, and medicine was about stopping hurt. Allowed to live, he would learn no lesson and continue to prey upon the weak and innocent. Good men and women would likely die if Pennywhistle showed leniency.

A yellow stain spreading slowly on Campbell's trousers made Pennywhistle's decision. Brutality matched by cowardice marked Campbell as the meanest of men. Pennywhistle's emerald eyes turned hard as he brought his pistol to the point. He fired directly at Campbell's chest, and the round lifted the large man a foot off the grass.

The pistol flew from Campbell's hand and his jaw dropped open in surprise. He hit the ground so hard that his expensive ivory dentures were jarred loose. The body lay there, inert, red seeping though the expensive cloth. Ogilvie rushed over to confirm the verdict of everyone's eyes. He put his fingers to Campbell's carotid artery and held them there, even as his eyes took in the severity of the wound. He shook his head.

Peel looked shocked beyond measure. The impossible had happened. Scotland's most feared duelist was dead at the hand of a callow 18-year-old who had never fired a shot in anger.

Gordon looked scared but not shocked. His cousin had a Quixotic streak a mile wide and would always do the right thing, not the smart thing. He heard the thunder of hooves in the distance. He had to get his cousin out of there, fast.

Pennywhistle stood transfixed, realizing that the taking of life had greatly dimmed the light in his heart.

Gordon dashed over and shook him smartly. "Tom, you damn fool! Do you hear that noise? Those are the horses of Argyll's bully boys, and they are not coming to throw you a garden party. He always sends them just in case his impulsive grandson should ever lose a duel. I tried to warn you, but no! You had to do the honorable thing!"

Pennywhistle's dazed expression changed to one of outrage. "Well, that's damned unsporting!"

"Damned unsporting? Tom, you idiot! You think a tyrant with unlimited funds possesses your exact regard for honor? Argyll cares nothing for the Code Duello and will only care that you stole the life of the last of his line. This is now a matter of Highland blood vengeance; the only *wergeld* Argyll will accept is your head on a pike. His reach is long and he will hunt you down without pity or remorse. You have about five minutes before his mob tears you limb from limb."

"Oh, my God," said Pennywhistle.

"Don't talk to God, listen to me! Take my horse, not that old nag you rode." Gordon dashed over to the black stallion he had tethered to a tree. He loosened the reins and walked the horse briskly back to Pennywhistle. "I thought ahead and rode Perseus instead of my usual mount. He is the fastest racehorse in my father's stable. Consider him an extended loan. Now mount up and ride like hell."

Pennywhistle glanced over his shoulder and saw that ten horsemen had just crested the brow of a low hill half a mile away. He put his left foot in the stirrup and clumsily threw his right leg over Perseus's rump, wishing he were a better rider. Gordon handed him a riding crop.

"Now use the crop smartly and don't look back!"

"Thanks, Steven! I shall never forget this."

Pennywhistle snapped the riding crop twice and Perseus shot forward, jerking Pennywhistle against the saddle. He clung to the reins with the desperation of a shipwrecked sailor seizing a floating spar, because he realized that his life had just changed forever. Grief flooded over him and he sobbed, not just for Caroline but for the life he was leaving behind. He was speeding to an entirely new destiny that even his great imagination could not foresee.

PART ONE: PREPARATION

"Out of every one hundred men in a battle, ten shouldn't even be there, eighty are just targets, nine are the real fighters, and we are lucky to have them, for they make the battle. Ah, but the one, one is a warrior, and he will bring the others back."

—Heraclitus *500BCE*

CHAPTER 1

HMS Bellerophon, 21st October, 1805
18 miles Southeast of Cape Trafalgar off the Spanish Coast

Bomp! Bomp! Bomp! 26 heavy cannons thundered violently backwards on their breeching ropes as hot jets of scarlet blasted out. The local temperature soared and shock waves roiled a calm sea. The sun vanished, blotted out by clouds of gun smoke. The lower gun deck broadside from a French 74 blasted away Tom Pennywhistle's regrets about the doctor he might have been and jolted his thoughts back to the sea-going soldier he had become.

Sea and sky were gradually assuming a diaphanous quality, resembling a screen of light gauze, as great thunderheads swirled skyward over the two-mile-long line of the Franco-Spanish Fleet. A sound like ripping canvas filled the air as a barrage of 36-pound shot tore through the sky at 1,600 feet per second. The air reeked of brimstone and the stench of thousands of unwashed bodies sweating profusely, the distinctive scent of fear mixed with the more prosaic one of exertion. Enthusiastic choruses of *Vive l'Empereur! Vive l'Empereur! Vive l'Empereur!* rose from several ships and carried clearly across the placid water.

The first serious broadside fired at *HMS Bellerophon*, 74 guns, from 1,000 yards kicked up waterspouts off her port bow a few feet shy of her hull. Previous ranging shots had not come anywhere close. British guns would return the French salutation with iron hail of their own, but the crews would reserve their fire until the range was closer and their broadside more deadly.

The battle Lord Nelson had long sought was at last underway, and Royal Marine 1st Lieutenant Pennywhistle was glad of it. He was about to confront combat for the first time and the long, slow approach to the enemy had made him skittish. The feeling of utter impotency angered him: the instruments of his death looming larger with each passing moment, while he could do nothing but watch. His primal instincts screamed *Act, act!* even as training sternly countered *Patience, patience.*

His brother's words echoed in his mind. "I should have preferred to purchase an army commission for you, Tom, but Argyll has too much influence at Horse Guards. He has none in the Royal Marines, so I send you there for your safety. Be not downcast, Brother. Your new profession is more fitting to a gentleman than that of a physician. Besides, the steady nerves and clear head that would have made you a good surgeon will make you a fine warrior. You merely have to accept that your heart has elements of darkness."

The day had dawned hazy, the wan sunlight making the sky suitable for a Turner painting. As the hours advanced, the weather had matured into a bright autumn day: a robin's egg blue sky, a few cirrus clouds, the mercury steady, the temperature a comfortable 70 degrees on the Fahrenheit scale. Visibility was nearly unlimited. The wind was light, although the sea was running with surprisingly heavy swells.

Pennywhistle had a clear view of the forest of masts directly ahead. With sails spread, the enemy ships looked like sky-scraping egg whites set upon a silvered sea; the black bludgeons lining the toffee-colored decks the only discordant elements in an otherwise pleasant vision. For a second, the talented artist within surfaced and noted that the view would be a fine subject for a watercolor.

He stood straight and tall, though the fifteen marines behind him in the forecastle kept low, as ordered. His men would probably see this as an officer striking a heroic pose, but he simply wished to have a better view.

His nervous energy overcame his resolve to maintain the statue-like stillness expected of an officer. He shifted his weight from foot to foot, the movements grounding his anxiety in the manner of a lightning rod. The fingers of his right hand commenced drumming a tattoo on the port carronade, while those of his left grasped and released the hilt of his cutlass. He felt himself a greyhound, muscles singing and straining at the start, compelled to wait until his superiors let him slip his leash.

The Captain had enjoined silence on all of the marines and sailors aboard *Bellerophon,* the "Billy Ruffian" to her crew. The only noises should have been the low hum of ropes stirred by wind, the quiet crackle of sails pressed against yardarms, the creaking of timbers rhythmically expanding and contracting, and the slow *swoosh swoosh* of waves meeting an advancing cutwater. Yet the anxiety of men facing a great test provoked sounds that were as natural as they were un-heroic: a discordant chorus of belches, farts, hiccups, and retching insulted the air. A few seconds later, the attendant stench assaulted Pennywhistle's nose.

He wanted to relieve his men's anxiety and thought a few well chosen words would help. He concentrated on locking down the fear in his mind, since it sometimes raised the voice a full octave. He turned to face his marines and forced a look of amusement that he did not feel into his face. "I dare say most of those French fellows are begging God's direct attention right now. What do you say that we arrange a face-to-face meeting for the lot of them?"

Snorts of amusement erupted, and a few low chuckles. Even those who remained quiet grinned. He blinked in surprise and smiled that his attempt at wit had worked. It was, he decided, less the remark than the intention; men welcomed an excuse to release their rising tension and were pleased that their officer had sufficient concern for their welfare to provide one.

His face flushed a deep crimson, just as it had done before the duel; his brain was commandeering extra reserves of blood to flood his muscles. He recalled reading somewhere that Richard the Lionheart's visage had undergone a similar transformation during battle.

Bellerophon had been lucky so far, but the distance to the French was shortening. Shots from the next round of broadsides would tell, and men would die. The sheer randomness of death frustrated him, as it had little to do with a man's virtue or want of it.

Riiiippppp! He looked up and saw a tear in the mainsail. A second later he heard a scream. *Bellerophon's* luck had just run out.

He checked the Swiss watch that had cost more than the price of a cavalry officer's mount. He wanted to note the starting time of his great personal test: exactly noon, the start of the nautical day. Eight peals of the ship's bell confirmed the verdict of his timepiece.

He noticed Mr. Scott peeling an orange and caught its scent. It trigged a recollection of the orange he had eaten at 2 a.m.—perhaps his final meal. In the wake of that memory, the events leading up to the present moment marched across the stage in his mind's eye.

His preparations had started in the middle of a sleepless night: sharpening his cutlass on a whetstone. That event now seemed centuries in the past; time was proceeding at the pace of treacle in an hourglass, and each passing minute seemed to add a year to his age.

He had started walking the quarterdeck at four bells of the morning watch when sleep refused his most earnest entreaties. Worrying alone in a dark, cramped, stuffy cabin had only turned small fears into great ones. He'd needed a friend; though an acquaintance would do.

He tried conversing with Mr. Douglas, the officer of the deck. "It looks like we will have fair weather for battle."

"Perhaps," Douglas replied laconically.

"I confess that the prospect of battle has greatly lessened my appetite."

"Indeed," sniffed Douglas.

"Have you had any thoughts of home this morning?"

"None."

Douglas lived up to his reputation as a dour Scot. Pennywhistle fell silent and focused his attention on the comforting light of the rising sun.

The test ahead was a crossroads of life, offering both the path of the conqueror and the cur. He knew he could kill; but dueling was stylized and orderly, while battle was rule-less and chaotic. In a duel, the only life you needed to worry about was your own. Today, 72 men were hazarding their fortunes on his judgment. As he gazed up at the brightening sky, he thought back to what his father had said about war.

Tobias Pennywhistle had commanded the 23rd Foot in the American War of Independence; part of the army that Cornwallis surrendered at Yorktown. He had eventually returned home, suffering the after effects of a mortar fragment to the head and crippled psychologically: plagued by melancholy and nightmares that often caused him to wake in the wee hours, shouting and soaked in sweat. He broke his silence about war on only two occasions, both in response to his son's determined questioning.

"War consists largely of boredom and waiting, grinding routine and endless paperwork, bad food and worse drink, interrupted at irregular intervals by occasions of blood-curdling terror," his father had said acidly.

"The words *moral, just,* or *good* should never precede any reference to it. War is easy to start, difficult to end, and creates its own agenda, unrelated to the reasons why it began. If war were a person, the appellations *cheat, liar,* and *scoundrel* would apply. War's cold fingers are agents of entropy and everything they grasp is reduced to dirt, disease, or death. War is Lachesis playing sport. It is my heartfelt wish that you never become a participant in her cruel games."

And yet here he was, Thomas Pennywhistle, about to live the very thing that his father had prayed he would never see. His father had died in pain and despair long before his time. Heroism exacted a high price never spoken of by poets and historians.

At least he was not alone in worrying, at this dawn of battle. He overheard Mr. Scott, the ship's second lieutenant, talking to Mr. Saunders, its fifth.

"I made my will last night," said Scott gravely, rubbing one heel against the other in a rhythm matching his words. "I am glad that I did so; although," bravado inserted itself into his voice, "I am sure that it was entirely unnecessary. Nelson knows what he is about."

"I wrote a letter to my sister," Saunders replied pensively, his index finger slowly twirling a lock of his blond hair. "She is a widow with two children, and I am her sole support. I assured her that our ship will shortly gain a great deal of prize money, and that if I should fall, my share will all be paid to her. I care less about my fate than the proceeds of this battle giving her a better life."

Pennywhistle meditated about his death from variety of perspectives, yet his thoughts did not spawn religious fervor or tearful contrition. While many on board were offering up silent prayers in hopes of cultivating the merciful attentions of the Deity, he did not do so. He conceived of God as a watchmaker who had set the Universe running, then stepped away to observe His handiwork.

His greatest allies today would not be God and the angels, but thorough training, good reflexes, and the staunchest friends of his intellect: reason, observation, and deduction. They had made possible the preparations which gave him a fighting chance of surviving the hours ahead. Those three warriors of wisdom would never desert him, no matter how seductively hot blood or cold fear beckoned them to do so. For Pennywhistle, clear thinking was a greater ally than the power of faith.

Two Royal Marine privates, Martin Combs and James Warwick, were industriously cleaning and oiling their Brown Bess muskets.

"I done some heavy praying this morning, Jim. I hope the good Lord was listening."

"Good for you, Marty, but the only religion I need is my Brown Bess and my bayonet. With them as my angels, ain't no French or Spanish devils I can't lick."

Warwick was a man after Pennywhistle's own heart.

Pennywhistle took several deep breaths to focus his mind on the many tasks ahead. He checked his Blancpain watch: 9:15. He stowed it, then unfurled his powerful Ramsden spyglass. Pennywhistle estimated *Bellerophon* was six miles from the enemy fleet. Though he could clearly see the topgallants on the closest ships, he wanted a better view than was available from the ship's forecastle. That could be obtained from the mainmast's fighting top, the platform where the lower mast met the maintop. Objects could be seen at 12 miles from that vantage point. While that was not as good as the 21 mile view from the masthead, the diamond shaped top was much steadier.

He furled his glass and compelled himself to walk rather than run toward the mainmast. Despite his eagerness, it was important to maintain a façade of gentlemanly *sang froid* for the benefit of the crew. Once on the ratlines, he embraced the eagerness and raced upwards with the speed of a monkey energized by a stolen pot of coffee. He emerged through the lubber's hole and made himself comfortable on the sizable platform. He unshipped his glass and swept it slowly across the enemy fleet.

"*Oooh, oooh, oooh!*" Jobu, a grey-faced Vervet Monkey that belonged to Midshipman Jewell, followed him up and leaped upon his shoulder. Pennywhistle was glad of the company.

His breath caught in awe as he beheld the Franco-Spanish fleet of thrice and thirty ships of-the-line; a seemingly implacable barrier of menacing black hulls with lines of gun ports marked by wide swaths of yellow, white, or ochre. Their hulls mounted a combined total of 2,636 guns and carried complements totaling 26,000 men. These impressive statistics he knew from intelligence estimates, but they had not prepared him for the visceral impact of seeing a fleet arrayed for battle.

Villeneuve's fleet sailed ESE in a line of battle that was really more an arc due to poor seamanship. Nelson's fleet was approaching their line at right angles in line ahead formation. The 27 British ships were divided into two parallel columns a mile apart, totaling 2,200 guns and 18,400 men, 2,600 of whom were Royal Marines. *Bellerophon* was fifth in line in Admiral Collingwood's lee division of 15 ships.

Pennywhistle remembered his father telling him that poor hearing was a common price paid by infantry officers who had been involved in heavy fighting. He could not fully conceive the sheer noise that today's heavy concentration of powerful artillery would generate. Many officers had reported that after the Battle of Blenheim, they were incapable of hearing anything for three days. Then, 170 cannons had been dispersed over a considerable area, and most had been of smaller calibers than the ordnance now present. Water also amplified sound. He wondered how many men would suffer permanent degradation of their hearing from today's confrontation.

The mastheads of the enemy fleet were adorned with colorful pennants marking the squadron commanders, but they drooped listlessly due to weak morning winds. The giant French Tricolors and red and yellow standards of the Spanish had not yet been hoisted, though Pennywhistle pictured them clearly in his imagination. Running up your national colors was a signal that you were willing to accept battle. The French and Spanish would likely do so only when the British ships were much closer.

"*Ooooh! Ooooh! Ooooh!*" Jobu begged for a treat. Pennywhistle obliged with some assorted nuts from his pocket. He had been munching on them throughout the morning to steady his nerves.

Directly below Pennywhistle, Mr. Thomas and Mr. Douglas, the ship's third and fourth lieutenants, had their glasses extended and were carefully observing the enemy.

"I am surprised, Mr. Thomas," said Douglas, the granite-faced lieutenant's loquacity a sign of his nervousness, as was the constant tapping against his trouser seam by the fingers of his left hand. "The French and the Spanish don't like each other much, yet look at their fleet. One French ship and one Spanish ship all the way down their line. I would have thought that they would have entirely separate squadrons."

"Actually, it is a sensible arrangement, Mr. Douglas," replied Thomas, his scholarly voice in perfect harmony with his thoughtful face. "The alliance between France and Spain is shaky and uncertain. My guess is that Villeneuve is using this arrangement so that he can keep a close eye on Spanish captains whom he does not know and does not trust. Admiral Gravina's fleet was added to the French less than a week ago. That means they have had no time to learn how to work together. The enemy possesses two minds and two wills, but Nelson has made our fleet a unified reflection of his genius." He smiled in admiration of the Admiral's strategy.

"The Spanish Captains have no faith in Villeneuve, either," continued Thomas. He scratched the top of his left hand with his right.

"I have heard that he ignores their concerns," observed Douglas.

"Indeed!" said Thomas. "The Dons think he is a man promoted beyond his competency, and that he will hazard their lives carelessly. The French scorn for the Spanish mode of fighting is well known. Bonaparte deems the Spanish Navy and Army relics of the past, unwilling to adopt more modern methods of warfare."

"Do you think the Spaniards will fight in a lackluster fashion, then?"

"Oh, they will fight, Mr. Douglas, and much harder than the French. Their ships are stouter built, and they battle with the fanaticism learned in their long struggle against the Moors. The French are more interested in *le vive* than *le gloire*. They generally surrender the moment it is clear that the day has gone against them."

"I wonder why Villeneuve has come out to fight at all," mused Douglas. "We have chased him across the Atlantic and back and he has always avoided a confrontation. "

"I think it is Bonaparte's will, not Villeneuve's. Bonaparte is impatient and seeks a decisive victory. Villeneuve has not given him one. Villeneuve probably suspects that he is about to be relieved in disgrace and wants to save his reputation by making one gallant attempt to bring on a general engagement. I almost feel sorry for him."

"Sorry? In God's name, why?"

"Bonaparte may be a brilliant soldier but he is no seaman. I think that he saddled Villeneuve with a very elaborate plan that looked good on paper but took no account of wind and weather. The chase across the Atlantic was supposed to lure Nelson away from Europe so that Bonaparte could launch his invasion barges across the Channel. But Bonaparte underestimated both the sea and Nelson."

Pennywhistle agreed with Thomas's reasoning. He panned his glass slowly across the enemy fleet and made deductions. You could tell a lot about a fleet's confidence, skill, and aggressiveness by how they displayed themselves and maneuvered. It was similar to taking the measure of a brigand by his posture, musculature, movements, and the cast of his face.

The set of a fleet's sails, general trim of each ship, crispness of course adjustments, and closeness of alignment among its member vessels, all furnished each fleet with a distinctive signature. Just as each man's autograph was unique, varying from bold to timid, so it was with a fleet's signature. A landsman's eye would see only a mass of sails; a mariner could deduce an entire fleet's personality.

If Villeneuve's fleet had been a man, he would have been tall and well made, but badly out of shape from a lack of exercise. The British fleet would have been a rangy, well proportioned athlete rippling with taut muscles that had seen a great deal of use.

Pennywhistle saw that the French and Spanish rigs were those of battle. Reduced speed lessened rolling and steadied the hulls as artillery platforms. Courses were furled; topsails and topgallants provided the locomotion, while spankers and jibs supplied guidance. Courses took a lot of men to work, and being close to the deck they became prime targets for any flaming bits of wadding. Topsails could be braced round quickly with far fewer men.

Thomas and Douglas continued their conversation. "Even though we are outnumbered in men and ships, Mr. Douglas, we will prevail. Nelson has made sure that we understand his tactical plan so that we can act decisively, even without orders. Villeneuve's captains likely have received no greater instruction than "fight hard." Once we pierce their lines and inaugurate a general melee, each of our captains can function as his own Nelson, using his initiative and our superior gunnery to crush any ships that come his way."

"I agree with you, Mr. Thomas, but I am worried about the many soldiers that the French and Spanish ships have aboard. I understand that at least 4,000 are French veterans just returned from a successful campaign in Italy. Our intelligence mandarins estimate that each Spanish ship carries at least 200 soldiers. Morale may be low among the sailors, but I fear the soldiers may not be affected."

"Your point is well taken, Mr. Douglas, but consider one thing: those soldiers are not trained to fight at sea. Many will be so wracked with seasickness that they will be of almost no use. Those able to stand will be greatly reduced in efficiency. I am confident that our Marines, accustomed to fighting and firing with the motion of ships, can handle them."

Pennywhistle was less confident. He would have felt far more sanguine if the Marine detachment had been at its allotted strength of 120 instead of the 72 present. Yet he could offer no complaint, since every British ship was shorthanded.

When *Bellerophon* broke the enemy line, she would pass between two ships carrying 400 soldiers. His men would be outnumbered 5 to 1, and many of the enemy 400 would be flinging grenades. Grenades were the weapons of the unskilled, but they could cause real problems.

Nevertheless, he thought that the power of volleys would keep most boarders off *Bellerophon's* weather decks, and bayonets would discourage those who gained them. A battle was first won in the mind, and he had wracked his brains to plan for the permutations of enemy boarding actions.

Naval battles were far more about men than about ships. Ships were hard to sink, and few ever went down in the course of battle. Some ships died days later of wounds, but the fate of a ship was generally sealed not by the strength of her timbers but by the character of her captain. Surrender came down to a question of will: deciding at what point a ship was so broken and her crew so weakened that further resistance became as futile as it was foolish.

Each of the 33 captains in the enemy fleet had a different answer about how long to continue resistance. Nelson was determined to know them all.

CHAPTER 2

Curiosity satisfied but his tactical worries intensified, Pennywhistle sprinted down the ratlines in an effort to burn off excess nervous energy. Jobu followed him down, then sped off in search of new adventures. Once on deck, he pulled out his Blancpain and noted the time: 9:50. The minutes seemed to be grinding by more slowly each time he checked his watch. He looked at sails and sea and made some careful calculations.

The British Fleet had the weather gauge and control of the opening phase of the upcoming engagement, but the westerly breeze was so light that the advantage was almost nonexistent. It would make Nelson's approach much slower than he had anticipated, and his ships would have to endure a torrent of fire before they could return broadsides.

Bellerophon was inching toward the enemy at two knots, roughly 45 feet per minute, so it would probably be just after noon when first blood stained her decks. Pennywhistle had plenty of time to wonder, worry, and die a thousand imaginary deaths.

He noted Edward Overton, the ship's sailing master, slowly walking the ship's waist with a troubled expression. He moved with a slight limp from an injury many years before.

He was fifty-five, tall and spare with a weathered face
that looked like it had been carved from old driftwood. His
beetling brows, steel grey hair, and stern jaw gave him an
imposing appearance that went well with the formality of his
uniform: black bicorn, double breasted blue tailcoat, ivory
waistcoat, white leather breeches, long silk stockings, and
buckled black shoes. Yet the twinkle in his brown eyes and
the pleasing tenor of his voice made him a man that sailors
not only trusted but liked.

Since the sailing master understood more about the ships
and the sea than any one aboard, it might be useful to find
out if he knew something that could affect Pennywhistle's
dispositions for the coming fight. He screwed on his most
pleasant smile and strode briskly toward him.

"You present the appearance of a man with a problem,
Mr. Overton. I should be happy to lend an ear."

Overton looked at him quizzically. "A kind offer, Mr.
Pennywhistle, but I doubt you need any additional worries."

"Bullets may kill me, but one more piece of information
surely won't."

"Very well then; it is the weather."

"What of it? Other than the swells and a lack of wind, it is
a beautiful day,"

"It is the heavy cross swells that worry me. I have counted
eight per minute for the last ten minutes. With no wind,
there is only one cause I know for such a thing to occur."

"What is that?"

"A very bad storm front. I believe one is headed our way.
If it is fifty or so miles away now, it will reach us some time
in the next twelve to twenty-four hours. I tell you, young
man, the last time that I saw swells like these was in the
Caribbean. The next day, a hurricane hit Barbados."

"I thought hurricanes which started in the Mediterranean
were exceedingly rare."

"Very rare; nonetheless, one happens every fifty years or so. I truly hope that I am wrong, but my intuition says that we are in for a very bad blow. It is absolutely the worst development for two fleets of dismasted ships."

"That is most alarming, Mr. Overton."

"You see," said Overton, "I should not have told you. I would ask you to keep this knowledge confidential, since I have not yet told the Captain. He has enough to worry about right now and it is possible that I am mistaken."

"I assure you, sir, not a word shall escape my lips."

"At any rate, I must take my leave of you. I shall go aloft with my glass and see if I might discover further proof of my suspicions. Good day to you, Mr. Pennywhistle, and good fortune in the fight ahead."

"And *bon chance* to you, sir!"

Though Overton's observations were worrisome, the heavy swells gave Nelson's fleet an advantage. Since the Franco-Spanish Fleet presented their beams rather than bows to the waves, they were bobbing strongly about and would have to time their broadsides exactly. If fired too soon, they would splash seawater; too late, they would skewer the sky.

10 a.m. The conclusion of his watch was confirmed a few seconds later by four peals of the ship's bell. He looked up and visualized marksmen shooting at him from enemy tops. His tall frame would be an easy target. He reminded himself to stand straight and defiant today; attend his duty rather than indulge the natural instinct to crouch low.

"Mr. Pennywhistle, Mr. Pennywhistle!"

The youngest officer aboard hailed him in a high, thin voice. 2nd Lieutenant Luke Higgins from Belfast had been in the Marines but eight weeks and had only joined the ship at the end of September. He was 16 years old, five-foot-four inches tall, with a rail-thin wisp of a body and a pinched, angular face that looked as if it had just been pried loose from a vice. His bright red hair and the avalanche of freckles on his cheeks made him seem an adolescent leprechaun. When he walked, his arms and his legs never acted in synchronization, and he always seemed to be sweating, even in cool weather. A less military presence could hardly be imagined.

"Mr. Pennywhistle, how are you this fine morning? Grand day for a punch up with Johnny Crapaud and his fleet of seagoing scoundrels, don't you think? Another chance for Nelson to humble them, even more than he did at the Nile! Perfumed Froggie bluster against John Bull courage! Ha ha ha! Like matching a nag against a thoroughbred! And the Spanish! I swear their donkeys smell better than their owners and have more intelligence. Ha ha ha! I am champing at the bit to have a good bash at the lot of them!" Each time he laughed he snapped the fingers of his left hand.

Oh good Lord! thought Pennywhistle. The boy seemed to be parroting nonsense from lurid tabloids. Higgins paid close attention when being instructed in how to fight, but apparently had not considered the difference determined foes could make. He seemed to think the great conflict ahead was just a giant version of some schoolyard tussle: king of the hill played with ships. Indeed, six months before he had been a schoolboy in Belfast.

"I shall smite those Frog and Don rascals smartly and lay them low. One Irishman is worth ten Frenchman and twenty Spaniards." He was so fired up with excitement that he did not even wait for Pennywhistle's reply.

A lack of fear was just as deadly as a surfeit of it. In his naïveté, Higgins probably believed that the sum total of the upcoming fight would be a few nicks, scratches, and scrapes; tattoos of bravery rather than debilitating wounds that turned men into cripples who ended up begging on the street.

"This will be a glorious day for England and her sister kingdom of Ireland!" His lilting brogue became more pronounced as his enthusiasm increased.

Glorious? As Pennywhistle half-listened to Higgins rattling on, he recalled a graphic description given him by Henry Darby, the captain who had commanded *Bellerophon* at The Nile in August '98. She had suffered 193 casualties, and after the fight her quarterdeck was slicked with blood and choked with orphan limbs, unraveled viscera, and amputated heads. Pennywhistle found himself in the odd position of a commander who had to instill a healthy measure of fear in a man, rather than armor plating him against it.

"I am surprised that those bumbling French dolts even got their fleet out of port. Their ship maneuvering puts me in mind of a bear trying to thread a needle. Ha ha ha!"

Pennywhistle felt as if he were witnessing an audition for the role of a buffoonish young squire in a badly written comic opera. He realized that Higgins was playing a part that had been taught him from childhood.

"Are you quite finished reciting your catalogue of insights?" Pennywhistle's voice was as sarcastic as his expression. Higgins grin vanished as abruptly as if someone had just dumped a bucket of ice water on him.

"Yes, sir."

"Good. Then I shall answer your original question. I think today is as good a day as any for a battle, Mr. Higgins, but any day a battle must be fought is not a good day, since it will be the last day for many men. We are heading into a battle, not a play. It is commendable that you are of sanguine temper, yet I caution you against letting blind optimism rule unreservedly. I am certain we will prevail today, but I do not underestimate our opponents. They will sell their lives dearly and exact hard payment for every ship we take."

Higgins looked affronted. "Sir, the French are a bad lot whose principal activity is making love with their faces to tarted-up women whose chief perfume is garlic; destroyers of order and tradition who want to spread their poison across Europe as a rabid dog bites those who cross his path. My father and friends say that a rabid—"

"Mr. Higgins," Pennywhistle interrupted curtly, "if you wish to beat your opponents, you must understand how they think. That is impossible if you regard them with contempt. You must appreciate their more admirable attributes and practices even if you decline to embrace them. Do not be what Virgil inveighed against: a man of zeal without understanding.

"But sir, *The Gazette* says that Frogs are just a gang of ill-bred regicides led by an upstart tyrant. Their Don lackeys are no better than bought dogs. Such low beings should pose no obstacle to the great Lord Nelson."

"Brag and bounce, Mr. Higgins, brag and bounce! Shakespeare said a warrior should imitate the action of the tiger, but he needs the cunning of the fox as well. Courage without craft is an engine unlinked to a piston. Those 'regicides' and 'bought dogs' you dismiss so casually will make very determined and skillful efforts to unburden you of the need for future plans. '*Vive l'Empereur*' is no mere slogan but a battle cry that makes Frenchmen fight like devils and puts fire into even the faintest of hearts.

"The man they cheer has cast his shadow large upon Europe and is an antagonist on the order of Caesar or Alexander. We may reject his pretensions and style him simply 'General Bonaparte' but he truly is the Emperor of French hearts and minds. Because of the force of his will, we face a fleet action today.

"As for the Spanish, though their glory days are past, the spirit that conquered the Americas still lives in them.

Spaniards may not fully approve of Bonaparte, yet the appeal of a gifted, successful leader should not be underestimated.

"The words you should heed are those of your drillmasters at Stonehouse Barracks and the commands that Sergeant Dale has taught you. I would also suggest that you carefully review that long list I gave you last week: tasks to accomplish before battle. Thorough preparation is the key to success in any enterprise. I am depending on you, as are your men."

The boy nodded in solemn understanding. Good, he was getting through! Pennywhistle paused and then set his face in as pleasant a cast as he could manage when about to utter a lie. "I have full confidence that you will distinguish yourself in a way that does signal honor to the Marines and your family. Events may well come to a critical nexus when my life and those of every marine on board will be placed in your hands."

Higgins chest swelled, he seemed to grow an inch, and his voice squeaked a little less. His face broke into a grin that was ingenuous and winning. "By God, sir, I will not let you down. I will do my duty and more. I will make you and this ship proud of me. I know I can lick those—"

"Excellent, Mr. Higgins. Save your energy for the fight ahead. Battle is the most draining experience in the universe. You eagerness is commendable, but let us review a few points to make sure that it is matched by your knowledge. You will be stationed on the quarterdeck today, along with Mr. Wilson. I trust you plan on using parapet fire."

Higgins brightened. "Absolutely! Just as you taught me; two lines formed behind the rolled hammocks lashed to the bulwarks. The first line fires, then kneels to reload while the second line fires. As the second line kneels, the first stands and begins the process anew. My men can also perform platoon fire and shift to it at a moment's notice." His green eyes seemed to flash copper for an instant. "We will give the

Frogs and Dons an unceasing wall of fire straight out of Hell!"

"And your primary tasks, Mr. Higgins?"

"Break up potential boarding parties with volleys, make enemy soldiers keep their heads down, and use individual marksmanship to fire through enemy gun ports to kill their cannon crews. When using individual marksmanship, the men are to take advantage of any available cover when reloading."

"And should the unthinkable happen and French sailors gain our decks?"

"Give 'em cold steel!" said Higgins with glee. "Zeal and bayonets! Ha ha! Thrust, develop, gore, recover! Ha ha! With the proper rhythm of course! Slow, slow, quick, quick!"

"Very good, Mr. Higgins. Zeal is good, but trained zeal is so much better. Always leave efforts to board the enemy to the sailors. Cutlasses, tomahawks, and half pikes work better on crowded enemy decks than our long muskets. Besides, if sailors carry the enemy ship, they can sail it, whilst we cannot.

"I wish to apprise you of one other thing. Normally half of our Marines man the big guns and are returned to the weather decks gradually, as replacements for the fallen. I plan on asking the Captain for the entire marine contingent to be present on the weather decks when the battle commences, since we will be outnumbered and the battle will likely be long."

Higgins eyebrows shot up and he smiled fiercely. "That is indeed a bold plan, sir! An excellent plan!" He punched his left fist into his right palm to underscore his enthusiasm.

"What it means, Mr. Higgins, is that you may have considerably more men under your command than you expected. Much is riding on your conduct today, though Mr. Wilson will be lending you his assistance. I know that Captain Wemyss wishes to speak with you, so I will detain you no further. Convey my respects and tell him that I shall need a few words with him about an urgent matter."

"Aye, aye, sir!" Higgins snapped to attention and saluted. After Pennywhistle returned the salute, he pivoted and looked about to break into a run that would express his martial ardor.

"Mr. Higgins! Walk, don't run. Act as if you are strolling to your bank, not charging into battle."

"Aye, aye, sir."

There was definitely hope for Mr. Higgins.

CHAPTER 3

Pennywhistle's reward for instilling a measure of respect for the enemy in Higgins was an increase in his own anxiety. His deep-set, emerald eyes darkened, he scratched his nose to banish an itch that would not go away, and puckered then relaxed his lips every few seconds. Though the temperature was moderate, he felt as if he were standing on an ice flow rather than a deck of oak. His heavy scarlet coat was no protection against a chill that existed only in his mind. He removed his plumed coachman's hat and let the slight breeze ruffle his sandy red hair. The sweat band was saturated.

"Finally going to meet the lion," he whispered to himself. He recalled that the expression for a man undergoing his first battle had originated at the Tower of London. Its menagerie was the only place in England where the King of Beasts could be viewed; those who did so felt they had accomplished something rare and remarkable.

His mouth felt as dry as his perspiring hands were wet. His stomach made ugly noises as lances of bile tried to skewer legions of butterflies. He extended his left hand and then his right, relieved that both remained steady and unwavering.

He had chosen the white wool trousers with the loops that extended under his Hessian boots; the loops made his trousers fit more closely and encouraged the illusory belief that the tighter the protective carapace, the safer the occupant. His men did the same by severely tightening the crossbelts that formed x's on their chests.

The twin rows of buttons on his swallow-tailed scarlet jacket, the single epaulette on his right shoulder, and the crescent-shaped gorget that hung suspended from a blue ribbon round his neck were islands of gold that would sparkle in the sunlight. The bright crimson sash round his waist added a conspicuous note that was completely intentional: it was important that the men be able to easily distinguish their leaders during the heavy smoke of battle.

Unfortunately, eye-catching attire invited the attentions of enemy marksmen as well. Some officers removed gorgets, epaulettes, and sashes before battle, but Captain Cooke would be wearing his dress uniform today with its truly splendid epaulettes, more concerned with being an inspiration to his men than his personal safety. He could do no less.

An officer might have greater privileges and prestige, but both came at a high cost that Pennywhistle had sworn an oath to bear. Officers were killed or wounded at sometimes double the rate of the men they commanded. Military *noblesse oblige* translated into two main requirements: correctly assess the moment of decision and danger, without letting sideshow sizzles distract from the main battle, then be first and foremost at that nexus. If necessary, show the men how to die.

Pennywhistle was also honest enough to be mindful of his personal ambitions. Promotion for officers in the Royal Marines went by seniority and was slow. It created something of a gerontocracy with captains and lieutenants that were often considerably older than their army counterparts. Success in a great battle when the government was feeling lavish with rewards was a way to circumvent that system.

He desperately wanted a beverage but needed his bladder empty when the battle commenced. Men wetted themselves in battle more often than most veterans would admit; the body clearing for action, just as a warship did. He would take no chances with anything that might impair the image that he must project to his men, yet a steaming cup of coffee danced merrily in his mind's eye.

"Mr. Pennywhistle. A word please! It is a matter of some moment."

He had been so lost in thought that the words delivered in a smarmy baritone almost made him jump. He turned to confront a face that reminded him that not all Britons possessed good hearts and admirable motives.

2nd Lieutenant Peter Wilson was a striking, broad-shouldered, twenty-five-year-old with flaxen hair, a strong jawline, and remarkable violet eyes. His diamond-shaped face was saved from perfection by a small purple discoloration just below his right eye. At six feet, he was considerably taller than most men on the ship. He perpetually wore an odd half-smile that suggested that he had just signed a pact with the devil yet retained possession of his soul.

Though he moved with the effortless grace of a dapper man-about-town and possessed refined manners and a keen wit, he nonetheless aroused distrust in perceptive people. Something was off about the man, even if no one could quite put his finger on what it was. He knew drill well enough and gave the right commands at the right moments with a manly presence, yet Pennywhistle had overheard several rankers discussing him this morning and their verdict had not been kind.

Hard discipline was accepted as long as it was applied fairly and evenly, but Wilson was sporadic and inconsistent. He had favorites and outcasts, and neither category seemed based on anything but caprice. The men sensed that he saw

them as ciphers unworthy of his concern, and thus he might
be extravagant in the surrender of their lives. Officers such as
Wilson sometimes "accidentally" got hit with bullets fired by
their own men.

Wilson was chiefly renowned for his prowess as a card
player who regularly relieved the ship's officers and
midshipmen of large sums of money. Pennywhistle found
cards slightly less interesting than watching a mole sleep,
and he disdained gambling. He wondered why men who lost
regularly continued to play; apparently, the thrill of an
occasional success was such a potent drug that it
overpowered common sense.

"Mr. Wilson," said Pennywhistle, his unctuous tone
mirroring Wilson's, "I trust you are not calling upon me to
wish me the compliments of the day. How may I be of
service?"

"Mr. Pennywhistle, I believe a serious error has been
made in my assignment for the coming battle. I should be
stationed on the poop deck with Captain Weymss, not
defending the quarterdeck. I am senior to young Higgins, so
by rights my place should be on the poop backing up the
captain." The hauteur in Wilson's voice and carriage were
more fitted for the role of a scheming staff officer. Yet battle
had a way of bringing out hidden talents. Pennywhistle
hoped that Wilson would surprise.

"While I appreciate your close attendance upon
established procedures, I must point out that Captain
Wemyss has chosen to alter tradition and place himself on
the poop, rather than the quarterdeck near Captain Cooke.
He is of the opinion that he should be present where the
greatest portion of marines are stationed. I am posted on the
forecastle, which would leave Higgins in charge on the
quarterdeck.

But he is a Johnny raw; your three years of service give
you a discernment that he lacks, so you will command the

quarterdeck with Higgins as your subordinate. In addition, you will be hard by Captain Cooke's side so that any gallant deeds that you perform will be observed and figure prominently in official dispatches."

Mention in dispatches was a plum for any officer, yet Pennywhistle could not shake the feeling that Wilson did not care. He wondered if Wilson actually did not want to be near the captain. A marine who lacked courage would not welcome the close observations of his commanding officer.

"I should insist upon precedent," Wilson said haughtily, "but I will subdue my regard for honor in the interest of the ship." He clenched and unclenched the fingers of his right hand as he talked. "Ah, things we do for England!" His tone implied that he was granting Pennywhistle a favor.

Pennywhistle replied neutrally, "I felt certain that an upright gentleman would quickly see reason." From the arch of Wilson's brows above cold eyes that had all the tenderness of a speeding bullet, and the pressing of his thin lips, Pennywhistle concluded that he had just made an enemy of a man who seemed to find amusement in sowing discord with barbed remarks. Nevertheless, he needed to be certain that Wilson understood his role today.

"I trust that you will make sure that the extra ammunition chests are brought up from the forward magazine. I am convinced that our men will exceed the usual forty rounds today. Use cartridges with the .670 balls rather than the .685 so fouling does not prove a problem. I would also suggest that two extra crates of muskets be brought up to replace those that become inoperable. Both can be stored under the overhang of the poop."

"Yes, yes, Mr. Pennywhistle," said Wilson impatiently. "I had already made plans to issue those exact orders."

Pennywhistle doubted that. Wilson was smart but careless, and it was easy to claim another man's idea as your own after it had been expressed. "Very good, sir. As I told

Mr. Higgins, leave boarding to the sailors. Our job is to defend, not attack." He could not picture Wilson leading a death or glory charge. "Doubtless many soldiers will be lining the enemy bulwarks, so it is important that you reduce their numbers quickly and keep them from doing any great mischief. Also be prepared for grenades. Make sure that every man has a moist chamois cloth to smother their fuses."

Wilson's expression was a combination of boredom and annoyance; a red flag in front of a bull to a perfectionist like Pennywhistle. Nevertheless he bridled his temper and spoke courteously, if coldly. "Have you got all that?"

"I do indeed, sir. You may rely upon me," said Wilson archly.

Wilson's manner banished the last of Pennywhistle's patience. He just wanted this annoying sack of puffed up bounce to go away. "Now, sir, if there is nothing further, I have many tasks that require my close attention. I trust you have many that compel yours. Oh, and a little extra drill for your men would not be amiss. Good day to you, sir."

Pennywhistle did not bother with a salute or further words. He brusquely pivoted and walked away, leaving Wilson with a surprised look halfway between confusion and irritation.

"Damned martinet will get me killed," he muttered.

As Pennywhistle walked away in annoyance, cheering and clapping erupted along the ship's starboard waist. "Get him! Get him!" shouted several sailors. Screwloose, the ship's oversized orange tabby cat, was chasing a huge brown rat along the gangway, his snapping jaws narrowly missing the rodent's tail.

Screwloose waged a successful campaign to rid the ship of rats, but one wily specimen had eluded him in the manner of an evil rodent genius. The men had named the rat Shredder for his depredations against sacks containing the captain's personal stores.

Shredder stopped abruptly and Screwloose overshot him. The rat pivoted and dashed down the rear companionway at the ship's waist. Screwloose screeched, dug his claws into the deck to check himself, and changed direction.

"Screwloose will bring him down, don't you worry none," said James Gill, at 59 years of age the oldest sailor aboard. "Shredder's just like the French; you can only run so long before you get cornered."

Pennywhistle smiled briefly. The odd interruption helped him realize that part of his problem with Wilson was that he saw in Wilson something he worried about in himself. The icy hand of fear gripped his soul; there was no disguising it. He refused to ease his mind by labeling what he felt as something that brought less shame. Once fear was out in the open, it could be fought like any other enemy.

He guessed the other officers were frightened as well, but no one was willing to directly own up to that fear. There was an unwritten code that no officer voice emotions which haunted the soul or made a man's stomach churn. That code reckoned it more knightly to joke about death and dismemberment with breezy lightheartedness than utter three simple words that a knave might speak without embarrassment: "I am frightened." Bravery was supposed to be as natural to a gentleman as flight to a bird.

Bravado and bonhomie were really no better than whistling when passing a graveyard at midnight, but both inspired confidence in the men. In a way, the code was a grand charade backed by the hope that if you pretended long enough to be brave, the day might finally arrive when you became so.

His ruminations were interrupted by the approach of a scarlet coat bearing temptation. Here came Dale, his sergeant, walking with the tread of a bulldog and holding a steaming tankard of coffee. The bewitching aroma chased away Pennywhistle's resolve not to drink as surely as a hound did a fox. His mouth exploded into a huge grin. God, it was such a relief to find joy in something!

"You should never go into battle with one boot off, sir," said Dale with a wry half smile as he handed the tankard to Pennywhistle. "It's not a good time to change your regular habits. Even the best steam engine requires lubrication when it is running fast and hard."

Dale was a solidly built man slightly above medium height, with a deeply lined face and scarred brows that showed he was no stranger to battle. He wore a crimson sash like his lieutenant, but the black line through its middle marked him as a sergeant. Three chevrons on the right sleeve of his double-breasted scarlet coat proclaimed that he had held that rank for more than five years.

"Thanks, Sarn't. You think of everything." Pennywhistle took a long gulp. The liquid of life flooded his veins and began working its magic, deadening fears and sharpening senses.

Dale's expression turned to one of concern. "I mounted the guard at 8:30 and briefly paraded the men at 9, sir. I am reporting to you rather than Captain Wemyss because... and it pains me to bring this up, sir, because of his condition. It is important that you know the men have noted his very poor health. His consumptive cough has greatly worsened in the last two weeks. I am sure that your observant eye has seen it, but you have been kind enough not to remark upon it. The men frankly wonder if he will be able to lead them.

"I saw him early this morning and he was so wracked with coughing that he was unable to rise from the wardroom table. Blood was plainly visible in the phlegm. He is a dedicated officer, but his body is betraying him. And so, Mr. Pennywhistle, when the battle commences, you will be the real commander of the Marines."

Pennywhistle frowned. "You may be right, Sarn't. His body is as frail as his spirit is strong. It pains me to place survival before the courtesy due a brave man, but with the lives of so many marines at stake, it must be so. I shall speak to him directly, and I am sure that we can arrive at an equitable arrangement that is best for all. He would never put his own pride ahead of the welfare of his men or the ship."

"Thank you for quieting my mind, sir." Dale reached into his pocket and produced a small case. He handed it to Pennywhistle. "I believe you will find these useful, sir."

Curious, Pennywhistle opened the case and saw two small objects shaped like circular pagodas.

"Ear protectors, sir, made out of the best beeswax mixed with pads of Egyptian cotton. The thunder of the big guns will deafen after a few broadsides, and you will need something to protect your hearing. I speak from experience, sir, since my own hearing is far from what it used to be."

"Kind of you, Sarn't. I had been speculating about the sound of massed artillery at close quarters, but I had entirely overlooked my own protection. I believe that the hand signals we have agreed upon with the men will obviate most of the need to hear well and will work better than drums, boatswain's whistles, or speaking trumpets. It is also fortunate that you and I are skilled lip readers.

"On my way here, sir, I observed several men practicing those signals."

Pennywhistle's system used various combinations of arms, hands, and fingers to indicate 33 basic commands and movements. The formation commands were typical: a raised left arm in an L shape with the hand open and the palm facing outward indicated a file formation, a left arm held out at 90 degrees with the hand in a fist indicated a line abreast formation, and an arm held downward at 45 degrees with the hand in a fist indicated a wedge formation.

"One other thing, Mr. Pennywhistle," said Dale, with an impassive face but a hint of amusement in his voice. "I am absolutely certain that no matter how many cups of coffee you consume today, your trousers will be as dry at the end of today's fight as they are now."

Pennywhistle's lips twisted and he blinked in surprise. "My worry is that obvious, Sarn't?"

"No, sir, but it's a common enough fear. I would actually suggest that you increase your consumption of beverages today, since we are likely to see heavy and prolonged action."

"I thank you for that endorsement, Sarn't. I'd appreciate it if you would have the drummers beat the assembly at six bells so that I might address the men. No harangue about duty, I merely wish to review practical actions which will save lives."

"Very good, sir."

"In the meantime, I plan on finishing this tankard very slowly. It may be the final contentment of a condemned man, so I shall savor every last drop. And I shall do so without worry."

"Very good, sir," said Dale. Rather than knuckling his round hat in the old manner, he snapped off a smart salute with the palm down; the new acknowledgment was fast gaining favor in the Royal Navy. He pivoted on his heel and briskly walked toward the quarterdeck.

The ship's bell rang five times, reminding Pennywhistle that by the time it rang eight, the ship would be engulfed in smoke and thunder. He sipped his coffee slowly, savoring its effects.

Despite his words to Dale, he dreaded the upcoming conversation with Wemyss. Regulations demanded that he do as he was told, regardless of whether it was right; but his conscience demanded that he do what was right regardless of what he was told. As long as the coffee lasted, he could pretend all was well.

CHAPTER 4

"Do you want me to fetch the old Jerusalem cross, Captain? You have always worn its silver around your neck in battle and it has never failed to bring you luck," asked Will Dobkins cautiously. Wemyss' servant had never seen his master in such a foul mood.

"No, damn it!" Wemyss roared. "No piece of family history is going to do anything for this aching body! Now get out!"

The servant skittered away like a bedbug suddenly exposed to light.

Wemyss opened the cartridge box, removed a small jug, and went back to drinking. The heated rum mixed with opium, onions, pepper, ginseng, peppermint, garlic, and molasses had subdued most of his coughing, at least temporarily. It was a traditional recipe from his time in Jamaica, popular with Voodoo *bokors*. Thanks to the potion, he was able to rise from his cot without being slammed back down by violent spasms.

He hoped the atrocious brew would keep his affliction in check long enough for him to do his job. He had already had two slugs of it this morning; this one and one more just before the battle commenced should see him through the day. The mixture had failed to banish the twitching of his

46

right eye lid, but that had more to do with stress than consumption.

It was not fear of battle that troubled him but a dread that he would be unable to fight at all. Certain Celtic family names occurred repeatedly in marine rosters, and Wemyss, pronounced Weems, was one of them. His father had stood next to Major Pitcairn at Lexington Green when the first shots of the American Revolution had been fired, and his grandfather had fought with great distinction at Belle Île in the Seven Years' War. He would do his utmost to keep that legacy burnished bright.

Wemyss was five-foot-ten and forty years old. He had dark blond hair, a square face with a lantern jaw, and a frame that inclined toward portliness; however, the reduction in appetite caused by his affliction had reduced his proportions. He spoke slowly and deliberately, which matched his style of command: a dependable leader rather than inspired one.

He had to be careful to drink just enough so that he could breathe without being wracked by paroxysms of coughing. He worried his breath might give away the game, but the onions and garlic asserted more influence over olfactory nerves than the rum.

Wemyss was an honest man for the most part, but he had lied several times when Cooke had questioned him about the seriousness of his condition. Telling the truth would have resulted in confinement to his cabin, or even being relieved of command. His duty, he told himself, was to be on deck issuing orders.

He knew his life energy was fading. It would take a supreme effort of will to command his body to perform the service it must, yet he was determined not to miss the honor and excitement of a fleet engagement. His men needed him and he would sooner face a den of lions than disappoint them.

A fleet action could forge a reputation that would echo for centuries to come. So much more glorious to die from cannon fire than consumption. By God, if he had to keep lying to Cooke, he would damn well do so.

Captain John Cooke slowly walked the quarter deck with quiet pride. His eyes took in everything and missed no detail. Heroic leadership was important, but being captain was primarily about being in absolute command of a daunting kaleidoscope of details. At any given moment, a captain needed to have an exact knowledge of his ship's stores, weapons, and personnel. Success in battle could sometimes turn upon a close acquaintance with the most obscure details.

He permitted himself a thin smile of satisfaction: something he did infrequently because he believed the majesty of command went ill with public levity. A captain appearing too much an ordinary man encouraged over-familiarity among the crew. Nonetheless, his smile widened because the universe furnished no greater enterprise than captaining a mighty warship in a great battle: a contest that would bring glory and safety to the British nation.

Mr. Stevenson, the gunner, approached, likely with a bulletin on the ship's powder and weapons.

Stevenson saluted. "Good day, Captain! Both powder magazines are squared away and ready for battle. The approaches have been dampened and all of the men issued slippers. I turned in my final report to your secretary for collation and he should be along with it directly." The Gunner's precautions were necessary to guard against the very real danger of stray sparks starting a fire.

"Very good, Mr. Stevenson," said Cooke. "Please continue making new cartridges. In theory, we have more than enough, but battle always creates surprises, and it is as well to be prepared for every eventuality."

"Aye, aye, Captain."

"I trust you have arranged for plenty of ammunition passers, Mr. Stevenson."

Only two cartridges per cannon were allowed on deck at any given moment to reduce the danger of accidental explosions, so the supply had to be constantly be replenished.

"Indeed I have, Captain. Should any fall, replacements will be available, though it means double duty for some, as we are so short-handed. There will be no interruption in the lines from the magazines to the weather decks. And they will all be adults, as you requested. My own wife will be assisting in that job," he said proudly.

"Good! Powder monkeys have no business handling live cartridges; one mistake could detonate a magazine and doom the entire ship." Powder monkeys were sometimes as young as seven, though most were closer to ten.

"I quite agree, Captain. All of the ship's boys and powder monkeys will be armed only with swabs. They have been instructed to keep eyes peeled for any stray bits of powder and to wet them down immediately."

"I am pleased to see that all of the weather deck weapon racks are stocked and all of the weapon's barrels filled, Mr. Stevenson. It will be a long contest today and our men will need quick access to both edged weapons and firearms. I trust that each gun crew is provided the standard weapons array?"

"Aye, sir. Each gun crew has received a boarding pike, two cutlasses, two tomahawks, and one pistol with a belt hook."

In each gun crew, six men were assigned additional duties: two as boarders, two as cutters, and two as firemen.

"Very good, Mr. Stevenson."

"Now, Captain, if you will excuse me, I must take my leave of you. A thousand and one details demand my attention."

"I appreciate your zeal, Mr. Stevenson. Good luck to you today."

Though Cooke had been captain of *Bellerophon* for only seven months, most of his crew had worked together for four years and had a fleet-wide reputation for solid teamwork. That teamwork would be tested to the limit today, because at 540 men *Bellerophon* was 100 short of a full crew.

Cooke was 42 years of age, of a medium build, with an ordinary looking face and a moon-shaped head distinguished chiefly by the bright blond hair that remained on his temples though it had deserted his crown. He had been in the Navy since age 11 and had fought in both the East and West Indies, notably at the Battle of the Saintes in 1782. In command of the *Nymphe*, he had engineered the daring capture of two French frigates almost in sight of Brest Harbor.

Cooke wished that he possessed some of Nelson's easygoing congeniality. He tended to be stiff and formal, even when off duty. He was a solidly professional seaman who kept mostly to himself. He knew himself to be prickly at times, a stern disciplinarian who engendered respect, not love. He liked to think he made up in dependability what he lacked in agreeability. The collegiality he left to his First Lieutenant; the quietly personable Cumby got on well with all manner of people.

The son of a long time clerk at the Admiralty, Cooke was a scion of the middle class, accepted into a Navy where fortune and distinction were more often earned by merit than by birth. The sea was a harsh mistress and meted out brutal sentences to those who sought to master her with pedigree rather than ability. Nevertheless, a good family name mattered.

He, for instance, had a sterling reputation; but no band of junior officers had tied their promotions and placements to his career because no one exerted influence on his behalf at the Admiralty. He cut no dashing figure and was completely devoid of the outsize flamboyance of a Cochrane or Sydney Smith.

He wore his best uniform today: white silk shirt, chalk-colored waistcoat, and double-breasted blue tailcoat of superfine broadcloth adorned with gold buttons and epaulettes. Ivory kidskin breeches and gloves, silk stockings, and black Hessian boots with gold tassels completed the outfit. His cravat of thick black silk was carefully tied in an Oriental Knot. The whole was topped off with a black *chapeau de bras* that he wore in a fore and aft rig.

He reached into his pocket, checking to make sure that the St. Christopher's medal resided within. He considered it a Popish artifact and had no belief in its ability to bring luck, but his wife had given it to him. It symbolized her love, and as such had great importance.

"Excuse me, Captain." It was Mr. Hazard, his secretary, the master of all manner of arcane paperwork. "Your signature is required on the final summaries of the boatswain's, carpenter's, and gunner's stores. I hate bothering you, sir, but I wanted to give you the most up-to-date information."

"Ah, Mr. Hazard, it is less terrifying to fight the French than confront the paperwork that constitute a Captain's lot. But the Admiralty has very particular ways of doing things, which must be observed. Cannons and muskets may be instrumental to victory, but the Navy runs on paperwork." He scrutinized the lists. "Good, good, Mr. Hazard everything is in order. You may add these to the twenty other forms I signed earlier."

Hazard held aloft a small portable writing desk with quill and ink pot. Cooke dipped the quill and affixed his signature to each document.

Cooke's ship was a typical 74 of the third rate: a floating fortress. Like 39 of her sisters, she had been copied from *HMS Bellona,* designed by Sir Thomas Slade. Such ships-of-the-line formed the backbone of Nelson's fleet.

British captains thought of their ships as women, and women had distinct personalities. Cooke saw *Bellerophon* not as the kind of flashy woman who would dazzle you with flirts and fluff, but the sturdy, unassuming type with whom you would settle down to build a life. She was stiff and weatherly, like himself; good at keeping a straight course with little drift to leeward. He felt certain that something more than chance had brought them together.

Bellerophon was a fast ship and had been nicknamed "The Flying *Bellerophon.*" The figurehead portrayed Bellerophon as a red-cloaked warrior, javelin upraised, riding the winged horse Pegasus. The Earl of Sandwich loved Greek and Roman mythology, and as First Lord of the Admiralty he had started a tradition of naming ships after men and beasts found in those tales. Her crew, however, understood little of Greek Mythology and suffered from the common British predilection for mispronouncing foreign words. To them she was simply "The Billy Ruffian."

Bellerophon was 168 feet long on the upper gun deck; 46 feet in beam; 1,600 tons burden and carried 1,200 tons of food, water, and supplies. She had cost £30,00, taken two-and-a-half years to construct, and 2,000 trees had been felled to provide her lumber. Her sails constituted more than two acres of canvas, and the rope in her rigging would be 25 miles in length if stretched end to end. She drew 21 feet, 1/7 of her length at the waterline, and could sail at 20 of 32 compass points. She was capable of 13 knots under ideal conditions though her average speed in fair weather was closer to 6.

Her armament consisted of twenty-eight 32-pound cannon on the lower gun deck, twenty-eight 18-pounders on the upper gun deck, fourteen 9-pounders on the quarter deck, and four 9-pounders on her forecastle. 80 round shot per gun were allocated for the 32's, and 100 rounds for the rest of her ordnance. Each gun was also supplied with 13 rounds of grape and canister. Power for those weapons came from 27,000 pounds of powder stored in three-hundred 90-pound barrels.

The two 32-pound carronades on her forecastle and the six 18-pound carronades on her poop were not counted as part of her regular armament. Carronades were shorter and stubbier than the great guns, and narrower at the bore than the breech. Much lighter than cannons throwing the same weight of ball, they employed slides rather than wheels to absorb the recoil. By greatly reducing the difference between the bore and the size of the ball, a carronade used a charge only one sixth that of a cannon to propel a round over a short distance. In fights so close that hulls nearly touched, the "smashers" were anti-personnel weapons that often proved decisive. Combined with her regular cannon, *Bellerophon* could throw a thousand pounds of iron in a broadside.

Her hull was black with two wide swaths of buff marking her gun decks; her stern displayed intricate gold filigree work: proof that art and war were not mutually exclusive.

Entering service in 1790, *Bellerophon* had compiled an admirable battle record. She'd played an important part in the Glorious First of June in 1794, but her most dramatic role had been at the Battle of the Nile in 1798. She'd single-handedly engaged *L'Orient,* the 120-gun monster that was the largest ship in the French Fleet. She had been severely mauled for her impudence: completely dismasted and with a long casualty list; but her sacrifice had paved the way for the gigantic explosion that had disintegrated *L'Orient* so violently that it was heard 22 miles away in Alexandria.

Here came Babbage, one of Cooke's five personal servants —every captain was allocated one servant per hundred crewmen. "Captain, I have your sword sharpened and ready; let me help you on with it. Your pistol is loaded as well."

"Excellent, Babbage. I trust that you checked the balls for roundness."

"I did indeed, Captain."

Cooke lifted his arms, as Babbage lifted his coat and buckled the sword belt round his waist. The belt also mounted a frogged crossdraw holster to the right of the sword. His razor sharp 39-inch sword was an exact copy of Nelson's, complete with ivory grip, hexagonal brass pommel, and five ball guard that could also function as a knuckle duster. His .50 caliber rifled pistol possessed twin brass barrels and was accurate up to 25 yards.

Screwloose raced by in a blur, still in angry pursuit of his nemesis, Shredder.

Cooke arched his heavy eyebrows in surprise at the feline's inexhaustible energy. He wondered why he was concerned about the fate of the ship's cat, but then, Screwloose was beloved by every sailor on board. He brought three or four rat corpses each day to his cabin as offerings. The midshipmen took care of the rodents, finding that when well fried they were not bad eating.

Two hours earlier, *Bellerophon's* six boats had been loaded with all manner of valuable miscellany, including the ship's livestock: pigs, cows, ducks, hens, and geese. Towed 100 yards astern, these boats were no longer a potential source of splinters, and they kept the livestock, if not completely out of harm's way, at least from causing pandemonium on the ship.

He had let Screwloose stay aboard because the huge orange tomcat had yowled his earnest determination to remain, pleading that he too was a member of the crew. Besides, sailors considered Screwloose a good luck talisman, and anything that boosted morale before a battle was welcome. He was not at all sure if there was a deity, but nonetheless said a silent prayer for the cat's welfare, then reproached himself for not first offering one for his men.

"Gracious Heavenly Father, Jesus my Savior, and Holy Ghost, Lord of all things spiritual and temporal, I humbly beseech you to keep all aboard this fine ship in your favor and mercy."

Fifty feet away, William Pryce Cumby, Wemyss' good friend and the ship's First Lieutenant, knelt in a prayer that he spoke aloud in quiet, reverent tones. He considered a supplication to Heaven essential preparation for the inspection that was the First Officer's prime duty before battle. He asked Christ for divine guidance that he might miss nothing untoward.

Cumby was a plain-spoken, modest man with sensitive eyes and a poet's mouth. A well proportioned, raven-haired man of 34, he was not given to ostentation. His double-breasted blue tailcoat and white trousers were of good but not exceptional quality. He sported a black bicorn with a sable cockade worn athwartships that was much less fashionable than the newer *chapeau de bras,* and he preferred jockey boots to gold-tasseled Hessian ones.

Cumby was a good Church of England man, pious yet worldly, and mindful of the responsibilities he bore. He asked the Almighty to protect his wife and two children and to lend him some of His strength so that he could discharge his obligations with honor and skill.

The sailor's nickname for Cumby was "the quiet man." You would have trouble distinguishing him in a crowd, yet sailors noted that when he came around things got done and performances improved. He and his captain had a relationship much like a Scots laird and his chief ghillie. The captain played the strict disciplinarian and planned the grand tactics, while Cumby spoke the kindly voice of moderation and took care of the small details.

Mr. Ames, the ship's master-at-arms, approached. Along with the boatswain, he performed the function of senior policeman aboard *Bellerophon*. "Forgive me for disrupting your reflections, Mr. Cumby, but you asked me to speak to you about any men under arrest at the time of battle. Seamen Barton and Hamilton got into a fight last night. I took them into custody and placed them in irons."

"What was the fight about, Mr. Ames?"

"Something silly, sir. Whether the French or the Spanish are the more dangerous enemies."

"I do not recall either having been in trouble before, Mr. Ames. I know that I commended Barton for his skill with knots, and I seem to recall that Hamilton has a way with the animals in the ship's manger."

"That is so, Mr. Cumby."

"Then release them and forego any punishment. They are sound men who got a little too carried away by their fighting spirit. We need such men today."

"Very good, Lieutenant."

Cumby had served on various frigates and ships-of-the-line, yet had never been granted the chance to test his mettle in battle. He enjoyed an inner confidence that he would acquit himself well, and even measure up to the ultimate test of command, should his captain fall. Their cause was righteous, their ship sound, and his sailors models of disciplined reliability. No officer could wish for more.

When he had breakfasted with Cooke at eight that morning, the captain had shown Cumby a memorandum from the Admiral. Nelson's instructions were clear and unmistakable. Two columns of ships would cut the enemy line at right angles. Captains were "to look to their particular line as a rallying point. If signals be neither seen nor perfectly understood, no captain can do very wrong if he places his ship alongside that of an enemy." Cumby thought the final sentence perfectly summed up Nelson's aggressive attitude.

At the same moment as Cooke and Cumby contemplated their ship's readiness for battle, Royal Marine privates Martin Combs and James Warwick were discussing battle in more basic terms.

"What do you think our odds are of making it through the day, Jim? That we are using the .670 cartridges tells me the action is going to be long and hot," said Combs.

"Battle is always a gamble, but ain't no folk on earth better trained than us Royal Marines. The enemy doesn't practice marksmanship, but we do, every day. Every one of us can hit a man's heart nine times out of ten at fifty yards; I think that gives us a real edge."

Combs was tall and thin, and bore the nickname Stringbean, while Warwick, short and squat, had been christened Stumpy. They disliked their nicknames, but marines loved to joke about personal attributes, and so they had learned to live with them.

Pennywhistle had taught them that one's weapon had to be kept in a pristine state at all times, so both men were cleaning and oiling muskets for their entire section, ones with browned barrels rather than the shiny-barreled ones employed for drill. There was no point in letting reflected sunlight give the enemy an advantage in pinpointing their position.

The .75 caliber, 53-inch Sea Service Brown Bess had a shorter barrel and simpler furniture than its Army cousin. Each was a smoothbore, weighed ten pounds, and fired a .685 caliber, 482-grain round ball. Propelled at 1,200 feet per second by 165 grains of black powder, the soft lead ball sometimes ballooned on impact to the size of a small pomegranate.

"I trust Captain Cooke," said Combs thoughtfully. "He's seen a lot of fighting. He will bring us through just fine. I think Mr. Cumby's a good man, too. I just wish that he had battle experience. You've been under fire before, Jim. What's it like?"

"Mainly it's a jumble of noise and confusion," replied Warwick, as a far away expression changed the cast of his face. "There is smoke everywhere, and besides the spit-spat of musket fire there is a lot of shouting, screaming, and crying. You can see the enemy faces at first, and you see that they are just as scared as you are. But after a few rounds, all you can see are musket flashes through the smoke, almost like watching fireflies. You just keep shooting at those fireflies until they go away, or until your officer yells for everyone to give them cold steel. Mostly you trust your commanders and remember your training."

"What do you think of our Marine officers?" Combs inquired.

"Wemyss knows his business, though his health ain't fine. Higgins is young but his heart is good, and I ain't never seen an officer so enthusiastic about everything he does. It's that rat's arse Wilson I don't like. That sneer in his voice and the contempt in his eyes bother me; there is more calculation than courage there. I worry that he is all jug and no handle. He's the kind of man always thinking first about his own hide and happy enough to sacrifice others to protect it." Warwick rubbed the cloth carefully along another barrel.

"Now Mr. Pennywhistle's a born warrior. His eyes I like. I seen them go from granite hard to soft as morning dew; character, but kindness. He puts his money where his mouth is, too. We are able to fire live rounds in practice because he funds them from his own pocket. That don't come cheap. All the government pays for is 16 live rounds a month."

"He knows more about guns than other officers I have met. How did he come to be so smart?"

"I asked the sarge that same question. He told me when Mr. Pennywhistle first joined up he persuaded the Commandant at Stonehouse Barracks to let him run some tests on Brown Besses to find out exactly what they could do. He and two other marine officers fired off muskets for two days straight and took measurements of everything."

"Just what did he find out?" Combs reached for another musket.

"What you and I know already, Marty. Our Besses are sturdy but they ain't accurate. Sarge said Mr. Pennywhistle discovered that while our ball could penetrate a one inch thick pine board at 100 yards, he could only hit a ten-foot by six-foot target 60 times out of a hundred at that distance. At 200 yards, he had to aim five and a half feet above the target to come anywhere near it.

"He also found out only 55 percent of his powder burned, which is why after thirty shots the leftover sludge makes it impossible to use the .685 round." Warwick hefted the gun in his hand.

"I am glad he's clever, but it's his attitude that impresses me. He's complimented me twice on the smartness of my drill, and I ain't forgot that. Wilson don't never speak to a man lessen it's to cut him up good with that nasty tongue of his."

"I worry about Higgins," said Combs. "I don't argue that he loves what he does, but he don't have no real experience. I ain't even sure if he has beard enough for a razor, yet he has my life in his hands." He rubbed his fingers along his own closely shaven jaw.

"Now I been watching Mr. Higgins real close, Marty. And you know what he does really well? He listens. He pays solid attention when the sergeant and Mr. Pennywhistle give him instruction. I seen some young officers so bloody arrogant that they never truly learn their profession. One bad officer did not even know how to maneuver his company when the battle was joined and had to ask his sergeant what commands to give. Pups like that think having a coat of arms makes them an officer by right of birth. Mr. Higgins takes his profession seriously, and that counts for a lot with me."

Combs looked dubious. "Maybe so, Jim, but I'd feel better if Mr. Higgins were a few years older." He scratched his head. "I wonder what the Frenchies are thinking about right now?"

"Probably wondering what the British are thinking!" Warwick laughed. "Or how badly they will get licked today. They are afraid of Nelson, rightly so. I'll hazard that a lot are thinking about wives and sweethearts, wine and cheese, and wondering if they will ever be able to enjoy them in front of a warm, safe hearth. They ain't as well trained or well led as we are, but the *matelots* doing the actual fighting ain't really so different from our lot. They are fighting for their mates and their ship a lot more than they are fighting for Boney. I almost feel sorry for them."

"Sorry for the French?" said Combs, scandalized.

"Why not?" replied Warwick defensively. "It's a lot harder to fight tooth and nail in a battle that you are probably going to lose than in one that you are pretty sure to win. I'll say this for the French: their casualty lists are always long when they fight us, and that don't come from men who lack courage. They ain't no quitters. They fight, get beat, rise, and fight again. And that makes our job tougher." He looked at Combs.

"The way I see it, it ain't necessary to hate a man to kill him in battle. You can fight just as well seeing your enemy as men, not monsters. The French want the same thing we do: the right to go home. On a distant anniversary of today's battle, the average *matelot* wants to be able to roll up his sleeve, show his scars as trophies, and tell the grandson on his knee, "These I got at the great Battle of Trafalgar. I done my part and never let my country down."

"You're a philosopher," said Combs with amusement. "That's not covered under The Regulations. It's dangerous to think too much."

"You have to think a little to keep your conscience alive. It's not hard to get carried away in battle. Killing is easy; knowing when to stop is hard."

CHAPTER 5

Sunlight glinting off two dancing cutlasses caught Pennywhistle's eye. It was gratifying to see the techniques of swordsmanship that he had begun teaching sailors four months before being practiced. Angus MacFarlane and George Jepson, the wielders of the cutlasses, had taken to swordsmanship as eagerly as cats to fish wagons. They moved back and forth with speed, precision and power: lunge, cut, parry, riposte.

He recalled the afternoon that he sprang his training surprise on the wardroom, smiling at how a foolish action had resulted in a good end. July 21, 1805, had been the third anniversary of the duel that had changed his life forever.

It had begun with a fight....

Pennywhistle's left forearm block slammed into the powerful right cross, easily batting it aside. He had seen it coming in Thomas's neck and shoulder muscles before it was launched. Without retracting his arm, he spread and locked the fingers of left hand and smartly jabbed his palm heel into his opponent's chin.

He did not add the force of his calf muscles, and he hit the side of the chin rather than coming up under it because he sought to demonstrate, not injure. His left hand glided down and grasped his opponent's lapel even as his right hand seized a wrist. He shifted all of Thomas' weight to his right leg and pushed him backwards at exactly the moment he shoved his left leg behind Thomas's right and kicked violently upwards.

With nothing to bear all of the weight, Thomas crashed to the wardroom deck like a brick that had tried to fly. His expression was one of astonishment, though he looked seconds away from passing out. He struggled to recover the wind that had been knocked out of him.

"No hard feelings I hope, Mr. Thomas, but you said you wanted a realistic test of *savate* against English pugilism. Had I added more force and redirected the palm heel strike, I assure you that you would now be dead."

"That was extraordinary," gasped Scott.

"I have never seen its like," exclaimed Saunders.

"Amusing," sneered Douglas.

Pennywhistle extended his hand and helped a shaky Thomas to his feet. "That fight was over before it began," Thomas said groggily. "It pains me to admit it, but your fighting art has merits that English boxing seems to have missed."

Thomas glanced at the hands that had thrown him and a look of shock passed over his scholarly face. "I say, sir, your hands are extraordinarily rough! Far rougher than a common seaman's, yet I know you to be a gentleman born!"

Pennywhistle surveyed his palms with satisfaction, realizing how discordant they were with his dress and bearing. "It is because I soak them in pickle brine for thirty minutes every day. It is a trick I learned from an old sailor. He did it so that his hands would be resistant to burns from fast descents on long ropes. I do it so that the striking surfaces of my hands become weapons even when I am unarmed."

He helped Thomas to the wardroom table and poured him a glass of wine, then addressed the other wardroom officers.

"There are three lessons to learn from that demonstration, gentlemen. A jab is a better opening move than a punch: it is faster to execute and unexpected. A palm heel strike spreads out the force of a blow more evenly than a punch and spares the knuckles. Balance is everything in a fight: remove it entirely from a foe and he is at your mercy."

The wardroom officers exchanged glances, as if a stage conjurer had revealed the secrets of his illusions. "You say this fighting art is a creation of the French?" Mr. Scott asked thoughtfully. "It's efficient certainly, but seems more fitted to street gypsies than gentlemen."

"You are both right and wrong, Mr. Scott," replied Pennywhistle with a scholar's eagerness to teach. "*Savate* is a compilation of fighting techniques from the back alleys of Paris and Marseilles. It is sometimes called *boxe française* and uses slaps, chops, backhands, and kicks in addition to punches. It is meant to kill, pure and simple. While it may be inelegant, I think most gentlemen care more about their survival than the origins of a useful art that can give them an edge in battle."

"How did you learn this... art?" inquired Douglas sourly. He shot the younger officer a look that suggested he fully expected Pennywhistle to frequent cathouses and involve himself in street brawls in the worst districts of Paris.

"From my tutor, Justin du Motier. He was one of the greatest swordsmen in France and he taught me the art of the blade. He was a refugee from the Terror given sanctuary by my father. Du Motier saved my father's life during the late American War—one Mason doing a good deed for another."

"I am impressed by *savate*, Mr. Pennywhistle, but how would your art fare against a knife?" asked Saunders with the delight of a child who has just discovered a new toy.

"Rather than telling, allow me to show you. You see that dirk that some careless midshipman has left on the chair yonder? Pick it up and come at me."

Saunders did as asked and cautiously advanced on Pennywhistle.

"Now stab me!"

Saunders slowly pushed the knife toward Pennywhistle.

"No, Mr. Saunders. Mean it! Stab; don't tickle."

Saunders thrust directly for Pennywhistle's stomach. Pennywhistle executed a sweeping low block with his right arm as he sidestepped. In one fluid motion, he grasped Saunders wrist and elbow jerked his arm skyward. Then to the wardroom's surprise, he abruptly stopped.

"At this point, I have two options, gentlemen. Slam his elbow down on my upraised knee and break his arm, or force his arm downward and plunge the dirk into his thigh. The important thing to remember is that men are most vulnerable where they are jointed."

He let go of Saunders's arm, then extended his hand, which Saunders enthusiastically shook. "Very impressive, Mr. Pennywhistle!" he exclaimed. "I hope that you will teach me something of your art in the days to come."

"I am glad that you gentlemen are impressed with savate's efficiency," said Pennywhistle earnestly. "I consider it an art form equal in its precision to the ballet. Yet while the ballet may delight the soul, it will never save a life. Since I have your attention, allow me to bring up a martial inefficiency that has troubled me since I came aboard five months ago.

"Mr. Stevenson told me that not a man in a hundred serving in this Navy can be found who can cut with a sword to effect at the right side of his opponent, or even make the attempt should the opening present itself. Few men can strike with the cutlass at any part except the chest or the head, and this with an awkwardness that is of no utility when opposed to one who is trained."

"Sadly, that is so," sighed Thomas in frustration.

"I could scarce credit my ears," said Pennywhistle with indignation, "but then I spoke to Seaman MacFarlane, a man recommended to me because he had fought in two successful cutting out expeditions. He confirmed Stevenson's judgment. I recall his words exactly: 'Don't remember anyone teaching me any special moves or stuff. I do what everyone else does. I run straight at a Frenchie screaming like a banshee and just shove the tip of my cutlass into his chest, like spitting a duck. If I swing and slash, I go for Johnny Crapaud's head.'"

Everyone in the wardroom nodded in acknowledgment.

"Considering the demanding training that our Navy gives gun crews and the unstinting drill my Marines perform daily, I found this situation as astonishing as it was intolerable. I found it repellant that the dead hand of tradition should allow good men to die simply because no one had the wit to train them properly.

"I worked out a solution for the problem, and for the past month have been putting it into action. I believe that now is as good a time as any to present it. I know that sailors are your responsibility, gentlemen, not mine, and I apologize for stepping on any professional toes. However, you have all seen me practicing with my cutlass day after day, in foul weather as well as fair. I know some of you have even laughed at my zeal," Pennywhistle saw looks of chagrin around the table, "yet I think that you will acknowledge that I am handy with a blade."

"Are you saying that you have developed a training program?" demanded Scott in astonishment.

"Indeed, I have, Mr. Scott. It is simple and easily learned if practiced regularly. I spent many hours studying fencing treatises and reflecting upon my own training. I have distilled swordsmanship down to a few essential evolutions that, if written, would occupy no more space than a child's hornbook. It is blade work designed for battle rather than the fencing salon and utilizes only the cutlass rather than the foil or saber."

"Is it a short version of the style of training favored by the great master Domineco Angelo Junior?" inquired Thomas.

"No, Mr. Thomas. Angelo teaches gentlemen how to fight other gentlemen on land, whilst I teach common sailors how to fight all manner of foemen on pitching decks. In my system, evolutions that require complex footwork or seek to trade distance for the perfect killing riposte are banished because deck space is limited. Any attack that requires more than two paces to execute I consider impractical. Blocks are hard and simple, best administered with the upper part of the blade. Feints are simple as well, since they generally constitute a game of opposites: your blade moving right when your intention is to strike left, or moving up when the final destination is down. To hit the heart pretend to go for the groin; to strike the groin, appear to go for the heart."

"That seems sensible," said Douglas, impressed in spite of himself.

Pennywhistle continued, emboldened, because even the crankiest man in the wardroom seemed receptive to his ideas. "I teach that the *forte* and *feeble* of the sword—the upper and lower parts of the blade—should be thought of as a shield extending from the top of your collar bone to just below your groin. The tip of the blade will take care of your head and lower leg. That same space in front of the enemy will form your principal avenues of attack.

"I have instructed sailors to think of the zone in front of them as two crosses atop one another. Holding your blade either horizontally or vertically as you move from high inside to high outside defends the first cross. Doing the same but moving from low inside to low outside would protect the second. I have focused on showing the men variants of 'The Rule of Four.'

"Men usually broadcast their moves before their bodies make them, so I have taught my trainees to pay attention to the shift of an opponent's hand on the hilt, the change in the tension of shoulder and neck muscles, and alterations in the cast of his eyes."

"I must say, Mr. Pennywhistle, you seem to have thought this out very carefully," remarked Scott.

"Thank you. I have to confess my talk and actions of the past thirty minutes may have seemed spontaneous but were carefully rehearsed, intended to guide you to a certain point of view. As with *savate*, it is much better to show than to tell. I have a dozen sailors standing by on the poop ready to show you what they have learned. I believe that you will find the display impressive.

"Wait!" said Douglas skeptically. "How is that none of us knows about this? "

"It is because I asked the warrant officers to divert any officers headed our way, or to alert us when my dozen practiced in the orlop: every day, one hour just after dawn. My volunteers agreed to keep their mates in the dark about their training as well. I apologize for this conspiracy of silence, but I did not want you to draw any conclusions before my men were ready. Now, gentlemen, I suggest that we repair to the poop where you can render a proper judgment."

MacFarlane, the leader of the trainees, stepped forward to address the lieutenants, knuckling his tarred round hat in salute. He was barefooted and dressed as most sailors aboard: white bell-bottom trousers, blue-checked shirt, red neckerchief, and short blue jacket with brass buttons. A giant of a man with hands like hams, his nickname was Gorilla and he had tattoos of the sun, the moon, and a mermaid on his heavily muscled right forearm.

"Good afternoon, Gentlemen. I have prepared a demonstration of what we dozen have learned in the last month. It will be as realistic as possible, so we will not be substituting singlesticks of stout ash for our blades. The cutlass is a heavy weapon and repeated practice with it not only makes us accustomed to its balance but builds strength in our arms. We can also fight with either hand, because battle fatigues muscles quickly.

"Since we realize that our enthusiasm could result in grievous injury, our blades wear carapaces of leather so that no one will bleed, though some will be left black and blue. Each of us will work with his partner, so you will see six matches proceeding simultaneously. It is the best way to show you a variety of possibilities in a very short time. When it is done, I shall explain to you the notions that underlie our training."

The sailors formed themselves into pairs. Pennywhistle dropped a silk handkerchief, and 12 blades swept through the air.

MacFarlane slashed at his opponent, Jepson, who parried the cut to his sternum with a low outside horizontal block. Jepson responded with a slash to MacFarlane's upper torso, which MacFarlane turned aside with a high inside vertical block. His returning cut at Jepson's groin was parried with a low inside vertical block. Jepson feinted at MacFarlane's chest, then cut at his thigh.

MacFarlane turned it aside and riposted with a straight line lunge to Jepson's chest, which connected solidly. "Ouch!" yelped Jepson. He grinned ruefully at MacFarlane and lowered his blade. The real life thrust would have been fatal.

Pennywhistle observed with satisfaction and consulted his Blancpain. The duration of the fight had been thirty-five seconds. The other five contests ended in the next minute.

The four lieutenants nodded and murmured in approval. The 12 swordsmen bowed in response. MacFarlane stepped forward.

"Gentlemen, on the first day of training, Mr. Pennywhistle said to us, "If you can dance a hornpipe, I can teach you how to fight. You just have to follow the Rule of Four."

We learned the box step from a new dance that is gaining popularity on the Continent but is little known in England: the waltz. The box furnished us way to both attack and retreat and is suited to the small spaces on deck where boarders can sometimes be packed as tightly as schools of herring.

Here is how the box step works, gentlemen. You may want to try it yourselves as I recite it." MacFarlane moved as he talked. "Start by bringing the feet together; step forward with the left foot, step to the right by swinging the right foot forward and to the right, then bring the feet together; step backwards with the right foot, then back and to the side with the left, then bring the feet together. To continue, redo the process from the start."

MacFarlane paused as the four lieutenants tried the box step. He was not surprised to see two of them smile when they finished. "The box step is for maneuver only. When we fight we observe the usual rules of the blade: pivoting grip for flexibility, side stance with even weight distribution to present the smallest target, and committing to a move only at the last second to outfox your opponent.

"We have even practiced blindfolded from time to time," he added.

"Why on earth would you do that?" inquired a puzzled Douglas.

"It's called *le sentiment du fer*, Mr. Douglas, and it focuses all of your sensibilities in your arm and hand so that your very nerves seem attached to the blade. With your vision blocked, you become more alert to changes in sound and pressure that usually go unnoticed."

"Sounds complicated."

"Beggin' your pardon, Mr. Douglas, it's not, once you do it a few times. Now if you gentlemen will recall the demonstrations just past, you will have noticed that we practiced several manifestations of the Rule of Four. Four steps forward and back go well with the four parts of the two crosses. Slow, slow, quick, quick, high inside, high outside, low inside, low outside.

"Feints come in fours as well. Feint high, strike low; feint low, strike high; feint inside, strike outside; feint outside, strike inside. We sailors have made a ditty of it: High low, low high, inside outside, outside inside. We use four stances, and employ our swords four ways: lunge, cut, parry, and riposte. We have been instructed in six cuts and eight parries, though we rely upon the primary four of each.

"When I look at an opponent, I see a large x on his body with a horizontal line drawn through the middle of the x. Slashing diagonally downwards or upwards from left to right is one half of the x: the other half is doing the same thing to the other side of his body. A straight slash from left to right or right to left completes our inventory of cuts.

"Mr. Pennywhistle cautioned us that while a straight thrust is more often fatal, it is also more likely to result in the blade being trapped in a target. The slash will kill fewer men but put more out of action, and requires less energy to deliver—an important concern in a long battle. "

"A remarkable demonstration, MacFarlane!" proclaimed an amazed Scott. He walked over to Pennywhistle and shook his hand vigorously. "You have outdone yourself, sir! My question is, can these techniques be taught to the rest of the crew?"

"My intent, Mr. Scott, is to make martial missionaries of my dozen, preachers of the Gospel of Four. I shall of course need your support, as well as that of the other lieutenants and Mr. Cumby when I present these ideas to the captain."

"And you shall have it, Mr. Pennywhistle!" said Scott. The other lieutenants gave varying indications of agreement.

Pennywhistle bowed. "I thank you gentlemen for your consideration. Courageous men can accomplish brave deeds, but brave hearts with trained hands are so much better!"

"Bloody know-it-all," muttered Douglas crossly.

"Excuse me, sir." MacFarlane's deep burr snapped Pennywhistle out of his reveries and back to present reality. "I just wanted to thank you for all that you have taught us. I've not said much, we Scots are not good at giving praise, but I could not go into battle without letting you know that every sailor aboard owes you a debt."

Pennywhistle's left eyebrow arched in understanding. "Praise to the face is open disgrace, eh, MacFarlane?"

MacFarlane looked at Pennywhistle like he was a mind reader.

"My mother is a Scot, so I understand. The privilege has been mine. It is only when a man teaches skills to another that his own reach their best fruition. *Manus manum lavat,* Seneca once remarked."

"Who's Seneca, sir?"

Pennywhistle chuckled. "Someone long dead who had a lot of opinions."

CHAPTER 6

"You say that Captain Cooke spent £100 of his own money to purchase this chronometer? Extraordinary!" remarked Roger Godwin, the ship's schoolmaster. The device that he was carefully examining was only slightly larger than the pocket watch that it resembled.

"Thomas Earnshaw's best," said Overton. "Chronometers are not standard equipment, and the Captain is much concerned with precise navigation. "

Godwin was finding that each day brought new knowledge of a world that was proving unexpectedly fascinating. Possessed of a hawk nose, brooding eyes, and an excessively lean frame, he had joined the ship a month before in poor spirits; angry that his frequent bouts with the bottle had forced him to accept a position at sea educating nine blockheaded midshipmen.

His reliance on alcohol had diminished with each day that he spent aboard because he was coming to have a real respect for the discipline and orderliness of this wooden world. Very little happened by chance; almost everything was the result of a well thought out procedure carried out on a daily basis.

He was the equivalent of a warrant officer and messed with the other warrant officers: Mr. Jewell, the Purser; Mr. Mart, the Carpenter; Mr. Robinson, the Boatswain; Mr.

Stevenson, the Gunner; and his new friend, Mr. Overton. All had specific skills. To function, a ship required every trade found in a great metropolis: coopers and cobblers, blacksmiths and bakers, tailors and tanners to name but a few.

"Latitude has always been easy to calculate, but not so longitude," continued Overton. "Longitude is related to time and the earth's rotation, and so requires a timepiece that is both accurate and sturdy enough to withstand the rigors of the sea. When Sir Cloudesley Shovel's fleet was wrecked off the Scilly Isles in 1707 because it was sixty miles from where he thought it was, the Admiralty offered a £20,000 prize for the creation of a truly accurate chronometer. Many tried and failed, including Sir Isaac Newton.

"The man who succeeded was John Harrison, a man of obscure origins who was not even a watchmaker but a cabinet builder. My point is that the sea furnishes unusual opportunities for men with talent, opportunities that exist nowhere else. I am a man of humble birth, yet here I am master of one of the most expensive pieces of the King's property. Talent is valued above all else at sea. In a storm, no one cares about your name, your court connections, or the color of your skin. What matters is skill and experience. I have been so long at sea that my very blood is salt water. You, on the other hand, are new. I should be very curious to hear your impressions of the sea."

Godwin rubbed his chin in thought. "I have conflicting outlooks, Mr. Overton. The sea is Janus-faced and I am both frightened and impressed by her. I understand why she is referred to in the feminine. In my short time aboard, I have seen her go from peaceful repose to sullen moodiness to murderous fury in the space of a few hours."

"Indeed," said Overton. "The sea has many moods and the wise mariner must always keep a close watch on her."

"What impresses me most, Mr. Overton, is her sheer power. Mighty warships are as a child's toys to her. She regards the works of man as men might judge an anthill: inconsequential and easily destroyed. I can see how men might be seduced by her allure, but to me she will always remain a mystery."

Overton smiled. "I have spent a lifetime trying to puzzle out that mystery and am no closer to solving it then when I first went to sea as a ship's boy. I have always wondered why it is called Planet Earth and not Planet Ocean. It is a foolish sailor indeed who does not regard the sea with wariness and awe.

"I must say, Mr. Godwin, that the sea agrees with you. You were seasick but a day when you came aboard, and you have nearly mastered the rolling gait which enables a sailor to navigate pitching decks. Admiral Nelson is a great leader but he is usually sick for a week when he goes to sea after an extended stay ashore."

"I find the sea air crisp and bracing," replied Godwin. "It is a great relief after the soot-laden air and dark skies of London. My father thought accepting this position would be my ruination, but I am beginning to see that it is actually my salvation. I am a scholar, not a seaman, but I confess that, like you, I am seeing *Bellerophon* as my home. I want to fight for that home. I never thought that I would be interested in testing my martial virtue, but I am interested now. I wish I knew of some way to be useful in the battle ahead."

Overton smiled. "Your resolve is admirable, Mr. Godwin. Messengers are always in short supply and play a vital role in any battle. A man with a fine memory would be a great asset to the Captain. Let me speak to him on your behalf. I do warn you though, that you will spend much time on the quarterdeck, likely the place of greatest danger. Are you sure you want to do this?"

"Very sure. I cannot sit idle while men are putting their lives at hazard. My young charges will also be risking life and limb today. I know I am not popular, but I should like to show them that their teacher is willing to share their burden. I promise you that if I perish under such circumstances, I will have no regrets."

While the world of wooden walls was a man's domain, each ship in the fleet was home to a few women: *Bellerophon* had two. Both were wives of warrant officers. Warrant officer status guaranteed them small cabins, which gave the women some measure of privacy.

Nancy Overton was married to Godwin's new friend, and Mary Stevenson was the spouse of the ship's Gunner. The two women were in their early thirties, twenty years younger than their husbands, both attracted to older men because of their stability of character. Nancy was tall and fair with long blonde tresses. Mary was short with curly, dark hair and olive skin.

Nancy wore a high-waisted grey dress with puffy sleeves, a shawl collar, and a muslin overskirt, while Mary wore nearly the same rig in blue. The dresses were sensible and sturdy, like the women who wore them. Both sported straw bonnets.

Ordinarily the women performed housekeeping duties such as washing, mending, or sewing clothes, but in battle they passed cartridges, made bandages, and assisted the surgeon in his gruesome work in the cockpit.

Nancy and Mary emerged onto the quarterdeck to listen to the small ship's band. Music was an important element in inspiring the men before and during battle. Cooke had retained the services of six professional musicians from Hanover and paid for them with his own funds. Considered a virtual Continental satrapy of the British crown, Hanover was famous for the skill of its bandsmen. Sir William

Herschel, the discoverer of the Planet Uranus, had originally come to England as a humble Hanoverian musician.

Franz Koenig, the band's leader and talented tuba artist, acknowledged the women's applause with a quick bow and a hearty "Danku, danku." Like his men, he spoke only broken English. He was a rotund, cheerful man who looked like a prosperous burgher in a Steen painting. His bandsmen played their instruments with a genius that delighted all and needed no translation. Their instruments were an English horn, a flute, a bassoon, a trumpet, a clarinet, and a tuba.

Koenig's men were dressed in the Bavarian fashion because Cooke thought it made his bandsmen stand out from the German musicians on other ships: Tyrolean hat, grey peasant blouse, red shorts, and green lederhosen.

In response to the women's smiles, they commenced an encore; a very loud version of the jaunty "Lilibolero."

"I hate the waiting," said Nancy. "The music helps a little, but the minutes pass so slowly. I just want this battle to be over and done with. Edward thinks that it's going to be a tremendous victory but a long, bloody fight. I think you should stay out of the cockpit today. It's a beastly place that can't be good for the child in your womb; I believe the unborn hear the sounds their mother hears. The surgeon will understand. I have heard that the roar of cannons can stimulate premature birth and I worry for you. You are not due for what...two weeks?" The sunlight glinting off a half pike blinded her for a second and she adjusted her bonnet.

Late pregnancy had given the four-foot eleven-inch tall Mary a gnome-like appearance and she could barely waddle. Her reply sounded as if she were slightly short of breath."Two weeks, yet I still aim to be useful. Keep the water butts filled and pass cartridges. Keep an eye on my man, too." Her hands were active as she talked, carefully stitching up a tear in her husband's waistcoat. Her sewing basket was rarely out of reach; when she moved about she carried it on one plump elbow.

"Do you ever wonder why you chose this life, Mary? I always do before a battle; the one in '98 was plum awful. It would be so much easier living in a little cottage with honeysuckles and hedgerows and having other women to talk to. I so dislike struggling to suppress my cries during the act of love because there is only a slender piece of pine separating me from men moving about."

"Civilians don't appreciate the privacy they enjoy," sniffed Mary. "It's a hard life, but it attracts a kind of man uncommon hard to find ashore. Edward is a bold soul, looking for adventure, not money. Growing old with a bottle in his hand moaning' bout what he might have been ain't in his future. He's been through the fire, a good father for strong children.

"We are restless people, Nancy," Mary continued, "so we don't want men who are homebodies, we want explorers. We want men itching to see what is over the horizon. Here I can be alongside my husband, and comfort him too. No lady of quality will ever have as exciting a life."

"That's true. I visit strange lands, with exotic customs and unusual people when most women never venture more than 20 miles from home. I think this ship has three monkeys and five parrots aboard. How often you see those in the English countryside? And the world here is ordered and disciplined. Even in the darkest recesses of the orlop, I feel safer than I would on a London Street in broad daylight. The men respect me and treat me according to my character. I am an admired stand-in for the wives and daughters they have left in port, and dearly miss."

"It's all about family," said Mary with confidence. "The sailors aboard are bound to you and me more closely than to many of their actual relatives." She finished the last stitch in the waistcoat and looked at her handiwork with satisfaction.

Nancy smiled gently. "I thank you for reminding me of that which I have always known. Sometimes, one needs a good friend to refresh one's memory."

The two women hugged each other, confident that whatever lay ahead, their womanly courage would see them through. Women instinctively understood better than men what the defense of hearth and home really meant, and *Bellerophon* was very much a home in their eyes. While the maternal instinct was often misrepresented by men eager to confine women to limited roles, it was also a wondrous force of nature that could conjure miracles. Nancy and Mary knew they would need to accomplish more than a few today.

CHAPTER 7

"Twelve more hours! Just twelve more hours! That's all I need!" snarled Wemyss. His words were addressed as much to his inner self as to a God that he only worshipped when times were bad. At least the damned coughing had stopped, though the twitching of his eyelid had grown stronger.

He unfurled a drawing of *Bellerophon's* poop, quarterdeck, and forecastle with the placements of marines marked in red. He smiled briefly. Focusing on the battle seemed to be lessening his misery; the flying buttress of duty shored up his unsteady structure as surely as a real one did to the wall of a cathedral.

The Marines would be stretched thin today; far too thin. With half assigned to the cannons, only 34 were left to defend 168 feet of deck. They would also have to cover the port and starboard sides at the same time, since the ship would be under simultaneous fire from both directions. The majority would be stationed on the poop because it was the highest deck and allowed unimpeded fields of fire.

The six carronades on the poop, and the two 32-pounders mounted on the forecastle, would help even the odds if they fired grape and canister to wreck men rather than wood.

He worried that the French intended to spoil marine deck defenses by mounting an aerial assault: storms of grenades thrown from the fighting tops. Some French captains crammed as many as 25 men into the maintop and slightly more than half of that into the fore and mizzen tops. Men positioned thus could throw a three-pound grenade about 30 yards. The fuses were of six seconds' length, lit by a piece of slow match in a metal case that could be attached to the hat. Men were supposed to whirl their arms three times before throwing so that the grenade would explode just after impact. However, in the excitement of battle most hurled them immediately after the fuse was lit.

Men in the tops were also useful for gunning down officers on the weather decks of enemy vessels, in addition to clearing the enemy tops of sharpshooters like themselves. The drawback was that muskets were hard to reload as the mast swayed, and bayonets were of no use; both were the meat and potatoes of Marines. It was a great relief when Cooke had told him that sailors rather than Marines would man *Bellerophon's* fighting tops.

On the weather decks, he would rely on disciplined musketry and bayonets to repel boarders. His subordinate Pennywhistle preached a new gospel of firepower like a martial George Whitfield. Though his True Believer harangues sometimes annoyed, he was an undeniably clear thinker. He had introduced not only chain order but a number of other routines that moved marines away from mindless tradition and enabled them to combine fire power and quick movement in smart defenses.

He had also pointed out the unexpected danger posed by enemy carpenter's mates. Such men in boarding parties often carried battering rams for punching holes in the deck through which grenades were dropped.

Pennywhistle's constant refrain was "discharge and dash"—Fight in pairs and change positions quickly and constantly. Trust the initiative of individual marines and rain bullets on your opponent from a variety of changing angles.

Wemyss considered himself a traditional officer but had to admit that some remarkable ideas were coming out of Shorncliffe Camp. His subordinate was the only marine who had passed the training course run by Coote Manningham and Sir John Moore that was revolutionizing the use of light infantry.

Wemyss' chief objection was that its discipline relied more on individual pride and self regulation than the lash. Trusting in the better natures of private soldiers required a leap of faith that he was not quite willing to make. In service to pride, Pennywhistle drilled the men hard. When one heavily sweating Marine had blurted out, "You're killing me," Pennywhistle had replied, "Then you'd best die now, as it would be hard to replace you during battle."

When Wemyss had remonstrated with Pennywhistle about his training methods, his subordinate had responded courteously yet firmly. "Captain, we are in business to demand the impossible: to let a man know that his only limits are self-imposed. With respect to drill, the virtue of moderation should be exercised only in moderation. If the men sweat more now, they will bleed less in battle."

The one thing that Wemyss had in common with his subordinate was a love of music, and both saw repelling boarders as a kind of symphony. Like a conductor, the Marine commander's job was to time movements expertly.

Carronades performed the first movement with the *thud thud* of canister: the *pop pop* of musket volleys dominated the second. The third movement consisted of the *clang clang* of bayonets meeting swords; the rousing final movement featured the *thung thung* of sailors boarding pikes, cutlasses, and tomahawks smiting enemy weapons and then sweeping them from the decks. Cheers, screams, and unintelligible cries furnished a loud counterpoint to the awful melody of each movement. Success would be greeted not by thunderous applause but by the cheers and huzzahs of men proud to have done their duty well.

"Aaahhhkkk! Aaahhhkkk! Aaahhhkkk!" His outburst sounded like the hoarse-voiced barking of a bloodhound. His frame shook with fresh paroxysms. Damn that bloody cough! He would need another dose of his "medicine" very soon. He managed to take a ragged breath, then another.

His subordinate's unstinting attention to duty made him seem a medieval knight embarked on a sacred quest for some object, or truth known only to himself. It would not have surprised Wemyss if someone told him that Pennywhistle was a secret Jesuit or wore a hair shirt under his uniform. Yet today he was glad that if he fell, his subordinate could assume command of the marines with skill and courage.

"Ahe...mm!" Wemyss' thoughts were interrupted by a discreet clearing of the throat: Pennywhistle. Even the man's hail was courteous. Wemyss had been so focused on his plans that he had missed the sound of his subordinate's footsteps. He was glad that his "medication" was hidden in a cartridge case. He hoped that his breath would not betray him.

Pennywhistle detected a faint odor of rum as he advanced. The twitching in Wemyss' right eyelid was very marked. This interview was not going to be pleasant. Where rum was in, reason was out. Odd, he thought; Wemyss usually drank no more than the average officer, but battle did strange things to people.

He had discovered early in life that he had a low tolerance for alcohol and had no real interest in it either. A sober head was proving to be a great asset in a Service where officers commonly drank prodigious quantities of beverages distilled from grapes and grains. An officer's consumption of wine at a meal was typically measured in bottles, not glasses: a commissioned gentleman labeled a sot had to have a head as big as all outdoors.

He enjoyed Wemyss' respect but not his friendship. Wemyss was a hail-fellow-well-met; a voluble man who ate well, drank well, and laughed much. Wemyss looked older than his years; his shallow chest, spindly legs, and sagging belly belonged to a man who lived life as heedless of tomorrow's reckoning as he was of the consequences of a bad bet in a high stakes card game. He was heavily in debt to Wilson, and Pennywhistle wondered if that caused him to look more favorably on the man than he deserved.

Pennywhistle knew his unwillingness to engage in riotous drinking bouts after a long evening of cards had gained him a reputation as a wet blanket, a man with as much starch in his personality as in the stiff collar of his uniform. Wemyss wanted merry lightheartedness in his evenings, not a man who brought the black cloud of responsibility to carefree occasions like a prim maiden aunt whose disapproval settled over every family gathering like a pall.

Pennywhistle was satisfied with the arrangement. Wemyss was a competent soldier, but a man lacking in imagination. The British military had any number of men who grew old and grey while still remaining captains.

Pennywhistle summoned every ounce of tact that he could muster and pasted a pleasant expression on his face that was completely at odds with the violent churning in his stomach. "Good morning, Captain. I hope you slept well. We have some important matters to discuss."

CHAPTER 8

Surgeon Alexander Whyte shook his head. "Definitely going to need more rum. Definitely!" he remarked aloud to no one in particular. Rum was a poor anesthetic but the only one readily available to Naval Surgeons. He estimated that he might have more than 100 customers today and his present supply was simply not enough.

He sighed in resignation as he fastened the ties of the leather apron that would shield his blue coat and buff trousers from blood. He was relieved that he had finally finished transferring all of the equipment in the sick berth to the orlop. Well below the waterline, the cockpit section of the orlop was the safest part of the ship, and the steadiest.

He had set up two makeshift operating tables; one made from a board laid across two sawhorses; one from a board across two sea chests. Lanterns hung from the deck beams and gave an eerie, uncertain light that would not be comforting to men moaning in agony.

He laid out the tools of his trade and was glad to see that they were clean and sharp; they would be neither by tomorrow morning. His kit contained one large and one small bone saw, eight scalpels and knives, seven straight and curved needles, a pair of bone-cutting pliers, three probes, and varieties of clamps, forceps, and tourniquets. Mr. Saunders had acerbically remarked, "Looks more fitted to a carpenter. Don't even think of laying a hand on me if I am wounded."

He would mostly be performing amputations today. Speed was the key, since the longer such an operation took, the more likely shock would set in and kill the patient. The one advantage sailors had over soldiers was that they were generally brought to a surgeon within hours of their wounding rather than days.

Whyte was not as fast as some surgeons, but he could generally remove an arm in two and half minutes and a leg in four. He had procured a small supply of laudanum paid for with his own funds; that pain killer would be reserved for only the most grievously wounded, and even so would not last long.

From the scuttlebutt on the upcoming battle, he deemed that he had about two hours before patients started arriving. He had one surgeon's mate, three loblolly boys, and at least one of the two women aboard to assist him.

All very fine, but he knew the main effort would rest squarely on his shoulders. He took a stiff drink from a bottle of rum; a hazard of his trade. It was the only way he could get through what might be 24 hours of horror with one surgeon and one assistant tending to uncounted wounded. Cutting, slicing, and sawing men seemingly without end caused a man to forget faces and see only damaged limbs without humanity.

Horner, a fifteen year old loblolly boy, suddenly appeared at his side. Whyte barked angrily at the four-foot, nine-inch lad, pushing on him all his personal frustration arising from the inadequacies of a tiny surgery asked to do a hospital's job. "We shall need more rum, Horner, at least ten more jugs. See to it! Immediately!"

"Yes, sir. Right away, sir."

Nancy's descent from the sunny quarterdeck to the dark cockpit was a journey from Heaven to Hell. The cockpit stank of mold and mildew when it was not being used for surgery, but today the smells of vinegar, turpentine, and hot tar—concomitants of amputations—would dominate the air. The only light came from swinging lanterns that lent everyone's faces a malignant aspect, as if they were Satan's servants. Though it was the place where some lives would be saved, its timbers were impregnated with death and suffering.

Two large buckets stood by the operating tables, ready to receive severed arms and legs. When the battle was done, they would be cast overboard without ceremony. Nancy's first task on arrival had been to help the loblolly boys clear space around the operating tables for the incoming wounded and unfurl an old sail to cover the deck. The heavy canvas was necessary to absorb copious amounts of blood.

Nancy sat down and began cutting linen bandages with heavy tailor's shears. She made them in three sizes: small for arms, medium for legs, and large for torsos. She had only six bolts of linen and dreaded that it would not be enough.

In the course of a long battle, it often happened that the bandages needed to be used several times, scavenged from the dead. It was not uncommon to see the wounded wearing bandages soaked in other men's blood, sweat, and urine. It repulsed her and she intuitively sensed that old bandages spread infection. But the watchwords in surgery were "make do", and she would extract the most from her limited resources.

She had also brought along a small tub of olive oil, standard naval balm for burns. Daubing scorched faces and limbs with it would be one of her chief functions today. In addition, she had prepared two homemade recipes learned from an old man in Gibraltar with a reputation as a healer. She hoped they would as effective in healing burns as palliating pain. One was a gel of extract of white oak bark.

The other was a thick liquid composed of honey, coconut oil, and apple cider vinegar.

She heard a kindly voice from behind. "How are you managing, Mrs. Overton? Might I assist you?" It was Thomas Jewell, the ship's Purser. He was a short man of quick motions, clipped speech, and precise habits. Perhaps because they normally doled out supplies and had no assigned post in battle, Pursers often administered rum to the wounded about to undergo surgery. Pursers were usually men of some education and resourcefulness, tasked with managing the ship's stores and finances. Sailors often suspected Pursers of cheating them on pay and food: the common term for the Purser was "the duck fucker." Assisting men in dire straits was a way to earn good will.

"I am managing, Mr. Jewell, but I have a great deal of work ahead. My stomach was upset this morning and I have eaten little. I still have no appetite, but I realize my body will need sustenance if I am to make it through the long hours ahead. I wonder if I could trouble you to fetch me some wine, stew, and biscuits."

"It would be my pleasure, Mrs. Overton. I admire what you are doing here. Many landsmen would pale in terror at your work. Those who believe women delicate vessels should spend a few hours with you here."

"I don't think it is about strength of character so much as it is about strength of heart, Mr. Jewell. The men I will help today are like my brothers. Though it is painful to witness their suffering, it would distress me far more to know that I could have helped them, but was cursed with a stomach too weak to do so. I think the worst thing that can happen to a person is to feel useless and unneeded when friends are hazarding their lives.

"Perhaps it is a strange way to consider the matter, but I see God as granting me a great honor. What greater responsibility could be given a person than helping the sick and comforting the dying? I feel God's presence here far more than I have in any cathedral on land. His light shines brightest where matters are darkest. It is amongst the dying that you truly come to cherish the spark of life. When I pass from this life, I will be able to look God confidently in the face and say, 'I helped men in need. My life made a difference.' I can think of no better epitaph than those simple words."

"That is a fine way to look at such a gruesome task," said Jewell, pulling his left earlobe in a nervous gesture.

"I am no mystic, but I feel God's hand upon me here: guiding my actions, sustaining me when I feel faint and even lending his eloquence to my lips. When your face is the last thing a dying man sees and your words the final sounds he hears, you have to trust the Lord so that your conduct can be what he needs to pass without fear. Alone, I am weak and brittle. With His touch, I am strong and resolute."

Jewell smiled gently. "Your words have power, Mrs. Overton. You would make a fine lay preacher, if women were allowed that role."

Nancy shook her head. "I could never do that. I am just an ordinary woman. I have no words to convey the power of the Almighty that I feel here. His grace encompasses all who pass through this sad place." She laid aside her sheers and steepled her hands in deep reflection.

"I have never forgotten a sailor named Leverett Jones. I held his hand as he passed after the Nile in '98. Just before his final breath his eyes lit with a joy and a calmness that told me he was seeing something marvelous in the world to come. He looked me straight in the face, said, 'Bless you,' and expired. I cherish those words almost as much as my husband saying 'I love you.' This is not just a sick berth but a school for my soul. Service here calls up the best parts of my nature."

Jewell scratched his head in thought, then spoke in subdued tones. "War is an awful thing, but God's grace allows people a chance to discover their hidden gifts and then the opportunity to use them for good or ill; to increase their humanity or diminish it. You have chosen wisely, and I admire you for it. The men are lucky to have you, as is your husband."

"You give me too much credit, Mr. Jewell, but I thank you for your kind words. Now I must return to my work, lest all my talk of God slow me in doing his work."

"It has been a pleasure and an inspiration, Mrs. Overton. If you will excuse me, I shall fetch you a small meal straight away."

CHAPTER 9

"Sir, you are unfit to command because of ill health. If you refuse to see reason and stand down, I shall relieve you on that basis. I know my duty, Captain Wemyss, and I must carry it out in spite of any personal feelings in the matter." Pennywhistle's voice was sad but firm. "In battle one must seize the fire, whereas you can barely stand. I have not yet spoken to Captain Cooke of this, feeling that I owed you the chance to arrive at the correct decision voluntarily."

"You traitorous dog! I—Aaahhkkk! Aaahhhkkk! Aaahhhkk!" Wemyss coughed and spat bloody phlegm for a full minute before resuming his tirade. "You traduce the honor of the Service in pursuit of naked ambition. It's always the quiet ones that do the scheming! They act oh so pleasant to your face, just before they shove the stiletto into your ribs. And to think I trusted you! I suppose I should not be surprised. A man who hates cards hates humanity!"

"I have the greatest regard for you personally, sir," said Pennywhistle with compassion, noting that the twitching of his captain's eyelid had increased in frequency. "I know you to be a man of courage and honor, but you are dangerously unwell. Even now, you illness only allows you to speak for brief periods before it tightens its iron grip round your chest. I would hate to see your affliction strike you down at a critical moment when marines are wagering their lives on you. I do not believe that you are thinking clearly or are capable of making sound decisions. In your condition, it is no disgrace to admit that.

"I would guess that you have dissembled to the Captain because you want to fight. I can applaud your motives while disapproving of your conduct. Sergeant Dale also knows the severity of your affliction, and the men sense something is badly wrong. The onions and garlic that make your breath disagreeable do not entirely hide the scent of rum. I think you have consumed an enormous quantity to repress your cough and put strength into your legs."

Pennywhistle stopped abruptly, pained to see the deep sadness in Wemyss face. He feared the man was about to burst into tears.

"Please do not do this. Grant me the chance to die with honor as a soldier facing the enemy. I beg you, sir, relent, and grant me my own kind of dig—" Another round of coughing began.

"I am sorry. I cannot relent, sir. My first duty is to the welfare of this ship. I apologize for being weak and not confronting you earlier, but I thought your native wisdom would prevail and you would stand down of your own accord."

Wemyss face flushed a deep crimson. He staggered over to the cartridge box, flung it open, and grabbed his medication. He popped the cork, pulled it to his lips and drank convulsively. The coughing stopped abruptly and his face became a picture of malicious resolve. He, or more likely the alcohol, had reached a critical decision.

His voice turned harsh and menacing. "This is mutiny, mister, pure and simple. And on the day of battle! You may not be loyal, but I have some among the men who will take my part and swear you that speak lies because of naked ambition. I have successfully answered the captain's inquiries about my health before, and I can do so again. I should remove you from command here and now and report your monstrous behavior, but frankly I need you for the battle ahead. There is much wrong with your understanding of fealty, but you can direct men in battle. I will make you a bargain. Speak no more of this and I shall not press charges after the battle."

A lightning bolt of pure terror lanced through Pennywhistle. He saw himself dying in disgrace, his legacy infamous. His attempt at doing his duty and a good deed had placed him in serious danger. Mutiny at sea was the most hated of crimes, and a capital offense.

His stomach shot a jolt of bile. The pain summoned his survival instincts. His mind turned icy calm and the sympathy in his face disappeared, replaced by an expression of unreadable neutrality.

Freed from the shackles of honor, his mind assessed the central problem. His evaluation of Wemyss' condition was sound, but his appraisal of the man's character had been dangerously flawed. A direct assault had failed. Guile was called for, a feint followed by a flanking maneuver.

Pennywhistle forced an expression of contrition onto his face that he most certainly did not feel, and spoke words of abject humility that came hard to him. "I am sorry, sir, to have overstepped my bounds. Understand that I did so because of a misplaced sense of duty. I see by your zeal and determination that I was mistaken about your fitness for command. I crave your forgiveness and beg leave that you still include me in your plans."

A look of triumph gleamed in Wemyss' eyes. "Consider the matter forgotten. You are a young man who misunderstood a situation, seeing it as more dangerous than it actually was. I may be a little off my game, but by God, sir, even on a bad day I am more than the equal of most officers on their best! Now attend me closely, and let me show you my plans and dispositions for the forthcoming engagement.

You will play a major part and have plenty of chances to cover yourself with glory."

"Yes, sir," Pennywhistle replied with studied calmness. "I thank you for your consideration. Might I atone for my misapprehension, sir?" It was as useless to reason with a drunk as it was to give a book to an illiterate. "Let me speak to the men on your behalf. There is no point in putting further strain on your vocal cords when you will need them in battle, to command and lead your marines. You have trained them so brilliantly that my task would be simply to remind them of their duty, the sense of which you have instilled in them. I would also be honored to speak on your behalf in the officers' meeting at seven bells."

Pennywhistle's flattery and apparent willingness to play the thoughtful subordinate got through. He could see the satisfaction in Wemyss' eyes.

"Your arguments make good sense, Mr. Pennywhistle, and I should be glad of the relief that you offer. If you will speak for me in these preliminaries I shall have voice and sword and pistols at the ready when the battle commences."

"I am pleased that we are in agreement," said Pennywhistle in an obsequious voice that he barely recognized as his own.

Claiming to act on his captain's behalf while actually undermining him was a rotten thing to do. Yet if he failed to act, men would die needlessly. His father had said battle was a wrecker of men, but he had not considered that it might be so in ways other than physical.

"Now, sir, I am most eager to see your dispositions for the battle ahead." That was true enough; Wemyss was a good planner. He would probably agree with most of the tactics, but in the end it would be his judgment that would prevail.

"Very good, Mr. Pennywhistle. I have added a few refinements to my original plan." He smoothed out his large drawing. "Now this is what I have in mind."

Pennywhistle settled in for a lengthy talk and was gratified to see a smile on Wemyss' face. He was clearly proud of his planning and eager for a fellow professional's approval. Wemyss' faith in him made the stain of what he was contemplating seem even blacker. Pennywhistle understood the pain in Wemyss' body was nothing compared to the pain that his soul would suffer if he missed this fight. Yet battle was intended to advance the fortunes of a nation, not provide a stage for martyrs.

Wemyss would simply be a battle casualty of a different sort.

The ship's bell struck six times. *Ask not for whom the bell tolls*, thought Pennywhistle.

CHAPTER 10

"Why aren't those ammunition chests on the quarterdeck, Corporal? I told you ten minutes ago. I thought I was speaking to man, not a tortoise. Well, perhaps you are a tortoise: as slow of understanding as you are of foot." Wilson's voiced dripped with acid, and he cracked his knuckles together in frustration.

"I put four men on it, Mr. Wilson. They should be here any minute. It takes a little while to unload the .685 ammunition and replace it with the .670 rounds, sir."

"An explanation, Corporal? I don't recall asking for one. Are you a seer or mind reader? Perhaps you belong in a carnival and not in a position of responsibility." Wilson was in a foul mood, and venting his spleen relieved his stress over the forthcoming battle.

Corporal Robbins was experienced enough to bridle his anger. "Very sorry, sir. If you will excuse me, sir, I shall attend to it personally right now." Robbins came to attention and saluted.

Wilson returned a lackadaisical salute. "If they are not here in five minutes, you will need a new jacket—one without stripes."

Wilson was worried. Not about honor, or his men, or his chances for glory. His concern was for money, pure and simple. He hated parting with the large accumulation of coins, bank notes, and IOUs that he kept in a strong box. But since his cabin had been dismantled, he'd reluctantly trusted the heavy iron container to Mr. Jewell for storage in the hold. A good portion of the IOUs were from Wemyss, and Wilson worried that the captain would die before he paid up.

The Royal Navy furnished splendid picking grounds for a professional gambler with a nose for bad players who believed themselves the opposite. He had schooled himself as deeply in his calling as the fanatic Pennywhistle had in the profession of arms.

Since childhood, he had displayed a genius for mathematics. The ability to break down each step in a card game into a series of precise, almost algebraic equations, coupled with his skill in counting cards, enabled him to make accurate guesses about the hands his opponents held. He also possessed a profound ability to precisely read his opponents' tells: subtle body movements and facial gestures that provided clues to their mental states and how they would play their hands.

Gentlemen in blue were easier marks than the civilians he had played against in London and Edinburgh. Most officers were foolish children when it came to cards. They gambled with the same reckless abandon that made their bravery in battle famous. Daring might be a wonderful thing in combat, but it was a dangerous conceit in a card game. And being part of a fleet where officers visited one another frequently had only increased his opportunities for money-making.

He took care to lose every so often so that his marks would not lose hope. Stupid men who won at odd intervals were like men addicted to opium; the exhilaration of a single win far outweighed a string of steady losses. Such men could never understand that card games of skill favored hard, steady calculation far more than the blind luck that some gentlemen believed in as fervently as Francis of Assisi trusted in the Virgin Mary.

Losing came unhandily to him. It was hard for an expert to play so stupidly that even a dull man might win. Slapping a debonair smile on his face afterwards was as difficult for him as a toothless man eating a steak.

His acceptance of IOUs with an easy grace performed two functions. It made impulsive men even more careless, and blinded them to the fact that he was a professional gambler. Allied to his breeding and polished manners, he appeared a gentleman who only played cards for the sport of it. IOUs posed no risks, because gentlemen always honored gambling debts to other gentlemen, even if doing so would greatly disrupt their lives.

No one ever seemed to notice that he drank only tea while they gulped copious amounts of alcohol. Drink rendered unperceptive men blind to the risks of extravagant bets.

He decided to take a walk to burn off some of the tension, though unlike his fellow officers, the sights and sounds of the ship brought him no pleasure.

The three most common types of sailors were plying their crafts: the joke-teller, the singer, and the yarn-spinner. All gave men a way to forget the ordeal ahead for a few blessed moments.

When the joke-teller in Wilson's path finished the punch line, Wilson frowned. "I've heard funnier jokes on Mr. Whyte's operating table."

A dozen Welshmen, to whom singing came as naturally as breathing, managed a stirring rendition of "Heart of Oak". When the dozen finished, Wilson tartly remarked, "I had no idea that *Bellerophon* had been invaded by crickets and bullfrogs."

He interrupted a yarn-spinner at a key point in his story. "Really, sailor, these men look a little old for fairy tales. I should have thought they'd prefer something more manly than Mother Goose stories."

Despite the noise of men preparing for battle, three sailors were fast asleep, leaning against the gun carriages of the quarterdeck 9-pounders. While most men react to stress with agitation, nervous energy giving rise to all manner of jerky movements, the opposite obtained in a few cases. Although it seemed counterintuitive, it actually made sense: facing a great ordeal ahead, a man's body shut down to arrest tension and conserve energy.

Wilson kicked all three in their rumps. "We are paying you to fight, not to sleep."

One of the groggy sailors muttered, "Man's itching for a bullet."

Some sailors sat mute and stared ahead, consumed by thoughts likely not pleasant, but most talked quietly with friends. One group, however, had produced a device that aroused merriment even as it demonstrated the ship's attitude toward the French.

The miniature guillotine blade crashed down and the young woman's head plopped into the basket. The cluster of watching sailors let a satisfied cheer, followed by contemptuous laughter.

"That's just what is going to happen to Johnny Crapaud today."

"Mr. Frenchman is in for one a hell of a whipping," another announced.

"About time old granny Villeneuve stopped hiding and fought like a sailor should," a third seaman said gruffly.

The guillotine was only a foot tall and had been carefully carved out of mutton bones; added bits of string and scrap metal made the device fully functional. Two soldiers of bone stood on either side of a pretty woman, prostrated at the guillotine's base with a detachable head. The sailors delighted in repeatedly executing her, imagining they were reenacting a moment of The Reign of Terror that had made revolutionary France infamous throughout Europe.

Their merriment irritated Wilson. He stalked over and looked down at the men with an expression that was part contempt and part ridicule. "You men look too old to be playing with toys."

Wilson heard their hisses clearly as he walked away. He cursed the day that he had come aboard.

He had smashed his promising career at the gaming tables with a foolish act of passion at odds with his usual calculation, fleeing Edinburgh two steps ahead of a breach of promise suit. Proving breach of promise in court was relatively easy, and a guilty verdict could relieve a man of a large part of his fortune. He'd never intended to marry the girl, but an engagement had been the price of stealing her virtue. He should have paid more attention to her father's combative temperament.

He retained a souvenir of his short engagement: a large gold ring with a perfectly rounded ruby in the center. He considered it a fair prize of war, since he had been forced to put up with ridiculous amount of insipid blather to get the girl into bed. It was an object of beauty and antiquity, and an odd legend associated with it promised both luck and death to the owner.

He had laughed at the contradiction, yet such was his superstitious regard for Lady Luck that he had felt compelled to purloin it. He'd come to consider the ring an indispensable part of any evening of cards. Though it was unlikely that anyone could identify it, he was a cautious man and wore it only when he gambled.

The engagement was the one time in his life where his loins had guided his actions, and it had blown up in his face. He had needed to disappear from society for a discreet interval, and the Royal Marines had provided a place to do so. He'd informed several prominent gentlemen whose IOUs he held that he would be willing to void their notes in return for a commission, and they had been only too happy to comply.

His want of interest in soldiering was matched by a lack of concern about earning a reputation that would blaze his name in history books. His weapons were charm and calculation, not ferocity and brawn. The men under his command were dull clots who bored him, though they served to confirm his belief in the superiority of his class. He learned drill readily enough but regarded it as a generator of ennui and so taught it in a perfunctory manner.

He finally spied Robbins and four men arriving with the ammunition chests.

"Ammunition is all here, Mr. Wilson. Packed right and ready to go. Are you sure two chests are enough?"

"Quite enough. I must say that I am not used to plant life questioning my judgment."

He was not looking for a mention in dispatches today. He just wanted to stay alive to spend his money. He did not think that he wanted for courage, but he was in no hurry to discover if he possessed any great store of it. He sought the position of least risk as a matter of logic, and that would not be under the observant eye of the Captain on the quarterdeck. He had to figure out a way to make good his escape, since that damned Pennywhistle had other ideas. Nor did he want the equivalent of a bull's eye painted on himself, so he would remove his epaulette and not wear either his gorget or his sash.

Two of the marine officers were no obstacle to his progress. Higgins was a silly goose, and Wemyss a sick man easily fooled by his faradiddles about striving for distinction in battle.

That irritating stuffed shirt Pennywhistle was the problem. The man would have made a good card player, since he was often hard to read. He was so damned earnest, utterly immune to polished charm and clever words.

A chance remark that Pennywhistle had recently made in the wardroom had sent shivers through him. He'd spoken of his sadness over the untimely death of a beloved cousin, and Wilson had realized that he was talking about the woman to whom he had been affianced. It was damned bad luck that the long hand of fate had reached him in such an obscure venue. He did not care to think of Pennywhistle's reaction if he discovered the truth.

Perhaps Pennywhistle would die in the hours ahead. He was the sort of man who welcomed danger, and such men often met an early end.

He reached for his watch to check the time and discovered it was not there.

"Ooooh! Ooooh! Ooooh!" Jobu held the watch in his paw; he had a penchant for shiny objects.

"Give it here, you damned imp!" Wilson hated the creature that seemed to delight in tormenting him.

Jobu flourished the watch about, almost in challenge.

He grabbed for the monkey, but Jobu leaped away as soon as Wilson bent forward, emitting a series of merry noises.

The cursed monkey was laughing at him!

CHAPTER II

"Pistols: loaded and with fresh flints. Done. Spare cartridges. Done. Interior of scabbard oiled. Blade slides in and out clean and easy. Done." Higgins recited aloud Pennywhistle's list of preparations as he followed them carefully. Now it was time to give one final sharpening to his sword. He placed it upon the whetstone and commenced pedaling to turn the wheel.

Officially, it was not his sword but a loan from Mr. Pennywhistle. It was a beautiful weapon with a curved blade and half-circle guard. He liked Mr. Pennywhistle a great deal, like the wise older brother that he had always wished for. He wondered why Mr. Pennywhistle had spoken to him this morning like an old granny warning a child away from a plate of freshly made scones. His motives were admirable, but he seemed unnecessarily pessimistic.

While Mr. Pennywhistle was probably right to warn that the French and Spanish would die hard, he seemed unwilling to place full faith in the skill of British arms. The wrath of the British Lion was a mighty and fearsome thing. What Shakespeare said about a medieval war was even more true today: "the King's cause is just and his quarrel honorable." With the great Lord Nelson arguing the King's Cause, how could they lose?

When he'd joined the marines, he'd resolved to become a hero. It was not just for himself but for his father. His father was from a poor branch of an old family who had done well as a haberdasher in Belfast. His father always wanted to be a soldier, but a club foot made that an impossible dream.

His earliest memories were of his father reading to him about great leaders, thundering battles, and gallant deeds. By the time he reached his 16th birthday, Alexander, Caesar, Richard the Lionheart, The Black Prince, and Henry V were as familiar to him as Lord Nelson was to the present generation. He embraced their stories as readily as man might a beautiful woman and wanted future generations to speak his name with the same awe and reverence as he spoke theirs.

Nature had cursed him with a runty body and a reedy voice, but he believed that he had a hero's heart, and at 16 had been old enough to qualify for an army commission. The problem had been that his father could not afford to pay £400 to purchase an ensign's commission in the infantry. That was the least expensive rank, but £400 was only slightly less than what his father earned in a year, just enough to be able to afford two maids, a groom, a horse and a modest carriage, above the ordinary expenses of a family.

The answer to his dream came about in an odd fashion. Charles Packenham was an ex-army officer and a frequent visitor to his father's establishment. He liked fine clothes and ran up impressive bills. He did not always pay on time, due to a strong affinity for gambling. Gentlemen scrupulous about discharging gambling debts were all too often less concerned about paying tradesmen.

One day, when his father was engaged in a particularly vexing exchange with Packenham about another month passing with his debt growing no smaller, Packenham made a suggestion. He had seen Higgins junior reading Vegatius in the store, had spoken to him, and was impressed with his desire to become a soldier. Later that same day, he'd watched him put a bully to flight even though that bully was five inches taller and several years older. "What if I could secure your boy a commission? Would you be willing to forgive some of my debt?"

His father jumped at the offer. The solution was the marines. Marine commissions were appointments. All that was required was influence at the Admiralty and four letters of recommendation from gentlemen, at least one of whom was or had been a military officer.

Packenham possessed all of the connections needed. Seven weeks after the initial conversation, Luke Higgins received an appointment as a second lieutenant in the Royal Marines.

"Woof! Woof!"

Higgins stopped the whetstone and turned round to see a happy beagle energetically wagging its tail. It was Archer, Mr. Douglas's dog and the saturnine Scotsman's only real friend.

"I know why you've come, you little beggar," said Higgins with a smile. "But your owner says that you should not have any because it gives you gas."

"Woof! Woof!" Archer's tale wagged even harder. He knew his man.

"All right, but this is absolutely the last time," said Higgins with mock sternness. He reached into his haversack and pulled out a round of cheddar cheese. The dog sniffed the air in eager anticipation. Mr. Douglas would have to put up with a lot of farts tonight. Higgins grinned. It couldn't happen to a better man.

"Only three pieces, no more," he said as he tossed the first chunk. Archer's face was pure ecstasy as he jumped and his jaws snapped open, catching the chunk in mid air. He chewed his trophy eagerly and then favored Higgins with a canine smile of delight. Odd that such a gregarious creature belonged to such a withdrawn man; perhaps opposites did indeed attract.

Feeding the dog calmed his nerves. The three chunks of cheddar vanished quickly. "Woof! Woof!' Archer cocked his head slowly from side to side, in earnest pleading for just one more chunk.

"No, that's all!" Now, be off with you."

Archer favored him with a seductive doggy grin.

"You little scoundrel! Alright, one more piece, but don't you ever think that I am an easy mark."

A week after his commissioning, he'd been on his way to Stonehouse Barracks in Plymouth. Three weeks of training only covered the bare bones of drill and tactics. Nelson's fleet was hungry for marines and it was deemed that new officers could complete training aboard ship under the practiced eye of a veteran NCO. Fortunately, he'd been assigned a manservant who had shared a lot of useful, out-of-the-way knowledge. On more than one occasion, a lesson he'd learned, not in class but from his manservant, had saved him from making a grave error.

He cast his mind back to his training sessions aboard ship with Sergeant Dale, and cringed in embarrassment at how inept he had first been.

Dale would settle for no less than the best. H constant refrain was, "No, young sir! No, no, no, that simply won't do. Let us try that again. Your normal marching step must be 75 paces a minute, not the 85 that you are demonstrating. Your steps are completely out of agreement with the drum beat."

Dale believed that any compromise of excellence was a bargain with the devil. "*Almost* good enough is something no marine should ever be. *Almost* good enough is what is said about mediocrities, and such men are not welcomed by the marines on *Bellerophon*. You will get the hang of things soon enough, but it takes practice, practice, and more practice. You are a gentleman and must be an example to your men.

You must be able to do everything they do, only faster and better."

While Dale provided the training in drill, Mr. Pennywhistle took him under his wing and gave him lessons with the blade. Higgins had several years of instruction that he thought stood him in good stead, but one sparring match with Pennywhistle showed him just how little he really knew. He would have been fatally skewered at least five times in the two-minute match if Pennywhistle had been in earnest.

After the match, Pennywhistle had looked at Higgins' sword with disgust. "The Pattern '96 Infantry Officer's Spadroon is a fine thing for a parade, but a poor weapon for naval combat. It is an infelicitous marriage of the gentleman's small sword for thrusting and the military broadsword for cutting. It does neither well; its blade is weak and the guard is too small to adequately protect the hand."

Higgins had felt like a child trying to read unfamiliar letters off his first hornbook. His face reflected surprise and puzzlement, because he had thought all swords could pretty much do the same things.

His bewilderment had caused his superior to soften his tones. "I realize that it is easy for a new officer to get to so carried away spending lavishly on a splendid uniform that he entirely forgets to allocate sufficient funds to purchase a truly fine sword. A pretty blade may stroke your vanity, but true steel can save your life. Rather than purchasing a dress sword and a working one, it is wiser and less expensive to purchase a single sword that is stout enough for combat yet has a comely enough appearance that it would not be out of place at a royal levee."

Pennywhistle examined his blade with the distaste of a master chef looking at a rotted piece of steak.

"This is an inferior specimen of the sword-maker's art. The leather in the grip is separating, the guard is loose, and the steel is cheap. I also detect some slight pitting. I must assume some unscrupulous veteran took advantage of your naïveté to rid his attic of a useless confection. This sword would shatter in under a minute of heavy use."

Higgins face fell at Pennywhistle's assessment of his blade. The blade's previous owner had said that the sword had protected him well in many battles. That was its problem: too many battles.

"Fighting on decks packed tight with men reduces your room for maneuver, so you need a shorter weapon with a heavier and wider blade," said Pennywhistle in the manner of a patient teacher. "The cutlass is favored because it is a superb hacking and slashing tool, a gutting sword that is easily carried aloft or in a boarding party, and strong enough to muscle through heavy ropes, canvas, and wood. Most have guards that can double as knuckle dusters.

"I would guide you in the purchase of a good sword, but it may be sometime before we call at a port. Until then, I have a spare weapon that you may use. It was made by George Blake, a superior craftsman who utilizes only the finest blued steel."

Pennywhistle turned round and picked up a sword and scabbard from the deck. He faced Higgins and handed both across with a care that could not have been greater if he had been handling the Crown Jewels. His solemn expression made it clear that he considered a good sword as much a sacred object as a deadly weapon.

"Use her well," Pennywhistle said quietly. The use of the feminine rather than the neutral told Higgins that Pennywhistle considered the blade a living entity. Admittedly, it did have the power to grant life or death, and so might be regarded as much more than an inanimate object.

Higgins drew the sword and immediately saw that the quality of its steel was far superior to his own. The weapon afforded good protection to the hand and felt sure and steady in his grip. The blade seemed an extension of his arm as he flourished the sword in several broad circles.

"It is the 1803 infantry officer's sword, which was specifically designed to remedy many of the problems of your present weapon, "said Pennywhistle sagely," and it is favored by many Marine officers. Its curved blade and hatchet tip make it particularly good for slashing off arms. The large crown escutcheon in the knuckle bow makes a very effective weapon against an opponent's chin.

"At 37 inches it is longer than ideal for the deck, but I purchased it when I was stationed ashore. The blade is well balanced and double-edged for its final seven inches. Those seven inches may come in handy for someone of..." he paused and his voice became tact personified, "your level of skill."

Higgins blinked as a realization hit him; sword and scabbard had been there all the time. The sword match and attendant commentary had been arranged to show Higgins what Pennywhistle had likely deduced on their first acquaintance: his training was as inferior as his weapon, and both would have to change. A lesser man would have used ridicule to make his point; though a lesser officer might have lacked sufficient perception to understand that Higgins's training and weapon were less than adequate.

It was clear that the word "adequate"was an obscenity to Pennywhistle.

"You will find, Mr. Higgins, that the grip sheathed in sharkskin will give you plenty of purchase. I would add that though I approve of the brace of pistols round your neck, Mr. Nock's toys by their look, you would be better off relying on the blade rather than the gun. A pistol is difficult to reload when men are packed tight and useful only at nose-to-nose range; once fired it becomes nothing more than an inferior club. A sword never misfires and is always useful; giving you the option of engaging at distance or close up."

Higgins was amazed at the amount of knowledge necessary to be a good officer. He had never really considered just how that knowledge was obtained. His initial thinking had bordered on the magical, as if an officer's commission and a gentleman's station gifted a man with arcane powers of perception that kicked at critical moments with exactly the right piece of information. A lot more hard work than he expected lay ahead. He did not want to remain the gentleman amateur for whom Pennywhistle displayed such a hard-favored contempt.

Pennywhistle had also schooled Higgins in military étiquette and gentlemanly manners, for although he had enjoyed a good upbringing based on Christian principles, it was a middle class one and unacquainted with certain subtleties of the gentleman's condition.

He was particularly in the dark about the rituals of courting a lady. He'd confided in Pennywhistle about Miss Lydia because he wanted to know how to most effectively to press his suit; he was certain that she was "the one."

Before departing Belfast, Higgins had obtained permission to write to Miss Lydia Travers, the 17-year-old daughter of Squire Travers, who did much business with his father. She was four inches taller than he, with a beautiful oval face, kind eyes of sapphire blue, and hair the color of gold caressed by moonbeams. Her smile caused the world to sparkle and her laughter moved the angels to rejoice.

They had only talked a few times, but he'd decided that a marine officer needed to be enterprising, and there was no better place to start than getting the attention of a lovely lady. He wore his new uniform when he boldly called upon her without receiving permission to do so, feeling every inch a gallant soldier as confident of conquering Irish hearts as he was of French ships.

She had been impressed, and so were her father and mother. She said she would welcome his letters and would be delighted to follow his progress "as he gloriously advanced toward admiral." He had not the heart to tell her that admiral was a navy rank.

Mr. Pennywhistle had advised caution and restraint.

He put the matter in a way that amused Higgins, even as its worldliness surprised him. "Mr. Higgins, men often under-estimate the importance of a well made boot. You spend most of your waking time in them, and yet many chose them on a whim, paying attention to nothing but the current fashion.

"I believe James Hoby to be the finest boot-maker in London; but no matter what his promises, before I take acceptance I insist on giving the boots a thorough walking. I want to make sure the fit is as good as it is comfortable. I want a boot that gives each sole her perfect content." He smiled briefly, then his expression turned avuncular.

"I understand that you are dazzled by a particular pair of boots, Mr. Higgins, but I suspect they are the first that you have contemplated. No doubt they are well made and attractive. But I think it premature to make a final choice in footwear when you have only walked bare-footed."

Higgins smiled at the memory of that conversation, then withdrew a small gold locket from his coat, opened it, and extracted a lock of Miss Lydia's hair. The golden strands smelled of cinnamon and sandalwood, and made his heart flutter. Mr. Pennywhistle was a man of the world, but he did not know everything. Higgins resolved afresh to honor Lydia and everyone else who believed in him today by becoming what he desired to be more than anything else: a hero. If he had to defy the gods, kill a score of Frenchmen, and suffer a dozen wounds, he would be one by sundown today.

"Mr. Robinson, it would quiet my mind if you would check the breaching ropes on the port forecastle carronade one more time. It's just a feeling, mind you, but I think they might be in need of a bit of tightening. I know I am being a mother hen about this, but you can never be too careful."

It was the Boatswain's job to check all ropes, rigging, and netting in the ship.

"No problem at all, Mr. Cumby. To tell you the truth, I was thinking the same thing. I shall attend to it directly. I have already rechecked the boarding and overhead nets, and the ship's fire engine is ready to go."

The boarding nets were designed to foul the weapons of enemy boarders and the overhead nets to protect crewmen from large chunks of falling wood.

"If you will excuse me, sir, I'd best be about my business." Robinson saluted and departed at a brisk walk.

Cumby had just completed his second inspection of the ship and was headed toward what had been the wardroom. Everything was in order: ropes, sails, carronades; small arms were in pristine condition, and ready to bring *Bellerophon* the victory.

Most importantly, the men were ready. He spoke with many during his inspections, hearing their concerns and offering words of encouragement. No one had any complaints; most of their concerns centered round having sufficient supplies to do their jobs if the battle proved to be a long one, as most anticipated it would. All were confident of beating the French, and as far as he was concerned that meant the battle was already half won.

He said a few prayers as he walked, hoping his righteous conduct in the battle ahead would make him worthy of being on God's side. He fingered the small gold cross that he wore under his shirt and thought of the loving wife who had given it to him. He did not try to foist his religion on a shipload full of men who were less than pious, but was happy to talk with any sailor who discovered in his heart a yearning for the Word of God. His captain never talked about God, and when he recited the Sunday service he sounded as if he were reading tide tables. It was a great pity that he had not seen fit to recruit a Chaplin. But the captain was a good man. If he fell today, he would surely find a seat in Paradise.

"Mr. Cumby, a word, if you please." It was Russell Mart, the ship's Carpenter.

"I am always happy to lend an ear to a conscientious man," said Cumby with the graciousness that made him so well liked. "How may I help?"

"Well, sir, I have thirty shot plugs of various sizes ready to fill in holes below the waterline, but I was wondering if that will be enough."

Cumby thought carefully. "Much as it pains me to say it, we should expect to take many hits today. I'd say you had better make at least twenty more."

"Very good, sir. I shall get on that right away."

Jobu raced up and offered Cumby a watch. He smiled and took the time piece. "Jobu, you really need to stop annoying Mr. Wilson."

"Excuse me, Mr. Saunders, mail boat just arrived," said a very cheerful Jepson. Saunders was just completing his final inspection of the big 32-pounders on the lower gun deck. "Last minute gift from Lord Nelson, and a right clever one, too. Nothing like catching up with the home folks just before battle. Mr. Cumby picked up your letters for you; six, I think, and says that they are waiting on the rudder housing, since the wardroom's gone. I heard that you were worried about you ma's health, so I got down here lickety-split, thinking they might bring some news."

"Thanks, Jepson! I pray these letters bring good tidings!" Saunders face was a mix of joy and anxiety.

Midshipman Walker stepped forward. "I can handle things here, Mr. Saunders. You've got half an hour before the meeting at seven bells, time enough to at least give the letters a quick perusal."

"Are you certain, Mr. Walker? "

"I am, sir! You have done your duty for the time being. Now it is time to concern yourself with family."

"Bless you, Mr. Walker." Saunders spun on his heels and dashed toward the companionway. It was entirely wrong for an officer to run, but he just did not give a damn. He had to know about his mother!

"I just wanted to say, Mr. Jewell, that you should be careful today. You are my best student and have the makings of a real scholar. Do not take any untoward risks." Godwin's voice quavered with emotion as he spoke to James Jewell, the second oldest midshipman and the Purser's son.

Jewell nervously clasped and unclasped his hands as he looked at Godwin. The schoolmaster usually regarded him as a trouble maker. Receiving compliments from the man that the midshipmen referred to as a thunderstorm waiting to happen was truly remarkable! "Thank you, Mr. Godwin. The mathematics that you have taught me will help make my section of guns the most efficient on the ship. I know I sometimes devil you, but I meant no harm; and I realize that you work hard to teach us important things. I'd be honored, sir, if you would shake my hand and wish me luck."

Godwin realized exactly what the gesture meant to the boy and it moved him greatly. No, not a boy; a man. He shook Jewell's hand firmly. "May God smile upon you, Mr. Jewell."

He had been wrong in referring to the midshipmen as blockheads. Though they sometimes engaged in horseplay that annoyed him, it was a characteristic of their youth to do so, and he had also seen them undertake tasks beyond their years and perform them creditably. The excursions that he conducted into grammar, rhetoric, logic, arithmetic, geometry, music, and astronomy carried little excitement, and they had signed on for adventure, not scholarship.

The Barron brothers, the youngest midshipmen on board, walked sheepishly up to him. Like many midshipmen, they sniffled and snuffled constantly, showing why midshipmen were often referred to as "snotties." Their blue uniforms with white flashes on the collars were ill-fitting; they seemed to be undergoing growth spurts.

"Mr. Godwin," said 13-year-old James with great earnestness," I do not want to go into battle without setting things right. That rotten act I committed, setting a sack of goat poo outside your cabin...well... it was just plain wrong, and I'd like to apologize." He nudged his 11-year-old brother. "Your turn, Thomas." He clapped his brother smartly on the shoulder to encourage his speech.

"I am most heartily sorry, sir, for placing that fart cushion under your chair, sir. It was not the act of a gentleman."

"It took courage to say that young, sirs," said Godwin. "Your apologies are accepted but I shall expect you both to turn over a new leaf by paying close attention in class tomorrow." His statement assumed that they would be alive the next day.

Several midshipmen would be commanding four-gun sections of cannon today, ordering about men more than twice their age. Others would be acting as messengers, relaying commands from the quarterdeck to other parts of the ship. Some would be posted aloft to observe the fall of shots so that the great guns could be better directed. All would be under heavy fire. Some would never see another birthday.

Jewell's action and the Barron boys apologies reminded him that the midshipmen had good hearts. Their past unruly conduct was likely due to a natural rebelliousness against a duly constituted authority with no nautical training. His stiff personality had not helped matters. Today he earnestly desired their respect.

Their esteem would have to be earned the hard way, but the battle ahead furnished opportunity. The captain had approved his request to act as a messenger. He had also volunteered to help pass cartridges from the magazine to the guns, replacing anyone who fell.

The parts he would play would be small ones, yet it was the aggregation of many little parts successfully carried out that brought a ship success. Though usually a loner, being part of a ship's company was teaching him the value of fellowship. Such fellowship promised the chance to become something more than the contentious snob that his father repeatedly belittled.

He hoped that his courage would be up to the challenges ahead. Though his job was not military, his warrant officer's rank made him feel a military man's sense of responsibility not to let the side down. He did not think himself any more or less brave than other men, but he could never again face the warrant officers that he dined with if he failed in his duty today. He did understand that he possessed the great advantage of serving alongside men whose courage was trusty and reliable. Courage was infectious.

"Baaaaaah!"

"God damn it! Nooooo!" Saunders shout was a combination of anger and despair.

Mrs. Taffy, the wardroom's goat, stood next to the rudder housing placidly chewing on a large bundle of paper.

Saunders recognized the remnant of his letters and dashed over to retrieve what little remained of them. He angrily tore the wad from her mouth, but what he got came apart in his hands. He dropped to his hands and knees and frantically tried to piece the remains together, but what Mrs. Taffy's teeth had not accounted for her saliva had.

"Baaaaaah!"

Scott had forgotten to give Mrs. Taffy her ration of rum that she came for promptly at 11 each day, and she had apparently decided to consume his letters as a substitute. She should have been put in the boats towed astern, but Thomas and Douglas had wanted fresh milk and so she had remained aboard.

Saunders rose to his feet slowly and drew his pistol. Worry and rage were controlling his actions, but they would not be denied. He put the gun to Mrs. Taffy's head and full cocked it. Just then Robinson's hand came out from behind; caught his wrist, and pushed it carefully away from the goat's head. "Easy there, Mr. Saunders, easy, the battle has not started yet. Save it for the French."

Saunders saw the worry in the Boatswain's eyes. He blinked as he realized just how insane he must appear. He put the weapon back in his holster. "She ate my letters, Mr. Robinson." His tone was halfway between despair and rage. "I have not had any mail from home in six months. My mother was gravely ill last I heard, and I hoped these letters would bring some relief. Now I will go into battle not knowing."

"I am very sorry, Mr. Saunders," said Robinson. "But remember she is a beast, no more, and has no idea what lies ahead. I would just say, don't let her get your goat."

"Baaaaaah!"

HMS Victory, *Admiral Nelson's flagship*

Admiral Nelson was pleased with his fleet. His men were performing as he had schooled them. It was time for one final public act of encouragement. "Mr. Pasco," he said to the lieutenant in charge of signals. "Run up the message I mentioned earlier."

Pasco replied uncertainly, "Aye, aye, sir."

"What is it, Mr. Pasco? Something is troubling you. Don't be afraid. I welcome suggestions. Tell me."

"Well, Admiral, in your signal 'England confides that every man will do his duty' the word 'confides' will have to be spelled out. That takes a lot of extra flags and consumes time. We have a single flag for the word 'expects'. If you change the message to 'England expects every man will do his duty' communications can proceed much faster."

Nelson thought carefully. "It is important that we get the message out before the first shot tells, so I will accept your suggestion. Make it so, Mr. Pasco."

Godwin heard the sound of cheering course across the weather decks and stopped in his tracks. Men were clapping each other on the backs and smiling broadly. He grasped the arm of a madly capering sailor and inquired what all the fuss was about.

"We just got word a message has been received from the Flagship. Lord Nelson says, 'England expects every man will do his duty.'" The sailor struck his palm with his fist and exclaimed, "By God, we shall do that and more!"

Godwin was amazed that a simple and obvious message could provoke such an enthusiastic response, but decided it was the sender that counted. These men worshipped Nelson.

Ten feet away, Warwick and Coombs had a different take on the signal. "So, Marty, had you thought about not doing your duty? Did you need any reminding?" said Warwick cynically.

"That's just Nelson's way. He likes the grand gesture that will look good in the history books. I think the signal is intended for future generations, not us. Maybe he is bit theatrical, but he's got a good heart, and he cares about us."

"I don't question he is a great man, Marty, but it annoys me that he thinks there is even a possibility we might need someone to tell us our duty. No one on board has any plans to let his mates down. If we haven't figured out that the folks back home expect us to protect them, telling us at the last minute won't do no good."

"Calm down, Jim. It's not worth bothering about."

"Sorry, Marty. You're right. I' m just keyed up right now."

Just then, Peg Leg Jones, the ship's cook, limped by.

"I was thinking how much better fixed for a fight Jones is then we are."

"How do you figure that, Jim?"

"It don't hurt at all to be shot in a wooden leg."

"Do you believe that story about Nelson and the boat cloak, Jim?"

"Ain't never heard it."

"The story goes that one night, years ago, he was leading some sailors on a cutting out expedition and a bad wind sprang up, turning the night bitterly cold. One of the sailors said, 'Captain, would you like me to fetch your boatcloak?' Nelson replied, 'That will be unnecessary, sailor. The heat of my patriotism keeps me quite warm.'"

"Balls and bang me arse, Marty! I don't believe that bilge for one second. It sounds like something a saint in a blue uniform might say, and you and I both know that King's Navy ain't got a single one of those. That has to be a myth invented by a landlubber who ain't never felt the chill a cold sea can put into your bones."

"I think the Whitehall gents feel the need to give heart to the home folks by making up tales that make a man seem like a British archangel with a sword. Personally, I think Nelson does just fine without any tall stories being told about him."

"I wonder what folks will say about us a century from now."

"I hope they will say we did our duty handsomely, Jim."

"Pretty sure they will, Marty. I bet historians will rattle on about how stalwart and fearless we were. Damn good thing my shaking knees will never make it into the history books."

Both men laughed. The idea that future generations would lionize ordinary men as martial demigods was hilarious.

CHAPTER 12

Warwick and Combs shifted their discussion to more prosaic concerns.

"Tell you what, Jim, if Johnny Crapaud takes me head off today, you take my stuff. If he takes your head off instead, I take yours. Sound fair?"

"It does, Marty. I got to tell you I wish I had a cup of grog right now. You'd think since I been in four fights the waiting would get easier, but it don't. It get's worse. It might even be easier for you. I know what lies ahead, and you don't.

"It's a sight harder being a marine than a soldier. On land, if you get real scared you can find some way to scuttle back and hide. Can't do that on a ship, especially since marines guard all the passages to the lower decks. When the air grows dark with lead, and believe you me, it does, you just got to keep going like you would through a blizzard."

"Hearing you say that makes me feel better, Jim. All of us are in this thing together. The ship is us, and we are the ship. That makes me feel less alone." Marty smiled. "And I do have a small flask of rum here that Sarn't Dale missed. I'll trade you a good pull for a chaw of that baccy you have."

"Well, ain't you the clever fellow!" Warwick laughed.

The men made the exchange quickly and no one noticed. All of their immediate neighbors were focused on their own fears and hopes.

Sailor's ears perked up at the *rat tat tat* of drums, but relaxed a few seconds later as they realized that the message pertained only to marines. Drummers could beat out 23 separate commands besides "assembly" that were understood by Marines but merely annoying background noises to sailors. Flashes of red raced past the sailors as marines hurried to the poop deck that served as their parade ground.

As the final notes of "assembly" died away, the last of *Bellerophon's* Marines formed up in two well ordered rows on the poop deck, the second rank one pace behind the first. All of the taller men were in the rear rank but both ranks were sized, with shortest men in the center. The ship's complement of red coats consisted of one under-strength company divided into two platoons: 62 privates, two corporals, two sergeants and two drummers.

Wilson stood on the right of the first rank, while Higgins took up a position behind the middle of the second. Pennywhistle stood directly in front of the entire assemblage. Wemyss was nowhere to be seen.

"Ten shun!" barked Dale in a command voice so loud that the French could probably hear it. The two ranks immediately became as stiff and straight as toy soldiers. Well, not quite as stiff as conventional soldiers, since marines had learned to use knees and feet to compensate for the pitching and rolling of a ship's deck.

The attention position was executed in accordance with Dundas's Manual. Heels were two inches apart and feet splayed at a 45 degree angle; belly drawn in, chest projected, shoulders squared. The little finger of each man's left hand rested on the seam of his white trousers, while his right forced the butt of his firelock tight against his shoe.

While battle was far more fluid than the precise evolutions of the parade ground, the smartness with which men performed drill gave a good indication of the skill with which they would fight.

Pennywhistle slowly swiveled his head from left to right, trying to gauge the men's readiness and their mood. Their brick-red coats had faded to a dusky reddish brown from exposure to sun and salt spray, and more than a few uniforms displayed patches. Some of the red and white plumes on the side of their black round hats had seen better days, and a few brass crossbelt plates were so scuffed that the marine insignia of a crown over a fouled anchor was undecipherable. The black gaiters that came to two inches below their knees were veterans of heavy service. Their shoes were in better condition than he'd expected—the Navy Board had a foolish penchant for purchasing cheap footwear—but the men had done their best to put polish to them. The firelocks gripped by their leathery hands glistened with gun oil, as did the hilts of bayonets that protruded above their scabbards. Their musket straps and cross belts looked to have been freshly pipe-clayed and glowed a pleasing white. The black cartridge boxes that held forty rounds had been carefully buffed with vinegar and linseed oil to keep the leather flaps supple for easy opening in battle.

The men's faces were mostly stoical; determined rather than grim, confident not arrogant. Smiles outside the regulations blossomed here and there, evidence of an eagerness to exercise their well-honed skills, certain that they would bring victory.

A surge of pride welled up in Pennywhistle. Whatever happened in the battle ahead, it was an honor to command such men. Like him, they were young. The most junior private was 16; the most senior, 31. Sergeant Dale at 36 was both the oldest and longest serving marine.

At six feet, two inches, Pennywhistle towered over most of his men. Their average was about five-foot-seven, though two were only five-foot-four. Most had been agricultural workers in their previous lives, but the company also contained a blacksmith, a tailor, and a cobbler. Their motives for joining varied, but were mostly practical rather than emotional. All were proud volunteers. The myth about many being jailbirds annoyed Pennywhistle as much the derisive nickname that wisecracking sailors had pinned on them: jollies.

He suddenly realized that he was keeping the men at attention longer than need be. Even at his most ill-tempered he was no martinet, and it was foolish to tax his marines' strength when a great battle lay ahead.

"Stand at...ease!"

A collective, quiet "Aaahhhh" arose as the men assumed more relaxed postures. Every eye fixed on him. It was clear that they expected words of wisdom, practicality, or inspiration: if all three could be managed, so much the better. The trick was to do it in a short space of time. British military men laughed at the long, florid harangues that French and Spanish officers favored.

He would have to mix practicality with passion; appealing as much to the measured reason he loved as to the raw emotions that he distrusted. He would also have to explain Wemyss' absence.

"Marines! I know that you are all looking forward to a dinner with fresh meat much more than enduring a short address from me." Cooke had advanced dinner from noon to 11 a.m. and had ordered several of the ship's bullocks butchered to save space in the boats. Usually meat came from barrels packed years before.

Pennywhistle's observation brought scattered snorts of laughter and a few smiles. Officers did not often acknowledge the basic needs of the men.

"I will keep my remarks brief, as I am neither Nelson nor Solomon. I will not remind you of the rightness of our cause, because I see that knowledge in your eyes. I will not make any special appeals to your professionalism, because I see your devotion to it in the exactness of your drill. I will not remind you of what you fight for, because every day I see your great regard for your mates and this ship.

"What I will tell you is that a hard battle lies ahead. We face determined opponents who will yield only after a stiff penalty of blood is paid. I ask you to do as you have always done. Trust in your training, your officers, and most of all, the gallant fighting spirit that lies deep within each of your hearts.

"Our job is to defend these decks with skill and honor. We will be outnumbered by the soldiers on the French and Spanish ships. Each of you must find the inner strength to fight as a dozen, though you are but a single man.

"The French and Spanish will likely try to board us, since they lack our skill with the big guns. Sailors will struggle valiantly, but the hard fighting will fall to us, and we shall contest every square inch of deck. The enemy will have numbers, but we will have volleys and bayonets, and the skill to use them with devastating results.

"Remember to fire on the uproll. Take advantage of any cover you can when reloading, and feel no shame if you must lie flat upon the deck to avoid a dose of enemy canister.

"You all have been trained to fight in pairs, and I would ask that you put your partner's welfare before your own, since he will surely do the same for you. You will also be the first to employ chain order firing. You should consider that both an honor and an excellent method for increasing your chances of survival.

"I want each pair to keep a sack full of grenades handy. Do not rely upon them, but if your firelock is disabled, a grenade toss at the last extremity may save your life. If one lands near you, do not attempt to throw it back. Make sure the cloths the sail-makers have fashioned for you are kept moist and handy to smother their fuses.

"Smother rather than run. The grenade is faster than your fleetest dash. Running from a grenade, already sizzling at your foot, is as pointless as heeding the words of a drunk with a beer in his hand lecturing on the merits of temperance!"

Utter silence reigned for a brief second, followed by entirely unmilitary laughter. Ready humor was not generally part of the lieutenant's make up.

Pennywhistle paused, pleased that his attempt at levity had underscored his point. "You will receive you final orders within the hour. There are a few details I must work out with Captain Wemyss and Captain Cooke. Then I will meet with the non commissioned officers. I am sad to say that Captain Wemyss is not here because he is consulting with Mr. Whyte, our surgeon. He has suffered considerable physical complaints of late, as you are all aware. I am in great hopes he will take his proper place before the battle."

That was a complete lie, but it was necessary to reassure the men. He would put Dale in command of the poop. He might be a non commissioned officer but the men trusted him, and his years of experience fitted him perfectly for the task.

"1st platoon will man the poop deck under Captain Wemyss. 2nd platoon, A section, will cover the quarter deck under Mr. Wilson and Mr. Higgins. 2nd Platoon, B section will be under my command on the forecastle. Those detailed as gunners will report to their 32-pounders after the first four broadsides."

Some of the men designated gunners looked puzzled that they should not immediately report to their crews on the lower decks, but they would leave the thinking to their officers. Innovation seemed the order of the day, so there probably was some clever wisdom behind the order.

Pennywhistle wanted those marine gunners available as soon as *Bellerophon* pierced the enemy line. Just as the first broadside was usually a ship's best one, so it was with the first volley. He needed maximum musket firepower as much for psychological reasons as tactical ones. He hoped his men and the ship's great guns would knock the enemy back on their heels so strongly that it would make them think twice before attempting to mount a counterstroke.

He was taking a chance that Cooke would listen to him, but one advantage of being a zealot was that it considerably amplified your powers of persuasion.

"I should also add that in the interests of conserving our man power, that sailors will be manning the fighting tops." There were slight murmurs of derision; no marine ever thought a sailor his equal in the use of a musket.

"The God of Battles considers you most worthy, as do I, and your country is grateful to have you as its guardians. I am happy if prayer brings you comfort, but while I have faith in God, I place my trust in your hands. I know that you will never let me down."

There was a second of absolute silence, followed by jubilant shouts and an energetic waving of hats. Not a single marine remained silent. "Hip hip huzzah, hip hip huzzah, hip hip huzzah!"

Extraordinary! He'd done nothing save speak a few truths that were obvious long before he opened his mouth. He was greatly moved, and struggled to keep tears from his eyes. Blood and death lay directly ahead, yet a moment of fellowship such as this was one for the ages: a treasure that gave meaning to sacrifices in battle far better than any medals issued long after.

"Ten shun!" Dale decided the jollity had gone quite far enough. As a good NCO, it was his job to maintain order and restrain excess enthusiasm. The force and confidence of his voice instantly recalled men to their duty. The ranks reordered and the pandemonium abruptly became complete silence.

It was time for him to give the men one last piece of information. "Because all of the mess tables have been stowed, you will be eating your stew by your action stations," said Pennywhistle. "Makeshift trenchers will be distributed near the galley stove. Detail an extra man to carry them. For now, I wish you good eating and good fortune. Sarn't Dale, dismiss the men."

"Dis...miss!" bellowed Dale. The ranks dissolved into small knots of men talking quietly and walking toward their battle positions.

Wilson briskly walked away, trying to conceal his irritation. Pennywhistle clearly possessed the "Nelson Touch." The men would follow him anywhere, while he had mostly earned their disdain. Normally he did not care, but when men emulated a leader like Pennywhistle, they took extra risks that put men like himself in extreme danger.

Wilson preferred to play the role of water carrier in a safe setting. It occurred to him that officers were sometimes accidentally hit by rounds fired from their own side. Despite training and the best of intentions, the chaos of battle ensured that some officers died thus in nearly every major engagement. Pennywhistle just might have to be numbered among them.

CHAPTER 13

The ship's bell struck seven times as Pennywhistle entered the wardroom. Since all of the thin pine partitions had been removed and stowed, there was no wardroom, just one long expanse of deck. Because the furniture was stowed as well, everyone was sitting cross-legged on the deck in the manner of Iroquois chieftains at a pow-wow. All of the officers wore their best uniforms, though the setting was the antithesis of formality.

Cooke and Cumby acted as the chairmen of the meeting. The four naval lieutenants, Thomas, Scott, Douglas, and Saunders sat on their right. Marines Wemyss, Pennywhistle, Wilson, and Higgins seated themselves on their left. Pennywhistle observed that Wemyss looked like death warmed over, and hoped that he might have a last minute flash of wisdom and stand down.

The general mood was optimistic, though the normally cheerful Saunders looked agitated. The only outward physical signs that this was no ordinary conference were the compulsive movements of fingers and thumbs drumming, scratching, rubbing, pulling, twiddling, and steepling. While all were understandably concerned for their individual fortunes, no one doubted that the ship would give a good account of herself or that the British would emerge the victors. Everyone had been long eager to bring the French to battle, and that day had finally arrived.

Cooke's steward placed biscuits and sliced Smithfield ham on a large plate on the rudder housing; it was the only thing available that could be used as a table. With the ship's cutlery and glassware in the hold, everyone was eating from wooden plates and taking long pulls of wine from cheap tin cups. Tension appeared to stimulate appetites.

Except Pennywhistle; he picked at his ham and biscuit. He knew in a general way what was expected of him, but listened carefully as Cooke outlined the full particulars of his plan.

Boom, boom, boom. Ears perked up. All knew what it signified. Pennywhistle consulted his pocket watch to mark the time: 11:40. Damn, he really had to stop checking his timepiece so often. It was dangerously close to becoming a ritual.

"*Royal Sovereign* is under fire, gentlemen," said Cooke gravely. "The great contest has begun. I know Collingwood and Rotherem will perform gallantly and I am also certain that your conduct will be every bit their equal. I welcome your questions, and if you have any suggestions, now is the time to voice them," said Cooke in a voice that was as confident as it was lacking in drama.

Many officers nodded, pleased that suggestions would be considered. Cooke was a stern disciplinarian but no tyrant.

"Nelson has made his design for the fleet very clear to all. There is not a man among you who does understand it in detail. Our fleet enjoys a perfect integrity, a unity of thought, purpose, and deed that the French and Spanish envy but will never duplicate. I wish to do the same with this ship. I have already spoken to the warrant officers about their roles. Mr. Cumby, have you anything to add?

"Just one thing, Captain. When we look for signs of a ship's impending surrender, it is important that we consider whether it is French or Spanish, lest we send a boat prematurely. The Spaniards will likely endure twice the casualties of the French before they consider capitulation. We need to make absolutely sure that we do not misconstrue an extended cessation of firing as acknowledgement of defeat."

"An excellent point, Mr. Cumby. Keep firing until you see a white flag or the Dons haul down their colors.

"Our strength today is our gunnery, particularly our 32s on the lower gun deck. The weather deck guns will aim for men and rigging; the two lower decks will focus on enemy hulls. Use red long grained powder for the first two broadsides, white long grained for the rest. When we close to musket shot, all crews will switch to reduced charges and alternate between firing on the uproll and downroll. That will generate the maximum amount of splinters and offset the enemy advantage in numbers.

"If the unimaginable happens and the French gain our weather decks, skillful use of lower deck guns can still guarantee victory. Our priority is to keep as many heavy guns in action as we can. If that means stripping men from other areas to replace losses, then we must do so. We fire faster than our enemies, and must not surrender that advantage.

"When we break the French line, we will have opponents in two directions; both starboard and larboard batteries will be engaged. Because of the lack of wind, our speed will be slow enough that we may be able to manage a good number of salvos. Since we have a limited supply of manpower, let me suggest that the starboard batteries fire first: then have the men dash across the deck to man those on the port side. I had considered have alternating guns on both sides firing simultaneously, but I think this arrangement will prove more effective.

"Mr. Saunders, you have a particularly critical charge, since you command the lower gun deck. I feel certain you will perform with distinction."

"I will indeed, sir!"

"You will have Midshipmen Fairbrother under your command, Mr. Saunders. He may be the only 45-year-old midshipman in the Navy, but he knows a great deal about gunnery. Make use of his knowledge."

"Aye, aye, Sir."

"Mr. Douglas!"

"Aye, sir."

"As with Mr. Saunders, your priority is to keep as many of cannon on the upper gun deck in action as you can. I would also ask you to be mindful of grenades tossed through the gunports. The French use them profligately. Keep swabs and ship's boys handy at all times to kill their fuses."

"Aye, aye, sir."

"Mr. Thomas, though you command the nine-pounders on the quarterdeck, I should prefer you take position on the poop deck so you can supervise its six carronades. I trust you have double-shotted them with canister.'"

Canister was a sheet metal container filled with anywhere from 44 to 200 balls, each projectile slightly smaller than a musket ball. It was exclusively an antipersonnel weapon and turned a carronade into a giant shotgun.

"I have indeed, sir," said Thomas. "The carronades will be as giant sickles and do great execution to the French."

"I will be on the quarterdeck," said Cooke matter-of-factly. "Three midshipmen will assist me as runners, and Mr. Godwin has graciously agreed to serve in that capacity as well. I would ask all of you to focus on keeping up a steady fire on the enemy.

"Mr. Scott, it is imperative you make the most efficient use of the 32-pound smashers located on the forecastle. We must make our first blows heavy and decisive. I shall leave it to your discretion whether you use grape or canister."

Cooke was eager to try out a new supply of grapeshot fashioned on the French pattern: a load consisted of nine golf ball-size projectiles mounted on three wooden disks around a wooden core. The whole was bound by cords, covered in canvas, and directed against both men and masts. It was an experiment, a grudging acknowledgement that sometimes Frenchmen had an idea worth copying.

"Aye, sir, the enemy shall receive a very stiff dose of the grapes that make only the wine of blood. My gun crews are distinguished for their speed, and we shall pound the enemy handsomely."

"I would ask that officers make sure that all men tasked to repel boarders are wearing their boarding helmets," continued Cooke."My compliments to you, Mr. Pennywhistle, for devising them."

Pennywhistle nodded in acknowledgement, though he had actually borrowed the idea from an American officer. The helmet was made of hard japanned leather upon which were laid two metal plates. It had a bill in front and fastened under the chin with two heavy leather straps, making sailors look vaguely like ancient gladiators.

"Now for the Marines. Captain Wemyss. Captain Wemyss. I say, sir, are you quite all right?"

Pennywhistle heard his cue and jumped in. "Captain, Mr. Wemyss is afflicted with a bad case of laryngitis and he has asked me to speak for him. He wishes to spare what remains of his voice for the battle."

"Commendable foresight! Mr. Pennywhistle, I have little doubt that your men's skill with volleys and bayonet charges will keep our decks clear of boarders. Do what you can to eliminate sharpshooters in the enemy tops, and make every effort to lay low cannon crews."

"Captain, if I might make a request?"said Pennywhistle with every ounce of tact that he could muster.

"Go ahead, sir. I have never known you to make a request that was not carefully thought through."

"Captain, we will be outnumbered by the soldiers on the enemy ships. While my marines are famed for their valor and training, stout hearts and skilled hands cannot entirely compensate for disparity in numbers. I respectfully request the maximum number of marines possible be made available to me.

"Although I know marines are needed for the big guns, I propose we should station all marines on the weather decks at the start, and wait until after the fourth broadside before sending any below. I know my proposal flies in the face of tradition, yet Nelson himself has frequently broken with expected procedures and his departures have brought much renown and honor to British arms.

"Our ship is in the position of a man confronting a pack of wild dogs. The best approach is not a cautious one. Stun the leader with a swiftly bloodied nose, put some stick about, and make the pack jump. We must chill the enemy ardor so they become cautious. I know fatigue takes its toll moving the great guns, but I am in hopes the gun crews can manage four rounds before weariness plays too great a part."

Cooke said nothing for half a minute; his face was grave. " I don't like it, Mr. Pennywhistle. Not one bit. We would not need the marines as gunners so badly if our ships were not so dangerously undermanned. But your point about Nelson is well taken. Battles can be lost due to conventional thinking. Since the numbers are against your marines, I will allow you temporary use of their full complement. But only four rounds, no more.

"One other thing, Mr. Pennywhistle. I hate saying this, but if the small arms fire from the French becomes too great and sheer numbers overwhelm, abandon the weather decks and husband the lives of your men. Form your command under the shelter of the poop and prepare a vigorous counter attack. Use French overconfidence against them. They will be emboldened by their initial success yet disorganized, ripe to be swept away by a spirited counter stroke."

"Aye, aye, sir. I had planned for just that eventuality, Captain, and am pleased that you see the sense of it," said Pennywhistle, the excitement that was heating his blood causing him to speak forwardly.

"To increase the strength of our resistance, I have developed some ideas that I think will find favor with you."

Pennywhistle felt the pressure of the group's gaze, yet rather than wilting, his spirit rose to the challenge. Instead of speaking with the calm tones of a man of science, the energetic voice that emerged from his lips became that of the persuasive orator.

"I have made a small supply of smoke grenades. I know there will be much smoke today, but it is still useful to have objects that can cloak a small area from the eyes of enemy boarders. I have also measured and marked distances to various points on the forecastle with small sticks topped in red, blue, and brown. They are measured from the point where my marines will first form up. Red is five yards' range, blue is ten yards, brown is twenty. They will be useful for men firing into smoke, since smoke often befuddles men's sense of depth and distance.

There were murmurs of approval. *Amazing*, thought Pennywhistle, *All the times I have been the subject of general amusement because of my concern with little oddments of knowledge, and now I am suddenly everyone's favorite officer.*

"I have placed a large barrel of thick grease on the forecastle, a byproduct of today's dinner given me by Mr. Jones. I propose to dump it when any French boarders are packed closely together. It may literally sweep them off their feet. I have warned my marines to keep well back when I dump it, so that they may fire a profitable volley into the reeling, disorganized crowd."

"Good, good," said Cooke.

"I have also prepared one offensive measure. If we become locked with an enemy ship, I propose to send small, fast men along its wales, tasked with cutting the ropes which keep its gunport lids aloft. If the ropes are slashed, it will slam enemy gunports closed. The only way they can then be opened will be by blowing them off. It may help to keep a number of enemy guns out of action for a time and give us a useful advantage. "

"Capitol idea, Mr. Pennywhistle, but those fellows will have to have fast feet and great agility," said Cooke.

"The men I have chosen spent time as circus acrobats, Captain."

Cooke looked pleasantly surprised. "Our Service contains truly remarkable men! And now, gentlemen, I would like to conclude by offering some general thoughts. Nelson's plan is brilliant, but it will require considerable discipline and fortitude on our parts. We will be under fire for some time with no ability to respond. We will suffer death and damage, but we must withhold our first broadside until we are very close. Even then, we may be fired upon by multiple ships attacking from various quarters. We will have to bear up to the pounding until our relief arrives. It will be up to you to explain to the men what is planned and set a good example by your own conduct."

He paused for a few seconds, as if in deep thought. He broke into a rare smile. "Gentlemen, I have cudgeled my humble brain long and hard and can think of nothing further to add. The only words that come to mind are simple ones, reflecting basic truths. I believe in you. I believe in this ship. I believe in Nelson. The sum of my beliefs is that we shall win a smashing victory today. I pray you Godspeed"—piety departed his eyes and voice, both now feral—"and God's might."

The officers were about to cheer, but the flat calmness in Cooke's final words stopped them. "We beat to quarters in fifteen minutes."

The officers quietly headed toward their individual assignments. *Time to meet the lion,* thought Pennywhistle. He wondered what was going through the minds of his fellow Marine officers, particularly Wilson. He would have to keep a weather eye on him.

I have to do this! thought Wemyss. He felt his eyelid and was pleased to note that the tic had stopped for the time being.

I can do this! thought an unafraid Higgins. He fingered the locket with Miss Lydia's hair.

I damn well do not want to do this, thought a resentful Wilson, stroking the ruby in his ring. He had been vaguely interested in discovering if he were a brave man, but had finally concluded it would be far more congenial to find out what it was like to be a wealthy old man. It was all fine and good if men wrote odes to your bravery and spoke your name with reverence, but both had little merit if they did so because you were dead. *He* was here for material advancement, not glory. He had lots of officers left to fleece, and it was annoying that a battle should get in the way of that.

He glanced at the gold ring on his left hand that brought him luck in cards and hoped it would extend to battle. He should not have worn it lest Pennywhistle connect it with his dead cousin, but he was scared enough to take the risk anyway.

Rather than rely on a talisman, he needed to figure out a way to skirt the dangers of the battle while avoiding the appearance of faint-heartedness. He needed to be in places where bullets were not flying, and convince everyone that he was speeding about on urgent errands for plausible reasons.

The Service punished outright cowardice in a most final way, but battle was confusion personified. Many eyewitnesses gave wildly differing accounts of an incident in battle because of smoke and stress. It would be hard to prove anything against him if he were clever.

The one person who might frustrate his plans was Pennywhistle with his damnable orders and zeal. A zealot could inspire ordinary men to insane acts of foolhardiness, and worse, to expect their officers to lead them from the front and absorb the first volley of bullets.

But a zealot approached from behind by a man with a grenade was an entirely different matter. The deadly orbs had a nasty way of appearing at exactly the wrong moment with no clue as to who tossed them. Crude weapons, yet a fine way of removing obstacles if you were not fussy. He most certainly was not fussy.

Pennywhistle walked a little faster to catch up with Wemyss. He hated what he had to do next. "Captain Wemyss, I wonder if we could have a word in private on the Captain's balcony. It is important."

"Of course Mr. Pennywhistle, I thank you for covering for me in the meeting. I do need to conserve my strength for what lies ah—" he broke into a fit of coughing.

Pennywhistle walked behind Wemyss as he wobbled out onto the balcony. "I am truly sorry," said Pennywhistle under his breath. He sharply jabbed his fist into the base of Wemyss' skull. The blow was administered to induce unconsciousness. Had he not pulled his punch, he could have caused death, but The Grim Reaper had already scheduled an appointment and Pennywhistle would let nature run its course.

He moved the body to a corner of the balcony, where he hoped it would be out of harm's way, though likely no one above decks would truly enjoy security for the next few hours. Anyone seeing Wemyss would probably think him the victim of a falling block or the deeply compressed air burst resulting from the close passage of a cannon ball. He exited the balcony and counted himself lucky that the tumult of preparing for battle had shielded his actions.

Pennywhistle walked very slowly toward his post on the forecastle, consumed by guilt, yet knowing he had done the correct, if dishonorable thing. He was coming to realize that duty and honor were not always synonymous.

There was another matter he needed to consider. In a well ordered ship, with everyone following closely prescribed rules and exhibiting predictable patterns of behavior, anomalies stood out like coals on snow. He had noticed Wilson wearing a distinctive gold ring that he had never seen on his hand before.

There was something oddly familiar about that ring. The pigeon-blood ruby occupying its center was a Sunrise Stone: famous for its clarity and the most valuable of that family of gems. The jackal's head of Anubis engraved on the right side of ring looked sinister, and was definitely not of contemporary design. The gold itself looked to be of great age. He was certain he had seen that ring before. But where?

The ring was significant somehow, but he could not figure out why. He hated mysteries and normally would have obsessed about the ring until he had pierced its secrets, but for now his mind was too preoccupied with the battle ahead to give it his full attention. It would eat at him over the next few hours, but he knew his subconscious was already working on a solution.

CHAPTER 14

The loud beating of drums kicked him back to reality and he realized that he had sleepwalked to his appointed position on the forecastle. The marine drummers energetically pounded out the rhythm to "Heart of Oak." Beat to Quarters: action stations.

The crew had done it hundreds of times, but this time it was no drill. Speed was important, but so was care. Men would die if actions were not performed with as much attention to safety as efficiency. The ship contained almost 14 tons of powder, and any number of careless actions could turn her into a giant bomb. It only took one careless man to destroy an entire ship, as had happened with Israel Pellew's frigate *Amphion*: a single gigantic explosion caused by carelessness had reduced her to floating bits of kindling. And that had occurred with no pressure of imminent battle.

Feet pounded, pulses raced, and men sweated. Commands were shouted, gun tackles adjusted, and cannon trucks squealed. Extra sand was applied to the decks. Excitement, tension, and more than a little fear seized control of sailors, yet their actions proceeded in orderly ways. There was also a general sense of relief: the great battle, long anticipated and trained for, had finally arrived.

The ship became a giant living organism: a symbiotic fusion of men and hemp and wood and metal. The ship was the remarkable product of the most complex industrial process on the planet, and the men who walked her decks were splendid specimens of fiery hearts subordinated to an exacting discipline. The resulting hybrid was far more powerful than the sum of its parts.

Higgins could think of no place in the world that he would rather be.

Wilson knew that he would never be ready and wanted to be anywhere but here.

Cooke welcomed the chance to match British valor and skill against French gallantry and élan. Cumby, at his side, shared his captain's enthusiasm.

Warwick and Combs checked the flints on their muskets one last time and were heartened by the look of assurance on Mr. Pennywhistle's face.

"I am going to give you a gift, Marty. It's something real special. It brings good luck, and it's seen me through four fights." Warwick reached into the pocket of his redcoat and brought forth something carefully wrapped in oil cloth. He handed it to his friend.

Combs gingerly unwrapped his present, revealing a small shriveled object. It smelled like the inside of a very old shoe. He wrinkled his nose in disgust. "God's death! What the hell is that, Jim?"

"It's an ape's paw, Marty, from one of them Gibraltar Apes. I bought it off an old gypsy woman and she said there ain't no better good luck charm. I paid a pretty price for it, but she was right. No bullet nor blade has come anywhere near me since I got it. I know it ain't a thing of beauty, but keep it in your pocket during the battle and you will come through just fine."

Combs looked dubious. "Well, if you've made it through four battles I suppose it must work. Thanks."

Macfarlane felt surprisingly calm. He had rehearsed his part as the loader of the port carronade on the forecastle many times; his gun crew was the fastest on the entire ship. His friend Jepson stood in the ship's waist, ready to man the braces if the ship needed to alter course.

Whyte checked his saws one last time to make sure their edges were as sharp as could be. He smiled a reassuring smile that he did not really feel at Nancy and Mr. Jewell. They returned equally false smiles with the best of intentions.

Mary would be passing cartridges today, part of a long line. The distant booming was growing louder. Standing outside the hanging magazine, she felt a sudden wetness at her feet. *Oh, shit.* Her water had broken.

Pennywhistle was proud of his ship and glad that fate had placed him in exactly the spot he now occupied. His pulse was steady, his hands unwavering, and his purpose as savage as his mind was disciplined.

He would rely upon three weapons, instead of the brace of pistols favored by most officers.

His unusual cutlass of 30 inches and 2.2 pounds was a hybrid weapon; both new and an heirloom. The 25-inch blade curved two inches from the straight and been made by Henry Osborn of Birmingham, cutler to the King. It was a short version of the Pattern 1796 Light Cavalry Saber: wider at its tip than its base and thinnest in the middle, it was capable of decapitation with a single blow because the entire strength of a man's arm was focused on its tip. The heavy brass clamshell guard that encased the hand had once belonged to Nicholas Pennywhistle in the 17th century and represented his indomitable spirit as well as family honor.

He considered the sword almost a living being and so had bestowed a name upon it: Nemo. He took it from the inscription on the blade: *Nemo me impune lacessit*—"No man attacks me with impunity." It was the motto of the House of Stuart, to which his mother's family was distantly related.

Osborn had also made the 15-inch dirk concealed in his right boot.

His .65 caliber Ferguson Rifle was also a lethal legacy: an inheritance from his father who had been a good friend of the inventor. The four-foot breech loader was only slightly longer than a Baker, though it was much faster to reload: a skilled operator could manage six shots a minute to the Baker's two. Like the Baker, it was short enough to reload kneeling or prone; it used the .615 round that was standard for the Baker and also took a 30-inch bayonet. Though not considered sporting, he planned to hunt enemy officers with it, starting with enemy captains.

The ship's second cat, known as "the other one," began rubbing himself against Pennywhistle's side and purring vigorously; the small feline had begun frequenting his cot three weeks ago. He had not been seeking a pet, but had apparently acquired one. The beast was affectionate, and he sometimes spoke to it at night, though he knew it was silly to do so. The cat was an Egyptian, with grey fur mottled with black starbursts, so Pennywhistle had christened him Mau —"cat" in ancient Demotic.

Pennywhistle petted Mau several times and it calmed his nerves. He then picked up the cat and handed him to Private Withers. "Take him to the cockpit, and be quick about it." The cat possessed a strange affinity for dying men; on three occasions he had seen the beast seek out and offer comfort to men who expired a few hours later.

"Mr. Franklin, run up the colors!" said Cooke to the signals midshipman. The 20 by 20-foot ensign soared proudly to the top of the mizzen gaffe: the Union Jack in the upper left quadrant of a large Cross of St. George on a field of white. It barely fluttered in the light airs.

The scholarly contemplative inside Pennywhistle departed. The warrior who took his place blazed with passion at the prospect of proving that he was as good in action as he was in training, to show that anticipation and reality were born twins. He knew the lyrics of battle and now he would demonstrate that he understood the music equally well. His emerald eyes turned from kind to cruel, his full lips pursed, and his nostrils flared. His breathing took on the steady, deep cadence of a hungry predator on the prowl.

The rising exhilaration that stirred his heart and heated his blood had nothing to do with the rationality that he prized. It was closer to the alcoholic intoxication that he disdained. The wine of battle was as sweet as it was powerful. *Bottoms up and God help the French!*

PART TWO: BATTLE

"When soldiers have been baptized in the fire of a battlefield, they have all one rank in my eyes. "
—Napoleon Bonaparte

CHAPTER 15

The band played "Rule Britannia" and other patriotic musical warhorses as *Bellerophon* crawled through the torpid sea like a lazy slug through heavy grass. She was 1,000 yards from the nearest enemy ship, and her speed had dropped to a single knot when the first enemy round stung.

Great bastions of smoke rose as enemy batteries spewed flame like magma bursts from angry volcanoes. The sound was hundreds of thunderstorms confined in a narrow canyon and pierced the ears like ice picks. The increasing smoke was rapidly diminishing Cooke's ability to see much of anything beyond a hundred yards. *Royal Sovereign*, *Bellisle*, *Mars*, and *Tonnant* had already endured the gauntlet that *Bellerophon* had entered and were through the enemy line.

Overton checked his watch the instant the first cannon ball hit *Bellerophon*; high noon. His Breguet was one of the most perfect time pieces available—a necessity for a very particular man who wanted to make sure any entry in the ship's log was accurate.

He had already fixed the ship's exact position by taking a reading on the sun's elevation with his sextant. He had then made a clean slate of the blackboard behind the ship's wheel. He quickly wrote upon it the most up to date information on wind direction, speed, and course heading, so that all might see it at a glance. Regardless of battle, ship procedures had to be followed.

He looked at the resolute faces of Cooke and Cumby standing a yard away, and then to the quartermaster, helmsman, and assistant helmsman positioned just behind them, and felt his confidence swell. The Barron brothers and Midshipman Pierson stood to Cooke's left, ready to carry messages. Mr. Godwin joined them a moment later.

He was grateful that *Bellerophon* contained such a marvelous set of human machinery, in which every man was a wheel, a gear, or a pulley, all moving with astonishing regularity and exactitude to the will of its master machinist— the all-powerful captain.

This was his second fleet action, and he wished that he did not know what lay ahead. He had been with Nelson at the Nile; the man was a born scrapper. He would not stop until the French and Spanish Fleets were wiped out as a fighting force. The affray ahead would be long and bloody.

Age was catching up with Overton. The sea was a hard life, and much as he loved it, it was job for youthful men. It was time to go ashore permanently, and he had made plans to do so when this cruise was over. He fingered the heavy parchment document in his coat pocket and thought the big surprise that he had prepared for Nancy might just make up for all the time she had spent at sea.

He had promised her he'd be careful, but his duty lay in staying close to the captain, and that guaranteed high risk.

His alert eyes detected a slight lessoning of shadows on the white caps; evidence the slight breeze was about to drop even further.

"Captain?"

"Yes, Mr. Overton."

"Wind's dropping a bit. Recommend you steer starboard a point."

"Very good, Mr. Overton. Make it so."

He just had to stay alive for a few more hours. Nelson's victory would undoubtedly bring him a good share of prize money, more than enough to finally put down solid roots.

The enemy fire was increasing in frequency and accuracy with each passing minute. So far, it was all round shot. *Bellerophon* was taking hits in her rigging and sails, but so far her men were unscathed. Three large holes blossomed in the foretopsail, while two small ones bloomed in the maintopsail. The mizzen flagstaff stay parted, as did the main topgallant stay. Neither of the two was critical, but the loss of any stays weakened the stability of the masts. A mast could endure huge chunks of wood being gouged out of it, but could not remain upright if it lost its stays.

"Unpleasant pounding this, Captain, but not unexpected," said Cumby to Cooke, his tone matter-of-fact. "We are under fire from at least four ships. I believe the two closest are Spanish, while the more distant ones are French. The Spanish carry 32-pounders as their heavy guns, while the French have 36s, so we are currently at the edge of their effective range. It will not be long before their bombardment becomes severe as their lesser guns are brought to bear. I'd estimate that with this wind we have fifteen minutes before we pierce their line."

"Indeed, we shall simply have to endure. Keep our course and nerves steady. We are ordered to penetrate the line, and by God we shall," said Cooke with quiet resolve. "I believe Collingwood has struck the enemy line farther South than Nelson expected. Given the fitful wind, we may have to hold our own against considerably superior numbers longer than expected. Our relief will come, fresh and eager, but it will be our task to smash up the enemy sufficiently so that their intervention is decisive."

Pennywhistle checked his watch as he puckered and unpuckered his lips, noting that the minutes were moving at the pace of crippled turtles traversing fields of molasses. He heard the tell-tale *riiiiippp* a second before a 36-pound shot ricocheted off the jib-boom and clipped the heads off of two of his marines, neat as one of Henry VIII's executioners. The bodies stood frozen for a split second as if they did not quite believe what had happened, then dropped to the deck like discarded old clothes. One deformed head lodged in the boarding nets to his right: its final grotesque expression that of an Aztec sacrificial mask. The other smashed into a sailor's forehead, crushing his skull.

Damn, thought Pennywhistle, *those deaths were my fault.* He was so eager to come to grips with the enemy that he had allowed his men to stand prematurely. "Lie down, Lie down!" He gave the palms down hand signal as well, to reach those deafened by the incessant booming. The marines promptly complied.

Dale came dashing up, his usual unreadable face betraying alarm. "Sir, we have a problem. Wemyss is on the poop shouting like a madman. He is yelling nonsense orders, telling the men to stand fast one second, then charge the next. The men are confused and scared. Thank God with all the noise the Captain has not heard him! I don't understand. I thought you had dealt with him, sir."

Pennywhistle scowled. "I was too mindful of his welfare. I shall be more drastic this time." He looked down at the prostrate form of Corporal John Madison. "Corporal, on your feet."

Madison jumped up and stood to attention. "Madison, you are in charge. An emergency commands me away. I trust I shall be back within five minutes. In the meantime, keep the men lying flat."

Madison looked puzzled but saluted. "Aye, aye, sir."

Pennywhistle barely heard his reply as he and Dale raced off, having to bob and weave as they dodged small knots of men at their action stations. The noise and smoke helped distract attention from their mad running, since sailors were focused more on the battle then the strange actions of two men.

They walked past Cooke and Cumby, who had their glasses out and were preoccupied surveying the sea ahead, likely trying to discern if any new ships had begun firing on them.

32- and 24-pound solid shot from the latest volley filled the air with splinters the size and sharpness of bayonets, but by some miracle no one was hit.

The marines on the poop had formed a circle around Wemyss. They reminded Pennywhistle of school boys gaping at freak of nature, like a two-headed frog or five-legged horse, and waiting to see the beast perform.

A hatless Wemyss was leaping up and down like a dancing goblin. The twitching of his right eyelid was like a metronome cranked up to top speed. He was waving his sword in circles and shouting, "Johnny Crapaud's picked the wrong Navy to fight, and the Dons will regret us accepting their invitation to a ball! We will mow them down like rotten wheat in a hurricane! I tell you all, we will win a great victory today, a victory like no other. Immortal fame awaits us. Why hasn't Nelson arrived? I must give him this news!"

A manic cackle accompanied the mad joy on his face. "It truly is to glory we steer, my lads. We will be ice water to kill French fire!"

Pennywhistle wondered with horror if his blow had caused this madness, but he had no time to indulge feelings of regret. He burst through the circle and grabbed Wemyss.

"Sir, you are not yourself. Let me help."

"Thank God, you have come, Mr. Pennywhistle, thank God." He smiled with the ecstasy of a drunk just given a bottle of rare Scotch. "Between the two of us, we can stop these Frog bastards. Things have been getting very hot here and I—"

Wemyss sagged suddenly, and Pennywhistle beheld the cause of the madness. A ragged hole, half the size of a shilling, had been drilled through the crown of the captain's head by a stray metal fragment. Pennywhistle could see the grey of his brain pulsating like a cerebral heart.

By all rights he should be dead or at least unconscious, yet the wound had energized him and affected his logic rather than his speech. It was a one in a million injury, but battles transformed the nearly impossible into startling reality.

"The captain is gravely injured!" shouted Pennywhistle. It eased his conscience greatly that he could tell the men the truth. "His skull is broken. The pain is driving him insane. He needs a surgeon immediately, and I shall lose not a second getting him below! Sarn't Dale, take over and get the men back into ranks. Commence firing when you judge best."

"Aye, aye, sir."

Pennywhistle glanced round to gauge the men's reactions. He saw shock in their faces that a dead man had been capering like an inmate of Bedlam and issuing insane orders that sounded the product of confidence.

He hoisted Wemyss over his shoulder and headed down the companion way to the quarterdeck. A bewildered Cumby confronted him. "My God, what happened to Wemyss?"

Pennywhistle thanked Providence that the lie that he that had been prepared to deliver could be discarded. "He took a hit on the top of his skull. I doubt the surgeon can do anything for him, but you never know. Can you get a couple of middies to carry him to the cockpit? I'd do it, but my men need me."

"Of course!" said Cumby, urgently gesturing to the Barron Brothers and Pierson. Just as they ran forward and snapped to attention, Godwin came dashing over. "Let me take him to the surgeon, Mr. Cumby. Mr. Wemyss has treated me well and I should like to return the favor. Besides,

I am bigger than these lads. It will be no problem at all for me to carry him."

Cumby did not hesitate. "Go, and bless you."

"Just make sure he gets plenty of rum for the pain," added Pennywhistle. That should at least arrest the frenzied shouting if he came to. He wondered if Whyte were familiar with metal skull plates to caulk such a wound, but decided that even if he were, such a delicate operation would require time that he did not have.

Godwin nodded. "I shall move so fast that Mercury will seem slow!" he said with a gallantry entirely unexpected by Pennywhistle. Godwin threw Wemyss over his shoulder like a large sack of potatoes and advanced toward the companionway at a fast jog.

It was ironic that the consumption Wemyss had long suffered and worked hard to conceal would prove irrelevant. He was being granted the death that he so earnestly sought. History would remember him favorably, because he died from a wound incurred while facing the enemy, his valor tested and found true. The actual moment of his death in a dark, un-heroic cockpit would mercifully go missing in the saga that historians would one day weave.

CHAPTER 16

Pennywhistle dashed back toward the forecastle. One problem was solved. Now all they had to do was beat the French. He smiled in relief as he ran, because no more subterfuge was necessary. He was in actual command of the marines. It was a heady feeling; daunting but exhilarating as well.

Vanity was a dangerous woman and right now she was whispering her seductions in his ear: all calculated to cleverly address the vulnerabilities of a young gentleman seeking to leave his mark on life. What man of modest years did not desire reputation, renown, and romance?

This was his chance to prove that his great promise was matched by sterling performance. He could build a reputation that proclaimed to the universe that he was a man to be reckoned with. He would attract the attention of maidens distinguished for their beauty.

Tremendously exciting prospects to be sure, yet a deeper part of him knew that most things lusted for out of vanity ultimately proved of small moment in the grand scheme of things. True glory and lasting honor sprang from reason and duty, and could not be hunted. Those who pursued them actively usually met the fate of the young men in "The Pardoner's Tale", in addition to leaving many innocent bodies in their wake. Keep your conduct righteous, your ideals uncompromised, and your heart selfless, and glory and honor would search you out unbidden.

Or he could turn out to be an utter failure; a conceited rogue who disappointed all, brought death to many, and disgraced his ship. No, damn it! That would not happen! Pride might goeth before a fall, but it was also a powerful driving force that kept you on the straight and narrow: determined to act bravely even as your instinct for self preservation shouted for you to do otherwise.

Wilson observed Pennywhistle's actions with interest, pleased that Wemyss was of out of action. "Death or glory" boys were the bane of clever men like himself. One less gallant voice to worry about gave him one more reason to believe that he might survive the next few hours. He kept to his position near the wheel, just under the overhang of the poop deck. It gave at least a little protection. He rubbed his ring for the tenth time.

Unlike the other 47 souls on the quarterdeck, his 20 marines were lying prone for protection, as their services were not yet needed. He wished he could join them in that posture, but it would be a glaring breech of officer comportment if he did so, attracting attention that he was trying to avoid.

The concussive discharges of cannon fire were growing louder and more frequent. A *crump, crump* caught his ear and a split second later, screams and shrieks on the poop directly above him announced that a 36-pound ball had claimed victims. Some of those who perished were probably marines, and it occurred to him that his initial idea of finding safety on the poop was mistaken.

A three-and-a-half-pound mass of grey matter plopped directly on his boots. A second later, a quarter of a skull landed six inches to the right of the slate-colored blob. He jumped, then shivered. There was no safe place anywhere on the weather decks! He had to find an excuse to move below decks.

"Courage, men, courage!" Higgins raised his left hand and twirled his index finger as he shouted: the hand signal for "Rally."

Wilson marveled at the stripling. Though his voice was high and thin, he did not lack for confidence and was saying the encouraging words that he himself should be speaking, since his commission predated Higgins. In spite of his cynical nature, he found himself admiring the Irish lad.

"Keep down and remain steadfast!" Higgins called out cheerfully as he slowly walked beside his men. "I know you are eager to have a go at the French, and lying on your bellies hardly seems the way to do it. But there is a time and a place for everything. Our volleys will do the most good when we can see the warts on their noses and smell the garlic on their breath.

"Remember the Rule of Four: aim low, be mindful of how many rounds you have, keep your cartridges dry, and cover your partner. With the bayonet: *thrust, develop, gore, recover*. Twist hard when you gore so that your bayonet does not become trapped in your target's belly."

Despite the noise, flying metal, and increasing clouds of smoke, Higgins was rather enjoying himself. Exhilaration seemed stronger than fear, though he knew what he was experiencing was the overture, not the main production.

Nevertheless he was bearing up well and fervently wished that Miss Lydia could see him now. He had promised her that he would recount in full the details of his first fight. It never once occurred to him that he might not be alive to pen that letter.

Cooke and Cumby stood on the starboard side of the wheel with their spyglasses extended, carefully observing *Tonnant's* struggle with the French. They were trying to gauge what they would face by observing the intensity of resistance shown her. Hazard stood behind the two, carefully writing down useful observations.

Cooke's best Quartermaster, Geordie Ferguson, manned the ship's wheel. Steering a ship was much more than guiding the helm; intuition and experience were just as important as sight and touch. The wheel could be as lovely and precise an instrument as a Stradivarius if a nautical virtuoso guided its progress, and Ferguson was certainly an artist.

Tonnant was fighting one French ship and one Spanish vessel, and both enemy vessels were maintaining a good rate of fire. *Tonnant* had replaced many of her deck cannon with carronades, so as the range closed her broadside would grow more deadly. Her ship's band was still playing "Heart of Oak," though only fragments of it could be heard in the intervals between broadsides.

Cooke's band was blasting out "British Grenadiers," *molto fortissimo*, yet still mindful of the tune's subtleties. Cooke noted that the bandsmen looked more determined than scared. They were artists, not warriors, but they appreciated that they would never have a more important or welcoming audience. Since this might be their final performance, they were performing with every ounce of gusto in their beings.

"Our band is playing well today, Mr. Cumby. Don't you agree?" said Cooke.

"Hearty and inspiring, Captain," said Cumby. "Our German's play better than their Germans."

Cooke and Cumby heard several whipping, snapping noises and instinctively looked up. The foretop mast standing stay had parted, as had the royal backstay on the mainmast.

"They are cutting us up badly aloft. The situation is becoming serious, Captain."

Ships were fitted with a complex series of ropes, stays and shrouds, to control and balance conflicting vertical and horizontal forces so that the ship achieved equilibrium while still moving forward. Anytime many of those ropes were severed, performance was reduced and the risk of sails, blocks, and even masts falling increased.

"The smoke is becoming oppressive and lessening visibility, Captain. I wonder if we can use it as our ally?"

"How do you mean, Mr. Cumby?"

A second before Cooke heard the distinctive *wuh, wuh, wuh* of whirling bar shot, the fore preventer stay on the foremast split in two.

"Captain, the reason we are moving so slowly is the same reason smoke is becoming a problem. The light, uncertain wind is not dispersing previous broadsides, and smoke is accumulating to the point where we can barely see anything at all. I know the first broadside is the most decisive and should be reserved for close range, but if we fired one now, we could use it to increase the opacity of the smokescreen, cloaking our approach. We just need to degrade the poor visibility a little further."

At that moment, a 24-pound shot landed just behind them; a missive from the upper gun deck of a French 74. It bounced once and smashed full in the chest of two of the seamen standing to the right of the ship's wheel. What remained was a messy pile that bore no relation to anything human. The wheel was unharmed. The ball continued under the poop and smashed two chests containing spare muskets into shards and kindling.

A second 24-pound shot grazed the mainmast and turned a fist-sized piece of it into a cloud of splinters. One man immediately below the impact point screamed and died, a four inch wood sliver protruding from his right eyeball.

"Confound it, Mr. Cumby, you are right. This hammering will only get worse if we do not take action. We have been lucky thus far that the heavy swells and troughs are impairing enemy marksmanship. As we close the range, we must expect more hits."

"Just a single broadside from the starboard 32's should be sufficient," said Cooke. "They have adequate range and are already loaded with twin round shot. Very well, Mr. Cumby. Pass the word to commence firing in two minutes. Tell the gunners to fire as they bear."

"Aye, aye, Captain."

Clunk, clunk. An 18-pound shot shaved the back end off the mainmast fighting top, missing a nearby seaman but compressing the air sufficiently to knock him on his backside.

Shredder and Screwloose emerged from the rear waist companionway, intent on escape and pursuit. They circled the quarter deck twice, then raced off along the port gangway. Laughter and cheers followed them. The chase was an ironic counterpoint to the fire and smoke; life continued its normal activity in spite of the extraordinary goings on of battle.

CHAPTER 17

Mary's contractions came fast and hard. She had maintained her place in the line of cartridge passers far too long. Two sailors offered to escort her to the cockpit, but she replied that she did not want to take them away from their place in battle. Despite the onset of labor pains, she made the journey by herself.

She knew a man on one of the 32-pounders who had once been a midwife; male midwifes were nearly as common as female ones. But he would soon be extremely busy. Mr. Whyte, the ship's surgeon, knew about birthing, but the lives of two were nothing compared to the survival of many. At least she could count on Nancy.

What a time to give birth, and what a place to do it! Her baby would first see life in a dark cesspool of hell. It was the reverse of the biblical adage, "in the midst of life we are in death." A life entering the world, even as many were preparing to depart it, schooled her that elemental forces were not contradictory but complimentary, part of a cycle that was as old as human history.

Whyte had just received his first casualty. A seaman hit in the upper arm stumbled into the cockpit, his face pale with pain, though his lips were silent. Stoicism was a hallmark of British tars. Whyte ripped off the man's shirt and sat him on the operating table. He examined the wound closely under the uncertain light. He smiled. This man was going to keep his arm.

A metal chip the size of a pistol lock plate was lodged just under the surface in his right forearm, immediately below a tattoo of a leaping porpoise. For its size, the damage inflicted was minimal; the shard had been almost out of velocity when it landed. Had it hit full force, the arm would likely be gone. Whyte had a limited supply of rum and laudanum; he decided that this wound merited neither.

"Hold still and brace yourself," he told the sailor sternly. He inserted his metal probe into the wound. The probe resembled a scissors with two half cups on the tips. It was important to extract all of the metal as well as any fragment of clothing carried in. Often it was the dirty clothing that provoked a fatal infection.

The sailor grimaced but said nothing as Whyte moved the probe slowly under the skin. After a minute, Whyte was satisfied that he had all of the shard and closed the cups round it. He retracted the probe with as much gentleness as he could muster and held it up to the lantern in front of him.

"Ah, yes. You are a lucky man, sailor. I got it all! I will have my assistant sew you up and you can return to duty."

The sailor nodded.

Whyte knew that every hand was desperately needed at his station. He wished all of his patients today would prove as quick and easy to handle, but that was as unlikely as a man walking through a puddle staying dry.

He looked at the empty bucket next to the operating table and the white canvas covering the deck. He wondered how long it would before one would be full of limbs and the other would be saturated in blood. The thought made him reach for his jug of rum. Just a quick shot, though: the day would be long and he needed to pace his drinking.

"Excellent!" said Saunders upon receiving Pierson's message from the Captain. His muscles thrummed with tension because of uncertainty about his mother; any action against an enemy that he could fight directly was welcome. This was his first battle, and he was honored that his men would fire *Bellerophon's* first salvo.

He wore his gold-buttoned dress uniform with his spanking new *chapeau de bras,* but the gun crews were all stripped to the waist; maneuvering and firing a metal and wood behemoth would quickly cover their backs and chests with sweat and powder grime.

With the gunports opened, his men enjoyed light and some relief from the usual stale air tainted with mildew. But when the guns fired, things would change for the worse. Choking smoke, stinking brimstone, furnace-like heat, hellish noise, and violently shaking decks would create a den of death that the devil himself would have shunned.

All of the sailors wore colorful bandannas around their ears to protect themselves somewhat from the awful noise of their guns. Many were already partly deaf just from the drills, and it was not uncommon to find several with bleeding ears and noses after a long battle.

Saunders saw the expectancy in his men's faces. To date, all of their efforts had been rehearsals. This was the command performance in the concert hall of history.

Number two cannon crew was the most efficient. Colin Ferguson was the Captain of its 14 men and had been with *Bellerophon* since before the Nile. Since the tompion had been removed, the gun lock attached, the gun already loaded and run in, only an abbreviated form of the loading procedure would be necessary.

Saunders called out the commands, which were relayed by the midshipmen and quarter gunners via speaking trumpets. Communication between the weather and lower decks was important as well. Only observant men on the upper decks could tell those on the lower if their shot had landed true and deadly.

"Run out your gun!'

Before Ferguson yelled "Heave!" he made sure the side tackles were hooked solidly to the carriage.

Everyone except the gun captain and second captain grunted, sweated, and shoved the ten-foot cannon forward with all their might. The crew stopped when the cannon's forward truck-wheels touched the hull and half the barrel protruded over the water. The trucks did not actually revolve, and care had to be taken lest they become entangled with the breeching ropes. The most physically demanding part was pitting manpower against 6,000 pounds of negative gravity each time the ship rose with the swell.

"Prime."

The gun captain thrust his pricker through the vent hole to puncture the flannel cartridge in the barrel. He next inserted a powder quill in the touchhole, then added powder from a horn to the gunlock's pan. He closed the pan and checked the flint one last time to make sure that when the hammer struck the frizzen, a healthy shower of sparks would result.

Determining a target and aiming came next, and this was where an experienced gun captain proved his worth. He had to know his weapon and its capabilities intimately, as well as being able to judge ranges, elevations, and the exact moment to jerk the lanyard and fire.

Ferguson judged the range to the optimal target at 700 yards; best to aim high and shoot for the masts and yards. To that end, he had a crewman entirely remove the wedge-shaped wooden quoin that controlled the barrel's elevation.

He sighted what looked to be a Spanish two-decker visible at brief intervals: the smoke really was a problem. Ferguson made it his target, and the two crewmen used the rear tackle ropes and handspikes to make the final adjustments of the cannon's trucks.

Satisfied, Ferguson took the lanyard in his hand and stepped well back from the cannon's recoil. The second captain full cocked the gunlock. Ferguson dropped to one knee and awaited the command to fire.

"Fire!" Saunders gave the command, but Ferguson did not immediately do so. Part of a gun captain's job was to determine the optimum moment to fire, and that might not be exactly synchronous with when the officer gave the command.

Boom! Five seconds after Saunder's shout, Ferguson's gun blasted back on its breeching ropes. A spear of red-orange flame shot out.

Bellerophon's broadside was not a simultaneous discharge but a series of blasts that rippled along her hull: a good thing, since firing all of the guns at the same moment put an enormous stress on the ship's timbers. The ship bucked, kicked, and gyrated with the equal and opposite reaction of Newton's Third Law, and the lower gun deck filled with vomit- inducing smoke. Most coughed, and few could see much of anything for a few seconds.

No one had told Pennywhistle to expect a broadside, and the recoil caught him off guard. The shaking deck planks caused him to lose his balance and it was only with difficulty that he stayed upright. When he recovered, he and Scott unshipped their glasses, exactly as Cooke, Cumby, and Saunders were doing elsewhere in the ship.

It took a full minute to assess the broadside's effect because the smoke parted only for brief seconds at a time.

Pennywhistle detected clear damage to one Spanish ship; its fore t'gallant mast had been knocked down.

Pennywhistle saw the sailors and marines in the forecastle eagerly looking at him, keen to hear a verdict.

"Well boys, our gunnery just blew a mast off a Don ship. Imagine the damage we will do closer in."

"Hip hip huzzah, hip hip huzzah, hip hip huzzah!" The men in the forecastle burst into excited cheering, acting as if the battle were already won.

Cumby and Cooke looked at each other in satisfaction as frenzied cheering erupted on the quarterdeck.

Wilson's expression remained dour. *So they had hit a Spanish ship. It meant nothing. Did these fools not understand that many of them were going to die soon? How could they be so blindly optimistic?* He nervously cracked his knuckles, then rubbed his ring.

Whyte felt the deep rumbles of the broadside in the cockpit and frowned. It would not be long before he had a steady and seemingly unending stream of customers. In his line of a work, a good day was one where he did not have much employment.

If only he hadn't been tricked into a get rich quick scheme by a foreign land speculator! Still, this was better than a debtor's prison.

Higgins grinned and struck his fist into his open palm in satisfaction. This was just how he had imagined battle: guns booming, men cheering, enemies being humbled. Why had Mr. Pennywhistle been so pessimistic? He was a commendably modest man; perhaps he was uninterested in fame. He once told Higgins that all glory was fleeting and that only fools made it the lodestar of their lives. Perhaps so, but parts of battle were certainly jolly good fun.

Higgins loved the idea of being famous. He would have plenty of opportunities to win glory today. He would impress his father, his friends, and most of all Miss Lydia. He briefly stroked the locket with her hair. He imagined the pride he'd feel being mentioned in dispatches, then thought it would be even better to see his name displayed prominently in *The London Gazette.*

CHAPTER 18

The heavy vibrations of the broadside increased the pain of Mary's contractions. The intervals between contractions were getting shorter; she just hoped she could deliver before the place filled entirely with whimpering, shrieking men. British tars were famous for their stoicism, but sometimes the pain of unimaginable wounds became so great that no amount of will power could prevent a man's lungs from making his distress public.

Nancy had found her a comfortable spot, though the word "comfort" could never really be associated with the cockpit on a day of battle. Her face was equal parts worry and compassion. "I was afraid of this. All of the firing has triggered birth too soon."

Mary smiled wanly. "Men say we are the weaker sex. I aim to prove them wrong."

The distance to the Franco Spanish line had dropped to 500 yards; point blank range for a 36-pound cannon. *Bellerophon* was drawing fire that was increasing in both frequency and accuracy as more and more of the enemy guns now found targets within their effective ranges. A Spanish ship ineptly maneuvered close to a French one to present a solid wall of wood that would prevent *Bellerophon* from slicing through the enemy line.

"Mr. Cumby," said Cooke calmly, "alter course a point to starboard. I'm not going to let that Spaniard ram us by accident because her captain knows nothing of subtle seamanship. They don't call this ship *The Flying Bellerphon* for nothing; we can outpace her. We will cut across that rogue Spaniard's stern." Cooke pointed and Cumby nodded, then brought his glass up for a closer look.

"I can just make out the ship's name, Captain: *Bahama*. She bears 80 guns and Commodore Don Dionisio Alcala Galiano commands. If I recall what the intelligence chiefs told us, he is an intellectual, not a fighting sailor: a nautical scholar of note and an explorer of some renown. Commanded a research ship in a round the world voyage in 1794."

"The clumsy way he maneuvers tells me that he has a many landsmen aboard," Cooke remarked. "*Bahama* makes an excellent target for our first real broadside. We will give Commodore Galliano the full force of solid rake, say in about ten minutes, given our present speed. Considering our slow speed and fast gunnery, we may be able to pour plenty of iron into her stern. Alter course to make it so."

"Aye, aye, Sir. Mr. Overton, bring us two points to starboard." The sailing master acknowledged the command, then relayed it to Quartermaster Ferguson at the wheel.

Moments after the course change was completed, Cooke and Cumby heard the distant *whup whup whup* of twirling chain shot. Both knew their rigging was in for a sound thrashing.

Chain shot consisted of an iron chain connecting two half-cannon balls, while bar shot used a bar to accomplish that purpose. Both were designed to slice up riggings, ripping stays and shrouds as easily as a pen knife cut paper. Because of their odd shapes, wind resistance was a problem and they could only be used effectively at shorter ranges.

"I am surprised they waited this long to switch to chain and bar," said Cooke, giving a professional appraisal of actions that might have caused intense alarm in a less seasoned officer. "They carry far more of that ammunition than we do, since it gives them a better opportunity to inflict hurt, then flee to fight again another day. Were I commanding their ships, I would have started considerably earlier."

"But, Captain," said Cumby dispassionately, "that's just the point: their captains are not like you. They are trained to be careful to the point of timidity, while our experience gives us the confidence to be bold, yet stopping short of recklessness. The Frogs and Dons are far more concerned with not losing ships than they about winning a decisive victory. The spirit of Bonaparte appears unable to cross deep water."

Suddenly a *whup whup whup* drew much closer and a loud crack announced that the foremast preventer stay had snapped. A *Wuh wuh wuh* followed hard upon it—the arrival of a 32-pound bar shot—and several t'gallant shrouds parted. The t'gallant mast's position was now tenuous.

"Death by a thousand cuts," said Cumby philosophically. "I do so wish Mother Nature would do us a favor and strengthen her breath just a little."

"Fear not, Mr. Cumby, *Bellerophon* endured much worse at the Nile. She is not just a survivor, she is a conqueror. We will soon have our chance to return the crude invitations of the Dons with our own tart responses."

Combs and Warwick were not supposed to be talking, but lying prone on the forecastle as the ship endured heavy fire loosened the bonds of discipline. They were mindful of the penalties for disobedience, but they might not survive the day to endure the punishment. They kept their voices low, barely above a whisper.

"This stinks: our ship getting punched about like a boxer taking shots from street urchin, and us not able to do a thing. I'd be so happy to rise up and slam a few rounds into Johnny Crapaud," said Combs in frustration. "I'd sooner have a tooth pulled than wait one more second for "the word."

"You wouldn't hit nothing but seawater at this distance, Marty. And don't be so all fired anxious to meet the lion. There will be plenty of blood and death real soon. Once the battle starts everything will become fast and crazy. You won't believe your eyes sometimes, and you will find your fingers fumbling on your firelock like you were an old man with arthritis."

"Silence there," commanded Pennywhistle's stern voice. "Any further chattering and I shall put you two on report."

The talking ceased immediately. Pennywhistle felt guilty condemning the men for something he was about to do himself.

"Mr. Scott," Pennywhistle whispered to the ship's second lieutenant. "I propose that we stand to in ten minutes. I judge that interval about right for our muskets and carronades to have good effect."

"I agree," said Scott quietly.

At just that moment, a gale of blood smashed into Scott's and Pennywhistle's chests, and narrow strips of skin gripped their uniforms, making them look as if they had just gone swimming in an abattoir. A 32-pound ball had landed square on the head of a sailor a foot off to their right. The man had not so much died as disintegrated.

The impact ripped out Pennywhistle's ear protectors and sent them flying over the side. Damn! His hearing would be unshielded for the remainder of the fight.

He reproached himself for his overconfidence. Maybe the battle had been already won in his mind because of his faith in solid training, but the butcher's bill would be ghastly.

His father had once told him men in battle were like watch springs. Wind them just right and they performed admirably. Under-wind and they ran down: over-wind and they snapped without warning. Pennywhistle thought his own tension level was just right. Though he was covered in gore and wondered if his expensive jacket could be salvaged, he found that his mind was clear.

His vision waxed remarkably acute as his body boosted systems most necessary for its survival. The blue of the sea, the black hulls of the enemy, and the white of the sails all became preternaturally bright. Details stood out in bold relief: the fouled anchor on the gold buttons of officer's coats, the number of twist's in a boatswain's starter, the mermaid's hair in a sailor's tattoo. Facial details of the men under his command suddenly seemed fashioned with the care of a Michelangelo. He saw scars, warts, and birthmarks that he had completely overlooked, though he had been training them for months.

His distance vision grew keener and approached that of his Ramsden. Usually at this remove, he could only see individual figures on enemy decks through his spyglass, but now he was doing so with his naked eye.

Sound traveling over water was naturally amplified, but something beyond that was happening with his hearing. It was a paradox: in spite of the thunderous crashes in the background, he could hear every breath of the marines lying on the deck. When enemy fire had cut some of the stays and shrouds, their snapping sounded as loud as cannon reports. Though Cooke and Cumby were on the quarterdeck and he on the forecastle, their conversation was as clear as if he had been standing next to them.

The reek of brimstone, the scent of damp rope, the smell of roast flesh, and the sickly stink of fear no longer merely tapped his nostrils; they pummeled him. The sum of the stench seemed an amalgam of the worst parts of sewer gas, dead fish, and rotting compost.

He could not say that he felt good, but the transformation was truly extraordinary. But such a great change was undoubtedly temporary and might demand a heavy payment when the battle was done. He would probably stumble like a tottering drunk and want to sleep for days. And yet that was a good thing: you had to be alive to do either.

Something odd was also happening with time. It seemed to be slowing down even more. The normal movements of men seemed so sluggish that he could break them down into a series of steps. Doing so enabled him to anticipate their movements in the seconds ahead.

He checked his watch. The second hand was turning at the proper rate. The time shift had to be illusory: the perception of a mind worried if its existence would continue. He stuffed his watch back in his pocket and resolved to quit checking the time so often.

He knew he would not have a complete answer to the question of his battle worthiness until the contest became much hotter, but he was pleased with the preliminary findings. Still, survival and leadership were two different things. It remained to be seen if men would follow him when things turned dark and hope dimmed.

Boooooom! A great shock blasted him off his feet. He flew through the air for an instant; his vision tunneled and stars charged at him. He landed with a jarring thud, feeling like a fly that had just been swatted. He saw double briefly, then objects snapped back to normal. There was a swirl of smoke rising in front of him and the air was thick with wood fragments. He heard shrieks and moans, though the sounds were muted.

The blast had thrown him back against the port boarding nets. He had landed in a sitting position, so he flexed his legs to see if they were both attached and working. They were, though he could see his toe tips, thankfully intact, where the tip of his left Hessian boot had formerly resided.

Damn, those boots would cost a pretty penny to replace! They were of a piece with his bloody scarlet coat, which now held a coating of tiny wood chips. He pushed out with his left arm in an effort to propel himself to his feet and found his hand was resting on another arm. This arm had a tattoo of a voluptuous woman and "Judith" beneath. The rest of the body was nowhere in evidence.

He rose and inventoried himself. Other than a few black and blue spots and the general feeling of being run over by a hippopotamus, he was intact. His sword, dirk, and rifle were still functional. He surveyed the damage to the ship and was shocked by what he saw.

The forecastle had taken two direct hits on the starboard side. A large, jagged gash in the bulwarks marked the intrusion of an 18-pound shot from the upper gun deck of a Spaniard, and a massive gap in the nettings proclaimed the calling card of a French 36. Two of the nine-pounders were in ruins, although both carronades remained untouched. Three grisly balls of bloody twine marked the remains of two sailors and one marine.

Two other sailors lay moaning, felled by splinters. One was impaled on the deck by a three-foot splinter to the thigh and was bleeding out rapidly. The other was pinned by a two-foot splinter that had passed through his upper arm. There was little blood, so it had missed the artery. That man could be saved.

Pennywhistle's medical training took over. He gingerly walked over, not quite certain if his own sense of balance was intact. He bent down and said calmly, "Brace yourself. This is going to hurt." He did not bother to inform the sailor of what he intended.

He wrapped the fingers of his left hand tight around the top of the splinter and pulled back hard and quick. The sailor gave a short "Uh!" as the sliver came out. Pennywhistle extracted a silk handkerchief from his pocket and turned it into an improvised bandage.

The sailor sat up slowly, a surprised look on his face. Pennywhistle noticed that the nearby sailors and marines were staring at him. He was puzzled by the attention. Bandaging was one of the first things any competent medical man learned. There was nothing extraordinary about it.

"Now sailor,' he said firmly, "get yourself to the surgeon and let him put on a better dressing. "

"Beggin' your pardon, sir," the sailor replied in a husky voice, "but I'd rather stay here and fight. I can do me job with one good arm and I'm itching to get back at those Dago bastards what done this to me."

Pennywhistle could hardly argue with such fighting spirit, and a few extra hours would not affect the fate of the injured arm. Besides, he thought ruefully, his silk handkerchiefs probably cleaner than any bandages in the cockpit.

"Far be it from me to countermand a man's patriotism. I admire your grit, sailor. Have you a name?"

"Able Seaman Jeremy Pryce, from Swansea. I thank you, sir, for your kindness."

"Pay my actions no mind, Seaman Pryce, but feel free to repay the Spaniards for their insult."

Pryce stood to his feet, saluted, and resumed his station as ventsman on the port carronade.

The marines and sailors on the forecastle looked about to cheer, but Pennywhistle's disapproving face forestalled that outburst. He just wanted to get back to business.

Scott walked over to him, a look of approval on his face. "You are a man of hidden talents, Mr. Pennywhistle. Warriors are rarely healers."

Pennywhistle replied bluntly. "I am not a healer, due to a serious error in judgment. How badly were we hit, Mr. Scott?"

"We have five dead, and the two wounded. Two of the nine-pounders remain operable, along with the carronades. The men are shaken but in tolerably good spirits. I daresay your demonstration has boosted morale.

"As for the rest of the ship, there is heavy damage aloft, particularly to the foretop and maintop sails. I used my spyglass and have spotted several dead on the quarter deck, and perhaps ten on the poop deck. Cooke still commands and the ship remains on course. I fear we may have to endure two more broadsides before we can return fire."

CHAPTER 19

"God's holy trousers!" Higgins was shocked. Two marines had been destroyed before his eyes. One had been reduced to a red mound of compost, while the other was a pair of smoking legs attached to a spinal column that ended just above the waist.

A third marine lay unmoving on the deck with no visible wound. Hoping that he was just stunned, Higgins bent down to help. He put his hands under the marine's armpits and began to lift. He gasped in horror as he realized that the man had no back. He was holding up a rib cage devoid of any organs. There was no blood, because the shot had acted as a cauterizing iron.

There was nothing heroic or glorious about any of the deaths.

It struck him as grossly unfair that the dead marines never even had the chance to fire a shot. It was if Fate were running some sort of ghastly lottery and they had drawn the wrong tickets. He wondered if they had loved ones back home who would grieve at their deaths, as his father and Miss Lydia would if he fell.

He was starting to see Mr. Pennywhistle's point that it was sweeter to live for one's country than to die for it. He was coming to understand that a high butcher's bill was not evidence of an officer's fighting spirit but, of his failure.

He suddenly realized that a lot of growing up lay ahead, and it needed to be accomplished at lightning speed, or many marines who had trusted him with their lives would die.

His peripheral vision detected something that the tales of his boyhood said should not happen. Men in battle always followed orders with eagerness and sought glory with determination. But one of his marines squatted a few feet away with his head down and his arms wrapped round the legs that he had drawn close to his chest. He was rocking slowly back and forth, almost like a human pendulum, cooing some unintelligible words to himself.

Higgins recalled the man's name was Edmonds, a former tinsmith from Swindon. He was perhaps 25, with black hair, dull features and a medium build. He spoke little but followed orders, and had never once been on report. He kept to himself and appeared to have no firm friends. He was the type of fellow easily forgotten. Indeed, most people barely noticed him in the first place.

The man had never been disobedient, but his posture now was contrary to orders and safety. Higgins was at a loss to understand why Edmonds was behaving thus, and walked over to solve the mystery.

"Edmonds," said Higgins gently, sensing that this was not a task for martinets. "Edmonds." Still no answer. Edmonds eyes looked pale and glassy. "Edmonds!" This time he barked it; not out of anger but simply to get the man's attention.

Edmonds slowly looked up at him, but his glassy eyes appeared focused on some other world that only he could see. He said nothing to acknowledge Higgins's presence.

Higgins wondered if he had been rendered insensate by a flying piece of shot: grazed on the head or struck in some odd place that was not immediately apparent. He surveyed Edmonds carefully, but could find no wound or mark of injury.

Higgins was at a loss as to how to proceed. The penalty for cowardice was death, but he was not sure if Edmonds was guilty of cowardice, insanity, or plain confusion. He had to maintain discipline, but what Dale had taught him of commanding obedience with your voice and attitude did not seem apply here. "Be strict, fair, and always consistent," was Dale's refrain, but Higgins had no idea how to do that in this situation.

Mr. Pennywhistle spoke of the importance of employing imagination and initiative; being willing to try something new when conventional methods failed. Perhaps it would work in this situation. Higgins sensed that Edmonds needed quiet understanding and gentle words, rather than threats of a cat-o-nine-tails or worse. He thought of the most compassionate soul that he knew, and Miss Lydia's face sprang to mind. When he spoke, his voice was infused with her kindness.

"Edmonds, what is the matter? Edmonds, I want to help but cannot do so unless you tell me what is wrong."

Edmonds looked at Higgins quizzically, not sure how he should regard his presence. He examined Higgins face, and its expression showed concern, not anger. Unlike Mr. Wilson, he never berated men, nor applied the flat of his sword. One of the older marines had told Edmonds that "no officer is ever your friend." But he desperately needed a friend right now, and young Mr. Higgins looked to be the only candidate.

"Wwwwwell, ssssssir, it is like thiiiiiiss." His old stutter returned. He tried to speak slowly and deliberately. "Wwwhen I ssssaw those Marines blown to ppppieces, something just ssssnapped in me. I lost my balance, and I don't seem to be able to make my legs work. I ain't no coward, but I think me legs might be." Tears filled his eyes. "I really don't want to let our boys down."

"So you want to stand, but cannot?" inquired a puzzled Higgins.

"Yesss, sssssir, that's abbbout it. I wwwwant to do my dddduty, bbbbut I am unable to dddo so."

Higgins had never heard of such a thing. Willful disobedience of orders was addressed in the regulations, but he had never heard of unwitting disobedience. The man did not seem malicious, just sincerely troubled. Yes Higgins could not do nothing, both because of duty and because the rest of the marines on the quarterdeck had focused their attentions on this odd conversation.

"Edmonds, take my hand and let me see if I can assist you to your feet." Edmonds nodded and Higgins extended his hand. When Edmonds grasped it, Higgins yanked him to his feet. Edmonds smiled for a second, then began to shiver as if he had been thrust into an icebox. His knees started knocking.

Higgins had no idea what to do, but Wilson, who came swaggering over, did. "I must say, Mr. Higgins, you are entirely too gentle and understanding. You might mean well, but it won't do. This man is a coward, pure and simple. Even worse, he is a coward in the hour of our marine's greatest test. The penalty is clear and unequivocal. An example must be made of him."

Wilson spoke with angry certitude, because he realized that he was actually describing himself. The best way to hide his nature was to divert attention by scapegoating another and making a loud show about his distaste for anything less than heroic.

Wilson pulled a pistol from the brace that hung round his neck. He looked at Higgins with a fierce and intimidating expression. "This is a time for swift and summary justice, Mr. Higgins. I will execute the sentence, if you are too faint of heart to do so."

Higgins was terrified. Officers sometimes shot men who ran, but it seemed entirely wrong in this case. He only wanted to kill Frenchmen and Spaniards. Mr. Pennywhistle had told him there were no bad soldiers, only bad officers. He had somehow failed Edmonds, and now Edmonds would pay the price for his incompetence. He reached for the pistol in his sash, but his own hand began to shake. His face reddened. *No, blast it, he would not do it.* There had to be another way.

Wilson viewed Higgins with irritation. He would have to do the job himself, though he did not like the messiness of death. Edmonds was a nonentity, and his execution might provide a useful cover for the less than gallant actions he had planned in the hours ahead. He full cocked his pistol and placed it against Edmond's temple.

An arm clad in scarlet shot out and a calloused, leathery hand gripped Wilson's wrist and jerked his arm skyward, then slammed it down onto a bent knee. The pistol clattered to the deck. Ooohs and aaaahhhs arose from the marine spectators. Edmonds collapsed back to the deck.

Dale stood firm, a human Rock of Gibraltar. The flinty look in his eyes made it clear that he brooked no disagreement. He had technically struck an officer, but none watching saw things that way; if asked, they would say they had no idea how Wilson had been disarmed.

Higgins blinked twice in surprise, but silently mouthed, "Thank God." Wilson looked incredulous that any non-commissioned officer would dare dispute his authority.

Dale spoke in a calm tone that were at odds with the sternness of his features. "Sorry to do that, sir, but I had to act before you made a mistake. I know a man of good conscience like yourself would not want an unnecessary death on his hands."

Dale knew exactly the kind of man Wilson was, but he also understood that presenting a favorable image of him to the crowd would limit Wilson's ability to retaliate.

Wilson was rarely at a loss for words, but he stood as tongue-tied as a callow swain asking the father of his beloved for her hand. Dale realized he could save Edmonds, if he acted quickly and offered a solution that helped everyone.

"Mr. Wilson, Mr. Higgins, you are both too new to the Service to have encountered a problem of the kind that Private Edmonds now presents. I have faced it twice before. Edmonds' case is akin to a man who sees a sight so horrible that he ceases to see at all. There is nothing wrong with his eyes: his affliction is caused by hysteria. While the problem is not physical, its consequences are. Edmonds is not a coward. He wants to fight. But right now, expecting him to do so makes as much sense as ordering a double-amputee to run a race."

Murmurs flitted through the crowd of marines. Heads nodded, chins were stroked, and brows furrowed. They were not vindictive, and Dale's explanation made sense to them. They were hard men but understood that sometimes even good men were affected by battle in bad ways.

Dale spoke to Higgins and Wilson, but his remarks were really addressed to all the marines. "Gentlemen, Private Edmonds desperately wants to be useful, so why not send him where he can be so? Put him where he will do good, even if he fires not a single round. Nursing your wounded mates is just as admirable as standing toe to toe with them in a hard fight. I know Mr. Whyte is short-handed in the cockpit, and Private Edmonds would be most welcome."

Dale looked directly at Edmonds, whose downcast expression had lightened noticeably during Dale's short speech. "What say you, Edmonds?"

Newfound starch appeared in Edmond's posture and voice. "Sounds real fine, Sergeant. Their ain't nothing I won't do to help my mates out today."

"Very good," said Dale. He turned to the officers. "Does this arrangement seem equitable to you, gentlemen?"

"It does indeed, Sergeant," replied a greatly relieved Higgins.

"Well, I suppose we must adopt whatever course enables us to get some use out of this man," said Wilson with ill grace and a sarcastic tone.

An undercurrent of hisses coursed through the assembled marines. Wilson returned the judgment with a sneer that was halfway between hatred and contempt.

Dale walked over to Edmonds. "Now, sir, the first test. Can you stand?" Dale extended his hand. When Edmonds grasped it, Dale did not have to pull hard. Edmonds did nearly all the work by himself.

Edmonds stood for a few seconds. He looked down at his legs and smiled. They were his friends again. "Sergeant, Mr. Higgins, Mr. Wilson. I thank you all for this second chance and shall always count myself in your debt."

The watching marines nodded in approval.

Dale faced Edmonds and said, in a voice that was surprisingly gentle, "To the cockpit with you, Private, and good luck."

A second later a whizzing cannonball neatly clipped off the top of Edmonds' head, spattering Dale, Wilson, and Higgins with his brains. Battle cared nothing for the solutions of men.

CHAPTER 20

Three decks below, Nancy spoke in a commanding voice that brooked no evasion. "Push, push! Put your heart into it!" Though her errand was tender, her tones were those of a gun captain ordering his crew to reposition their cannon. "Come, Mary, don't slack off now! You have been doing so well."

Nancy was actually far more frightened than her friend, who seemed abnormally calm. She hid her fear by maintaining a gruff timbre in her voice. She feared her lack of knowledge and experience might prove fatal to her friend, or her baby, or both.

Mary's husband could not be present because today would be the busiest of his life; an entire ship was hazarding its life on his ability to deliver cartridges in a timely fashion. Mary would enjoy no privacy, but it was a fair bargain to surrender her womanly modesty in return for being in the safest place in the ship.

Birth and its attendant complications killed far more young women than any disease. The sailors manning *Bellerophon's* decks were statistically safer than Mary. But Nancy drew comfort from knowing that her friend possessed an indomitable spirit and a hardy constitution, both strengthened by service on *Bellerophon*. "Again, Mary!"

Her friend huffed short quick breaths and her stomach muscles convulsed. Though Mary's cotton birthing sheath was soaked in sweat, Nancy took heart that events were unfolding as Mr. Whyte had told her to expect. Mary's contractions were strong and regular.

She prayed no complications would develop. Her greatest fear was of a breech birth: the baby's feet coming out first instead of the head. Such an event was almost invariably fatal to the child, and frequently to the mother also.

Nancy did not know that a chore that she performed hours earlier now worked in favor of her friend's odds of survival. Pummeling dirt out of her husband's small clothes in a vat of lye soap had resulted in her hands being spotlessly clean.

She mentally recited the steps that Mr. Whyte had told her to follow, and remembered the force of his final words. "Your friend trusts you utterly because you care greatly for her. You may lack knowledge, but you do not lack power. Friendship cannot be over-estimated in bringing an operation to a successful conclusion."

Whyte could not act as Mary's birth instructor because a trickle of wounded had changed into a flow, and his duty lay in the employment of his scalpel, saw, and sutures. He steeled himself to ignore the incessant human moaning that seemed a hideous parody of the natural resonance of a ship's timbers.

He looked at the man lying on his operating table. He had seen him any number of times, but knew nothing about him. One of the loblolly boys who held him down said his name was Jenkins. The heavy calluses on his feet indicated he worked aloft: a topman. He could not be more than 20.

He had an unmemorable, trusting face, fair hair, and was manfully fighting the pain and the urge to cry out. What really mattered to Whyte was that Jenkin's teeth were in good shape, and that he was lean and muscled. Oddly enough, good dental health was a strong indicator of a man's general well being, and a fit body signaled that the individual could withstand the shock of an amputation.

The wound just above Jenkins right kneecap was bad and deep. A lance of pine and dirty cloth had intertwined themselves with his musculature so securely that it would have taken the power of a Titan to yank it free. Even if he had been a civilian doctor with all the time in the world, there was no way this limb could be saved without risking a fatal infestation of gangrene.

Thank God, the sea was calm and the ship's motion through the water steady. Surgery in a stormy sea was like trying to thread a needle while riding a bucking horse.

Whyte wondered how Jenkins had managed to descend from the tops and to the orlop unaided. It must have been an agonizing process, but it spoke much about Jenkins strength and will. Strong-willed men were men who survived.

He had given Jenkins one of his small supply of laudanum balls and told him to suck on it. The effect was almost immediate. Jenkin's eyes glazed over, and the tension in his muscles slackened. The instinctive jerking motion that occurred when steel cut into flesh would be diminished and make the task of the two loblolly boys holding him down easier.

Whyte fastened a tourniquet above the wound and checked his supply of turpentine and his bucket of hot tar. He grasped his scalpel and his saw, and heated each over a candle.

Nelson had complained that, when his arm was amputated, the coldness of the surgeon's implements had added to his distress. He'd therefore enjoined the fleet's doctors to heat their instruments before operating. His motives sprang from the humanity that made Nelson so beloved, but his concern conferred a practical benefit that, unbeknownst to the surgeons, saved lives. Heating instruments at least partly sterilized them.

Whyte took longer than most surgeons to heat his scalpel and bone saw: half a minute for each. Later, when business increased, he would cut that time in half.

He checked the pocket watch lying next to his instruments. Every operation was a race against time: the longer the procedure, the greater the damage done by shock. The watch reminded him to keep the pace speedy. His first amputation today had taken three-and-a-half minutes: far too slow. The man had struggled mightily, but that was no excuse, since an obstreperous patient was a hazard of his trade.

He nodded to the loblolly boys, who increased the force of their grip. He looked down at Jenkins. "Hold tight, this may sting a bit." Jenkins tried to smile at the surgeon's lame jest. The pain would be as terrible as childbirth.

Amputation was like peeling an onion. You had to get past several layers of muscle and tissue before you arrived at the heart of the matter. He checked his watch.

He thrust the scalpel deep into the man's thigh and began to slice through layers of skin, tissue, and muscle, thinking of nothing but the practiced motions that he knew so well. He worked his way clockwise around the circumference of the leg, and when he had reached the noon position, he glanced at his watch. 90 seconds gone. Much too slow.

He glanced at his patient's face. The grimace told the tale, but no sound issued from the man's lips; a good sign.

He pulled back everything that he had cut in the manner of man removing the husk from an ear of Indian corn. The naked bone lay exposed. He had carved the flesh just right so that a flap of skin would cover the stump. He put down his knife and picked up his saw. He checked his watch. Two minutes elapsed. Damn! What was the matter with him!

He began sawing as energetically as if felling an oak tree. White flecks flew up like wood chips from a saw mill as his saw hummed back and forth. The limb came free. He grabbed it and tossed it unceremoniously into the bucket at his feet. His ears listened for the man's respiration. Steady and regular: good. Three minutes gone; he was improving.

The next part required every ounce of his manual dexterity and taxed his small motor skills to their limits: tying off the smaller vessels and artery with waxed ligatures of horsehair. He concentrated and his fingers flew. He then scraped the edges of bone until they were smooth. He pulled the flap of skin over the stump and sewed quickly, leaving the ligatures dangling free; to be pulled out when the wound was sufficiently healed. He finished in two minutes. Five minutes gone since his first action.

The patient's breathing grew shallow but his pulse was sure and steady. The only sounds he had made during the entire procedure were a few grunts and groans.

The play was done; only the epilogue remained. Whyte released the tourniquet to let the blood flow unimpeded. He dipped a brush in turpentine and swept it slowly across the stump. He sank a wide-ended stick similar to a tennis racket into a bucket of hot tar and applied it carefully to cauterize the wound.

He frowned when he checked his watch. Seven minutes gone. He consoled himself with the fact that while he might be slow, craftsmanship invariably took more time than butchery.

The loblolly boys helped Jenkins off the table. He was groggy, but far from unconscious. They put his arms on their shoulders. Jenkins hopped uncertainly to a spot of canvas where he could lie down. One boy held a tin of water to his lips and he drank feverishly. Then they abandoned him to his own devices, because many others needed their services. Jenkins would have to watch scores of others endure the same agonizing process.

Whyte took a quick sip from his rum bottle. He deserved a small reward. He wiped his hands on his leather apron and noted the blood splotches on it were small. In a few hours, the leather would be saturated. God, this was going to be a long day. He should have listened to his mother, who had always told him that he would make a superb barrister.

Mary continued to push and push. "Breathe, Mary, breathe!" exclaimed Nancy. "I can see it. I can see the baby!" Nancy could just discern the crown emerging; not long now.

"Oh, God! Oh, God! I don't think I have the stuffing for one more push!" Mary wheezed.

To Nancy's surprise, a sailor lying next to Mary who had drifted in and out of consciousness several times over the past hour suddenly became wide awake. His blue eyes were distant, as if guided by a vision and a power that were not his own. He reached over and gently took Mary's left hand in his.

"Mrs. Stevenson, give that one last effort. All of us are cheering in our hearts for you. We all want to see a little nipper come into this world so's we can pretend to be his godfathers. Ain't that so, boys?" His voice carried surprisingly far.

An anemic cheer rose from the twenty wounded in the cockpit. What that cheer lacked in volume was compensated by the love and sincerity it contained.

Nancy felt tears roll down her cheeks, partly from gratitude for the sailors' support and partly from relief that the baby's full head was now visible.

Mary huffed and puffed.

"Almost there, dear Mary, almost there! Just one more push!"

"Ah ah ah!" Mary gave one final, gigantic push. The sailor's hand tightened on hers.

A minute later Nancy exclaimed with glee, "It's a boy! It's a boy! The spitting image of John!"

The anonymous sailor's grip went slack. A smile blossomed on his face even as his eyes closed forever.

"Praise the Lord!" said Mary in exhaustion. "Thank you, Nancy, thank you. I will talk to you more..." she said in a whisper, "after I have slept for a century." She drifted off into the realm of Morpheus, as Nancy severed the umbilical cord with her tailor's shears. She then wrapped the baby in a plaid blanket and gently cradled him in her arms.

Since the child had been born in battle, a rare and remarkable occurrence, whatever Christian name the lad received would forever be eclipsed by his nickname: Son of a gun.

The orlop timbers shook as the ship absorbed another broadside. Nancy had counted two previous hurricanes of iron. Her husband told her *Bellerophon* was a strong lady, but how much more pounding could the ship stand? Nancy held the precious new life gently and close, but wondered with irritation how long it would be before *Bellerophon* meted out some death of her own.

The answer she sought lay not long in the future. She was far from the only one aboard who wanted vengeance.

CHAPTER 21

"On your feet!"! barked Pennywhistle. Normally Scott would have given the order, as he was the senior officer, but he was busy calculating shot trajectories. As a skilled mathematician, he might be able to increase the lethality of the forecastle's guns. Besides, Pennywhistle's deep voice carried better than his own.

The men smiled at each other, pleased that they would finally have a chance to strike back at their tormentors. Not a man aboard expected that retaliation to be anything less than terrible.

Pennywhistle's patience had died twenty minutes before and the time since then had been as tedious as it was oppressive. He felt like a thoroughbred straining at the starting gate, but commanded to wait while it swung open in slow motion. But Cooke's decision to defer the first full broadside until the range to the enemy was close was the correct one, and consonant with the behavior of the other captain's in the Fleet.

The forecastle was nothing like the pristine arena it had been a scant hour ago. The deck was slicked with blood and entrails from the corpses. The non human detritus had already been cast overboard: chunks of wood, javelin size splinters, and misshapen cannon barrels, but there remained the unrepaired wrecked bulwarks, severed ropes, and torn bitts.

Despite three separate blasts from the French and Spanish, the two-foot, six-inch-thick oak hull was not easily harmed. Two of the cannon had been dismounted but the rest were set to go, their crew's eager to fire. Pennywhistle's marine's muskets were loaded.

He conferred with Scott, then gave the order everyone dreaded. "We must clear the decks! Marines of the first chain and sailors designated boarders: heave those bodies overboard. Now!"

The men did not like it, but understood. The decks had to be kept clear. Sentimentality and sadness could not be allowed to impair the efficiency of the forecastle as a fighting platform.

With low mutters and hot tears, sailors and marines prowled the deck, picking up large and small pieces of what had once been human mates, chucking them unceremoniously over the side. Hands became sticky with blood and tempers grew short.

All those cleaning up the remains would have wished them a proper burial at sea with a service read by the Captain. Their names would have at least been spoken aloud, and their deeds recalled.

Seamen Blunt picked up the head of his messmate, Seaman Dawkins, and looked closely into its frozen eyes. He could not tell if its final expression was one of fear or surprise. They were of the same age, 28, and came from the same small fishing village in Devon. They had grown up together and enlisted within a day of each other.

Blunt would miss his friend, especially his quirky sense of humor, which had brought him through many bad times. He struggled to think of something appropriate to say.

"Well, Joe, this is going to be a dull ship without ye. When I get home I'll talk to your ma, tell her you died a hero.

I know the angels will look after your right proper. Goodbye, Joe."

He grabbed the head by a hank of hair, cocked his arm as far back as it would go, and hurled it over the side. When he saw it splash, he put the memory of his friend to rest, turned on his heel, and resumed his designated position as the ventsman on the port carronade.

Jepson, a dozen yards away, used a different method to dispel the agonizing tension. He spied a rope that had been severed from the bitt to which it was anchored. He scrambled to his feet; his friend MacFarlane had recently taught him the bowline knot and he was eager to try it out. He dashed over, and took a good look. Yes it would work!

He remembered the rhyme about the rabbit hole and slowly tied the rope to the bitt with a bowline knot. He glanced at the finished product and was pleased to find he had tied it well. The knot was tight, firm, and could bear any strain.

Several splinters the size and thickness of chair legs whizzed past his head.

"Get back down here, you damned fool!" shouted a boatswain's mate. "Are you trying to get yourself killed?"

Jepson raced back and crouched down, a crooked smile on his face.

"You don't never do anything on this here ship without someone ordering you to do it! You got that?" The mate was more exasperated than angry.

"Aye, sir," aid Jepson, unable to keep the pride in his small achievement out of his voice.

MacFarlane on the forecastle carronade wondered how his friend Jepson was adjusting. He had to be scared right now; he was new to the nautical life and had never seen battle.

"Sailors, stand to your guns." Scott's command instantly caused MacFarlane to dismiss thoughts of Jepson. His world now was the six-foot circle round his 32-pound carronade. Nothing else mattered but doing his job fast and right.

"Marines, to your posts!" Warwick came to full alert when he heard Mr. Pennywhistle's thunderous voice. Warwick was the right flank man of a four-man firing chain that included his friend Combs. The marines would be spread loosely after discharging three regular volleys, employing chain order for most of the fight.

The essence of chain order was to keep the enemy under a continuous hail of lead. Two sub chains made up a full chain. After the first man fired, the second man advanced four paces and fired. The third man advanced four paces beyond the second then discharged his weapon. By the time the fourth man had completed the ritual, the first man was again ready to fire.

The marines had also learned to execute a reverse version where they discharged their weapons and retired. That was a necessity given the ebb and flow of enemy boarding parties. Such a system provided each man with covering fire, and Pennywhistle made sure that the members of each four-man chain messed together so their bonds of friendship would be strengthened. It was easier to trust a man with your life if you ate meals with him and slung your hammock next to his.

Warwick saw the fear in Combs' eyes. Natural enough; meeting the lion was a big event. Silence was enjoined so commands could be heard clearly, but that did not prevent Warwick from silently mouthing, "You'll be fine." Combs was his partner in chain order firing.

The message got through and Combs let out the breath that he had been holding. If his friend Jim said things would be all right, he could trust that everything would indeed work out fine in the end. Besides, he had the ape's paw. He tapped it.

His friend's final words had reminded him to trust his training and Mr. Pennywhistle. Combs resolved to do so, and set his face in a terrible cast that dared the Dons and the Crapaud's to do their worst.

CHAPTER 22

Higgins watched the Captain and Mr. Cumby anxiously. Surely the command to open fire could not be more than a few minutes away. His marines were formed up in well ordered ranks, their numbers sufficient to deliver volleys that packed real punch. For his own part, he was ready. Seeing death had finally made him feel real fear, but he was not debilitated by it.

He looked over at Mr. Wilson a few yards away and was surprised that his expression was that of a man uncertain about his next action. He would have expected just the opposite, since Wilson was so confident and debonair playing cards. No matter; Wilson would come through. Higgins could not conceive of a gentleman letting the side down.

Wilson was glad that his knees had stopped shaking. His nerves were on fire and he wanted to run, but the sight of the boy Higgins standing firm put enough resolve into him to keep him fixed in place.

He would do nothing until the confusion of battle took over and he had a safe opportunity to disappear. There would be plenty of wounded, and a large splinter held in place by a suitably bloodied bandage would give him the cover to exit the deck as yet another sad casualty. All he had to do was stay on deck long enough to give two commands: "Fire" and "Reload in quick time." He could manage that.

The ring on his finger seemed to glow faintly, though that was probably his fevered imagination. He also could have sworn that he felt a slight vibration in it when he was contemplating ways to outfox propriety. It was ridiculous how superstition played tricks when your life was at stake. Whether the ring was a bringer of good fortune or just a bauble with a legend, it was soothing to believe it his ally, since he needed all the luck he could get.

Bhummp, Bhummp! Two French round shot bounced twice and smashed open the spare ammunition chests, spraying powder onto the deck. Two alert ships boys rushed over and began industriously swabbing the powder with wet brooms to ensure that it stayed inert.

Cooke was operating on instinct now, using his intuition to judge the exact moment to open fire. He briefly fingered the St. Christopher medal in his pocket and thought of his wife. "Steady as she goes, Mr. Cumby, no further course adjustments." His first officer relayed the order to Overton, who in turn passed it to Ferguson at the wheel.

Cooke had chosen his course expertly. A three hundred yard gap had opened between *Bahama* and what appeared to be *Montañés*, a virtual sister ship. He had navigated his vessel to pass through its exact center. The range to both Spanish ships would be musket shot: 150 yards.

The wind had almost vanished. The lack of wind had been a problem all morning, but now it would be an advantage. The ship's speed was slow enough that Cooke would have the opportunity to rake *Bahama's* stern with several broadsides and pour an equal weight of metal in to the bow of *Montañés*.

Bellerophon had taken damage aloft, mainly severed stays and shrouds, the principal visible result being the dangerous swaying of her mizzen t'gallant mast. But her sails were still functional and the casualties among the crew were fewer than he expected. The men's spirits were excellent; if anything, they were even more eager than he to have a good long bash at the enemy.

Cooke realized that he was blessed with a moment that all captains prayed for but few were ever granted. He was engaged in a major fleet action with exactly the right weapon, at precisely the right spot, at just the optimum moment to deliver a devastating fusillade which might well be talked of for centuries. He was a modest man who had never sought fame; yet if it came, as fortune seemed to be promising, it might be quite a pleasant thing.

Almost time now. He could see faces on the enemy decks when the smoke parted for brief intervals, but it was best to think of the Dons as ciphers rather than actual human beings. He saw a well dressed officer on the quarterdeck of *Bahama* pointing a glass at him and assumed it was Commodore Galiano, curious about his opposite number.

A spark of inspiration shot through his brain as intuition, calculation, and experience all came together. His voice spoke in bland tones completely at odds with his racing pulse. "Mr. Cumby, open fire, if you please. By divisions, port side first."

"Aye, aye captain," replied Cumby, in an equally calm voice. "Fire!" Cumby's sword flashed down. The command was relayed via midshipmen with speaking trumpets to all of the ship's decks. Every gun captain awaited the best moment for his piece to speak its deadly words.

Five seconds later, the ship roared as *Bellerophon*'s judgment of fire gave a blistering reply to a morning of Spanish and French insults. Every gun was double-shotted: two rounds of canister for the weather deck guns and solid shot and grape for those on the gun decks. The port side guns fired in groups of four, creating a rippling fire that raced down her hull. Crews then dashed over and manned the starboard guns, discharging their lethal contents within fifteen seconds after the port weapons had completed their depredations.

Rippling fire was more psychologically disheartening to the enemy than a single broadside, since it created the illusion that they were under fire for a substantially longer period of time. British infantry did the same thing, preferring rolling volleys by platoons so that the enemy had not a second's respite from hurtling metal.

The deep bass voice of 72 cannon and eight carronades created a sound that was a cross between the *buzz* of enormous swarming bees and the *whoosh* of a giant geyser. The air turned black with lead and *Bellerophon's* temperature soared ten degrees. Clouds of smoke and the reek of brimstone made stunned men feel that they no longer trod the deck of a ship but walked the footpath to Satan's throne.

Gun crews coughed, and smoke temporarily blotted out the effects of *Bellerophon's* fire. The *bomp bomp bomp* of hammers smashing wood was drowned out by choruses of shrieks, screams, and primal ululations drifting across the water. *Bellerophon's* opening salvos had hit the enemy hard.

Bellerophon's guns struck *Bahama's* mostly unprotected stern, the sweet spot that every captain prayed his enemy would expose. The stern of a ship had the weakest scantlings, only about a foot thick. *Bahama's* twenty-five large windows sacrificed strength for light, allowing the illumination of the captain's cabin and wardroom.

With all of the partitions removed, *Bellerophon's* shot slashed through *Bahama's* decks, losing little of their velocity. The broadside traveled the entire length of her lower decks unimpeded; smashing timbers, spraying splinters, and dismounting cannon while dismembering any humans in its path.

A full one-sixth of *Bahama's* crew went down. Three officers died, significantly weakening her command. The First Officer was struck in the thigh by grapeshot. As he bent forward in agony, a nine-pound shot cut him in two.

Montañés took severe damage to her bow. The ropes attached to the jib-boom and bowsprit that anchored the rigging geometry of the entire ship now hung in tatters. Her flying jib and jib had been shredded, and her spritsail was wrecked. The loss of those sails would seriously reduce her ability to navigate what was becoming a confused melee of ships suddenly popping out of thick smoke like deadly reefs on a lee shore.

Pennywhistle's marines fired when the forecastle guns cut loose with a deafening broadside, focusing their attentions entirely on the *Bahama*. They discharged a second volley 18 seconds after the first, and a third 19 seconds after that. Despite the term "musket shot," men hit at 150 yards were generally victims of bad luck; aimed musket rounds were usually only effective at 100 yards or less. Aiming would have made little difference anyway, since the marines could only see their opponents for split seconds through the thunderheads of smoke.

"Keep it up, keep it up!" bellowed Pennywhistle. "Good work, lads, keep firing on the uproll!" The marine's fire was a continuous series of *pop, pop pops*; unimpressive compared with the thunder of the great guns, yet their fire gave the enemy no respite from iron.

After his initial words of encouragement, his men needed no further instructions. Practiced technique and trained initiative guided their actions, giving him the opportunity to do some officer-hunting. He dashed to the side and took up his Ferguson that he had carefully wrapped in canvas and placed at the base of the foremast.

Satisfied that everything was dry and ready to go, he shoved the muzzle through the boarding nets and let them take most of the barrel's weight, giving him the equivalent of a firing stand. He swiveled the barrel in a slow arc, knowing he would only have time for a snap shot when the smoke parted.

The port carronade crashed out and slammed another double round of grape up the *Bahama*'s derriere. The crew then dashed over and delivered the same greeting to *Montañés'* bow.

After what seemed an eternity, the smoke in front of Pennywhistle's Ferguson thinned and parted. The snarling face that he saw did not belong to an officer, but the ship's boatswain was an important man; he would do. Pennywhistle gently squeezed the trigger a split second before the enemy ship began her downroll. A blotch of red appeared just below the boatswain's throat, then he was swallowed by a wave of smoke.

Pennywhistle knelt and reloaded his piece in ten seconds, glad that the breechloader's lack of a ramrod made reloading time less than half that of a musket. Though his weapon was efficient and deadly, the expense necessary for its manufacture made it uninteresting to a British government that placed frugality above other concerns. Much as he wished that all of his marines were equipped with them, you could make ten Brown Besses for the cost of one Ferguson.

He shoved the Ferguson back through the boarding nets and this time did not have to wait for a target. Directly across, a lower ranking officer was trying to assemble some sea-going soldiers to fire a volley. The soldiers looked green —not just with training, but sea sickness. Knock the officer down and it might spare *Bellerophon* the volley. He sighted his weapon on the officer's chest, then tickled the trigger. The officer jerked and stepped backwards, and to the obvious consternation of the soldiers, collapsed onto the deck.

The carronade roared again, and this time the smoke was dissipated by a burp of wind. Pennywhistle saw the effects of the blast, and it sickened him. He reloaded by touch, his eyes riveted on a file of soldiers who had been blown down like pins struck by a bowling ball. What remained looked more like a trail of thick, greasy paste than anything human.

A Spanish officer dashed up to the mess and froze in horror, making him an easy target. You noticed odd things in battle, and as the man fell Pennywhistle wondered what order of chivalry he wore upon his left breast.

The Sea Service muskets continued their incessant chirping, and Pennywhistle saw enemy sailors go down when the smoke parted after a discharge. He guessed his men were doing steady damage, but decided that sound was a better indicator than sight. The awful chorus of the condemned was growing louder.

Battle excited him. His heart beat fast but steady, and the feeling of having it in his throat had long since departed. He felt detached, yet focused. It was as if he were outside his body, merely a visitor to a macabre art gallery. Mind and body seemed two different things, just as Descartes had said. Or was his imagination putting Descartes before the hearse? Dying men seemed falling puppets, and wounded men shredded rag dolls. Though he saw his Marines' faces clearly, he was treating them as assets to be husbanded or expended, based on the needs of battle rather than the strictures of humanity.

He reloaded his Ferguson and snapped off a shot that only wounded a puppet, rated an army subaltern. He would have killed him but an unexpectedly harsh roll of *Bellerophon* disrupted his aim and his round went high. It impacted on the top of the man's left arm, leaving that appendage limp and useless. He had often tried to explain to prideful army officers that shooting at sea was quite different from doing so on land, but usually ended up feeling exasperated.

He spied a portly petty officer on the enemy foretop firing directly at him. He could not help but take it personally. Hitting a small target on a swaying mast was nearly impossible for most marksmen at this distance, but he enjoyed the challenge. It was a matter of timing three things exactly: the rhythm of the mast's movement, the downroll of the enemy ship, and the uproll of his own. The sailor cooperated by maintaining a relatively fixed position as he steadied his own aim.

Pennywhistle felt the sportsman's thrill of executing difficult shots under adverse conditions, not the fanatic's rage. He preferred fishing to hunting, but stalking game that fired back was an entirely different matter and possessed an undeniable exhilaration.

Steady, steady, he told himself. *Just another second. Let that slight puff of wind pass. Elevate just a little higher. By God, I have you now!* He squeezed the trigger with the care of a Celtic monk creating an Illuminated Manuscript. A few seconds later, the fat petty officer cried out. He clutched his chest and fell off the top like a drunk plunging over the edge of a cliff.

Pennywhistle felt respect for the men that he killed. It was one thing to prate loudly about patriotism, quite another to put your life on the line. Right now, the cause the Dons fought for mattered less to him than their courage. Seneca had cynically written,*"Fur fures congnositur:"*One thief recognizes another. The same could be said of fighting men. Fortitude and honor were universals and knew no allegiance to a particular flag.

He reloaded and tracked what looked like a midshipman running; probably carrying a message from the quarterdeck. Damn, he was just a boy. Boy or no, cutting the flow of orders from the captain was important. The boy took the bullet in his left pectoral and spun like a top before collapsing on the deck.

He briefly pitied the midshipman, but a heart too kind was a dangerous liability on a battlefield. He was in the position of a man undergoing surgery after ingesting a dose of laudanum. Instead of screaming as the knife rent his flesh, he could regard it the motion with an objective curiosity about the cutting capabilities of the sharp edge.

He heard the low whistle of a bullet close to his left ear. By its sound, it was almost out of velocity. Had it struck him, it would have given him a bad headache and left a large black and blue bump. The Spanish might not be skilled, but they were trying hard.

Though his face had been a bright crimson during the approach to the enemy fleet, once *Bellerophon* fired her first rounds his tanned skin had whitened: vaso-constriction limiting the flow of blood to the face so that wounds would prove less damaging. It struck him that his kinder emotions had undergone an analogous suppression to prevent damage to his soul.

His Marines were performing well, employing initiative brilliantly. They were definitely aiming, and to his surprise many were hitting their targets, though the distance was now 125 yards. Even the ones that missed their target hit someone, since the enemy decks were crowded with sailors and soldiers.

"Keep it up, boys! Keep it up! Good work! Good work! Hit 'em hard! Hit 'em hard! Slam it into 'em!" The strength of his voice pleased him. Sometimes, officers new to battle were so rattled that their words came out in high-pitched, garbled spurts that were virtually unintelligible.

The men responded with a quick cheer. They were pleased that their officer was not only killing just as they were, but was doing it faster and more skillfully. He raised his rifle in acknowledgment.

His terror of failing his men had vanished. What remained was a generalized fear that was healthy and manageable. His mind was active, his fingers nimble, and his movements quick. He did realize, though, that he was puckering both his lips and his anus.

He reloaded and fired again, but this time it was a clean miss. Damn, he hated wasting a bullet, but the downroll of the enemy ship had been slightly different from the one before. He liked to think of each shot as a mathematical equation. Since he hated cards, Mother Nature seemed to take perverse delight in reminding him that she considered each shot a card game and that she always held the wild card. The naval lieutenant he had aimed at went down, but it was a tumbling ship's block that felled him.

Boom! There was a tremendous explosion on *Bahama,* just abaft of her waist; strong enough to induce considerable vibration in the deck planks below Pennywhistle's feet. Arms, heads, torsos, as well as oddments of metal and wood, hurtled skywards and shot sideways. Some unrecognizable human remains smashed into the boarding nets next to Pennywhistle. The only thing he could identify was a man's bloody hand, still wearing a gold ring.

A huge pillar of smoke engulfed *Bahama's* main and mizzen masts in a grey-white fog. Pennywhistle thought her aft magazine had detonated. No, that explanation wouldn't serve. The explosion of an entire magazine would have sent her masts flying and turned her hull to kindling. *Bellerophon* would have been severely damaged as well.

Not even Pennywhistle's vivid imagination could have imagined the comedy of terrors that had resulted in the blast. *Bellerophon's* solid shot had been indirectly responsible. Solid shot did not explode, but the concussive force of one 18-round possessed the equivalent kinetic energy of three Boulton and Watt steam engines running at full power: all compressed into 5.17 inches. One such shot had crashed into *Bahama's* quarterdeck, bounced twice, and knocked over two sand tubs containing slowmatches on linstocks. One of the burning matches had ignited a chest with two cannon charges. Sparks from that explosion had leapfrogged and detonated a second ammunition chest.

The second explosion ignited three men, turning them into blazing scarecrows. These scarecrows did not stand still like their namesakes, but stumbled crazily about as flesh burned and crisped. To the ship's misfortune, every one of them collapsed close enough to other ammunition chests to trigger more explosions.

All that mattered to Pennywhistle was that *Bahama* was badly damaged. Her wheel was intact, but he could see no one manning it. All three t'gallant masts had toppled, and there were severe tears in her topsails.

The t'gallants had the effect of anchors on *Bahama's* forward motion. The wind was light and the swells considerable, so she slowly began to swing away from *Bellerophon.*

There was a flurry of activity on her quarterdeck. Many of her crew had been temporarily stunned, frozen in shock and disbelief. They were just now snapping out of their trances and beginning to carry out damage control functions. Several quartermasters raced to man her wheel, and men with axes hurried to cut away the mass of ropes, sails, and general wreckage impeding her ability to maneuver or fight.

Pennywhistle had been taught that a gentleman never kicked a man when he was down, but that was exactly what you wanted to do metaphorically when the same thing happened to a ship.

He reloaded his rifle with machine like precision; his flying hands a marvel of swift symmetry that needed no prompting from the mind. A sneer crossed his face as he thought of fellow officers who belittled his concern with constant and realistic training. This was where the hundreds of hours of hard rehearsal paid off.

Boom! Boom! The two nine-pounders fired a second time, and the deck shook. Two more rounds slammed into *Bahama's* forecastle. The gun captain of the second nine-pounder thought it a damned shame that the two guns on the starboard side had been dismounted and could not administer a similar punishment to *Bahama's* sister ship.

Crump! the port 32-pound carronade fired a third time, and its double dose of grape severed the breeching ropes of cannon three on *Bahama's* forecastle. The freed beast rolled about like a drunken rhino and crushed half of its crew. The rounds also disrupted *Bahama's* damage control parties.

Cooke might lack dash, but he was a fighting man to his core and would likely alter course, close with *Bahama*, and do as Nelson directed: lay his ship alongside that of an enemy and finish the job that he had so admirably started.

CHAPTER 23

Bellerophon's forecastle gunners cheered after they blasted another round into *Bahama*. They then dashed over to the starboard carronade, reloaded it in twenty seconds, and let fly a blast of grape that dug several large chunks of wood out of the base of *Montañés* foremast. Those chunks generated an attendant storm of large splinters, which felled four seamen on the deck below.

Above the din, the band played on, but now only five remained alive. The melody was "Jolly Mortals Fill your Glasses", a popular drinking song.

Pennywhistle debated whether to keep his marines firing. The distance had opened to 300 yards. Rounds still possessed sufficient velocity to kill at 300 yards, but muskets were not accurate at that distance and would only have minor nuisance value as the range increased. The prudent thing to do was to conserve ammunition for the fight ahead, so he told his marines to stand down. He himself would continue firing with his rifle, because he regularly scored hits at 250 yards. The freshening wind opened a window of opportunity: a clear view of the shattered enemy quarterdeck.

He saw just what he desired: a tall officer in a blue coat and red trousers waving his sword and shouting to some sailors covered in blood. In a badly damaged vessel, a single officer with presence of mind might be the brightest jewel in the ship's crown. Pennywhistle could not have asked for a more worthy target for a tricky shot.

A hit on land at 300 yards would require no wind, a stable platform, a sound eye, and the steadiest of nerves. The pitching and rolling of ships complicated matters, but he relished challenges. This was where his grueling program of training would bear its sweetest fruit.

He probably had less than a minute before the window snapped shut, and he did not hesitate. He noted the wind, the wave troughs, the pitch and roll of his ship and that of the enemy. The officer was walking, gesturing energetically. Pennywhistle factored in his movement, speed, and probable course heading.

Timing was critical: the difference between pulling the trigger at almost the right moment instead of exactly the right moment was the difference between completely missing one's target and deadly accuracy. In a split second, a complex series of calculations distilled itself into an absolutely opportune moment to squeeze the trigger.

His ship was on the downroll; five more seconds till it would rise. His concentration deepened. The bow of *Bellerophon* was coming up like pendulum moving toward the outer edge of its arc. A surge of eagerness hit him, but he peremptorily batted it away as a guard dog would an intruding cat. His composure was unruffled by any emotion save a disinterested curiosity if his calculations were exact. Almost there.

Perfect! His mind blanked out all sound to his ears, but a klaxon blared in his brain that this was the moment. He held his breath, let it out slowly, and squeezed the trigger with the gentleness of a mother wiping the mouth of a newborn.

He felt the recoil punch his shoulder, but his mental filters caused him to miss the actual sound of the shot. The smoke cleared a few seconds later. He saw a sight that should have filled him with human sadness, but instead gratified the artist within. The young Spanish officer was staggering, hands clutching his left breast, trying to stanch a spreading stain of purple on his bright new uniform.

He looked a noble and intelligent fellow, the kind of man Pennywhistle might have called friend in better times. But these were hard times, requiring ruthless choices. The tall officer had sworn an oath to King Ferdinand to do all in his power to destroy his sovereign's enemies; it was Pennywhistle's duty to make certain such vows proved costly. As the officer crashed into the deck, a smile creased Pennywhistle's lips. The chances of *Bahama* staging any kind of a rally had just become a lot more unlikely.

Seven men he had killed thus far. Sadness, pain, and remorse had laid no claim upon him. He felt none of the sick joy of the sadist, but he was pleased that his final shot had been a minor masterpiece of his craft. The blood and gore affected him less than most officers, because he had witnessed numerous dissections at university in Edinburgh.

Yet, while the contents of his stomach remained secure, his moral sensibilities were less so. It was a much better thing to put men back together instead of tearing them apart; but the duel had made his bed and he would have to lie in it.

His soul felt empty, though his senses remained on high alert. He had taken lives, yet it had seemed more like pest control, a gamekeeper dispatching a pack of wolves that threatened his flock of sheep. When the wolves died, you neither rejoiced nor wept. It was simply a duty that had been discharged.

He was meeting the test of battle well by conventional standards; thinking coolly, acting logically, and viewing men as mere numbers in a vast equation. He assured himself that his detachment from emotion was not permanent. His emotions were merely in hibernation, like a bear seeking a cave at the onset of winter. They would rise again when safe times returned, like the first roses in spring.

He looked once more in the direction of *Bahama,* but she had been swallowed up by the smoke and not even her masts were visible. Round one of the battle was done.

"You think entirely too much about every trifling matter," an exasperated fellow officer once told him after he'd suggested one more repetition of a common drill. "You need to regard life more lightly; look upon it as something to be reveled in, not endured with manly fortitude. Good god, man; laugh a little, dance to the Pipes of Pan, and let Bacchus banish your cares on occasion. Glory in sport and women, and don't treat every damned thing as a cosmic issue. I know not why simple frivolity frightens you, but I do know that it must be very difficult to be you."

The officer in question meant well, and had been both right and wrong. Strength and weakness were not always opposites: they were sometimes flip sides of the same coin. Introspection and deep thinking were generally reckoned liabilities in the military profession because they could transform a Caesar into a Hamlet, agonizing over so many possibilities that he could never come to a quick decision. Yet the energies that made a man introspective were the same ones that fueled his imagination.

That imagination had conferred upon Pennywhistle what Bonaparte called *Le coup d'oeil*—literally, the stroke of the eye—a gift that enabled him to immediately size up a dangerous situation and devise ingenious solutions that would forever elude conventional thinkers. He took satisfaction in applying a line of Hamlet to both his personal qualities and the deeds that he had just carried out: "Nothing is good or evil but thinking makes it so."

He noticed the men staring at him, uncertain smiles upon their faces. Damn and blast, he had been so enslaved to his private musings that he had forgotten his first duty. The marines looked to be expecting some sort of praise. It was well deserved, and ordinarily he would have given it freely. But right now it was far more important that he attend to business than distribute laurels. Round one was done, but many more lay ahead. He did not want his men getting comfortable and complacent.

At least the smoke had cleared enough from the deck that he could see his men clearly. Elsewhere, the gigantic thunderheads formed from thousands of cannon discharges grew worse with each successive broadside. You could discern most vessels only by the scarlet muzzle flashes of their big guns. The blobs of light blinking on and off reminded him of the bioluminescent jellyfish he had seen in the Caribbean.

"If you were expecting knighthoods for you conduct, I must disappoint you," he said more gruffly than he intended. "You did your duty, but King George does not reward men for simply doing what is right and expected. You must attend to that duty many more times today if we are all to see sundown tonight. The Spaniards will return at any moment, likely bringing considerably more firepower than this ship enjoys. And we have yet to try conclusions with Johnny Crapaud, whose ships carry many veteran soldiers."

He tried to keep his voice pitched at a conversational level but the continuous *boom booming* from the other ships in the great melee made that impossible. He found himself shouting, as if he were speaking to miners in deep shaft during a thunderstorm. If the noise got much worse, he would be reduced to pantomiming.

"I want an immediate weapons and ammunition check. Examine flints, frizzens, fowling, and touchholes with the utmost care. Your life is forfeit if your musket is not at peak readiness. Be sure your barrel contains no unfired charge: misfires often go unnoticed during the noise of battle. Make certain a pull of the trigger ensures a shower of sparks. If not, you each have two spare flints in your cartridge boxes; do not hesitate to replace the current one if its dull edges even hint at a misfire. Employ your vent picks freely and keep the touchholes clear. Application of some extra gun oil on your ramrods would not be amiss to ensure they slide in and out of their channels a little easier. Fouling should be handled by," he paused slightly, "the usual method."

Pissing down the barrel was a time-honored expedient.Uric acid dissolved unburned powder.

"Refill your cartridge boxes when the ammunition chest is brought forward. I am quite certain that you will expend all of its contents over the next few hours.

Once you have done all of that, you may rest. Conserve your energy, for you will need every ounce of it in the struggles ahead. I shall not summon you again until new enemy sails manifest, and then I shall require every bit of spirit you possess. For now, you are all dismissed."

The men broke up into their component two-man sub chains.

Warwick wondered why his officer felt compelled to remind the men of things that they knew by heart. He decided that while Mr. Pennywhistle sometimes repeated messages too often, it was because he was conscientious, and that was better than an officer who was careless about details.

Combs and Warwick talked quietly. Combs wormed out his venthole, while Warwick dropped his trousers and emptied the contents of his bladder down the barrel of his musket. "Mr. Pennywhistle sure ain't like he usually is, is he Jim? I thought we done right well. He's being as miserly with compliments as a pawnbroker valuing a rich heirloom. Never would have expected that from a man that always has kind words for those who do well at drill."

Warwick *ahhhed* in relief that his bladder was now empty and hitched up his trousers. "He's not being hard, Marty, just smart. He wants to keep us on our toes and remind us not to let our guards down. This ain't drill: this is war. It's the difference between conning a boat in harbor and commanding a real one at sea. He's being tough on us because he wants us to come through this day with our hides intact.

"It don't fret me none that he ain't given to big compliments. A real leader is not a popinjay but a determined man who gets the little things right and makes sure his men do the same.

"I ain't never come across an officer like Mr. Pennywhistle. Most officers are brave enough, but they don't want to spill blood by their own hand. Oh, they will defend themselves if attacked, but they prefer to leave the infliction of cheap, common death to lowly devils like us.

"Mr. Pennywhistle ain't just willing to kill, he has practiced to be good at it. You saw how he used his rifle: watching him take down Dons was like watching a beaver cut stripling trees. Gutting a man takes courage, but it's a lot better if you use skill to kill at a distance so he can't never get close."

He shook the barrel of his musket vigorously, then dumped the contents over the side. Most of the fouling was gone.

"I think at his heart Mr. Pennywhistle would rather be wearing a horned Viking helmet than the Royal Marine round hat. He may be a gentleman, but his lack of squeamishness signifies he don't consider himself superior to me. Anyway, Marty, you seen the lion. How are you faring?"

Combs was not a reflective man, and it took him a few moments to reply. "I wanted to flee as bad as someone with the runs needs to find the nearest head, but damn if my feet would move only in accord with this chain order stuff. My body seemed to know what to do without me thinking at all. I also didn't want to let you down."

Warwick laughed. "It's training, Marty, pure and simple. Your body had to obey in spite of the fear. The same energy that could have been used to run was instead used to confound the enemy. And I felt the same about you. I did not want you thinking that I was a talker, not a fighter, and that what I had said about my experience in battle was so much hot air."

"Well, Jim, you sure were right about battle being confusing. Even now, I can't see much beyond the jib boom, and the air smells like passel of dead fish dumped in a crate of rotten eggs. But you didn't tell me how hot the air gets, or that my lips would feel like old parchment left out in noonday sun."

Bahama's mainmast stump suddenly appeared out of the smoke four hundred yards away.

"Mr. Cumby," said Cooke," bring her larboard half a point. Put us alongside *Bahama's* starboard beam. We have knocked her about smartly, now let's close in and finish her as a fighting platform."

"Aye, aye, Captain, a pleasure. Two or three good broadsides should give us our first prize of the day."

CHAPTER 24

Higgins and Wilson were both alive and unwounded on the quarterdeck, but the conclusions they drew from the fight just concluded were diametrically opposed.

Wilson was white as a sheet and his left index finger was twitching badly. He was soaked in sweat, but at least his legs supported him; no knocking knees or trembling muscles. He was surprised that his bladder and bowels had stayed continent. The last few minutes were a blur to him, and it took a mental effort to figure out how he had survived.

He had apparently yelled the right commands at the right moments. The marines had poured wave after wave of volleys into the Spaniards on the port side. The Brown Bess barrels were hot to the touch, and the marines were cooling them as well as relieving their bladders by "the usual method."

They had fired low and kept silent, in contrast to the loud cheers emanating from the Spanish ship before *Bellerophon* had opened fire. With all of the smoke, he had no idea of their volleys' effects, but there had been plenty of screaming after each discharge so at least some rounds had hit home.

He'd wanted to run when the battle commenced, but the path to the companionway and safety was completely blocked. Short of kicking and elbowing, he could only stay and face the fire. He had felt panic enveloping him like a straight jacket, and not an ordinary one, but a garment soaked in water and then quickly dried so it would shrink to three quarters of its original size.

Wilson hated to admit it, but the only thing that had stopped him from shrieking and bursting into unmanly cheers had been Higgins' conduct. Though small of stature and high of voice, Higgins had stood resolute and firm. As the shot, grape, and canister flew thick and fast, he kept repeating to the men, "Steady, boys, steady" in a voice that bewitched with its quiet sincerity. The men kept their ranks and looked upon him with respect and more than a little affection. Higgins was the well-meaning underdog who made up with heart and determination what he lacked in training and experience.

Wilson found the spectacle strangely affecting, even though he cared little for anyone but himself. He felt ashamed that he should be outmatched by a mere wisp in a scarlet jacket, and a small shred of dignity that he did not know he possessed floated to the surface of his soul.

Sometimes Corporal Robbins had called out the commands slightly ahead of Higgins, his words serving as prompts, though Higgins had mostly done things right. Robbins' eight years of experience made him nearly as good a drillmaster as Dale. Wilson had added his voice, echoing the commands.

The act of yelling had proven cathartic. He had come through his first fire fight unscathed, though with a slight nose bleed and muted hearing that made him feel as though a bale of cotton had been stuffed in each ear.

He had been lucky, plain and simple. As a gambler, he learned early on never to push a streak of luck and always leave before the cards turned cold. Battle, however, was an unforgiving game where his clever calculations could do nothing to even the odds. You were forced to play out your hand until you either stood triumphant or lay flat, bloody and unmoving. He could not depart unless his exit could be explained and made to appear decorous.

Then it occurred to Wilson that he might play an adult version of the child's game "let's pretend." He might be a fraud as an officer, but there was nothing wrong with his memory; he still knew how to speak the words of command, as he had proven earlier. The blackness of his heart and the yellow in his liver might matter less than his ability to simply fake his way through the charade of war.

The same acting skills that he used to fool women and gamblers might be employed to bamboozle these men. He knew his lines, his marks, and the expected actions of the other players. He had a manly voice and his costume fit well. He just needed to transfer that same easy self confidence of the gentleman gambler to the part of the gentleman warrior.

He did not have to think. He just had to get the men to stand firm and fire. And be mindful to include at appropriate intervals, "Well done", "Steady" and "Good work" because they sounded like the things heroes said.

It was at that moment that his ring to started to pulsate and its ruby to glow a very unusual shade of red. He stared at it in feverish amazement, convinced that his fear and overheated imagination were playing tricks on him. The damned ruby was bizarrely mesmerizing; you could lose yourself gazing into its depths. Yet it was strangely reassuring. Its energy seemed to be telling him he could do this.

He'd never noticed the details of the jackal image on its side until now. He wondered why that seemed important. He searched his memory for what Caroline had said about it. He had paid little attention at the time, dismissing it as the vapid maunderings of a woman with too much time on her hands. Her words came back to him in a flash, and a shocked expression chased away his usual cynical half smile.

"The image is Anubis, Peter," Caroline had said in the sweet, lilting voice that was her only charm beyond a pretty face and the body of a goddess. "In ancient Egypt, he was the God of the Underworld and the patron of orphans and lost souls."

Wilson haled from a good family but had been orphaned early and raised by distant relatives. He'd learned to make his way on his own; charming many, trusting none, and relying upon his wits rather than his heart. He fit many people's definition of a lost soul.

Whether it was from magic, shame, or desperation, Wilson vowed to make it through the next round of fighting before he sought an exit. He might not be able to change his nature, but he could suppress it for a short time. Three marines had been blown to bits in front of him and his stomach had lodged nary a protest, so there was hope.

His resolve was about to be tested, for here came Higgins with a smile on his face and his hand extended.

"I say, Mr. Wilson, we did rather well, I think. Saw those Dons off to a fare-thee-well and left them with a fine load of lead in their backsides." His smile faded and his expression turned pensive. "I have to admit I was scared something awful. How about you? I heard your voice clearly but I could not see you through the smoke."

Wilson could not help but admire the boy's candor, his callowness allowing him to admit an emotion that many officers denied that they had ever tasted. He wanted to unburden himself and say, "Damned true! I have never been so appallingly scared in my life," but honesty would undermine the imposture he had decided upon.

"Well, I admit I was more agitated than I would be when holding a bad hand in a game of whist, but I thought the excitement was rather bracing." *Yes that sounded like the thing a devil-may-care gallant might say.* "It's a change from the dullness of blockade duty." *Oh please, please bring that dullness back! It brings me so many sheep to be sheared! Officers always find cards the best way relieve their boredom. The greater the boredom, the higher the stakes."*

"It seems to me," Wilson continued, "that battle divides men into two categories: those who can stand the fire and those who cannot." *At least battle has clarified my defects and stimulated my brain into giving me an honest picture of what my survival requires.*

He was speaking loudly, hoping that his talk would improve his reputation among the men. Higgins in his innocence was lapping up his words and nodding in sincere agreement, but the marines' faces showed only three expressions: skepticism, derision, and contempt. It was time to toss out a few compliments. He would start with Higgins. The men liked him, and his good will might help the men see him in a different light.

"I must say, Mr. Higgins, your conduct has been most admirable: bold but prudent, audacious yet measured, gallant without flamboyance." *God he was piling it on with a heavy shovel!*

Higgins grinned like a schoolboy. Most of the men were not buying it, but at least a few softened their expressions. It was time to throw a few kind words their way. He turned to confront an assemblage of cynical faces black with powder grime.

"Marines, I want to compliment you on your conduct. Mr. Higgins and I are grateful for your courage, loyalty, and steadfastness. Any laurels that we accrue today properly belong to you. I am proud to command you and know that you will continue to bring great honor to King George."

The silence was deafening and not a marine smiled at the praise. No one could recall seeing Wilson lead from the front, but there was so much smoke that it was possible that they had missed something. His voice at least had been heard, and it had said the right things. They knew a man talking rot when they heard one, but his compliments were welcome, as many officers said nothing at all about their men's conduct.

Wilson noted the marines' faces were a trifle less hard; his words had at least bought him a second chance. They did not like or trust him, but they were not quite willing to give up on a man who at least sounded like a gentleman and did not try to steal all the glory for himself. Wilson realized that he was on probation, and for now, that was good enough. It was so much easier to bamboozle men who were not pitched to a steep angle of suspicion.

CHAPTER 25

"For God's sake, Mrs. Overton, hold him tighter!" Whyte did not mean to scream the command, but his desperation overwhelmed his natural regard for the fair sex. Indeed, regard for any kind of propriety seemed fatuous in this pit of death.

"I'm trying, I'm trying!" shouted Nancy, fighting back tears that were as much a product of frustration as they were of grief. She was cradling Mary's crying newborn with her left arm and using her right to hold down a sailor.

The big man was not an example of the stoical British tar. He thrashed about on the operating table as violently as a beached whale drenched in acid. Three men were trying to pin him down, and Nancy had been dragooned into helping simply because an extra arm was needed and she was near.

Whyte moved his bone saw back and forth almost faster than the eye could follow, yet he knew at least thirty seconds remained before the man's right arm came off. Thirty seconds was an eternity for a surgeon with an industriously struggling patient. The man spat out the wooden plug that he was supposed to bite on for the pain and screamed, "No, no, no!" with a hideous resolve that excited pity in a few but disgust in most.

Whyte had exhausted his small supply of laudanum and was nearly out of rum. The man had been given only a third of the usual dose. Whyte sent a desperate order for more rum from the ship's stores, but it would probably not arrive anytime soon.

He was taking the arm off just below the shoulder. The higher up a limb was amputated, the greater the need for speed to prevent the onset of shock. The man's frenzied contortions were slowing him; twice he had been forced to withdraw the saw blade lest it bounce out of its groove and strike healthy flesh higher up. God, he wished that he'd never left London: a debtor's prison seemed very welcoming about now.

Mary's baby reacted badly to the thrashing sailor's shrieks. His cries changed to loud wails. Wounded sailors showed little sympathy for the struggling sailor, but tears began to form in their eyes over the infant's distress.

"God's blood! That's enough," shouted Nancy in loud, stern tones that she barely recognized as her own. Wounded men awaiting surgery perked their heads up in shock; the voice was that of an angry Valkyrie.

Nancy's resolve was pure maternal instinct. A child under her care was being harmed, and she could not permit it. She did not so much let go of the struggling sailor's arm as hurl it aside. Still holding the child, she drew back with her right arm as far she could and made a fist. That fist shot forward with a fury that would have done credit to Gentleman Jackson and connected solidly with the man's chin. His eyelids fluttered briefly, then closed.

Whyte stopped his sawing and stared at Nancy in shock, as did many in the cockpit. Wounded sailors could scarcely credit what they had seen.

The looks angered Nancy. Did they expect her to stand idle? "Well, someone had to do something!"

There was a brief pause, then the cockpit erupted in laughter. Not loud, because these were wounded men, nonetheless the laughter was hard and deep, and they all benefited from that moment of merriment; a man could not feel pain when laughing hard.

"Thank God!" Whyte sighed in relief. He resumed his energetic sawing, and forty seconds later the man's right arm dropped into his nearly filled bucket. He finished the rest of his surgery on the man. He had no idea if the man would live, but at least he had done his job. Just then, one of his loblolly boys arrived with an additional supply of rum.

Whyte spoke to Nancy in a voice that was both respectful and amused. "I hope that we will not need your furious fist again, Mrs. Overton. Yet, by stopping that man's movements, you may just have doubled his chances of surviving."

The baby responded to the men's laughter and stopped crying. Indeed, the child wore the hint of a smile. Nancy responded with a smile of her own. "It was not fair for the child to suffer, Mr. Whyte. You and I and all of the men are here for a reason, but this innocent neither asked for this nor deserves it. I am sure that, years from now when he is told the curious circumstances of his birth, he will scarcely credit that I am telling the truth."

"No doubt, Mrs. Overton. Truth is far more *outré* than what finds its way into novels. I just hope all of us survive the day to be able to tell him the story. And that we are sane enough to tell it correctly."

"I have decided on a name to suggest to Mary for the child," Nancy confided.

"Something noble, like Nelson, perhaps?"

"No, Mr. Whyte. Trafalgar."

CHAPTER 26

The band moved to the port gangway and commenced playing the chief melody from Handel's *Water Music*. They were down to four musicians, but each death seemed to increase the determination of the remaining members to continue. Their martial version of Handel's masterwork might not evoke George II gliding down the Thames with his courtiers, but they could see that it brought relief to hardy British tars fighting for their lives.

Without warning, a towering dragon thrust her head out of the smoke.

"Holy Mother of God!" shouted Robinson in shock.

"It can't be!" mouthed MacFarlane.

"Bloody hell," murmured Warwick.

"Marines, down and brace for impact!" Pennywhistle yelled.

"Not this!" Cumby said under his breath.

"Back top'sulls and t'gallants, immediately, Mr. Cumby!" commanded Cooke urgently.

As French t'gallants pierced the curtain of smoke, a puff of wind dispersed some of the brimstone fog. The stern of the ship materialized, formidable and unmoving. Only ten yards off *Bellerophon's* starboard bow, *Aigle's* ornate gold and vermillion backside towered over *Bellerophon's* jib-boom.

Her design marked her as younger than *Bellerophon;* not only bigger, but carrying guns of larger caliber.

Bellerophon desperately needed to slam on the nautical equivalent of brakes to avoid a collision, but Cooke's orders to back sail came too late.

Robinson, MacFarlane, and a recently escaped slave of the Barbary Pirates, Piers Jansen, acted instinctively. Without orders, they leaped from their forecastle stations and raced to grab ropes to release the forecourse as a brake. They pulled hard, but *Bellerophon's* jib-boom crashed into *Aigle* just abaft of her mainmast. *Bellerophon's* foremast yards jammed themselves hard against *Aigle's* mainmast yards, creating the equivalent of a pine padlock. *Bellerophon's* stern began to drift toward *Aigle's* bow.

205 feet and 1,600 tons of British oak slamming into 220 feet and 2,100 tons of French oak generated an enormous amount of kinetic energy. The impact knocked sailors on both decks off their feet. The better trained and more experienced men of *Bellerophon* recovered first.

"On your feet!" Pennywhistle shouted to his marines as his outstretched, upraised palm moved quickly upwards; the hand signal to rise. "Two volleys, then grenades!"

For the first time, the marines could see lots of potential targets close and clear. French sailors were yelling, waving cutlasses, and assembling two boarding parties. French soldiers behind them formed themselves into three ranks, ready to lay down suppressing fire when the sailors made their move.

Marine muskets crashed out and Pennywhistle saw that many bullets found a ready mark. The Marines reloaded and their weapons volleyed a second time. Pennywhistle noted with satisfaction that several men had glanced at the colored markers denoting ranges before lining up their shots.

Seven marines laid their muskets down as gently as if they were babies and grabbed grenades from the large canvas sack. Each man inserted a precut red fuse, lit it with a slow match taken from a small metal case tacked onto his round hat, waited the regulation three seconds, then threw with all his might.

The grenades landed among French sailors and detonated with large thumps that sounded like giant paper bags popping. The marines were gratified by the screams, groans, and curses that shortly followed.

Pennywhistle remembered the name of the ship's captain, Pierre-Paulin Gourrège; a tough, former Breton merchant skipper with a reputation as a never-give-up fighter. If he could render the enemy captain *hors de combat*, he could slow their boarding plans and cause at least a brief interval of indecision before the First Lieutenant could take over.

He searched the enemy decks for a forty-three-year-old man wearing an ornate uniform and a fancy *chapeau de bras* but found no one matching that description. Then he realized that Gourrège was the probably the opposite of a showy gallant and would likely wear a basic rig, disdaining gaudy epaulettes and stylish headgear.

He swept his gaze over the enemy quarterdeck. After a minute that seemed like a millennium, it settled on a short, squat man with a green spyglass in his right hand. He had a round, florid face with more character than comeliness and wore a double breasted, blue serge coat that reminded Pennywhistle of a pea jacket. The coat was roughly tailored, of a civilian cut with a free fall collar; inexpensive brass epaulettes had been tacked on as an afterthought. Instead of a grand hat, he wore a red *bonnet de police* with a tricolor rosette; a common fatigue cap in the French army.

The captain was giving orders calmly, using his left hand energetically to underscore important points. His lined, weathered face matched what one would expect of a grizzled, no-nonsense sea dog.

The deck shook heavily as *Bellerophon's* lower batteries blasted into *Aigle's* hull at less than pistol shot range. The impact of the broadside was attenuated however, because *Bellerophon's* hull was at 70 degree angle relative to the enemy hull. All of the enemy guns bore directly on her while few of her own could return the favor.

Boom! The double round of flying canister from *Bellerophon's* port forecastle carronade did not just kill men of the enemy boarding parties; it wiped thirty men from the face of the earth as if they had never been born. Flesh, uniform, and steel dropped to the decks, and the air grew thick with a red fog.

The fighting halted briefly, as stunned Frenchmen struggled to make sense of the vaporization of thirty good men.

A pair of short, nimble men raced up to Pennywhistle. Their names were Parker and Perry, but everyone called them Punch and Judy; partly because of their circus background, but mostly because they argued often and occasionally came to blows, though each considered the other his best friend. Unlike many saddled with nicknames, they liked theirs because they might one day look good on a theater's marquee.

"I think the time is right, Mr. Pennywhistle," said Punch earnestly.

"I agree with Punch," said Judy sturdily. "There is plenty of confusion right now that will make our jobs easier." Both he and Punch brandished edged weapons which were more than knives but too short to be called swords. Their wide, razor-sharp blades would cut through even the thickest rope.

"Three ports disabled will do," said Pennywhistle. "You business is sabotage, not taking an enemy out of the fight."

"We understand, sir. Don't we, Judy?" said Punch with a wry half-smile that contained more determination than humor.

"We sure do," said Judy. "I want to tell my girl back home what I done. Her folks always said she had no business taking up with a circus man, and I aim to prove them dead wrong."

"The smoke grenades will give you extra cover," said Pennywhistle with more hope than certitude.

He motioned Warwick and Combs to come closer and pointed to the bag of special projectiles. "Toss six of these things as quickly as you can. You don't have to be accurate, just fast."

"Aye, aye, sir!" Warwick and Combs chorused. The two men laid out six grenades ready to have their fuses lit. The bottom of each grenade was coated with a mixture of tar and pitch so that it would stick to the enemy hull. The marines looked at Pennywhistle for the signal to start.

"Go!"

They dispatched their grenades. Clouds of dirty grey smoke rose thickly and the enemy hull disappeared from view.

"Off with you, now. Good luck and keep moving." Pennywhistle worried that he had just condemned two men to death. But they had volunteered, and the task was worth undertaking. Anything that reduced the enemy's vastly superior firepower, even temporarily, was a godsend.

Punch and Judy threw their grappling hooks. They did not need to see their target; it was enough that they knew the distance and the shapes of the two ships. The hooked steel heads lodged on the enemy bulwarks, and the two former acrobats swung across the short distance between the ships with the skill of squirrel monkeys traversing a rain forest.

The smoke and the disorientation of the French worked in their favor and they faced no gun shots. The instant their feet touched the enemy wales, elevated horizontal bands that strengthened the hull, they released the ropes and went down on all fours. They commenced scuttling sideways like spiders navigating a tightrope.

Pistol shots rang out from the first gunport they approached. They dodged and skittered to the next gun port, which offered no resistance. Punch pulled the port lid outward, while Judy cut the rope. Punch let go and the lid slammed shut. Shouts and curses issued from behind the lid. Both men laughed and moved left toward their next target.

Pennywhistle saw his acrobats were off to a good start and again focused his attention on Captain Gourrège. He aimed his Ferguson and made the necessary calculations, slowing his breathing and taking the measure of the rhythm of the ships and the man. All of the smoke, thunder, and confusion of battle dropped away as his concentration deepened: his only goal in life became the death of a short man in an inexpensive serge coat. He lined up the sights on the captain's chest, let out his breath slowly and caressed the trigger with the sensitivity of a man stroking a lover's cheek. The rifle barked and a puff of smoke obscured his vision briefly.

Pennywhistle lurched. The smoke cleared and he frowned. Nature had played another trick on him, for his ship had rolled at the last instant. What was meant to be a kill shot had only wounded.

Gourrège rolled around on the deck, clutching his stomach. Being gut-shot almost always guaranteed a painful death, but one hours, even days in the future. Pennywhistle was saddened that a worthy adversary would suffer, but he had accomplished his mission of taking the enemy captain out of the fight.

Boom! The forecastle carronade thundered forth a double round of canister. 400 pieces of hot lead, sounding like legions of madly flapping bats, pulped 20 French sailors into blue, red, and white remains of valor and dreams of glory.

"Fire!" yelled Higgins on the quarterdeck. Dale on the poop shouted the same command. Their marines were sweeping the enemy decks, but because of the angle of *Bellerophon* to *Aigle* their fire was far less effective than usual.

Wilson crouched under the poop deck overhang; his mind flitting between his earlier resolution and fresh panic. The sudden, terrible proximity to French resolve, steel and lead meant it was high time to look to his own safety. When the confusion became great enough, he would slip away down the quarterdeck companionway. The marine sentry guarding it would not challenge an officer.

"Mr. Cumby," said Cooke urgently, "get below and tell all the gun crews to focus their intentions entirely on *Aigle*. I've spotted another French ship moving toward us, but *Aigle* is the real threat."

"Aye, aye, sir," said Cumby tersely. He remembered not to run, but his walk was uncharacteristically brisk. He rubbed the cross under his shirt. His resolve strengthened as God helped him to remember that he was not alone.

Cooke took up his spyglass and panned it toward the port side. Another ship was moving toward them. It was *Bahama*, the one that they had savaged and had been preparing to finish off. The fox was turning on the hound. *Bellerophon* would soon be under cannonade from three ships firing from two different directions.

For the French *Swiftsure* had also opened fire. She had simply appeared a minute before out of a thunderhead of cannon smoke. Cooke recognized her because she was the sister ship of *Bellerophon*. Having captured her five years before, the French had declined to change her English name. The original name galled British hearts, because the Royal Navy rarely lost a ship-of-the line.

Just after Pennywhistle's marines fired a fourth volley, the French counter-effort began. Grenades flew from the maintop of *Aigle*. Pennywhistle could see it was crammed with upwards of 25 men, and they looked to be lighting grenades.

The first three exploded not five feet from him. Fragments peppered his hat and pock-marked his jacket like Swiss cheese, but to his astonishment his flesh remained intact, protected by the heavy wool of his uniform. Whizzing fragments badly wounded two marines and two sailors. Several iron orbs were smothered by marines using their wet cloths.

He wracked his brain for a way to defend against the aerial assault, but none presented itself. The distance and angles were all wrong for his marines to shoot at the men in the maintop, and the sailors possessed only edged weapons. Lucky shots from the forecastle carronade might make the mainmast unsteady; a supremely lucky shot might topple it. But a lot of French soldiers were sensibly aiming their small arms fire at gunners, doing their utmost to kill the carronade's crew.

By their black gaiters, grey trousers, and single breasted blue coats with red collars, cuffs, and piping, Pennywhistle recognized the soldiers as members of the veteran 67th Regiment. He could not quite read the battle honors on the regimental flag, well to their rear, but the flag displayed at least three, and those were never given lightly.

Ping, ping ping. Bullets kicked up chips of wood around Pennywhistle as three ranks of the 67th delivered a well-ordered volley. Two sailors were slightly wounded, one in the shoulder and one in the forearm. That the volley did not do greater damage was entirely due to the fact that soldiers were creatures of the land. They had no idea how to fire from one rolling platform at men who were on another rolling platform.

Pennywhistle noted many of them displayed the pasty white complexions of men suffering from seasickness. Three actually vomited at the volley's conclusion. It put him in mind of bears that he had seen at county fairs. It was not that the bears danced well, but that they danced at all. Nevertheless, if British sailors and marines remained standing, many would fall before they could retaliate. He decided the threat from above was greater than the menace in front. His mind fixed on a compromise.

"Everybody down except Chain One!" He pushed his left hand, palm open, violently downward several times. "Warwick, Combs, Howell, Page: keep on smothering those grenades!"

The French would undoubtedly try to board over the jib-boom, and the grenade-tossing would have to cease before boarders advanced. The boarders would have to advance along the jib-boom in narrow files; they could be picked off by marines. The range would be very close: even smoothbore muskets would be effective. Then at close quarters, the sailors and marines on the forecastle could make a difference with cold steel.

Two grenades landed right at his feet, fuses sizzling malevolently. *What a stupid way to die,* he thought, staring bemusedly at them. But Warwick and Combs threw wet cloths on the fuses, killing them at the last second.

"Much obliged," said Pennywhistle, struggling to keep the relief out of his voice."

"Just doin' what you taught us," said Warwick with an almost impudent grin.

Pennywhistle glanced at Howell and Page: six grenades lay smothered at their feet. The French were acting with more eagerness than experience, tossing the grenades immediately after lighting, inadvertently giving their opponents enough time to snuff most of them out. It was a lucky development, but good luck mostly favored the prepared.

Chain One had rendered a dozen grenades duds, but there will still plenty of live ones flying about. He glanced at Scott. Hand gestures were exchanged. He looked at the jib-boom, and inspiration took fire.

CHAPTER 27

Ten boarders were crossing the jib-boom, brandishing cutlasses and pistols. The boom was narrow and slippery, so all were barefooted for better purchase.

The boarders wore the dark blue jackets, red waistcoats, and white breeches common to French sailors, each topped off with a Liberty cap featuring a tricolor rosette. Their leader looked to be a quartermaster, judging by his tailless coat, black glazed hat, and the two yellow chevrons on his right sleeve. He held a six-foot boarding spear in front of him, jabbing the air every so often as if to clear invisible opponents.

Warwick raised his musket to shoot the quartermaster, but Pennywhistle caught his eye and gave him the hand signal to stand down. Let the French gain a little confidence. He made a suggestion to Scott lying next to him.

Scott replied, "It can be done. Robinson, MacFarlane, and Jansen are the men to do it."

The French boarding party reached the spritsail yard and spread themselves sideways so that all would have a chance to discharge their pistols at the same time before making the final advance. The yard creaked under the weight and yawed slowly back and forth.

Pennywhistle saw that their lack of experience did not allow them the quick rush that would have been their safest bet, no matter how slippery the jib-boom. He nodded to Scott, who in turn made hand gestures to Robinson, MacFarlane, and Jansen. The three smiled wolfishly and drew their cutlasses.

Scott's hand flashed forward giving them the "Go" signal.

The three rushed forward, but the sailors were not their target. When they got close they dropped to their bellies and slithered over the side of the jib-boom, hanging by one hand like orangutans and slicing energetically with the other. They hacked away at the braces that supported the spritsail yard.

Like so many other parts of a ship, the spritsail yard needed the support of braces to counterbalance conflicting geometric stresses. When the final brace parted, gravity took over.

The spritsail yard wobbled, then swayed. Alarmed, the French dropped their weapons and mimicked the actions of circus acrobats on a high rope. Their clumsy attempts at balance were as futile as hippos trying to dance a ballet, and nearly as entertaining to Pennywhistle's men.

By ones, too and threes, the advance boarding party lost their footing and splashed into sea. Heads and hands bobbed frantically for a few moments, then disappeared. Like their British counterparts, few French sailors could swim.

British amusement changed to satisfaction. Ten fewer Frenchmen to contend with, and all accomplished with cleverness rather than British casualties.

Whyte felt swamped by the casualties from French grenades. Large grenade fragments were easy to spot, but ones the size of hat pins were the devil to find and remove. The same was true with wood splinters.

He was sweating so hard that it was becoming difficult to see. He asked that some tallow candles be lit to increase the light. Naked candles were dangerous on a ship, but men were dying and rules sometimes needed to be bent. "Closer! Closer!" he shouted at one of the loblolly boys.

The boy moved the candles so near his face that he felt their heat. When he completed the amputation five minutes later, he wiped his hands absentmindedly along his forehead. He noticed something was wrong. What was it? He had no eyebrows! The candles had been held so close that the heat had singed off the fine hairs.

Nancy walked among the wounded, stopping to treat burns and contusions with her oak bark, olive oil, and honey salve. The men she was treating were not likely to die, but they were in excruciating agony and many would suffer lasting disfigurement. Some uttered quiet "Aaaah"s and "Oooh"s when Nancy's touch temporarily reduced their pain.

Saddest was a blond lad of twenty with bad burns about the eyes. He was a strapping country youth of great manly beauty who Nancy thought belonged strolling down a rural lane with his best girl's hand clasped in his. It would be a miracle if his sight ever returned. As she applied the ointment he squeezed her hand and murmured, "Take me home, please, take me home. My Pa needs me for the harvest. He ain't strong."

Her eyes misted over, but all that came out was a hoarse whisper. "I will try. I will try."

Punch and Judy scampered along *Aigle's* wales. Punch noted that the French ship was drifting toward *Bellerophon* and the two would shortly scrape hulls; a good thing, since it would make the return journey easier.

He and Judy kept sheered off at any sign of resistance. French cannon crews were firing at will rather than attempting any kind of coordinated broadside, so the two never knew when a gunport would erupt in flame. Fortunately, French crews were less than half as fast reloading as their British counterparts.

Punch and Judy moved up, down, and sideways so quickly that small arms fire could not pin them down. They dodged pikes and spears by scuttling sideways at the last second.

Pennywhistle had said three closed gunports constituted success. They needed one more, but words of warning were being passed along *Aigle's* lower deck. Each time they approached a gunport, shouts and curses rang out, followed by pistol shots and a frenzied thrusting of edged weapons. And they were only halfway down *Aigle's* side.

Punch had an inspiration. Mr. Pennywhistle frequently said surprise was a warrior's best ally. The French expected them to continue down the hull until they reached the stern. Why not do the unexpected and head back the way they'd come? The French who had already been annoyed would not be expecting a return visit and their guard would likely be relaxed just a little. A little meant a lot in a desperate battle, and it just might be enough to get them home.

Punch pointed back the way they had come. Judy pantomimed acknowledgment. Both felt that this show was far more exciting than any they had staged at county fairs. Being shot and thrust at was more of a thrill than dazzling an audience. Before, they had been mere entertainers, exciting only applause and amusement. Now they were earning the respect and admiration of fellow warriors.

They scuttled sideways, moving closer to *Bellerophon's* jib-boom, locked in its embrace with *Aigle's* foremast. The cannon and small arms fire were making things so smoky that they would soon not be able to see anything at all.

Judy traced a 2 in the air. Punch nodded. They converged on gunport 2. Judy's hunch was rewarded; they were not detected.

Punch held the lid and Judy cut the ropes. The job was done! Now they just needed to escape.

The two acrobats groped in vain for the grappling hooks and ropes that had brought them there, but they were nowhere in evidence.

Punch and Judy were trapped. Though they had been warned that this might be a one way trip, they were sorely disappointed that they would not be able to return and enjoy the accolades of the marines who were now the only audience they cared about.

But luck had not deserted them. Pennywhistle spotted the two men with his Ramsden, looking like bedraggled flies stuck on the wrapping paper of a molasses pound cake. He made some quick calculations. The men were about thirty feet away.

A sailor with strong arms and a sharp eye was needed to cast them a rescue rope, and more men would be needed to haul it in. Thirty feet was a long way to throw a heavy mass of hemp, but the one man who could was conveniently close: "Gorilla" MacFarlane, who had severed the spritsail braces with the strength of his arm and a sharp cutlass.

Pennywhistle eyed the boarders on *Aigle's* deck. The failure of the first boarders had induced caution. There was perhaps enough time.

Pennywhistle shouted for MacFarlane and explained his plan. MacFarlane in turn summoned ten of his mates, then found a suitable rope and made ready to throw.

Pennywhistle knew that shouts and hails could not be heard through the din of battle. He needed something startling and dramatic, something that would command instant attention.

A blue signal rocket! Yes, that would do. Two were kept for emergencies just behind the ship's wheel. He dispatched Grimes, his fastest man, and told him, "Run like you feet are on fire. If any man disputes your errand, tell him that men's lives absolutely depend upon its completion."

It seemed an eternity until Grimes reappeared, rocket in hand. MacFarlane signaled Pennywhistle he was ready.

Higgins' Marines on the quarterdeck and Dale's on the poop poured fusillade after fusillade onto *Aigle's* decks. The effects of their volley's grew more deadly as the distance between the two ships decreased. A heavily rolling sea and interlocked yards pushed and pulled the two ships toward each other.

But the decreased distance actually brought more advantage to the French. Clouds of grenades from *Aigle's* tops landed on *Bellerophon's* decks with such speed and numbers that even whole squads with damp cloths could not have extinguished more than a fraction of them. There was a continuous *pop popping* on the two aft decks of the British ship. Sailors and marines fell thick and fast like insects caught in a cyclone.

The rocket's fiery tail lit the sky with distinctive flair. The trapped acrobats looked upward.

"It's a miracle," Punch gasped.

"No, it's Pennywhistle!" shouted Judy. "Get ready; a rope or grappling hook will headed our way faster than shit through a goose."

Sure enough, a rope coursed through the air. MacFarlane's arms proved their worth yet again, and the rope flew straight and true.

Punch caught the rope's heavy end with an "Ooof!", his acrobat's strength and reflexes accomplishing a feat that few could have managed. Even though he tried to move with it, he was going to have a bruise from the impact.He grabbed Judy, pulled him close, and wrapped the rope around their waists. Punch leaned back, hoping tension on the rope would transmit that he and his mate were ready.

MacFarlane had already tossed the rope to the ten strong sailors, who gripped it in their heavily calloused hands.

Pennywhistle extended his Ramsden, saw that the two men were ready. "Pull for all you are worth!" he shouted in a voice that rippled so heavily with emotion that he barely recognized it.

The sailors gave a mighty heave and Punch and Judy shot off *Aigle's* hull like they were rockets themselves. They flew through the air and crashed hard onto the deck.

The sailors shouted cries of congratulations as they untangled the two intrepid acrobats. Even Pennywhistle's face was emblazoned with an uncharacteristically broad grin. A second later faces darkened and several men murmured, "Oh, no."

Punch was fine, but Judy was dead. A three-inch wood splinter protruded from the back of his neck. His luck had held until the last second, but in war a second could hold the difference between life and eternity.

Heavy and accurate small arms fire from the French tops drove the sailors in *Bellerophon's* tops to take cover. Five sailors had been killed, including the three best musket shots. Every time a British sailor stood to retaliate, a hail of bullets warned him of the foolhardiness of his act and he quickly plopped back down.

The best the survivors could do was lie prone and squeeze off an occasional shot to at least serve notice that the British were not quite toothless. They were downcast that their puny efforts could offer no relief to their mates on the decks below.

Cumby's face betrayed alarm as he returned from his errand. "Captain, the lower deck guns are pounding *Aigle*, but it looks like we are getting the raw end of the battle on our weather decks."

Cooke was too busy to immediately respond. He took aim with his double barrels at an enemy marksman who was targeting him and fired. A billowing wall of smoke caused the man to disappear from sight and Cooke had no idea if his rounds had hit anything; on the other hand, the same wall obscured him from the enemy's sights.

"Yes, Mr. Cumby, the situation is troubling. We need a way to reduce their advantage in numbers. I hate sending you dashing below decks again, but hard times call for risky measures. Have the crews of all of the lower deck guns remove the wheels and quoins from their pieces and elevate them at a forty-five degree angle; reduce powder charges to the minimum as well. We need to fire directly upwards into *Aigle*, killing her people not her hull."

"I concur, Captain. I also noticed *Aigle's* closing many of her gunports. There is only one reason why they would do that, Captain."

"Yes, yes, Mr. Cumby, I know. They stand a fair chance of taking our ship if they can add their gun crews to their borders. We need to hold here and push with our 32's; destroy the cannon crews before they get to *Aigle's* quarterdeck."

Cumby saluted and dashed away. The need to keep up heroic nonchalance was gone and all that mattered was getting below decks as fast as possible.

Cooke fired his double-barreled pistol again, and this time he was absolutely certain that his bullets killed a French petty officer. He handed the weapon to his servant for reloading and took up his glass.

He swept *Aigle's* decks and saw two boarding parties of roughly eighty men each forming, *Bellerophon's* quarterdeck their apparent target. The *matelots* were armed with boarding pikes and cutlasses, and many carried two grenades in bandoliers that criss-crossed their chests.

CHAPTER 28

The first French boarding party breeched *Bellerophon's* forecastle just after 1 pm. Scott ordered his sailors to use the eight-foot boarding spears to fend off the first wave, but that only worked until follow-up boarders swelled French ranks to a critical mass. Men behind simply pushed the front rank forward.

Five *matelots* fell to their deaths, impaled on the long spears, but their very falls pulled all five spears down, and a passageway opened. Frenchmen tumbled through the gap onto *Bellerophon's* decks by twos and threes.

The cascade of grenades from above had wrecked havoc on Pennywhistle's marines. All but two had fallen, dead or wounded; but Pennywhistle, Warwick, and Combs, kept firing at any warrant or petty officers they could find. A round to the head from Pennywhistle's Ferguson had killed the sole commissioned officer.

"Fall back!" yelled Scott to the sailors holding the spears. The wall was breached, and the spears were too unwieldy for close quarter fighting. The battle ahead would be fought by men packed tightly into what was essentially a rectangular box 42 feet long and 46 feet wide. The sailors dropped the spears, and a line of 15 determined British sailors opened briefly to allow their mates to pass through. The spearmen dashed to the weapons barrels and drew cutlasses, then assembled themselves into a second line of defense behind the first 15.

The air rippled with tension, yet the sailors stood with the easy, ineffable looseness that only veterans displayed. The cant of their heads, the set of their jaws, and the smoldering slow matches in their eyes warned the French that this was not their first fight, and that they were unworried by *matelots* who had never seen battle before.

They were quiet; unlike the French, who were vigorously yelling all manner of jeers and defiance. The only sounds issuing from the British side were the swishing of cutlasses moving into positions of attack and the huffing of breaths that were heavier than normal.

Their boarding helmets added to their menacing appearance, and increased their confidence that they could survive blows to the head. The French would quickly understand the helmet's function and would wonder why their own commanders had not thought of such a clever thing.

Pennywhistle noted that half the boarders were soldiers. His trained eye saw what he expected: sweating from nausea, and unsteady, wobbly legs. Seasickness was proving a British ally.

The five-foot long French Charlevilles could not be reloaded in a swirling, closely packed body of men, and the bayonets would be afforded no room for efficient use. Soldiers could block and thrust vertically with the butts of their muskets, but that was a poor use of their weapons. The army veterans would chiefly add weight of numbers to the attack, but the real danger would come from edged weapons in the hands of *matelots*.

A French sergeant, a muscular man in his forties with a ruddy complexion and deep scars, leaped to the deck of *Bellerophon* bearing a gold eagle on a pine pole. He thrust the eagle high in the air so that all of his countrymen might see and draw inspiration. *"Vive l'Empereur!"* he shouted triumphantly. He vigorously pumped the pole up.

The Eagle of the 67th Regiment was the symbol of the regiment's honor and an icon to be defended to the death. While traditionally the eagle was an army symbol, it seemed curiously appropriate, since all of the boarders came from a ship whose name meant eagle. The raptor was purposely patterned after those used by Rome's legions, and was made of bronze covered in gold leaf. It served as both an inspiration and a rally point. Eagles were presented to their respective regiments by Bonaparte himself, and served as constant reminders of his imperial glory.

The gilded raptor put Pennywhistle in mind of a portly parrot, but his artistic judgment mattered not at all. Symbols had great power in battle. Conversely, when men invest so much of their hearts in symbol, its loss can damage their morale.

The French were damn fools to risk such a thing. He felt temptation rising.

Scott signaled a question, and Pennywhistle nodded vigorously. Aggression was best; hit the boarders while they had no officer and were disorganized. "Charge!" yelled Scott.

Pennywhistle watched avidly as he reloaded. Now he would see the results of the cutlass training that he had labored so hard to devise.

The sailor's charge was no pell-mell rush, but an advance resembling a soldier's quick time. Pennywhistle had instructed each man to pick out an opponent well in advance of contact so that he would be fully on balance to strike the first deadly blow. If that was not decisive, every man possessed the full set of skills to fight an extended battle.

"You die, Crapaud!" "Fuck you, Johnny!" "Boney rot in hell!" Sailor's lungs roared to life and all manner of imprecations flew in the direction of the French. They sudden change from silence to shouted defiance startled the enemy. The boarders hesitated for only a moment, but that gave an opening to their British opponents.

The defenders stopped a foot-and-a-half in front of the boarders, a good distance for the use of their blades. The 1804 pattern Royal Navy cutlass, nicknamed "the lead cutter", had a straight, wide 29-inch blade; the variant used by *Bellerophon's* men featured a basket hilt of heavy iron that not only afforded excellent protection but made it a jaw-wrecking weapon if used to punch. Pennywhistle had emphasized that in a very close fight, a reinforced punch could be just as fatal as an energetic slash or thrust.

MacFarlane singled out a burly *matelot* with a huge mustache and a tattoo of a growling tiger on his left arm that was of a piece with the snarl on his face. The Scotsman had been trained to look for weakness and saw it now. The Frenchman held his sword too low and too far out from his chest. His balance was poor; his feet were too close together, his shoulders hunched, and his chest thrust too far forward. Before his training, MacFarlane would have missed all of that and just taken a good whack at the man's angry face.

He tightened the hempen sword knot round his wrist as well as the stout leather straps binding a Brown Bess bayonet to his left forearm. The bayonet not only enhanced his ability to block but could be used as a talon.

When the *matelot* cocked his sword arm, MacFarlane anticipated where the blow would fall. Everything seemed in slow motion as the *matelot* thrust for his right pectoral.

MacFarlane turned aside the thrust with a high outside vertical block with his sword, then ripped a deep furrow with his bayonet. The blows pushed the man's sword arm so far to the right that it left his torso defenseless. MacFarlane slashed sideways and gauged an eight inch trench just below the *matelot's* stomach. The man gasped, dropped his sword, and his hands flew to the cut, unsuccessfully trying to shove back in the grey-white intestines peeking out.

MacFarlane pivoted to avoid a heavy blow to his shoulder from a gap-toothed Frenchman. He brought his blade high and chopped down hard, severing his opponent's sword arm just below the elbow.

MacFarlane spied a Frenchman about to skewer a British sailor from the rear. He took two *quick quick* sidesteps and his blade gouged a chasm from the man's throat to his floating ribs.

Next, the Scotsman saw and stomped hard on a bare French foot to his right. The man howled in pain and instinctively bent forward toward the injury. MacFarlane only had to advance his blade a few inches to allow the man's momentum to spit him on its tip.

He smiled as he had an *Aha!* moment of understanding. All of the usually barefooted sailors on the forecastle had been required to show supervising petty officers that they sported footwear. He had donned a pair of brogans with angry reluctance. Now he was glad of their heaviness.

His peripheral vision noted his mates on both sides were employing their cutlasses to good effect: fast, economic movements of both attack and defense, making their French counterparts appear clumsy and uncertain.

Another blade shot at him from out of the crowd. He pivoted forty-five degrees at the last second and the blade missed his head by half an inch. He spun back to face the man, sidestepped, and executed a quick rake across the man's floating ribs. The man howled and dropped his sword. MacFarlane followed up with a thrust between the ribs. With no bone to block it, his blade continued unimpeded to the *matelot's* heart.

A red-haired Frenchman cut at his thigh, and he parried with a low horizontal block. Jansen on his left feinted toward the man's groin and the *matelot's* blade jumped vigorously to defend his manhood. MacFarlane redirected his blade; it ripped a gap between left and right pectorals as easily as if it had been cutting warm butter. The Frenchman gurgled and collapsed.

A short, stout *matelot* drew back his sword arm to cut at MacFarlane; the Scotsman punched him in the face. He felt the cartilage crumbling beneath his knuckles. Unconscious, the man fell back into his mate's arms.

MacFarlane felt a wild, mad contempt for death that thrilled him, though his conscience understood it was abnormal. He had no idea where the fury was coming from, but it was exactly what he needed to perform the one duty that overrode all others: kill the French. Kill them fast, kill them hard, and drive them off *Bellerophon* like a herd of frightened cattle. Don't stop until rivers of blood were all that remained of the French presence.

This would all make a fine tale to tell his brothers back in Kircaldy!

A Frenchman thrust at his right side. He executed a high outside vertical block, then elbowed the man in the Adam's apple after stomping his right foot. The man dropped his saber and his hands flew to his throat. He made pathetic, wheezing noises that would continue until asphyxiation finished him.

Two bullets whizzed near his head, but he knew from the sound that they had been at least a foot high.

Pop! Pop! Pop! Zippt!! Zipppt! Two flights of lead insects followed. One British sailor was killed, and two wounded.

Most of the boarders carried two pistols in a bandolier, and they had just discharged all of them, the volleys intended to unman and disrupt before a charge. The .69 caliber weapons were difficult to aim on a rolling deck, however, especially while being jostled by closely packed fellow *matelots*. To avoid hitting friends, all of the Frenchmen had aimed their shots at British heads but forgot to allow for the rise of the ball; most rounds met empty air or miscellaneous bits of rigging. The shots mainly just added to the choking clouds of smoke and ear-shattering noise; sowing confusion that benefitted neither side.

Throwing grenades with friend and foe so tightly packed was insane, but battle itself was insanity and played havoc with judgment. One French sailor had just ignited a fuse when a bullet shattered his upper arm. He dropped the projectile like a hot coal. It exploded at his feet and shards of metal pelted his groin, gelding him.

Combs smiled. Four grenadiers hit so far. He had also killed a sailor with a battering ram, since Mr. Pennywhistle warned him of the special danger of carpenter's mates.

Combs and Warwick kept targeting potential grenade throwers throughout the sword fight. The two marines had loaded most of the spare muskets in the weapons chest just before the forecastle battle commenced and laid them just astern of their firing positions, giving each man ten muskets ready for use.

As soon as a musket was discharged, it was passed to one of four powder monkeys in the rear for reloading. The efficient weapons delivery system meant that the two marines kept up a steady volume of skilled fire that was almost the equivalent of a full squad.

Soldiers at the back of the crowd of boarders were pressing everyone forward, but were having no luck at all bringing their long muskets to the horizontal so that their bayonets could be utilized. They were fiercely shouting *"Vive l'Empereur"* at the tops of their lungs while elbowing and shoving vigorously. *Matelots* yelled at them to stop pushing; their yells of protests only contributed to an air of general chaos. French soldiers and sailors fought very differently, and the limited time spent in each other's company had not been   enough to devise any semblance of teamwork. Together they were a predatory animal with one instinct but two brains.

OneFrench corporal found an opening in the screaming whirlpool of humanity and managed to stumble to the front. He reversed his musket and stabbed downward at a sailor, like a harpooner aiming at a whale. To his surprise, the British seaman parried the bayonet, then thrust his cutlass into the man's thigh. With the femoral artery pierced, a geyser of blood shot skyward and color drained rapidly from the soldier's face as energy departed his limbs.

The soldiers continued shoving. The congestion increased with newly arriving boarders, and it became increasingly difficult to do much other than make short jabs with the edged weapons. The range was close enough that backup knives and dirks were drawn on both sides; nasty weapons at eyeball-to eyeball range. Men were wounded and killed, but no bodies reached the deck because the press kept them upright.

MacFarlane pulled out a midshipman's dirk that he had won in a card game and shoved it into the underside of a *matelot's* jaw. He continued pushing until it pierced the Frenchman's brain.

A feeling like the crisis in a play flooded the air. This emotional storm front did not pass, but instead became stationary and taut. It drove both sides into a killing frenzy. Men who are jammed together and feel they have nowhere to retreat will always fight harder than men who feel they have a way out. Men not only slashed with steel but punched and kicked. A few even buried their teeth in sword arms when one passed close.

Everything became simple and primal: one side wanted to hold the deck; the other wanted to sweep it clear. The battle had a life of its own; a writhing, formless creature that infected everything it touched with madness and terror like some martial version of rabies. It defied any human agency to bring it under control; it was every man for himself.

At least it was on the French side; every British sailor remembered to protect the man on his right. Even in the midst of insanity, trained muscles remembered, even if minds went blank.

British skill with blades had enabled the *Bellerophon's* crew to hold their own far longer than ordinary sailors, but now numbers were beginning to tell, and they were slowly being pushed back. The Britons were wearing out. The French sailors, though greater in numbers, were in no better shape: the seasick soldiers were pictures of misery.

Pennywhistle continued firing his Ferguson, picking off men whose faces and postures indicated the strong will necessary to swing a battle their way. His philosophy was brutally simple: slay the best men and let fear infect the rest. It took all of his willpower to resist the urge to dash into the fray with his Osborn, but he needed to restrain his passions and keep a clear head for the counterstroke ahead.

"Mr. Pennywhistle, Mr. Pennywhistle!" Fourteen-year-old Midshipman Charles Barrows dashed toward the marine, likely with a message from the Captain. Pennywhistle appreciated the lad's keen intelligence and considered him a youthful friend.

"Mr. Pennyw—" Barrow's head was suddenly enveloped in a dark cloud of canister. When the cloud cleared, Barrow still stood, but his lower jaw was gone and bone, tongue, and teeth had fused together in an awful parody of a face. He looked to be trying to speak and seemed puzzled that no words came forth.

Bile rose in Pennywhistle's throat; he knew that the boy would die a lingering death from malnutrition, but he forced it down and commanded himself to focus only on things that he could affect.

Scott dashed over for a consultation with Pennywhistle. Both agreed it was time for the secret weapon. Pennywhistle mentioned the additional refinement, and Scott smiled coldly at the idea. Robinson's whistle would be used to sound the retreat. The spare muskets were loaded and ready. Sailors had nothing like the musketry skill of marines, but at such close range they could do the job just fine. "Mr. Scott, three minutes, and then give the order. "

"Sounds about right, Mr. Pennywhistle."

Both men took out their watches and looked at the second hands. "Three minutes from... now!" said Pennywhistle, unable to keep the thrill out of his voice. Both men dashed to their agreed-upon positions.

Scott alerted Robinson, who took out his whistle.

Pennywhistle spoke urgently to Combs and Warwick. "I have only one chance to make this work. My life depends on your following my instructions precisely."

But the next three minutes did not work out as expected. As Bonaparte repeatedly warned his own troops, the best laid plans vanished in the first minutes of battle. The chasm between design and execution defies all expectation, and so it proved with Pennywhistle's plan.

CHAPTER 29

He did not hear the footfalls astern because of the deafening noise, but a slight alteration in the air pressure caused his intuition to apprehend movement. He spun round and confronted four French sailors with expressions that mixed anger, contempt, and brutality in equal parts.

All bore scorpion tattoos on their right forearms that he recognized as hallmarks of The Brotherhood of the Violet Scorpion, a vicious gang that had plagued the Marseilles docks for years. He gathered that these men had been captured and had preferred service at sea to the censure of Mademoiselle Guillotine.

Their faces and postures were those of hell raisers, men who delighted in killing a gentleman simply because they hated anything resembling an aristocrat. Their expressions turned mocking; clearly they considered Pennywhistle someone who would be amusing to slay—unless they decided he was more valuable as a prisoner to be ransomed.

Pennywhistle looked behind them to make sure that they had not brought additional friends. They had not. Looking up, he deduced they had used grapnels and ropes to swing from *Aisle's* main yard to *Bellerophon's* foreyard, then stealthily descended the rat lines. They must have crossed at a moment when the lookouts in *Bellerophon's* foretop were distracted by gunfire or blinded by smoke.

He was damned if he would be outmatched by nasty brigands who had happened to find shelter under the benevolent flag of the French Navy.

"*Rendez-vous, damnés rat!*" demanded the tall one, whose ugly face featured a lively competition between smallpox pits and ditches gouged by cheap knives. His posture suggested that he was the lead male in a pack of vicious dogs.

Despite the thunderous noise, Pennywhistle heard the demand clearly. His hearing underwent a sudden increase in acuity as his body prioritized its defenses and boosted his brain's capacity to filter and interpret noise. The ragged *matelot's* ignorant patois was as offensive as his choice of words.

The lead Frenchman waved his blade menacingly, as did his three friends. He evidently expected a sensible—or terrified—gentleman to yield. His narrowed eyes suggested that he wished to bring home a live prize, for probably no better reason than the reward of a large tot of rum, but not before his prize was subjected to a few degrading kicks and punches.

Pennywhistle startled them by smiling and responding in perfect Versailles French. "I might be willing to accommodate your request, monsieur." He executed a bow that was as correct as it was mocking. "It is just that I believe you have a pressing engagement"—his voice dropped an octave, turning as hard and cold as granite—"in hell!"

He whirled his Ferguson from his shoulder, brought it to the point and discharged it. The rapidly spinning .615 ball ploughed into the tall Frenchmen's shocked face and ballooned upon impact. A shower of blood and gore splattered his mates like a crimson thunderstorm.

The shock froze the remaining sailors. In that interval, Pennywhistle thrust his rifle to the deck, whipped out his cutlass, twirled the sword knot round his wrist, and lunged.

The straight line thrust pierced the heart of a pig-faced *matelot*. As the man sagged, Pennywhistle yanked the blade free to pivot on his left heel and swung his blade in a fast, hard slash at the sailor who stood to his right.

The man's evil harlequin face froze in terror as the Osborn ripped a deep canyon from his right shoulder to his groin. His blood spattered Pennywhistle, adding to the gore on his scarlet jacket. The expensive garment had absolutely no future.

The remaining sailor cut at his face with more quickness than skill. Pennywhistle parried the blow and ended the man's life with a particularly violent slash that carved a second mouth two inches above the original.

A *matelot* charged Pennywhistle headlong. Pennywhistle sidestepped at the last second and the man shot past like a rocket, the back of his neck conveniently exposed. The Osborn's edge sliced through and lifted his head off so smoothly Pennywhistle's arm scarcely felt the resistance.

The sailor's body continued a few steps before it collapsed. The kinetic energy of the wayward head caused it to bounce several times before coming to rest directly in front of Warwick. He blinked in surprise. "Well, Marty, that's one less Johnny to worry about!"

Combs nodded. "Makes our job that much easier."

The time for the counterstroke was almost upon Pennywhistle, but just then he was shoved aside by jostling fighters and fell to the deck. The fall saved his life. Cold steel whizzed through the space where his head had been a second ago. Rolling, he turned and saw one boot of the blade's owner lay within reach.

He drew his dirk from his own boot and stabbed down hard through the stranger's toe. A scream rent the air as the enemy boot mated itself to the deck. Pennywhistle grasped the Osborn and corkscrewed to his feet, happy that he would face a stationary target.

Damn! It was just a boy, maybe a dozen years old: an over-eager powder monkey who had followed the Frenchmen, probably without their knowledge. The boy held a pattern 1780 hanger far too big for him in a shaking hand. He was fighting back tears and trying to look fierce.

Pennywhistle could not do it. The boy was no warrior, though his conduct said he longed to be one. He admired the boy's courage, and it seemed unfair that he should die for it. His death would make no difference in the battle's final outcome, but it would make a great one in whether he ever slept again with a clear conscience. Truly, the quality of mercy was not strained.

He extracted the dirk and the boy gave a slight yelp. The wound was painful but not serious: the boy could walk. The marine inserted the dirk back in his boot and looked the frightened lad directly in the eye. His French words were brutal but his tone kind. "Go back to your ship. You are a child trying to do a man's job. If you pull such a foolish stunt again, the next British officer you meet will cut you down without a second thought. *Comprenez-vous?*"

"Oui, oui, monsieur." The boy's look of gratitude was the best repayment Pennywhistle could have asked for.

"Now be off with you!"

The boy darted off like a frightened mouse. Pennywhistle followed him with his eyes until he reached the foremast ratlines. The boy waved at him, then began the long climb upwards.

Pennywhistle's act of clemency had distracted him at a critical moment. Turning, he saw a sight that made him blanch.

"Reed, you got any goddamned idea what you are doing?"

"No, but I shoved plenty of stuff inside and know that if I pull this here lanyard, all hell is about to rain down on somebody!" Reed's hand was scant seconds away from discharging the piece.

Pennywhistle wanted to scream a warning, but the landsmen were facing away from him and the tremendous noise of battle made shouts seem whispers.

Pennywhistle looked in horror at the ranks of closely packed men, British and French, in the path of the carronade, and his fear spawned inspiration. If his own people could be made to duck, and if the carronade blast was even marginally accurate, the French would suffer far more than the British.

Luck came to his aid in the form of Robinson, who nearly bumped into Pennywhistle.

He grabbed the startled man forcibly by the collar. "Blow the command 'All hands down' as loud as you can. Immediately!" Robinson looked shocked, but did just that.

The high, trilling notes pierced the noise like a soprano rising above a chorus of bass singers. Training compelled obedience; sailors and marines hit the deck even as Reed yanked the lanyard.

The huge stirring of air caused by the grossly overloaded 32-pounder's recoil knocked Britt and Reed backwards as if they had been slapped hard.

They were too ill-trained to know that the four rounds of canister that they had shoved in the gun and the six charges that they had crammed in to power them should have exploded the barrel. Yet such were the skills of the Falkirk engineers who built the weapon that the barrel remained intact, and the massive blast of metal hit the roiling mass of *matelots* and soldiers dead center.

"If that don't bear all!" said Britt.

"Everyone back home will think I am telling a tall tale," said Reed.

The blast vaporized a good many of the French boarders and crushed most of the rest into a gigantic, shapeless blob of red and blue, smoldering at its edges. A few things vaguely recognizable as legs jerked spasmodically. The few who were unscathed stood aghast. One of them was the Eagle bearer, but he had only one bewildered soldier alongside to aid him in the standard's protection.

Most of the prone British sailors were paralyzed from a mix of shock, fear, and concussion; a few were limp with relief; none of them would be any good to anyone for the next few minutes. They would not be able to retire and provide covering fire, as Pennywhistle intended, but because the surviving Frenchmen displayed equal shock that might be unnecessary.

Luck and preparedness gave Pennywhistle one perfect moment before reinforcements arrived and what was left of the French recovered their wits. He could make a dash for 67th's Eagle, but seizing such a prize was useless if it could not be brought back. Frenchmen might dispute its loss with vigor, and he needed something to trump that. His initial design had relied upon an anchor of a kind.

He raced over to Combs and Warwick. Thank God, they had not been unmanned by the blast, and they remembered his earlier instructions. "Dump the barrel in thirty seconds. I know you lack watches, but counting 1000, 1001, etc. will be close enough. Once I have the Eagle, unravel the rope from the bitt and pull me in with every ounce of strength you have. And just in case, have a couple of loaded muskets ready."

Warwick flashed the hand signal for "I understand."

Pennywhistle raced to bitts nearest the foremast. He picked up a severed rope and wound one end around his waist. He calculated the amount of slack necessary for his short journey, then tied the other end round the nearest bitt with a bowline knot. He tugged at his waist; the rope's grip was secure. He checked his watch. Ten seconds! He snapped it shut and shoved it back in his pocket.

He counted the last few seconds under his breath. "Four, three, two, one!" Warwick and Combs were right on time and spilled the barrel of thick cooking grease. The buff-colored sludge engulfed the forward third of the forecastle.

The decks were sanded, but the movement of many feet meant that the remaining coat of sand was thin. The thick ooze formed a top layer that was as slick as ice even if considerably more messy, rendering the surface congenial to a human sled.

The dazed Eagle bearer and his helper tried to retreat, but the sludge engulfed their feet. They slipped, and what would have been crashing fall was more of a *splat!*

Pennywhistle aligned his body on a direct heading with the Eagle bearer and threw himself forward and down on the slicked deck, like a human arrowhead. He shot forward far faster than anticipated and crashed into the Eagle bearer's side so hard that he drove the sergeant's breath from his lungs with a loud *"Ooommpph!"*

The sergeant was dazed, but his grip on the shaft was one of iron. Pennywhistle tried to pry it loose with all of his considerable strength, but with no success. He had no time for a battle of endurance, since he could hear shouts from French reinforcements growing louder by the second.

The sergeant rolled back to face him, fire and hatred in his eyes; a zealot defending a holy relic. The sergeant was naturally strong, but fanatics often summoned reserves of strength that made them seem superhuman, and that was true now. Pennywhistle met his blazing eyes. He respected such a man, but that respect could not be allowed to compromise his duty.

The boot dirk came easily to his hand and he shoved it up under the man's chin, ramming it mercilessly into his brain. The man's hard eyes blinked in surprise, then the light went out like someone had snuffed a candle.

Pennywhistle gasped in revulsion. This was death at its most personal; eyeball-to-eyeball with a man making the transition from living being to corpse with no banners, drums, or cheering men to adulterate the sheer indignity of the conversion. He had wondered what battle was like, and he had just received an answer that he would never forget. He would see those dying eyes many times in future dreams.

A fist striking him in the cheek recalled his training. *Savate* took over, and Pennywhistle batted aside the next punch, then tensed his own right hand into a spade. His brine-hardened finger tips were like an iron wedge that dug hard into the man's right eye socket. The man screamed in agony and his hands flew to his face.

The first rule of s*avate* was that a man who could not see could not fight. Since this man posed no further threat, Pennywhistle could show him mercy. A man with one eye might still enjoy a life.

Pennywhistle grabbed the eagle pole and held it close to his chest. The bird looked cheap and tawdry up close. He flashed a quick hand signal. Combs and Warwick heaved on the rope.

The combined pull of their heavily muscled forearms lifted him up a full foot from the deck and he flew through the air, landing hard with an utter lack of dignity and a complete loss of breath.

His back hurt and he felt as if he had just been run through a clothes wringer. He hoisted himself slowly to his feet and briefly contemplated his prize: a mere piece of wood and gilt.

"You did it, sir," said Warwick, clearly in awe.

"I will tell my grandchildren about this," said Combs with pride.

Pennywhistle looked back whence he came and saw that the French were not yet ready to quit.

Loud of cries of *"Merde, merde, merde!"* rose from at least twenty French on *Aigle*. They began to shove forward in anger and defiance, intending to make violent amends by recovering something that only the Emperor could bestow.

It was then that Lady Luck chose to make a terrible intervention. A flaming wad from one of *Aigle's* cannons landed atop the sludge covering the forecastle and ignited it. A hot grease fire roared into life. Men barely alive screamed in terror as flames engulfed them. Others, unwounded, knew that it was mere seconds before they suffered a similar fate. The primal fear of fire united both French and British sailors in terror as they tried to crawl away or pull themselves upright.

Pennywhistle watched in revulsion as his bright idea became bright in an awful way. He had indirectly brought about the thing most feared in wooden ships at sea. Vomit rose in his throat.

But Lady Luck attracted an opponent called Providence. A 36-pound solid shot flying through the air smashed two large barrels of sand into kindling. The barrels had been left in front of the foremast because Cooke had thought the battle might be very bloody one. The large cloud of sand that swirled through the air came to rest directly on the blossoming fire, suffocating the blaze.

The whole sequence from the start of the fire to its extinction occupied less than ten seconds; nevertheless, ten men burned to death, three of them British. Several more had burns over half of their bodies and likely would not survive the night. Still, were it not for the sand, the fire would doubtless have spread to consume the rest of *Bellerophon*.

There was absolute silence after the fire went out, as men considered the awful *what might have been*. Then a recall bugle sounded on *Aigle* and the French began crawling back whence they came. The British were too tired and shocked to cheer.

The law of unintended consequences had saved the British. The French were not easily deterred, yet fire, it seemed to Pennywhistle, had paradoxically chilled the resolve of brave men in a way that bullets and bayonets had not. No, he needed to be sure.

He unshipped his Ramsden and swept *Aigle's* Deck. *Damn!* The recall was sounded because the French were massing for an even greater attack on *Bellerophon's* quarterdeck and needed every spare man for the effort.

There was on odd cessation of sound as well. What was it? Of course! Most of the 36-pounders on *Aigle's* lower deck had stopped firing. The French were losing the battle of the big guns and had probably decided to use the lower deck gun crews to beef up the boarding parties.

Pennywhistle again swept *Aigle's* deck and saw an extraordinarily large boarding party. More were joining it each second. He needed to round up the survivors and speed them to the quarterdeck as fast as possible.

A visibly shaken Scott shuffled up to him as if his feet were made of concrete. "Horrible, just horrible, Mr. Pennywhistle. Seeing men die like that..." His face went white and he bent violently over as his stomach heaved.

He wiped his mouth with a silver silk handkerchief and spoke with embarrassment. "Damn sorry about that, Mr. Pennywhistle. Won't happen again. I promise."

"Already forgotten, Mr. Scott. I came deuced close to something similar myself. The important thing is we finish the job that we have started here. The forecastle was the soup: the meat course is the quarterdeck. It is there we must direct our attentions."

CHAPTER 30

Young Lieutenant Higgins felt overwhelmed. Nothing in his experience had prepared him for this all-out assault on his eyes, his ears, and his very soul. His fingers felt clumsy and oafish. He unsteadily fired off both of his pistols. Ten feet was the limit for smoothbore pistols and his targets were at least fifty feet away, so both rounds were clean misses. He threw the pistols away in disgust, realizing that Mr. Pennywhistle had been right about their limited utility.

Aigle had lost her foretop, maintop, and mizzen top masts, to Higgins it seemed as if some gigantic, invisible lumberjack had decided to practice his trade at sea. The fallen masts reversed *Aigle's* drift, pushing her stern toward *Bellerophon's* stern instead of toward her bow. The damage gave Higgins hope that British gunnery on the lower decks might still decide the battle.

His men were falling fast as leaves in an autumn wind and the storm of iron showed no signs of abating. The marines had been firing almost continuously since the battle began and they were definitely doing some good, just not enough good.

His marines were laying down covering fire on behalf of the sailors now repelling a very energetic French boarding attempt. He could see that the volleys of his Marines were at least hampering efforts of the French to swell the numbers of the boarding parties. It frustrated him that the splendid efforts of his marines could only play a supporting role.

A second later he heard shouts that induced sheer terror. "Fire! Fire! Fire!" No more frightening words could be spoken on a wooden ship crowded with miles of greased and tarred ropes. The main t' gallant and mainsail from *Aigle's* fallen mast were blocking the gun ports of *Bellerophon's* upper gun deck, and a flaming wad from one of the cannons had ignited them.

Cooke's insistence on rigorous training saved the ship. Rather than panicking, the sailors designated as firemen raced to the hoses on deck. They quickly formed themselves into a line, lifted the long hose, and shook it vigorously. A ripple coursed along its entire length to the men at the pumps, who began pumping with all the strength they could muster.

A powerful jet of water spurted from the end of the hose. It was sprayed back and forth on the burning sails until the blaze was extinguished. Then the men designated as cutters sprang into action.

The cutters chopped with vigor, but it took a full five minutes to rid *Bellerophon* of the intruder's sails. The upper gun deck had to cease firing during that time, so French sailors firing through open gun ports focused their attention on the cutters. That only two cutters were hit was not due to bad marksmanship but smoke. It was hard to see much of anything for more than a second or two.

Higgins' relief turned back to anxiety when he heard a sharp crack and Bellerophon's main t'gallant went over the side.

Cooke looked up in dismay, but there was nothing to be done. At least the sails were not blocking any guns. Cutting them away would have to wait. Manpower was so depleted on the weather decks that he had funneled all of the remaining cutters into the parties now repelling boarders.

One of his servants handed him his reloaded pistol, and Cooke nodded in acknowledgement. His sword remained sheathed, which was a good thing; no enemy had ventured close enough to require its employment.

Wilson could not understand why he remained alive. He should have been dead twenty times over. Right now he was so terrified that his legs simply would not move, though he had never wanted to run so badly in his life. He stood tall and immobile, at least giving the appearance of good officer-like conduct.

Wilson's anxiety was morphing to panic. He had survived the first encounter with the enemy without overtly disgracing himself, but the current onslaught of concentrated fire from the bulwarks and tops of *Aigle* made that outing seem a Kew Garden picnic. *Bellerophon* was under cannon fire from three ships: *Montañés*, *Monarcha*, and *Swiftsure*. The intermittent roaring sounded like eruptions of a continent full of angry volcanoes, and the billowing thunderheads of smoke made it seem as if all the forges on the planet had exported the sum of their airborne effluvia to one four square mile rectangle.

But rather than cannon balls, it was the grenades from *Aigle* that were doing the principal damage. They were slapping *Bellerophon's* decks like giant hailstones, and there was a constant *pop popping* as they detonated.

The accompanying *zippt zippt zippt* of musketry from soldiers lining the enemy bulwarks made Wilson think that he was standing in the path of hundreds of angry hornets. Several puffs of air pressure battered his cheeks and it was only by a miracle supplied by a prankster God that prevented his bladder from venting itself.

A marine next to him was pierced by a splinter to the face, and a second a few feet away absorbed a grenade fragment in the left thigh and lost his balance. The quarterdeck was littered with broken men screaming, groaning, and crying as they tried to limp, crawl, or roll, to a place of imagined safety that did not exist. Several flopped about like beached fish and gasped madly for air.

"Stand fast! Stand fast!" yelled Cumby. Higgins echoed his cry in his reedy voice and added, "Briton's never yield!" Wilson wanted to scream from fear anyway and this gave him an excuse, as long as what came out sounded vaguely heroic. He could only think of the damn fool who got him into this mess. "Remember Nelson!" he shouted. To his complete surprise, that man's name elicited a hoarse cheer, with even a few of the wounded joining in.

A French 16-pound cannon ball blasted forth from *Aigle*'s quarterdeck. Starting life in 1798 at the Armory of St Etienne, it been loaded aboard *Aigle* at Rochfort in 1800. Propelled by four pounds of powder, the hurtling ball accelerated to 1,500 feet per second. It punched through *Bellerophon*'s bulwarks, generating four large wooden splinters which killed two, then glanced off a nine pounder, dismounting the barrel and killing the gun captain. Slowed somewhat, it hit the deck and bounced once.

The second bounce would have taken off Wilson's head, but for carelessness on the part of a powder monkey. The ball landed on a stray wet mop, which absorbed enough energy to deflect it slightly. It missed caving in Wilson's head, but it left a bruise on his cheek.

Wilson shuddered as he touched his hand to his face. He swore that if he outlived this day, he would resign his commission as soon as the ship made port. It had been three years since the breach of promise suit, and matters had probably cooled off in Scotland. Even if they had not, the loss of fortune seemed a lot less frightening than forfeiture of his life.

As the casualties increased, the marines on the quarterdeck gradually withdrew toward the ship's wheel and formed themselves into blocks of ever decreasing size. Only ten marines remained standing, and Wilson felt like they were ducks in red conveniently grouped for hunters to take pot shots at. The marines were so well trained that they reloaded without prompting and he merely give the command "Fire!" at regular intervals.

His knees started to shake slightly, and he knew that would soon become noticeable. It was time to go.

In times of great stress, a man reverts to his basic nature and the fundamental configuration that experience has impressed upon that nature. Wilson had a gambler's gift for mathematical calculation and knew that if he had been in a card game, it would be time to cash out. The card deck of his life was as cold as the quarterdeck was hot. The odds against survival would continue to get worse until they became none at all.

Inspiration hit him when he saw a private's open cartridge box. The marines were down to five rounds from forty, and the reserve ammunition had been destroyed. Someone needed to bring spare cartridges up from the magazine. He did not have to play until the deck was done; he just had to outplay the man next to him. That man was Higgins.

"Mr. Higgins, "he said breathlessly, "we are almost out of ammunition. We cannot spare a marine and his musket in this great contest, so I take it upon myself to bring more from the magazine. I am reluctant to forego even a single second that could bring me honor, but this job needs to be done." The magazine would provide him the stoutest protection in the ship.

Several more musket balls whistled by his head, reminding him that the French certainly were not out of ammunition.

Gunner Stevenson might be a problem. He was a man fundamentally opposed to any kind of gambling and he was a stickler for protocols, because he routinely dealt with materials that could destroy a ship. He would ask a lot of unwanted questions, but a good bluff in the form of aristocratic hauteur and some blather about honor and necessity would make him play Wilson's game rather than the other way round.

Higgins was entirely focused on the battle and it took a few seconds before Wilson's words sank in. Several bullets whizzed by his face before he spoke. "Uh, uh, cartridges, yes. By God, sir, you are right! We will need more!"

Wilson's luck was in; the impressionable Higgins put the best possible face on Wilson's action. "Go, sir, go! I can handle things here. Ask Mr. Saunders if he can spare a few marines from his crews. We need reinforcements!"

There was a huge cracking sound and the fore t'gallant mast slowly toppled over the port side, causing a second disaster. The foretop mast wavered, then joined its mate in a journey over the port side. All that remained of the ship's masts were three tall stumps, slightly more than half the size of the masts that had propelled her into the battle.

"Right, Mr. Higgins. I am counting on you!" And so he was, but for more than Higgins could know.

The marine rankers looked skeptical, but did a quick check of their cartridge boxes and reluctantly conceded Wilson's point. A musket would be missed, but an officer flashing a sword would not.

CHAPTER 31

Wilson wanted to flat out run, but that would be inconsistent with the part he needed to play. He instead walked briskly, though the sound of bee swarms close to his ears tested his willpower.

Cumby saw him go and was puzzled. Officers with all limbs intact limb did not generally exit a hot quarterdeck unless carried off. He shouted to Higgins, "Where has Mr. Wilson gone?"

"Cartridges, sir! Reinforcements, too!"

Cumby wondered why an enlisted man had not been sent, but decided that an officer was probably better fixed to correctly estimate the number of rounds needed dismissed Wilson from his mind. The curious actions of a single red-coated officer were of small moment when his ship was in imminent danger of capture.

Dale also saw Wilson go. He scowled and snarled under his breath, "Son of a bitch!" *I have to help a wounded friend, carry a vital message, get more ammunition.* Dale knew every excuse used by rankers to run, but he had never seen an officer employ one.

Pennywhistle would never have permitted such an action, but young Mr. Higgins had clearly been played. He naïvely believed that a fellow officer would seek honor as instinctively as a woodpecker sought wood.

Wilson raced down the companionway, deftly avoiding the functionaries who were headed to the weather decks. Fear gave a man surprising agility. It became harder to see as he descended the decks, since the only pale light came from small swinging lanterns that cast brooding shadows. His mood lightened as he descended: each step bringing him a little closer to the safety of the aft magazine.

It also got smokier and smokier as he went downward. The booming 18-pounders on the upper gun deck made his ears feel as if they were being pounded with cricket bats, and their collective recoils gave his feet the impression they were dancing during an earthquake. The heat from the guns caused him to sweat as heavily as if he had been in a Turkish bath. The gun barrels themselves sizzled. The heat from repeated discharges had amplified gun recoils so strongly that the guns sometimes jumped high enough to collide with overhanging deck beams.

He could not see more than five feet in front of him and extended both arms as he tried to find a path through the smoke. He proceeded with the deliberate pace of a toddler taking his first tentative steps.

The smoke parted for a brief instant and he saw that *Bellerophon* was so close to the *Aigle* that the barrels of their run-out cannons nearly touched. He could see some *matelots* through the open gun ports, shouting all manner of exhortations and imprecations, though he could not distinguish words above the ear-crushing noise. Some of the French gunports were closed, indicating a gun was out of action or the crew had given up. It wasn't just cannon or shot the damned French were unleashing; grenades issued from the still open gun ports and seemed to be killing quite as many men as the splinters or cannon balls.

One grenade exploded three feet away, felling five men of a gun crew. Wilson feared that he would see the damn sight in his dreams for years to come. He felt heat on the third finger of his left hand: the ruby in his ring suddenly seemed a facsimile of a grenade, and he could have sworn it emitted a brief burst of luminescence.

Another grenade exploded and peppered the shoulder of a loader with red-hot shards. The man screamed and batted madly at his back. A second later he jumped out the gun port, hoping that the sea would provide relief from the pain.

A *matelot* raised his pistol and Wilson grimaced, knowing he was the target. But then a wad of goo hit the *matelot* in the eye and his shot went wild. Jobu screamed and capered with delight as he continued hurling clods of his own feces.

The situation Wilson met on the gun deck below was even worse. The noise and smoke from the giant 32s made their 18-pound cousins seem mere ordnance adolescents. There was no coordinated broadside; the guns were fired at will, each gun crew trusting to the judgment of their gun captain. Wilson estimated that each gun was being discharged about every four minutes, owing both to fatigue and a reduction in the size of crews from casualties.

The French guns were also firing sporadically, perhaps one shot every eight minutes. At least half of their gun ports were closed and many of the open ones displayed cannon in various states of disrepair. It seemed as if many of their crews had abandoned them in favor of tossing grenades.

Wilson jumped as two of the cursed globes bounced past his feet. Lady Luck still favored him, and they exploded against a nearby bulkhead. He increased his pace and started down the companionway to the magazine on the deck below.

He heaved a sigh of relief when he reached the bottom, thinking that he was safe at last. He started toward the magazine; the door was open to allow passage to gunner's mates bearing cartridges. Stevenson stepped out to speak to one of them. He looked startled, then puzzled, when his eyes alighted on Wilson.

"Mr. Wilson, I am surprised to see you here. I gather some emergency has arisen on the quarterdeck that compels you to depart from your usual duties. Is it some technical question whose answer only I can give?"

There was suspicion in Stevenson's voice. He had served at the Nile, and Wilson feared that he knew a coward when he saw one. Wilson's explanation suddenly seemed lame. His bluff had just been called: an officer was supposed to command, not function as an errand boy or a two-legged pack horse.

Wilson maintained the noncommittal expression that he used when he received a bad hand in a card game. Time to raise or call; he struggled to think of a convincing riposte. Then he heard a hissing sound, followed by a series of slow thuds. His heart froze, because he knew exactly what it was. Stevenson and his mates turned white; they knew, too.

A grenade had bounced off the lower gun deck through some odd combination of ricochet and excess kinetic energy. Gravity was causing it to *thud thud thud* down the companionway steps like the dread gait of some approaching ogre, delivering doom.

Wilson heard it land behind his feet. It rolled in front of him and its trajectory would take it directly into the powder magazine. His life flashed before him. The complete, total, and absolute annihilation of *Bellerophon* was spinning at his feet.

Wilson's ring seemed to glow for a brief second, and he acted with a lightning speed that he did not know he possessed. He snatched up the ominous orb before it rolled out of range. He frantically beat at its fuse with the expensive kid glove on his left hand. The glove singed and darkened, but the fuse died. It had been survival instinct, not courage, but Stevenson and his mates in the narrow corridor stared at him like he was some kind of hero.

He was so startled at being regarded as the ship's savior that the incipient shaking of his hands and legs died as completely as the grenade's fuse. The irony of the situation was not lost on him. He had sought safety from the showers of grenades on the quarterdeck, but his flight had put him in the greatest peril imaginable. His avoidance of a personal appointment in Samara had just spared the 1,300 souls, on two ships from the same dread rendezvous, for had *Bellerophon* exploded, *Aigle*'s proximity would have doomed that ship as well.

He laughed; softly at first, then harder with each passing second. His laughter strengthened as he saw Stevenson and his mates looking at him with something like awe. They actually thought he was laughing at danger.

Suddenly his request for cartridges seemed entirely reasonable: a man who had saved a ship could never in a million years be thought to have a cowardly bone in his body. His perceived courage had just given him an ace in the hole. He called his considerable acting talents to the fore: time to be the modest paladin of virtue.

"Mr. Stevenson," he said with the perfect aplomb of a gambler accustomed to being a gracious winner, "I am glad I was on hand to render some small assistance, but I cannot be long from the quarterdeck. I am in great need of cartridges, since my marines are nearly out of them. I would rather die than see their efforts hampered by a lack of ammunition."

That was all a pack of nonsense of course, but it was very, very gallant nonsense. Stevenson was normally terse and stern, but his faced beamed with admiration and his voice became almost obsequious. "I quite understand, Mr. Wilson."

Stevenson and his mates quickly packed an ammunition chest with enough rounds to sustain an entire half-battalion of marines. Strangely, Wilson felt an urgent need to get the additional rounds to the quarterdeck. He had done something undeniably heroic. He was not planning on any future feats of daring, yet it warmed his cold heart that his conduct had benefitted the very men he frequently disparaged.

He looked at his ring and it was as always: exotic, striking, and exquisitely crafted; furnishing no evidence whatsoever of supernatural properties. The legend promised luck or death to its possessor. Did that mean death was the outcome if the ring's warnings went unheeded? He *had* reacted with a swiftness that was almost unnatural.

Mysticism was beyond Wilson, but he understood luck. The belief in luck was part of the unacknowledged contradiction that gave accomplished gamblers the will to risk what the casual gambler would not. "Trust Allah, but tether your camel," an old Arab trader had told him in Ceuta; the ring would stay firmly tethered to his finger for the remainder of the battle.

He was so caught up in rejoicing over his survival that he nearly forgot the second part of his mission. Almost as an afterthought, he said to the Gunner, "I am badly needed up top. Please convey an urgent message to Mr. Saunders that we are in dire need of some of his Marine gunners as reinforcements."

"I will move heaven and earth to make certain that your message is received and understood, Mr. Wilson," said Stevenson with the greatest respect.

CHAPTER 32

Wemyss' return to consciousness was gradual. He felt like he was at the bottom of a murky lake slowly swimming upwards towards a weed-choked surface. Shapes and sizes of objects seemed weirdly distorted, and people's faces were grotesque masks straight out of some ancient and vicious fertility cult.

The deep thudding of cannon made the planks under his back vibrate so hard that he felt like the deck was being torn apart by inhuman hands. A low moaning echoed off the cramped bulkheads as if the ship herself were wounded. The noises told him that the ship was still very heavily engaged and that casualties were severe.

The air reeked of vomit, urine, excrement, blood, and fear. The air was so hot and stale that it seemed as if it had not been fresh for many centuries. For a second he thought himself in Hell, but realized that a ghost did not draw breath. His tattered scarlet coat smelled as if it had been marinated in a pot of ammonia, and his white trousers as if they had been dragged through a field of cow pies.

Strangely, he felt euphoric, though he had no idea why, considering that his head throbbed as if it were being hit by a boulder every few seconds. His vision was slightly blurred but his hearing seemed unusually acute. He slowly sat up and was only a little unsteady.

There was no trace of the tearing cough that had plagued him the past few weeks.

His memories of the past few hours returned in a flood, and he realized he had been taken to the cockpit to die. So far, Death's outriders were slacking off. He still had some fight in him, and decided that he might have a good hour before he exited this vale of tears.

The cockpit was so jammed with sweating, coughing, mewling, powder-caked bodies that no one paid any attention to him. There was a long line of men awaiting the surgeon's knives and, unlike himself, some of them could be helped.

All of the alcohol that he had consumed was likely masking the pain, and that was a good thing. He would simply will his legs to take him to the quarterdeck. He was in no fit shape to command, but he could still do something with a gun or a sword.

He hoisted himself unsteadily to his feet and leaned against the port bulkhead. A second later he shoved himself away from the bulkhead like a ship launched from a slip and took a few lurching, uncertain steps. No one had bothered to take his sword, and he drew it to make sure it was still intact. He reminded himself of his vow that once he had drawn the sword he would not sheath until it was covered with the blood of many enemies. Today it had accounted for none, and that was just wrong!

He hoped Mr. Pennywhistle was still alive and that fate was being kind to young Mr. Higgins. He wondered how Wilson was standing the test of battle. The man was certainly no fire-eater, and his occasional remarks about his desire to win glory in battle had always sounded hollow and rehearsed. Still, it was unfair to judge a man before seeing him perform.

It saddened him that he would not be able to pay off the £300 worth of IOUs indebtedness to Wilson. A gentleman never defaulted on his debts; but battle rendered its own accounts and sometimes forestalled men from carrying out the duties of everyday living. It was a pity he was going to die; his share of prize money would probably have made it easy to clear all his debts.

He lurched forward a few more steps and found to his satisfaction that his gait steadied. No one remonstrated with him or made any move to stop him exiting the cockpit.

He slowly climbed the steps to the lower gun deck. As he hoisted himself up the last step, he nearly collided with an astonished Wilson carrying a large ammunition chest.

"Fancy meeting you here, Wilson! Should have expected you'd be busy on the quarterdeck. Couldn't Robbins have fetched more cartridges? Must be a hell of a scrape upstairs if we are dipping into the reserve ammunition supply."

Wilson felt like he had seen a ghost and his first words sprang from his lips without any supervision by his brain. "Aren't you de—"

"Everyone seems to think so, but by Jove, sir, I still have some vinegar left in me and am not ready to quit life without seasoning some Froggies. Lend me your shoulder and assist my journey to the quarterdeck."

Wilson did as asked, though he wondered what earthly good Wemyss could do on the quarterdeck. Nevertheless, he admired Wemyss' grit and courage and wished he possessed some of each. Perhaps those qualities were infectious; certainly, heroically assisting his dying commander would look good to the men.

His experience with the grenade had put heart into him. Instead of hiding in the magazine, he was at least performing the duty he'd said he would. He had never before received anything like the admiring looks of Stevenson and his mates, and in an odd way he did not want to let them down.

Wemyss' was huffing and puffing as he slowly ascended the final companionway to the quarterdeck, but his steps did not falter. He apparently was commanding his body by sheer willpower, and Wilson admitted that it was an impressive thing to witness. He himself would have stayed confined to the cockpit for the battle's duration if he'd received even a minor wound. But then, he did not have the reputation of an old military family to uphold.

The appalling noise grew in intensity. Wilson's stomach lurched and he fought down the urge to deposit his last meal on the steps. He looked at Wemyss' and saw his captain's face bloom into a radiant smile. That was insane, but Wilson knew that battle itself was a form of insanity, and men who embraced that probably handled its stresses better.

The whizzing of bullets, the thudding of cannon, and the *klunk klunk klunk* of colliding metal fragments reached a crescendo as Wilson and Wemyss stepped onto the quarterdeck. Wemyss motioned Wilson to release his arm, intending to endure whatever lay ahead under his own power.

Things looked bad to Wilson. Dale stubbornly had refused to evacuate the poop but ordered his marines to lie on their bellies. It took considerably longer to reload a musket from that position, but the marines were managing.

The rest of the marines and majority of sailors were crouched under the poop's overhang astern of the ship's wheel. *Aigle* had just lowered boarding planks and Frenchmen were forming up at their ends. Higgins' marines were in a tight knot near the wheel, and the sailors clustered around Cumby.

Wilson wondered where Pennywhistle was. Much as he disliked the fellow, he would have felt safer with his presence on the quarterdeck. Then he noticed sailors racing back from the forecastle, eyes ablaze, and his question was answered. Pennywhistle would likely be where the fighting was hottest.

Wilson remembered what Pennywhistle had said about repelling boarders. Bullets zipped past his head like dark streams of insects, and he instinctively bent forward as a man would if beset by a swarm. He rubbed the ruby in his ring vigorously.

Wemyss smiled as he stood tall and firm: a man exactly where he had always wanted to be. The whine and whistle of bullets, the juddering of the deck planks, the *thumps* and *crumps* of large pieces of iron striking wood, and the roaring thunder of cannons looked to be as pleasurable to him as a Beethoven symphony to a connoisseur of music.

Where in God's green earth do they find such men? wondered Wilson. It was one thing to endure danger, quite another thing to court it. Wemyss was going beyond courting, almost daring every stray piece of lead to make his close personal acquaintance. It truly crossed the line into madness; but then Wemyss was going to die anyway, so what did he have to lose? Yet even when perfectly healthy, lifelong warriors like Wemyss desired a heroic death.

Wemyss' heroic posture had not gone unnoticed. The marines under the poop were cheering him loudly, though it sounded faint in the infernal din. Higgins looked to be shouting loudest of all.

Wilson snapped himself back to reality and remembered his vital cargo was needed more than ever, since repelling an all-out boarding attempt would require a lot of rounds. He put his dignity in his pocket and made a mad dash across the quarterdeck with his heavy burden.

He felt a huge rush of air at his back and instinctively turned toward its source. What he saw astonished him, though it should not have, considering Wemyss' had been taunting Fate. Fate had finally had enough.

A swarm of lead locusts engulfed Wemyss from head to toe, devouring his flesh with a rapidity so ferocious that in a few seconds only a fine red mist remained in the shape of a man. That mist was carried off by a breath of wind an instant later. It was as if Wemyss had never existed.

Wilson shuddered when he thought that the leaden swarm had nearly caught him as well. Then he scowled, as he realized that blast had just annihilated £300 of his own fortune. If he survived to reenter civilian life, he would never again issue another IOU. Thank God his ring might give him that chance to carry out his new cash-only policy.

CHAPTER 33

Since the Captain commanded the ship, it was the First Lieutenant's job to repel boarders. Cumby judged the moment right and ordered his sailors to charge. Shouting variations of "Death to the French!" they all obeyed. The sailors collided with the enemy boarders, and *clang, clang, clang* rang out as steel met steel. The sudden press forced the dozen boarders who had gained the quarterdeck back onto their boarding bridges.

The starboard quarterdeck bulwarks turned into a seething, writhing mass of men that resembled two arrays of rival wasps contending for control of one nest: one tasked with defending a queen, the other committed to establishing a new one. The fighting was savage with no quarter given and none asked, guided by primal instincts about territoriality.

The formal weapons were all edged: cutlasses, boarding axes, and half-pikes. Firearms and grenades could not be used because they might just as well injure a friend as a foe. Informal weapons included fists, feet, knees, and even teeth. Men slashed, cut, and lunged, but also punched, clawed, kicked, and bit.

The lower hulls of both ships collided repeatedly and rhythmically from the motion of the waves. The tumblehome of *Bellerophon's* and *Aigle's* sides meant that the weather decks actually curved away from one another. Three four-foot wide bridges of broken spars had been thrown across the gap between the two ships. The narrowness of the bridge fronts and the impatience of both sides to get at one another created three large traffic jams. Each passing second brought more men forward, pushing and shoving for a chance to fight.

A line of British sailors clad only in bell-bottoms and bandannas shoved boarding pikes into the stomachs of any *matelots* who made it to the fore. Since each bridge allowed only three men to come forward at any given time, the British defenders faced only nine attackers and could gore each man with boarding pikes and injure those immediately to their rear.

Those impaled generally fell off into the sea, though some needed the additional motivation of kicks and punches. Several of those falling never reached the water but were mashed into red pulp when the two ships' hulls crashed together.

Eight *matelots* jumped from the bridges and secured handholds on *Bellerophon's* bulwarks. British sailors responded by smashing their groping fingers with fists or the heavy wood of the pike poles, or simply amputating entire hands with cutlasses. All eight men fell into the water, but they had kept the British defenders occupied long enough for an additional four jumpers to gain *Bellerophon's* quarterdeck.

One swarthy French lieutenant cut hard at Lieutenant Thomas's wrist, severing the sword knot and sending the weapon flying. The lieutenant thought he had rendered Thomas defenseless and launched a killing stroke.

An afternoon from months ago flashed through Thomas's mind, and he did as Pennywhistle had done unto him. He blocked the Frenchman's sword arm with his right forearm and shot a palm heel strike under the man's chin. With the full force of his calf muscles behind it, the blow lifted the Frenchman off the deck and snapped his neck.

Before Thomas had time to congratulate himself, a passing shard of iron nicked the top of his bicorne. The fragment missed his skull, but had sufficient force to knock him unconscious.

Another French lieutenant with a beaky nose and a pointed chin identified Cooke by his uniform. As he advanced, cutlass at the ready, Cooke saw him out of the corner of his eye. The Captain swiveled and fired his pistol. The twin balls took the Frenchman square in the chest, batting him off his feet. The *matelots* accompanying him backed away in the direction from which they had come.

Cooke looked at the deck littered with wooden and human wreckage. "They shall never take you from me! Never!" he murmured fiercely.

Cooke's elimination of the lieutenant attracted the attention of an enemy marksman in *Aigle's* maintop. He had been loudly cheering that officer and swore when Cooke killed him. He fired in revenge. The bullet struck Cooke in the chest, right of center.

Cooke looked surprised, then collapsed. Sailors rushed to his aid. Fourteen-year-old Pierson knelt down to help. "We will get you to the cockpit, Captain, don't you worry." Pierson's voice wavered with hurt and confusion. Captains were supposed to be immortal!

The younger Barron brother raced over to assist, but a four-foot-long splinter impaled his chest and he fell a foot from Cooke.

Higgins saw Cooke fall. He cast an agonized look at Wilson, who reluctantly said, "I can spare you for a minute, Mr. Higgins, no longer." Higgins dashed over to Cooke, and was horrified by what he saw.

"No," said Cooke weakly. "I do not need help. Just let me lie here a minute." He turned his head to the side and his eyelids fluttered. His left hand pulled the St. Christopher medal from his pocket. He put his right hand to the wound and let out a low, indecipherable whisper. And then he was gone.

Higgins kept his face as impassive as he could, but worried that his trembling lower lip undermined his efforts. His belief in British invincibility was wavering badly. He had never thought it possible to be so scared. He flirted with the idea of fleeing to the lower decks; but that moment passed. He was in this to the end and would not leave his post until relieved by victory or death.

"Get Mr. Cumby, immediately!" Overton shouted at Pierson. The boy jumped to his feet and raced away.

Higgins dashed back to his post, bursting with the need for vengeance. The battle had just become very personal. He was so keen on retaliation that he completely forgot that Wilson was in actual command. He commenced issuing orders as if Wilson were not there.

Word of the captain's death spread like wildfire. Sailor's repelling the French *matelots* began to chant: "Cooke, *Cooke*, **Cooke!**" as their savagery rose to a fever pitch. They cut and slashed at the French with a fury that made their former actions seem those of kindly men.

The Frenchmen felt the change, and it was too much for them. They lost heart in an instant of fearful comprehension. They backed slowly away for a few seconds. Then, infected by mad panic, they abruptly turned and scampered back to their ship, more rabbits than men.

But Cumby knew the respite could prove a false one. He said a quick, silent prayer, touched his cross, and began issuing orders. The first thing he did was recall his sailors and again have them shelter below the overhang of the poop. No sense in exposing them to enemy fire unless absolutely necessary.

Captain Cooke was dead, most of his marines were down, and the ship was rolling badly from the loss of her masts. The *Bahama* had materialized out of a brimstone mist and maneuvered herself 30 yards off *Bellerophon's* port side to unleash broadsides into *Bellerophon,* though their impact was attenuated by a lack of gunnery skill and a shortage of men.

Cumby was hard pressed to cope with the expanding emergencies. He needed junior officers to exercise initiative and lighten his burden in whatever ways they could. Besides being sandwiched between *Aigle* and *Bahama, Monarcha* and *Swiftsure* had opened fire on *Bellerophon's* stern from 500 yards away; *Bellerophon's* 74 guns were up against an enemy total of 296. Their fire was inaccurate, but the occasional hit added to the air of swirling chaos and his growing feeling of helplessness. If they closed, raking fire would be the end of the ship and nearly everyone aboard.

Wilson looked confused, and Pennywhistle was occupied on the forecastle. Dale was preparing for a last ditch defense. Everything was up to him. He had begged God for a chance at glory, and God had answered. He should have kept his mouth shut!

Higgins' men were in desperate peril, and he was out of options. They could not just stand there and be cut down like stalks of wheat, but he had no idea what to do. He fought back tears of frustration and despondency.

.

Each time a broadside slammed into *Bellerophon,* despair became an increasingly powerful French weapon. Bonaparte had stated that in battle morale was to the physical as three was to one, and his observation was proving true. Blizzards of serrated metal, jagged wooden lances, and human detritus shredded, impaled, and crushed men in ways so grotesque and unpredictable that even stalwarts were reduced to faint hearts. The human confetti that rained down upon survivors was particularly dispiriting. Shrieks and sobs of pain and terror added to a thunderous sound. As their eardrums were being wrecked, sailors and marines found it difficult to frame coherent thoughts: they were reduced to their most basic animal instincts.

Then the situation got immeasurably worse.

A quartermaster trying to re-hoist *Bellerophon's* battle ensign plunged to the deck. A flag was not only important for morale but symbolized that a ship had not surrendered! Since the flag had first fluttered to the deck, ten minutes before, two attempts had been made to jury rig the 20-by-20-foot ensign to the mizzen gaffe. Both had been stopped by French marksmen.

A collective groan arose from *Bellerophon,* followed by French cheers. The task of getting the flag back up was clearly a forlorn hope, but the attempt needed to be made.

Understandably, volunteers for a suicide mission in the midst of battle were hard to come by. Cumby wanted to put heart into his men, and deeds could do what words could not. Enlisted men had failed; time for an officer to act.

In the midst of the confusion and horror, Screwloose the cat raced onto the deck, engaged in his apparently eternal contest with Shredder. A stray splinter caught him in the back. The feline mewled, sank to the deck, and moved no more, and an even louder groan arose from the men. They had lost not only their ensign, but their mascot!

Tears dripped down Higgins's cheeks, plowing narrow furrows through the powder grime on his young face. He angrily wiped his eyes with his sleeve. His men were staring at him, yet it was with compassion, not contempt.

"They killed our cat, but I am damned if am going to let the bastards kill our flag!" His anger deepened his voice a whole octave. "By God, I will get that flag up if it is the last thing that I ever do!"

His few remaining marines cheered.

He smiled fiercely and saw Miss Lydia's face in his mind. His blood became fire and his will tempered steel. By God, he could do this!

"Corporal Robbins, take over and keep firing!"

"Very good, sir. Best of luck. God be with you," called out Robbins, but the lieutenant could scarcely hear him.

Higgins stripped off his shoulder belt and frogged scabbard, since speed and maneuverability were of the essence. He ordinarily wished he were taller, but now his scant height would prove an advantage. A short, fast man could weave his way through the crowd more adroitly than a tall man, and a short man was a much poorer target.

He took one last look. The quarterdeck was a mass of men's gore and broken ship's parts, with screaming, shouting men who appeared and then vanished as the caprices of gun smoke acted as a thick, drifting fog. The deck was slick with blood: it flowed so freely that it had washed away the sand and there was no sure footing. He'd have to be as careful as he was fast.

He broke into a run and felt the wind of several bullets just astern. The French were working hard to get his range and nearly succeeding. He bobbed and weaved like a footpad evading Bow Street Runners. He had never been well coordinated, but suddenly he was moving with the focus and agility of a jaguar ascending a jungle tree.

He grabbed the ladder up to the poop with a strength that he did not know he possessed and rocketed to the top. He caught Dale's eye and a wealth of understanding flowed between the men in an electric current.

"I'll cover you," shouted Dale. "There's a marksman up there in an old cocked hat; he's the one that's done the damage." Dale's voice rippled with an uncharacteristic anger. "But I have his position now and I can bring him down. Don't worry about anything but the flag, sir!"

Higgins gathered up the huge flag as quickly as he could. The 400 square feet of silk was heavy, unwieldy, and kept threatening to pour out of his arms. A bullet nicked the deck just by his foot. He glanced up and saw a Frenchman in an outrageously large cocked hat cursing.

He glanced to his right and saw Dale lining up a shot. From the expression on Dale's face, he could see this had become personal. He suddenly felt a surge of confidence. A veteran of Dale's skill and experience was a bad man to cross. Dale fired, but as he did so the ship rolled and a wounded marine fell against Dale. The shot went wide. Dale looked disgusted and set about reloading. At least all the motion and commotion was also queering the sniper's aim.

Higgins wrapped the flag around his scarlet tunic as tightly as he could. It was the only way that he would have full use of his arms and legs in the climb.

He started up the ratlines as briskly as he could, but felt like he was walking through thick mud with lead weights on his legs and arms. Every pull was difficult, hampered as he was, and as he got higher he realized just how exposed he was. He was as naked to gunfire as a newborn baby to the elements. On the other hand, if he succeeded his triumph would be very public, and a hero needed recognition.

Hero? What rot! He just wanted to survive.

He felt the silk quiver every few seconds and realized the flag was shielding him from rounds that ordinarily would have buried themselves in his flesh.

The choking smoke made breathing difficult, and so he paused on his climb several times. But each time he faltered, he smelled the cinnamon and sandalwood in Miss Lydia's hair, felt her touch on his arm and heard her voice. "There is nothing that you cannot do, Luke. I believe in you." An unexpected reserve of strength opened; he kept going and finally reached the base of the gaffe.

Some presentiment of danger caused him to turn his head; he saw the Frenchman in the cocked hat smile. He had Higgins dead to rights and was about to pull the trigger. *Well, I have done my best, and at least will die in the performance of my duty.*

Then the cocked hat flew high in the air and the back of the Frenchman's head exploded. The body pitched forward and plunged toward the deck.

Higgins glanced down at the poop and saw Dale wave in acknowledgment. Dale's marksmanship was as good as its reputation. Apparently there was something to be said for an early career as a poacher.

Higgins began crawling on his belly along the gaffe of the spanker. His progress was slow and encumbered. Strangely, he felt no wind from bullets aimed in his direction. He turned his head and was surprised to see Frenchmen in the tops staring at him but making no moves to raise their Charlevilles.

He reached the outward edge of the gaffe and wondered why he was still alive. He unwound the flag, and over the next five minutes carefully tacked it to the gaffe, using bowline knots. It was slow work and should have afforded the French plenty of opportunities to blow his head off. When he finished, he again looked at the French in the tops and saw what he took to be expressions of approval.

What an amazing thing! For some reason, appreciation of his gallantry had suspended all the strictures of their duty. It was not logical in the least, given their almost fanatical devotion to eliminating the enemies of their beloved *Empereur*. Higgins wondered if his being an officer had anything to do with it, but decided that his status made the French actions even more curious. The French despised anyone they considered an aristocrat, and though many British officers bore no private title greater than gentleman, the French often styled an English officer a *milord Anglais*.

Perhaps it was just not his time; but if so, Nature had an extraordinary way of bending men's minds to her will.

A realization struck him that in this moment he was more a symbol than a man. In the midst of all of this madness and destruction, the French were deliberately sparing him because he spoke of something excellent in the human spirit. For a few brief minutes, flags and allegiances mattered less than applauding a brave man doing a fine deed under circumstances that should guarantee certain death. It was queer: the gallant behavior of his enemies accorded him the recognition that he so devoutly wished from his friends.

The French were indeed a strange people; but then, the words *chivalry* and *gallantry* originated in their lexicon. He was embarrassed by the stupid way that he had spoken about them earlier in the morning. But he had been a mere boy then.

Satisfied the flag was now fixed firmly in place, he slithered back along the gaffe. He descended the ratlines at a moderate pace. As soon as his feet touched wood, bullets began to sing past him. His temporary immunity had expired.

Dale greeting was rough-voiced but sincere. "Well done, Mr. Higgins."

"I owe my life to your marksmanship, Sergeant, and shall always be in your debt."

"Consider the debt paid in full, Mr. Higgins. The heart that you have put into my men and everyone on *Bellerophon* has a value beyond the price of rubies."

Higgins saw the truth of Dale's words in the grime-covered faces of the remaining marines on the poop. The light in their battle-worn faces meant more to him at this moment than anything else that he could possibly think of... except words of praise from Miss Lydia!

Just then a bullet grazed his arm. It ripped his scarlet coat but only plowed a slight furrow in his forearm. It felt like a hornet sting and he knew it was not serious. Still, it was a hard warning. On the other hand, it would give him a scar that could be shown to the welcoming eyes of Miss Lydia.

CHAPTER 34

Pennywhistle assessed the ship's situation with his Ramsden. The quarterdeck was a shambles, the masts were down, and two more enemy vessels looked to be on an intercept course. Things were definitely touch and go. A plan came into his mind, as fully formed and as resolved as Athena emerging from Zeus's skull. He spent a few crucial moments giving orders to a number of sailors, who darted away to carry them out.

Pennywhistle spotted a group of five soldiers that had broken off from the main band of boarders. They were lead by a gigantic officer sporting a wide black bicorn featuring an oversize blue, white, and red cockade with a small silver imperial eagle at its center.

The men's faces looked seasoned by hard life: lined cheeks, crooked noses, and more scars on their faces than would be found on a dozen smallpox survivors. They carried Pattern 1780 hangers instead of Charlevilles and held their 26-inch swords like veterans who knew what they were about. Each man carried a sack of grenades, and they were bound for the ship's waist. They meant to descend the rear companionway and pitch grenades into the backs of unsuspecting gunners on the upper gun deck. If they could not disable an enemy's cannon, they could kill the men manning them.

Bellerophon's men were holding their own against the enemy boarders, but only barely. *Aigle's* efforts to clear *Bellerophon's* poop and quarterdeck with small arms fire and grenades were dangerously close to success. Not a man could be spared to meet this new threat. He'd have to handle the job alone.

Two could play at the grenade game. He snatched a grenade from the bandolier of a dead French *matelot,* as well as his supply of fuses. He reined in his excitement and slowed his pace to a brisk walk, careful to maintain a distance between himself and his targets. The odds of success would decrease if they saw him coming.

His targets reached the top of the companionway. One of them tossed a grenade prematurely, bringing an angry rebuke from their officer. They advanced their blades and descended the steps, wary of an ambush from below. They never imagined danger lay astern.But he had perhaps been too cautions: he was too far behind to catch them as they descended.

When he arrived, they had already reached the bottom of the companionway. The were conveniently bunched together. Pennywhistle lit his grenade, counted to three, and dropped it on their heads.

The grenade plopped directly behind the group. They all turned swiftly at the familiar hissing sound, but it was too late. Two absorbed most of the fragments and died instantly. One fell to the deck, crying out in pain and rolling in agony as his thigh spurted blood, his femoral artery pierced by one of nasty shards.

Pennywhistle's blade flew from its leather prison and danced to the point like a martial scrying stick that had divined hot blood. He clattered down the stairs and the tip of his blade pierced the Adam's apple of the remaining soldier before the private could raise his hanger high enough to block. The man folded like a discarded concertina, leaving only the officer to fight. His expert stance challenged Pennywhistle to try conclusions.

The officer was a major of the 67th; at least five inches over six feet, well-muscled yet sinewy, moving with the grace of a leopard. He outweighed Pennywhistle by thirty pounds at least, and had the advantage of three inches in height that gave his sword arm an exceptionally long reach. He was in his mid thirties, with a patrician face that was complemented by a finely tailored uniform. One small object told his tale in a way that Pennywhistle could respect and admire. On his left breast, *la Légion d'honneur* shone like a beacon of nobility. That was never awarded save for conduct of the highest merit.

Quite as remarkable as his height was his sword. It was a hybrid weapon, as was Pennywhistle's own Osborn. It was, however, a foot longer: a big weapon for a big man. The twin shell guard and stag horn grip were distinctively French, but the double-edged blade had not come from Europe. Pennywhistle recognized the curve and style of the blade as having once been part of a katana; it had probably found its way to Europe via the China Trade. It would be a contest pitting reach against speed, French and Japanese artistry against English craftsmanship.

Emerald eyes locked with thunderhead grey ones in the manner of knights greeting each other before a jousting match. Neither man's eyes held malice, but both sparkled with the thrill of the hunt. There was mutual respect, but not a hint of compromise. This was a fight to the death.

The Frenchman snapped his blade vertical, its pommel above and behind his left shoulder. Extraordinary! The man was both a southpaw and ready to fight in the Oriental fashion: two hands upon the hilt. Pennywhistle speculated that a two-handed grip might reduce the speed of his opponent's thrusts.

The French major's katana flashed down with the speed and power of a lightning bolt. Pennywhistle had anticipated the chopping cut, but its swiftness was so unexpected that he blocked it only with difficulty at the last second. The impact of doing so pushed him back. He had been badly wrong about a two-handed grip affecting speed, and it certainly added to power.

The Frenchman was not only enormously strong but kept his blade moving, almost as if it were a living entity with a mind of its own. The Marine had barely recovered from the first cut when the Frenchman again chopped hard at him. This time Pennywhistle met the blow earlier and yielded only a few inches.

Most of the open waist area of the ship's upper gun deck was clear of impediments, so he had space to maneuver in; he would need it against this man's raw power. A third powerful hack he deflected upward and away, yielding no ground.

He turned aside a cut to his thigh and slashed low. The Frenchman stepped back quickly, but not fast enough. Pennywhistle's cutlass took a deep chunk out of his left ankle and elicited a loud *"Merde!"* The Frenchman riposted with a lateral slash to the head that missed the marine's right cheek by a fraction of an inch.

The contest swayed back and forth with advantage to neither side. Lunge, cut, parry, riposte; blurred movements and discrete actions that were the result of training and instincts, not conscious thoughts. The exact movements of a sword fight were often as hard for the victor to recall as the many pairings of partners in a grand ball.

A blast of tiny wood flecks blinded Pennywhistle for a split second, but the *sentiment du fer* saved him. His blade deflected a likely fatal cut to his throat that he sensed rather than saw. When his vision returned, he lunged at the Frenchman. His blade missed the Frenchman's sword arm by a whisker. His opponent was as nimble as he was powerful.

Since he had been trained by a Frenchman, Pennywhistle recognized and anticipated a number of his opponent's moves. Nevertheless, he felt the heavy breath of defeat perilously close.

Their blades met and locked three times. Pennywhistle could not match his opponent's strength and got shoved back twice. On the third occasion, he kicked the man's injured shin and sent him reeling back. The Frenchman stumbled but did not fall, and recovered sufficiently fast that he easily blocked Pennywhistle's follow up thrust.

Four more cuts and blocks had Pennywhistle breathing hard and backed against a bulkhead. His left hand felt a barrel of sand next to the bulkhead: Cooke had placed extra barrels throughout the ship to soak up excess blood. He noticed that the major's footsteps were the slightest bit uncertain; he was unaccustomed to fighting on a rolling deck. The Frenchman was getting angry as well, apparently not used to someone close to his level of skill. Angry men were foolish men.

Neither had made any mistakes, but it was time for Pennywhistle to commit an apparent one in order that his opponent would make a real one.

He made two lunges at the major's stomach and sternum: they were parried neatly. Then he flashed the Frenchman a look of weariness that was only partly feigned, and saw the gleam in his opponent's eye. It was the same gleam that a leopard displayed when it cornered a gazelle.

Pennywhistle blocked the next low and high slashes, but he did so with a slowness that was calculated. When the expected lunge to the rib cage came a few seconds later, Pennywhistle made no move to block it, but sidestepped at the last possible moment. The great power of the Frenchman's killing thrust worked against him and the tip of his blade slammed into the barrel so hard that the sand imprisoned it as if it had been thrust into concrete.

Pennywhistle had only a second before his opponent's towering strength wrenched the blade free. The marine launched a short, hard jab with his left at the major's throat and was rewarded with the sound of a collapsing windpipe.

He let his cutlass dangle from its sword knot and whipped his dirk out from his right boot. From that crouch, he corkscrewed upward and plunged the 12-inch blade under his opponent's sternum and upwards with every ounce of strength from his powerful calf muscles.

He stood almost nose to nose with the Frenchman and saw the surprise in his eyes. He gave a short exhalation, staggered backward, then fell over like a human mainmast hit by too many cannon balls.

Pennywhistle breathed hard, trying to recover his strength. Had the fight continued much longer, the great strength and endurance of the Frenchman might well have prevailed. He was alive because he had seen the sand barrel as a weapon, rather than mere staves of wood. Also because he kept a secondary weapon handy. There was much to be said for foresight and guile.

He ordinarily was averse to the souvenir-hunting that was nearly as common among officers as it was among the men, but thought he would make an exception in this case. He unfastened the Legion of Honor from the Frenchman's coat and put it into his pocket. The trinket had little monetary value but great symbolic importance. It would serve to remind him that in the midst of mindless savagery and carnage, honor and gallantry still counted for something.

He looked into the major's sightless eyes and wondered what kind of man he had been, but could draw no satisfying conclusion, since corpses were like bird cages without the bird. He examined the Frenchman's sword and speculated on how the blade had come into his possession. Though the sword was valuable, he decided to leave it with the major as a gesture of respect. Probably a quixotic action, considering some fellow would likely appropriate it after the battle, but he nonetheless felt obliged to pay homage to an opponent who had fought well.

The jury remained out on whether the cutlass or katana was superior. In the final analysis, victory was more about the superiority of the swordsman than the superiority of his sword.

He carefully wiped the blood from his sword and dirk with a heavy chamois cloth. He returned the sword to its scabbard and the dirk to his boot, satisfied both were clean enough to be drawn quickly.

The thundering noise of battle assaulted his ears. He blinked, realizing that he had been so focused on his fight that he had utterly blanked out all but the sounds necessary to win. Reality slapped him hard in the face and he snapped back to duty. He raced up the companionway and dashed along the gangway. He wondered how bad things were on the quarterdeck.

Two Frenchman leaped at him and slammed hard into his left side. The blow knocked him off his feet and drove the wind from his lungs. The men had been crouched behind some large bitts and were probably the rearguard for the party that he had just defeated. Pennywhistle rolled right and onto his back. One Frenchman towered over him; sword upraised and face ablaze with mad glee.

But his face was not important; his knee was. Pennywhistle locked his left boot behind the man's left ankle and launched his right boot hard at the man's left knee. There was a sickening crunch as the joint shattered. Pennywhistle was on the fallen man like a wildcat on a rabbit. He jammed his dirk into the man's left ear and pushed hard until it emerged from his right.

The second Frenchman had apparently expected his mate to prevail, because he had just begun to draw his sword. Pennywhistle leaped to his feet and, before the hanger cleared the scabbard, he had drawn his own Osborn. He slashed at the Frenchman's wrist, severing the man's hand. A second later he cut the man a crimson necklace that nearly decapitated him. The Frenchman gurgled and fell backward to the deck.

Pennywhistle breathed heavily for a few seconds, then wiped the blade and sheathed the sword. He swiveled his head to make sure that there were no further surprises.

The powerful surges of fear and excitement triggered a flash of memory: the ruby ring on Wilson's finger flashed into his head. Of course! How could he have been so dense! It had belonged to his dear cousin Caroline.

Her father fancied ancient Egyptian curios and had visited the Land of the Pyramids on two occasions. He had presented the ring to Caroline at the start of her coming out season. The Peter Wilson of the Marines was the same Wilson who had jilted her so cruelly.

It was the height of arrogance that the smarmy cad should wear that antiquity into battle. Was the damned fool wearing it as a talisman, for luck? Caroline had told him some hoary tale of the ring's professed supernatural powers; had she told the same to her fiancé, and had he believed it? What typical gambler superstition!

Pennywhistle felt his hot blood run cold with fury. This was the man who had betrayed and abandoned his beloved cousin. He had just killed a good man and an effective leader. It seemed terribly wrong that the major should die simply because he wore the uniform of an upstart emperor rather than a hereditary king, while a man without honor, an unscrupulous gambler, womanizer, and, Pennywhistle was fairly certain, a coward, should continue to live. And amidst mass carnage, no one would scruple much over how a disliked man, even an officer, met his end.

He was not thinking sanely, and he knew it. Anytime your mind understood an action was wrong yet added an enabling "but..." your moral compass was seriously askew.

The problem with killing in battle was that it made all killing easier. Summon the Devil and he might not wish to relinquish his foothold in your soul once the crisis was past. It worried him that his first victim today had caused little soul-searching, and subsequent ones none at all. His personal tally of bodies was rising rapidly, and remorse had made no appearance. His survival instinct possessed no ethics whatsoever, for it understood that regret would likely reduce the odds of staying alive.

Kill one man in a private quarrel and you were an outlaw. Kill many under the coverlet of a commission and you became a hero. War gave the worst excesses in man a way to hide behind the pretensions of higher authority. Personal responsibility for all manner of outrages could be evaded by saying, "I was following orders."

Wilson was a bounder, a knave, and a coward in roughly that order. Some might call Wilson's cessation murder, and so it might be, in time of peace. But war changed things. The elimination of a man who dealt as falsely with his oath and his men as he did with an inamorata would be a public service to the Marines and mankind in general. War was licensed murder anyway, and he only had to make that license slightly more elastic to justify his actions.

He broke into a run. But when he reached the quarterdeck, thoughts of personal vengeance vanished. In his absence, the specter of irremediable defeat had seized center stage. This was no time for self-indulgence. He was exhausted, but by God, he had just begun to fight!

CHAPTER 35

"God, no!" exclaimed Nancy as she watched two burly quartermasters carry her barely conscious husband into the cockpit. She dropped the cloth she had been using to wipe the brow of a sailor. She wanted to race over to her husband. Instead she took take small, careful steps to avoid disturbing any of the wounded

Her stomach lurched. His face was deathly pale from severe blood loss. His right leg below the knee had been shattered by grapeshot and was a repellent red tangle of bone, sinew, and flesh. He kept saying, "No, no, no!" to the sailors transporting him, recoiling from Whyte's operating table.

Boom! Boom!Boom! The bulkheads of the orlop shook as *Bellerophon's* 32-pounders on the deck above fired another broadside. The pressure waves made Nancy's head feel as if it were a walnut in a nutcracker.

Her husband looked up and smiled wanly when he saw her. "I tried to be careful, Nancy, honestly I did. Don't bother Whyte about me; there is a long line of men who need his services more than I. Nothing to be done for me now. Cutting off my leg won't change things, and I'd rather leave this world with all my limbs intact. Just make me comfortable. Don't cry, Nancy. At least I have you by my side. Not as good as dying at home in our own bed, but a sight better than what most of these men here face."

Nancy brushed aside her tears. "Gently, you men, gently. Follow me and I will tell you where to lay my husband." The cockpit was filling up fast; the space she chose was not very private, but most of the wounded men were in their own private hells and would pay no attention to another dying man.

But a general groan of regret echoed off the cramped bulkheads as men realized that the sailing master was badly injured. He was not only a father figure to many, but the man who probably knew more about the ship than her designer. The loss of his skills was a major blow to morale.

The quartermasters took special care and laid him down as softly as if they were handling fine porcelain. Nancy found some wadded up rags which had only a little blood on them and used them as a crude pillow. She retrieved her wet cloth and began to lovingly wipe the beads of sweat from her husband's brow. Underneath the powder grime, his face had a sickly pallor that she had seen all too often today.

"Don't go, Edward. Stay. It's not your time. I need you. The ship needs you." Nancy fought back her tears, but she could not keep the anguish out of her voice. She needed to put heart into her man, not give him the idea that she had already accepted a conclusion that grew more obvious with each passing minute.

The small, grey cat that usually went unnoticed began rubbing itself against her husband's side and purring. He began to idly stroke its fur.

"I wish that were so, Nancy, but I've been a sailing master too long not to know when a vessel's hull is ripped so bad that there isn't any way to keep her afloat. I am bound for a safe harbor on a kindly sea; the Great Heavenly Navigator has fixed my course and set my sails and there is nothing I can do about it. I never told anything but the plain truth to every captain that I have served, and I owe you the same honesty."

"All of our plans, Edward! That place we were going to buy with your prize money. You remember; that brown and white cottage outside Portsmouth with the thatched roof and the big kitchen garden."

"And you shall have it, my dear!" He slowly reached into his right coat pocket and extracted an official looking document, which he handed to his wife. He fought back the pain that made him feel as if he had fallen into a pit of spikes and managed a brief smile. "Rather than tell you, I wanted to wait until we reached England and present it to you as a grand surprise."

Nancy read the purport of the deed. Her mouth fell open and she blinked twice in utter astonishment. She could not have been more surprised if she had been told that she had been proclaimed a duchess of the realm. The little cottage and the acre surrounding it now belonged to them. "But how, Edward, how?"

"A while back, Mr. Pennywhistle, who knew of my fascination with spyglasses, asked if I could make a few adjustments on his Ramsden. I was happy to oblige him, and we struck up an agreeable friendship in the days before we departed Portsmouth. I had been nattering on about the cottage, saying how my dear wife considered its possession her life's dream. He listened attentively, and at the end of my long rattle he inquired what funds would be necessary to secure its possession. I quoted him the figure of £100 for the freehold.

"To my astonishment, he stated, 'I could have a draft of such funds from Counts Bank ready the day after tomorrow. Would that be soon enough? I gather you would want to conclude the deal before we depart for the Mediterranean.'

"I told him that I could not accept such as sum, as it was what I earned in a year and I did not know when I would have the means of repayment. And you know what he did?

He laughed. He laughed!" The pain in his face diminished for a few seconds, and his dry lips gave an anemic smile.

Nancy smiled back. Her husband's enthusiasm for his story had sparked a brief rally in his body. "Why would a gentleman do such a thing?"

"I asked him the very thing. He said, 'Money matters little compared to friendship. A sailing master has the welfare of an entire ship in his hands, so it is no risk at all to trust him with a few spare pounds. Besides, a man who wishes to buy a home is likely a reliable soul who will do his utmost to ensure the repayment of any loan as soon as possible.' I again stated that I had no idea of how I could repay the funds. And he replied, 'I will make that easy for you. Allow me to invest your saved prize money in my brother's copper mines. They are reliable enterprises and a sound harbor for your £85. The price of copper rises daily, thanks to the antics of Bonaparte. Your money will be as safe as in a bank with a return that is considerably greater than any interest.' You can imagine my astonishment."

Overton smiled up at his wife. "His counsel has proven wise. I have been following the price of copper in the newspapers that the ship receives from time to time. Since it is the major element in the brass cannon barrels used by the army, demand is nearly insatiable, and I calculate that we have almost tripled our money."

Nancy's heart fluttered with hope. As her husband warmed to his subject, his grimaces of pain had grown fewer.

"You will be able to pay him back in full when the ship reaches England. You will have enough money left over to buy that lovely satin dress in the shop on George Street that you have so often remarked upon. It makes my soul soar to think of you wearing such a fine dress!"

"That dress, Edward? It is a beautiful confection, one befitting a grand lady, which I am not. I am not sure I could wear it without thinking myself an imposter."

"Do not talk that way, my dear. No finer woman ever walked the planet. There is no dress that can imitate the beauty of your face, your figure, and most of all, your character. You have put up with unnumbered privations living at sea; it is time to go ashore and claim your well-earned rewards.

"Running off with me took you away from the status that should have been your lot. Buy the dress, revel in it, and consider it my small way of making amends. Blue is a fine color for you. When you wear it, think of the joy that you brought into my life, and know that I love you every bit as much now as I did on the first day of our marriage."

He grimaced. "Never, ever, wear the black of mourning on my behalf. Such a color ill becomes you, and I would not have my memory associated with sadness. We have many friends on this ship, and they will look after you when the ship is docked for repair. I am only sorry that I won't be there with you."

Nancy started to cry. "Oh God, Edward, just when we can have what we have always wanted, this has to happen. It is not fair. It is just not fair!!"

Overton held his wife's hand gently. His tone was resigned. "No one ever said life was fair, Nancy, but we have had a good ten years. We understand each other in a way that few couples do. We finish each other's sentences, and that has brought us delight rather than irritation. No marriage has been stronger than ours, and we have seen and done things most married couples do not even dream about.

"This is not a bad way to go, having done my duty in a great battle, and translating to the next life alongside my shipmates. I just wish I could have lived to see the extent of Nelson's victory while holding my newborn son. I do regret we never managed to have children. But Nancy, I need you to promise me two things."

"Anything, Edward, anything!"

"You can't help me, but you can help these men here. Don't let grief win: stay and keep bestowing upon them your tender mercies. The Captain's down, probably dead by now, so you'll need to warn to Mr. Cumby."

"What do you mean?"

"Cumby can't read the signs like I can. A storm is coming, a big one. The Trafalgar Shoals are dangerous. Tell him to anchor just as soon as he can after the battle ends. Cumby must anchor. He must!" In his earnestness, Overton tried to surge up. The grey cat yowled faintly and nudged against his hand.

"Tell him to re-ballast quickly, too. The use of tons of powder and shot today will have shifted *Bellerophon's* center of gravity: with the damage we have sustained, a readjustment is critical! I would never want it said that this fine ship sailed like a crank garbage scow. Promise me, Nancy, *promise* me, that you will do all I ask!" He spoke as emphatically as his weak body permitted; even in his last moments he was a through-going professional.

He began coughing violently and his spittle contained a great deal of blood. Nancy grasped his hand as strongly as she could. She had seen enough death in the cockpit today to know her husband's was imminent.

Boom! Boom! Boom! The cockpit shook hard as *Bellerophon* fired another broadside. The pressure waves made Nancy's head feel as if it were in a vice.

When Edward stopped coughing, his breaths turned raspy. He was losing life with each passing second. She could not stop his death, but she might be able to give him an extra measure of peace before his passing.

"I promise Edward, I promise; with all my heart! I won't let our shipmates down! And I have a surprise, too. You were worried that you would be the last of your line. That's not going to happen. I..."

"You're with child?"His voice was frail as an infant's, but the joy in it was unmistakable.

"Yes, I am. I spoke to Mr. Whyte yesterday, and he is certain. If it is a boy I will name him after you, and if a girl, after your mother."

Edward coughed again, and bubbles of pink froth formed on his lips. He was trying hard to smile but could not quite manage. "The Lord be praised, Nancy. Just make sure you tell our child about his father. Tell him that he died well, and for something worth fighting for." He made a motion to pull his watch from his coat pocket, but his hand was too weak to complete the task.

Nancy understood and extracted his watch.

"I want our son to think of me whenever he notes the time and understand the inscription on its case is what I wish for his life and yours: *A fair wind, a righteous course, and a steady hand on the wheel.* Tell him my last thoughts were of you both."

His voice grew calm and soft, and his eyes lit for a second with an unearthly glow, as if seeing a prospect not granted to the living. He smiled briefly. "Let us cross over the river and rest under the shade of the tree...."

His grip relaxed and his lungs gave a short rattle. The light faded from his eyes, like the transition from sunset to darkness in the tropics.

Nancy sobbed quietly and gently stroked his cheeks. She continued both for a full minute as the reality of his death sank in. She took a piece of sailcloth and lovingly covered his face. The little grey cat that he had been stroking now moved closer. His gentle pleadings in almost human tones persuaded her to begin petting him. It proved comforting.

She took a deep breath, wiped her red eyes dismissively, and shoved aside her grief. She had made a promise to her husband and by God she was going to keep it.

Boom! Boom! Boom! The 32s again roared their destructive message.

Her friend Mary called over from where she lay, still recovering from childbirth. "I am so sorry, Nancy. And I am so happy for you. Your baby won't make up for the loss, but he will be a wonderful reminder of the fine man your husband was."

Nancy wiped away incipient tears. "Yes I know that he will grow up to be a man his father will be proud of. I feel certain that a generous God will allow Edward to view his progress from heaven. May I ask a favor? I would like to hold your son for a while. He reminds me that joy still lives in the world and that a blessed event awaits me."

Mary handed her the baby, and Nancy cradled him lovingly. "He really is beautiful, Mary, and the exact image of his father." She stroked the child's forehead and the baby let out an approving coo.

It's time to go ashore, settle down, and make a proper life for my son. I aim to have him delivered by the best physician in England." Nancy looked around at the dark horror that confronted her from every angle. "Heaven forbid he should ever have to see a slice of hell like this."

"When the ship reaches England, I will ask John to resign. He could be a foreman at any powder mill in England just for the asking. After all we've been through, I want peace and safety."

The baby made some pleasant gurgling sounds as if in agreement with his mother's sentiments. Both women smiled.

"Wisdom from the mouths of babes," said Nancy.

"A great pity that men in power do not heed it," said Mary.

Nancy handed the baby back to Mary with some reluctance. Holding a new life truly was a tonic for an injured soul. She briefly surveyed the 40-by-20 resting place of 100 specimens of damaged humanity, and formed her lips into a line of stern purpose. "Now, I can do my duty."

Boom! Boom! Boom! The guns thundered their baleful melody. Nancy would hear that noise in her sleep every night for the rest of her life. She looked at the engraving on her husband's watch and realized that if she could give her child those three things, no matter how much he might wander, he would never be lost.

CHAPTER 36

"What do you think, Mr. Pennywhistle, one hundred boarders?"

"I make it one-twenty-five, Mr. Cumby."

"More than double our numbers, Mr. Pennywhistle. I am surprised that the French are taking so long to get organized, but I am grateful for every second of reprieve that we can put into preparation."

"True, sir, and Marine reinforcements have arrived. They may be few in number, but to me it is as if Caesar's Tenth Legion had just joined our cause."

Pennywhistle checked his watch and noted the time: 25 minutes past one. *Bellerophon* had been in action for just under ninety minutes. He looked at the faces of the sailors and marines behind him under the overhang of the poop. There was worry, but determination as well. These men had fended off two boarding attempts, and their hard faces proclaimed that they could manage the feat one more time.

"We will just have to double the ingenuity of our tactics to meet their numbers, Mr. Cumby. I do not mean to overstep my authority, but I anticipated our present situation and have taken certain measures."

Cumby looked at Pennywhistle with surprise. "Really? Well, I am never offended by initiative. I take most seriously any advice proffered by a man who has captured an Eagle.

Pray give me some idea of the shape those certain measures take."

"I sent the strongest men on the forecastle not designated as boarders to the magazine and told them to bring up three chests of muskets," said Pennywhistle. "I also appropriated the swiftest powder monkeys and told them to carry the necessary extra ammunition. 60 extra muskets will enable my marines to triple their firepower, and render trifling the time between volleys. Here they come now!"

Each chest contained ten muskets and weighed close to one hundred pounds One man grasped the front handle of each chest, and another man the rear. The sailors covered the distance from the rear waist companionway to the quarterdeck in spurts and starts, since the deck was being peppered with musket balls fired from the French tops.

"Come on, come on!" The sailors beneath the poop knew what the crates contained and cheered on their mates with lusty yells.

Powder monkeys bearing cartridge cases raced alongside the sailors, weaving nimbly enough that the French muskets could not get a proper bead on them.

It took less than a minute for the men and boys to reach the overhang of the poop. The great amount of smoke had acted as a partial cloak, and to everyone's delight both people and cargo reached their destination unscathed.

The sailors pulled open the crates and the powder monkeys deposited their cartridges on the deck. Every able-bodied sailor grabbed a musket and a cartridge and began to load. Since they would not be firing, they wanted to assist the Marines. Speed was imperative, and the sailors wasted not an instant.

Pennywhistle glanced at his watch again:1:28. The checking of his watch had become an obsession, he fretted. It had to stop.

Pierson dashed up. He was badly out of breath, but simply bursting to convey his message. He burbled his words so fast that Cumby could barely understand him. Cumby spoke in calming tones. "Slow down, Mr. Pierson, slow down. As Drake said, there is time to finish our game of bowls and still beat the Spaniards."

"Right, sir. Message from Mr. Saunders. *Aigle* has closed up every single one of her lower gun deck gunports: just upstick and away!"

Cumby turned to Pennywhistle. "That's where all the extra boarders have come from. They have stripped every last man from their big guns."

"They are conceding us victory in the artillery duel, Mr. Cumby, confirming our late Captain's wisdom. They are gambling everything on this last effort. Beat this, and we've got 'em."

"I gather from the expression on your face, Mr. Pennywhistle, you have already formed some design to go with the increase in musketry."

"Its all about firepower and steel, Mr. Cumby. My marines will be gateposts to fix the French in position, while the sailors will act as a swinging gate and sweep them off the deck like a steel broom. Let us both use our glasses to make one final survey of the enemy."

French sailors were shouting and screaming like jackals, waving sabers and axes. But religion was hampering French preparations for boarding action. Because of their zeal to give all bodies a Christian burial, they were not tossing overboard the corpses that clogged their decks. Moving the bodies consumed precious minutes. The French dead were actually rendering yeoman service to the British cause.

Pennywhistle noted only a few pistols; most were carried by petty and commissioned officers. They would have no answer to the concentrated firepower of marines. Marine bayonets also had a superior reach compared to the relatively short-edged weapons of the French.

The training he had given *Bellerophon's* sailors in swordsmanship should at least partly compensate for the disadvantage in numbers. The capstone would be a blast from one of the poop carronades, though they were deserted just now.

Higgins could handle his part just fine. And Pennywhistle needed to use Wilson, though it would have given him great pleasure to simply shoot him. He wanted to place him where he could do no harm and maybe some slight good, but could not think exactly where that might be. Dale disliked the man intensely, so perhaps stationing Dale nearby might put some starch into Wilson's jellied backbone.

Wilson viewed with alarm the growing bellicosity of the French and the look of feral satisfaction on Pennywhistle's face: the combination portended potentially lethal trouble for him. He again thought about faking a wound after the first volley, but that would probably not fool Pennywhistle, who just might place him front and center as punishment.

He did not want the French to take his ship, yet the French treated captured officers decently enough, he reflected almost wistfully. As a POW who had given his parole, he would probably be sent to Verdun, where he would have plenty of chances to play cards. French officers were probably just as easy to fleece as as British ones.

And then, Pennywhistle approached.

Pennywhistle took Wilson aside when he finished his instructions to the rankers. He kept a pleasant expression on his face as he spoke, aware that men were watching. Regardless of his personal estimation of the man, it was important that he not detract from the status Wilson should enjoy as an officer.

"I debated whether to simply kill you, Wilson," said Pennywhistle, with an icy calm and a sunless smile. "I doubt anyone would inquire closely into the manner of your passing."

Wilson's perpetual half smile deserted him and the shock in his eyes was plain. Pennywhistle was a killjoy prig and might have been a friend of Savonarola in times past, but he was no murderer. He was a thoroughgoing gentleman and such men never.... Oh my God, he knew. He knew.

"I finally made the connection. You should not strut about with such a distinctive piece of jewelry." Pennywhistle's lips thinned. "Love and reason keep small company. Truer words were never spoken.

"I have solved a mystery that has perplexed me for some time; why a man of your... ah... character elected to join the marines. But there it is: James Murray's solicitors would have brought a breech of promise suit as airtight as it would have been ruinous."

Wilson looked as dumbfounded as if he had been grazed by a falling spar.

"Killing you, however, while likely a service to good men everywhere, would be wrong. Caroline made the choice to end her life, though the provocations you gave her were cruel and great. Besides, a dead man is no use to me, while even a creature of marginal value may furnish some utility in the fight ahead.

"I am giving you a second chance. I do not expect you to be a hero; just stand and give the appropriate commands. That means echoing my words for an engagement that I believe will be hard and quick. Surely, you can manage that. Well?" he looked Wilson in the eye and his voice rippled with challenge. "What say you, Wilson? Gentleman or knave?"

Wilson wanted to lash out with the foulest expletives imaginable, but much as he hated to admit it, Pennywhistle had a point.

The cold mathematical calculations of the gambler took over. Pennywhistle might be a Jesuit in a scarlet coat, but his plans were generally well formed; a bet on him was pretty much a sure thing. Following his designs might actually be safer than trying to outguess the vagaries of battle. Unlike men, battles had no tells that he was capable of reading.

He stared at the ring and it seemed to glow with a quick flash of acknowledgment. Yes, he could do this. He was good at playing parts, and this play had a very limited run.

"Very well, Mr. Pennywhistle, a gentleman it is." He spoke with a magisterial confidence that he most certainly did not feel, but he was damned if he would give Pennywhistle the satisfaction of letting him know just how scared he was. "I will do my duty."

"You will be stationed on the left flank of our small line," said Pennywhistle curtly. "Higgins will be in the center, and I will take position on the right. I will place Dale close to you. Look to him and listen carefully to anything he says. Remember, our only objective is to kill every Frenchman who sets foot upon this deck."

"I understand Mr. Pennywhistle," he said calmly. And strangely, he did. It was similar to risking everything on a spectacular bluff. He was betting that he could bluff his way through the next engagement and meet any calls made by the French.

Pennywhistle turned to his men and drew his Osborn. "Marines, to your posts. Volley fire by ranks when I give the command. Move!"

The 30 marines moved to their assigned firing positions. There were no collisions or jostling, because they all moved with a grace that was the result of frequent training; each man knew the path to his spot as well as a salmon knew his way back to the stream in which he had spawned.

The redcoats assembled themselves into two ranks of 15, forming a solid block between the wheel and the quarterdeck companionway entrance. They had slightly less than 2,000 square feet of deck to defend, roughly the same area as three cricket pitches, though the shape was different. Each man in the front rank shifted slightly right to the "lock on" position, leaving a small gap so that the man in the rank behind him could discharge his weapon safely.

Every man loaded his musket with a special round consisting of one ball and three buckshot: another of Pennywhistle's experiments to increase the lethality. With a 17-inch socket bayonet attached, each Brown Bess became a five-foot, eight-inch pike as well.

Each marine unslung the twin muskets burdening his shoulders and laid them alongside his right foot for easy access. The French were in for a nasty surprise if they expected any respite between volleys.

The redcoats stood with their weapons held horizontal at a 45 degree angle in the classic stance of marines awaiting an attack. Left foot in advance of the right, bodies upright but not rigid, weight equally distributed. Their right hands, slightly in advance of their hips, gripped the small of the butts of their weapons. Their left hands gripped their muskets an inch in advance of the balance.

Pennywhistle believed God a watchmaker, but wondered if He departed that role on occasion. The smoke had thickened in the last few minutes, a Godsend, acting as a cloak sheltering his men from the attentions of French snipers.

Warwick selected as a target a short *matelot* with curly blond hair and a crooked nose who put him in mind of a ferret crossed with a poodle. He knew the range to his target and just how much he should allow for the rise of the barrel and the arc of its ball. He had spent hours whet-stoning his bayonet's tip to a razor-like sharpness equal to the blade of Mr. Pennywhistle's expensive cutlass. Though it was not regulation, Pennywhistle had told his men to sharpen their bayonet's edges.

Combs took heart from the calm expression on Warwick's face and cheered himself with the knowledge that he and his mate had been skilled enough to assist in capturing an Eagle. The ape's paw in his pocket smelled to high heaven, but it had certainly done its job today. He was still scared witless but knew his training would carry him through. He muttered "Slow, slow, quick, quick," without realizing that he did so.

He did a quick review of "Pennywhistle's Pointers." Aim for the widest possible surface on your target. Squeeze your musket's trigger gently at the bottom of your exhale, never jerk it, and make sure the butt is seated firmly against your shoulder. Ram the ball hard to make sure it is closely compacted with the powder, and always return your ramrod to its proper channel lest it be fired by accident. Never reverse your musket and club, but use its butt freely to block enemy thrusts. Always receive an attack upon the wooden portions of your weapon; the bayonet point is best used to attack; the edges best to riposte; twist smartly as you recover.

Though a small part of him wished that he were back in Portsmouth holding a warm beer with one hand and a hot woman with the other, he was mostly glad to be exactly where he was, defending the "Billy Ruffian". It was a wonderful feeling to be granted such an honor. If he survived this day, he would have such stories to tell that he would never have to pay for a drink again. Some of the dockyard dollies in Portsmouth were not without patriotic impulses, and his tales might win him some horizontal refreshment as well.

Dale made his calculations about the number of boarders and the amount of volleys necessary to bring them down: six should do it. With already loaded spare muskets, they could dish out that punishment in a little more than two minutes. Any bleeding scarecrows left standing would be given cold steel.

Dale looked over at Higgins and could see he was ready. He felt very protective toward that young man and thought he would make a fine officer if he remained in the service. He did not think he would do so, however. He had once overheard him talking to Mr. Pennywhistle about his Miss Lydia, and Dale suspected that once Higgins's heroism was established for all and sundry, that lady would never again allow him to risk his life.

He looked at Wilson and hoped a blade or a bullet was emblazoned with that scoundrel's name.

Higgins thought he should say something brave and heroic, but his mouth was desert-dry and he was not sure his tongue would work right. He surveyed his men and his chest expanded with pride. No, nothing need be said. They were ready.

Wilson's knees commenced slow shaking, and several of the men noticed it, judging by some quick glances of contempt directed his way. *Damn their bloody hearts!*

Pennywhistle yielded to temptation and checked the time. 1:35. He slammed his watch case shut in irritation. French shouting had increased in volume and was now peppered with barbed taunts and spirited jeers. Taunts and jeers were great French tells. Once those started, the assault would soon be launched.

Under the poop overhang, Cumby talked quietly with his sailors. He understood the dangers of over-familiarity, but he had come to believe that the carefully measured social distance between officers and men should be bent on occasion so that each side could see the other as just a little bit more human. His philosophy was paying off handsomely: officers and men reposed absolute trust in each other.

A sailor made a mad dash across the quarterdeck and breathlessly came to a halt at Cumby's side. Cumby searched his memory for the man's name; he was one of the landsmen. Ah, yes, Jepson was the name.

"What are you doing here Jepson? This isn't your station."

"I know, sir, but the ship is fighting for her life and I could not just stay where I was and let things play out. I took Mr. Pennywhistle's sword training, it made no sense to me that I should not put it to use."

"You may have signed your own death warrant by coming here, Jepson."

"Not worried about that. With us getting hit so hard from so many directions there ain't no safe place on the weather decks, Mr. Cumby. My mates are putting their lives on the line, and I aim to stand alongside 'em."

"Commendable, most commendable. Jepson. Find a place and have your cutlass ready. We will be attacking shortly."

Jepson swaggered up to his friend MacFarlane with what he hoped was a warrior's confidence. MacFarlane asked with amusement, "What took you so long?"

"I ran into a little trouble on the way here. Dodging slivers and lead slows you a bit. I will be at your side in the fight ahead. I can't let you have all the fun."

Ragged cheering erupted from deep in the bowels of *Bellerophon* and rose upwards like a chorus of men celebrating their release from Purgatory. It was so at odds with the tension under the poop that both Cumby and Pennywhistle diverted their attention from the approaching French horde towards the rising noise. What they saw put heart in both of them.

Bahama was sheering off and taking herself out of the fight. Her sides were pock-marked with holes and she had only stumps for masts.She had jury-rigged two sails that gave her limited propulsion. Cumby could not be sure, but she looked to be riding lower in the water than she had an hour ago. Best of all, the two other ships that had been firing on *Bellerophon* from a distance had been set upon by newly arrived British vessels. Because of the light airs, a substantial portion of the British fleet had not yet made it into action, but now, instead of one ship against four it was one ship against one.

As a parting salutation, *Bellerophon* fired a broadside at *Bahama* that caught her square in the stern. *Bahama* was still afloat, but she would not be bothering anyone for the rest of the battle.

Cumby spied another figure racing toward the poop.It astonished him that it was the man aboard closest to a civilian: Godwin. He had been serving as a messenger, but by now he should have been safely ensconced below decks.

"What are you doing here, Mr. Godwin? I thought you'd be helping in the cockpit." Cumby was genuinely puzzled.

"I was. The sad tidings that I bear are the reason I am here. Mr. Overton just died."

"Blast!" said Cumby quietly. "I knew he was hit badly, but I thought he would recover. He was so sturdy of heart that I always thought he would live to be a hundred. Men like that form the soul of a ship. I cannot think why Jesus did not look upon him kindly." His left arm brusquely wiped away tears.

His countenance brightened just a little. "Well, perhaps Jesus did look upon him kindly; calling him home because He needed a good old tar to welcome all the victims of today's fight to the Pearly Gates. Yes! That must be it! But, Mr. Godwin, while I appreciate being informed of his passing, you did not have to endanger yourself to bring me the news."

"I have seen much of death today, Mr. Cumby, and Mr. Overton's was the one too many. I have watched the midshipmen directing some of the great guns and putting themselves in all manner of danger. I decided that I had to do something active to help them, since schoolmasters are supposed to be an example to their charges. I claim no great skill with a sword, but my father insisted on lessons growing up and I am in hopes some of that knowledge will come back to me."

"Every hand is needed in the crisis ahead, Mr. Godwin, so grab yourself a cutlass from the arms barrel."

"Aye, aye, sir," said Godwin.

Chapter 37

A burst of heavy smoke caused the French boarding party to vanish from view like a coin from a conjurer's hand. Smoke had been both an enemy and a friend to Pennywhistle's men all day. Though it now protected them from snipers that would have provided covering fire to the boarding party, it also made it impossible for his men to employ their marksmanship. He debated whether to have his men volley into the brimstone fog; if they fired low they were bound to hit something; but he decided to exercise patience in the interest of inflicting higher casualties, firing only when they could at least see the outline of a target.

Two loud French voices echoed over the deck and Pennywhistle blinked in astonishment at what he heard. Apparently, two officers were having a violent argument that was as inappropriate as it was dangerous.

"You fool, we must advance immediately! Attack now! It is what the Emperor would do. Audacity! Audacity ! Always audacity!" The voice spoke in a backwoods Breton patois, raspy and deep.

"I am in command here, and you will follow my orders. We would be sending our men on an idiot's errand if we charge when we cannot see a thing." This voice spoke with a gentleman's accent, though it was shrill and callow. "We must wait until there is a break in the smoke. Besides, not all of the lower deck gunners have arrived."

Divided command was a recipe for disaster but a godsend to Pennywhistle. He guessed he was listening to a disagreement between an between an experienced petty officer and a newly commissioned *enseigne de vaisseau*: one sure and eager for action, one untested and biding his time for the ideal opportunity.

Pennywhistle knew the result would be hesitation when the French advanced. Men needed to have absolute confidence in their officers, particularly men who, like the vast majority of French sailors, had never seen combat. Men uncertain if their officers knew their trade fought less well and broke earlier than those who believed their officers.

"I do not dispute your authority, *Monsieur le enseigne*, but it is far better to attack; men who sit still become corpses, not warriors. You must trust me."

"No, we have attacked twice with many casualties but no success. We need more men."

"And those attacks have made the British tired and reduced their numbers. Now is our time!"

Pennywhistle detected a low murmuring of complaint from French sailors.

"We have more than enough men, *Monsieur le enseigne*.

"No, we need more..."

A blast of wind whipped away enough of the smoke so that both sides could see each other again.

"Charge! Yelled the man with the deep, raspy voice.

"Present!" Pennywhistle's men leveled their muskets. He waited a few seconds before completing the order. Concentrated firepower worked best against masses of men, so he delayed until *matelots* were bunched together on the boarding spars and ten Frenchman had crossed over.

"Fire!" Pennywhistle's cutlass flashed down, and all hell broke loose. 30 dragon's tongues of scarlet flame lashed out. A devil's whip of zipping lead tore into the mass of boarders on the spars and Bellerophon's deck.

The volley stopped the advance cold. Pennywhistle detected puzzlement as well as fear in the boarders' cries, yelps, and curses. Since some had been allowed to board unimpeded, he wondered how many had believed the petty officer about the British being weary. Doubtless many were wondering if the *enseigne* had been right about needing more men. Pennywhistle waited five seconds for the marines to switch muskets.

"Follow me! Follow me!" yelled the callow *enseigne* as he waved his sword. The French cheered. Whatever was going through their heads, they were still game. They made another rush, but it was slower than the first, as they had to step over the dead and wounded.

"Fire!" Brown Besses kicked, flames bloomed, and a hurricane of lead knocked down another swath of boarders.

Pour it on, fast and relentless, thought Pennywhistle. French voices cried out in pain and terror. French and British alike coughed from the swirling smoke from the volleys. The wind had dropped again and smoke was accumulating, so Pennywhistle could not see more than a foot ahead of him. It did not really matter, however, because he knew where the French were. As long as his men fired low, Frenchmen were going to die.

"Fire!"

It took about a minute for a marine to load three muskets. Pennywhistle wanted to keep the pressure on the French, but he did not want to frighten them off. He did not want to blunt the boarding attempt; he wanted to annihilate it. He needed to lure them in close.

"Marines! Retire five paces." He knew his order would confuse the French. He hoped they might suspect that the British had run short of ammunition. Some of his marines were probably confused too, but this was where trust paid its most valuable dividend.

The marines reformed in their new position.

"Reload in quick time," Pennywhistle bellowed

Meanwhile, *Bellerophon*'s sailors had made it to the starboard 18-pound carronade on the poop and were reloading it with the frantic speed of men who knew they had only seconds before they came under deadly sniper fire.

A fitful gust of air fully cleared the smoke: the odd, fluky winds were playing havoc with tactics today. Pennywhistle flashed three fingers in Cumby's direction and Cumby acknowledged with three of his own: the agreed upon signal for the sailors to attack after three more volleys.

A second wave of *matelots* were leaping to the deck, but Pennywhistle noted a diminution of enthusiasm. The battered, bleeding bits of humanity underfoot were inducing revulsion and its natural concomitant: caution. That caution slowed the second wave's movements and furnished Pennywhistle the best gift of all: time.

Combs performed the eighteen separate motions necessary to load a musket with a disciplined care that did not sacrifice a second of speed. Pennywhistle had told them shortcuts were dangerous; though he used none, he had his three muskets reloaded in 55 seconds. His fear retreated with each succeeding volley. He assumed there would be a bayonet charge thereafter, and checked to make sure his bayonet was firmly anchored to the forward nub on his musket.

Warwick grinned in satisfaction at the effect of the volleys. His pulse raced and a wave of exhilarating heat enveloped his face. There was a certain truth to the expression "the joy of battle," at least as long as you were winning, and unharmed. He had never been in a battle where his side had the enemy dead to rights at such close range. Even the allurements of the best whore in Portsmouth could not compare to the excitement of his present post.

Dale was pleased with the men's conduct, but checked the bad apple in the marine barrel to make sure he was doing nothing to spoil it. He had expected Wilson to faint, fall, or feign injury, but he was still upright, looking startled that he was still alive. He was at least waving his sword and pointing in the right direction. Dale doubted that any men were drawing inspiration from his motions, but at least he was not detracting from the reputation of British officers.

Cumby was enough of a humanitarian to feel a twinge of sadness at seeing his enemies sliced up like cutlets of beef, but it in no way blinded him to his duty. He had sympathy for his enemies, like the good Christian he believed himself to be; but his primary duty was to defend his ship and he would do so with every ounce of his heart and soul. He would launch his counterattack, and he was confident that it would be devastating.

The five sailors on the poop had just finished loading the 18-pounder when the first of their number was struck by a bullet. It entered the crown of his head and flattened as it bored forward. When it burst from his forehead it removed most of the top half of his face. His brains splattered his friends, who froze in shock. Musket balls hitting the deck like a squall of hail snapped them back to reality.

Only one man was needed to fire the weapon, and the others might now retreat to the safety of the poop overhang, except there was the distinct possibility that the one remaining man might be killed before he could fire the weapon. All knew the carronade was to play a key role, and so all resolved to remain where they were, part human shield, part reserves.

Pennywhistle estimated fifty new boarders had joined the ten who still stood from the first wave. They were readying to charge the sometimes visible sailors in the distance, but their officer must have decide to lead form the rear, and without his command to advance they hesitated. Thirty more remained on *Aigle's* deck: a sure sign that the infection of caution was spreading. He assessed his men and saw they were reloaded and ready.

He bellowed the words his men were eager to hear. "Present!" Two lines of wood and metal cobras went to the point. "Fire!" The scarlet whip again lashed out. one tenth of the new boarders were struck down, and those left standing began to very slowly edge backwards. Their confusion deepened; they had been led to believe the this boarding effort was just a mopping up operation.

"Fire!" The disciplined volley hit the French low and five more souls departed the earth. The rearward movement of the remaining *matelots* quickened.

"Fire!" The third volley extinguished any sense of order that remained in the boarding party. The survivors abandoned any pretense of discipline and turned toward the spar.

Higgins' blood was on fire and his heart was racing like a thoroughbred spying the finish line. By God, they were giving Johnny Crapaud a damn fine thrashing! This was what he had signed on for. He was leaping and laughing like a leprechaun on a drinking spree. The stories he would tell his father and Miss Lydia! "Give it to 'em, boys! Slam 'em! Crush 'em! Smash 'em hard! They won't stand!" The irony of him addressing men nearly double his age as boys was utterly lost on him. His men liked his enthusiasm and speeded their reloading.

Wilson increased the frenzied waving of his sword. He hoped it was the right thing to do, but he was really doing it to burn off excess nervous energy. He looked down at his trousers and saw a demeaning yellow stain. Damn! Still, the obscuring effects of smoke might conceal it; and anyway, the men were far too preoccupied to notice.

His side looked to be winning. No thanks to him, but at least he was keeping up appearances. He thought of all of the money that he had won on this cruise. Just a few more minutes and it would all be his to spend in a very long and very safe life.

Godwin watched the slaughter of the *matelots* with satisfaction. It surprised him how quickly the death of Overton had turned his heart dark. He might not have much skill with a cutlass, but all he could think of right now was burying it deep in French flesh. Revenge might not be admirable, but it had a marked effect in reducing fear.

Pennywhistle knew the boarders were reeling and primed for the knockout blow. He blew a staccato blast on the boarding bugle and a sailor jerked the carronade lanyard.

Boom! The weapon spat a dragon's breath of 400 balls on to the crippled, frightened rabble of Frenchmen trying to flee *Bellerophon's* deck. The hail of metal swept the boarding party. All but twenty of the French were as mangled as if their bodies had been forced through an immense sieve. The survivors were frozen in horror, and many of them retched.

A few of the British retched as well, but none dropped out of line.

"Charge bayonets! Advance!" Pennywhistle kept his voice strong and steady, devoid of the excitement stirring his blood. The more the extraordinary was made to seem a mere stroll in the park the better his men would do.

The marines moved forward with slow, precise steps; their discipline as awesome as the line of sharp steel that they held in front of them.

"Stall and hook," whispered Combs to himself.

"Stall and hook," whispered Warwick.

Entirely unbidden, the rest of the marines took up what seemed almost a medieval prayer.

"Stall and hook!" It acquired the rhythm of a Gregorian Chant.

"Stall and hook!" grew in volume and certainty as the Marines moved forward. It evolved from a low rumble to a menacing growl.

Pennywhistle had never heard a melody so beautiful.

As the marine bayonets converged on the boarders, *Bellerophon*'s sailors attacked, yelling imprecations. *Die, sons-of-bitches! Devil take you! Fucking whoresons! Shit on Boney!*were the milder insults. They held their weapons at the ready as they dashed forward, and the expressions on their faces proclaimed that they were confident that nothing could stand before their onslaught.

So great was *Bellerophon*'s *esprit de corps* that anyone who could hold a cutlass joined the charge. That included five ship's boys, three of Cooke's servants, Hazard his Secretary, and a sailor who had the worst case of dysentery imaginable. That sailor had removed the seat of his trousers so that he could defecate as he ran.

The sailors and marines crashed into the knot of Frenchman at the same time but from different angles. The marines hit them head on; the sailors on the flank. The effect was to place the boarders in a closing nutcracker made of British steel.

"Slow, slow, quick, quick," Warwick muttered as he moved. He used the wood of his musket just aft of the balance to parry a savage thrust to his head by a *matelot* who towered over him. His confidence soared because he knew that only amateurs cut at heads. The Frenchman's perceived height advantage was actually a liability, because Warwick could reach the man's vitals quicker than his hands could protect them. Warwick shoved the bayonet into his belly and reflexively recited the section of The Rule of Four that he had turned into his personal catechism. He gave his bayonet a sharp twist and it came out as easily as it had gone in.

He saw the next blow coming before it was launched. He paid attention to the stubby Frenchman's shoulder and neck muscles and they positively shouted that the target of their owner's sword would be Warwick's stomach. He was on guard before it arrived and knocked it up and away. He slashed sideways at the Frenchman's throat and was rewarded with a mighty jet of blood when he severed the carotid artery.

A slash at his leg was deflected with a low inside block and he retaliated by burying the point of his bayonet in the *matelot's* thigh. He did not wait to see the man fall before engaging a fourth Frenchman.

This time he made a straight line thrust to his opponent's heart so fast that the man had only begun to raise his blade in defense.

Combs beside him parried a slash at his legs with the butt of his musket. A red-headed sailor screamed words at him he could not understand, though their purport was clear. Combs responded with utter silence and quick action. He shoved the butt hard into carrot-top's groin. As the man gasped and bent forward, Combs retracted his musket and used his bayonet to gouge a furrow down the Frenchman's face that continued to slice open the cloth over his sternum and the flesh beneath, pressing forward so the sharpened edge went deep. The Frenchman fell back, his screams of fury changed to wails of pain.

Combs' peripheral vision detected an incoming slash at his shoulder. He pivoted and parried it with a vertical high outside block. His riposte was to slam the butt of his musket hard into the man's left ribs. He heard bones snapping. He swiveled his weapon quickly: the tip of his bayonet dug so deeply into the man's right ribs that bone became visible. The *matelot* made a horrible wheezing sound that Combs would never forget.

Twenty feet away on the left flank, MacFarlane blocked what seemed to him a very slow cut at his throat. He executed a high inside vertical block and took the weight of the enemy blade on exactly the right portion of his own. He guided the enemy's sword away from himself and then punched the man hard in the nose with his own heavy guard.

There was an explosion of cartilage and the man staggered backwards. The pain caused him to bend his neck at an odd angle that was most inviting to MacFarlane's blade. MacFarlane had been cautioned not cut at the head, but he had also been instructed to strike at any vital, unprotected surface.

His blow hit the Frenchman so hard that it nearly severed his head. His head appeared attached by only a few tendrils of flesh and it puzzled MacFarlane how he remained alive. His question was answered a second later as his head drooped to a highly unnatural angle and the light fled his eyes.

The next sailor was a skilled fighter and MacFarlane found himself hard-pressed. He cut at the man's stomach and it was blocked. His opponent then lunged at his leg and he parried it aside. He cut at the man's neck and it was deflected. The Frenchman returned the favor with jab at his diaphragm, which he batted away.

They were evenly matched, and MacFarlane could see a certain respect in his opponent's eyes which oddly gratified him. He won the fight by sidestepping a lunge at his left ribs and riposting with a slash the amputated the man's arm and continued on into his lungs.

Jepson's skill was less than his friend MacFarlane's. He missed a block and his mistake should have proved fatal, but his cumbersome boarding helmet saved his life. The heavy blow landed on its left metal plate just above the bill and glanced off. He felt dizzy and there was a distinct ringing in his ears, but he remained upright and functional.

His opponent gazed at him in amazement; his blow should have cut the Englishman's brain in two!

Jepson might not be skillful, but he was fast. His opponent's moment of confusion was just enough. Jepson feinted at his throat, then slashed at his stomach. The blow ripped a foot long furrow and the man's pulsating intestines cascaded out.

He wasted no time celebrating his good fortune, but stabbed the tip of his sword into the kidneys of a sailor who had unwisely presented his back to him to fight someone else. There was nothing dishonorable about stabbing a man in the back during general melee; in fact, it was wiser than trying to do the same to his front.

The French grenade-tossing had stopped during boarding, since explosions do not discriminate between friend and foe packed closely together. But in every war there is always one man who somehow fails to get the order. That man had a strong arm and threw his grenade far. It sailed slowly through the air, headed directly for Wilson's head.

Wilson had just finished wiping the vomit from his uniform induced by viewing the carnage caused by the carronade. He only saw the grenade at the last second. He instinctively turned away and brought his hand up for protection. It landed squarely in the palm of his glove, still sizzling evilly. He looked at it in horror; he seemed a magnet for the damn things.

For a brief second a roaring anger hit that he was going to die. He moved to pitch the grenade at the chief author of his misery, Pennywhistle. He had him in clear view, but to his great surprise, he instead pivoted and threw the projectile overboard. It exploded in mid air before it struck the water.

He had actually done the right thing. It was a shame that in the noise and confusion of battle no one noticed.

His reward for his good deed was a bullet to the right temple. It was a spent round that did not penetrate the skin; nevertheless, the pain was awful: spent rounds hurt worse than ones that actually penetrated. He staggered for a few seconds, then passed out. As he lost consciousness, he wondered if he would survive, or if the rig's protection had failed him at the last.

Dale saw him fall but had not seen the grenade. He noticed the vomit on Wilson's collar, the urine on the trousers, and the lack of any holes in the body. Just as he suspected! The faint-hearted bastard had lost his nerve and passed out.

Higgins advanced, sword drawn, on a French Lieutenant who looked old for his rank. He slashed hard at the Frenchman's stomach then his chest but but both blows were parried with a grace that suggested his opponent was a swordsman of experience and skill. The Lieutenant riposted with a slash at Higgins' sword hand, but the crown escutcheon in the knuckle bow deflected the cut.

The enormous energy of the blow shoved Higgins' sword back so powerfully that its lion's head pommel was now a mere inch from his nose. The Frenchman retracted his blade and readied a strike.

Higgins had no time to cock his arm to deliver his own slash. A look halfway between confusion and fear rippled over his face.

The Frenchman saw it and laughed derisively, likely believing that he faced a no-account boy merely impersonating an officer.

The contempt angered Higgins, and the Frenchman's open mouth sparked an idea. His blade was seven inches longer than the Frenchman's, and every one of those inches was double edged. He turned his weapon sideways and thrust it forward in the short, hard jab that Pennywhistle had taught him from *savate*.

The Lieutenant blinked in astonishment as the Irishman's blade burrowed under his tongue, bisected his gullet, and exited out the back of his neck. Higgins oscillated the blade violently, cutting the Lieutenant a bloody clown's mouth. *Who's laughing now?* thought Higgins.

Higgins anger fled when he saw life depart the Frenchmen's eyes like windows suddenly shuttered. It was an awesome sight but his fixation on it allowed a French petty officer to come at him from the side, undetected until the last second. Higgins clumsily batted his blow aside but it left him off balance.

Dale watched Higgins fight with alarm. The Irishman blocked two cuts to his chest and inflicted a gash on the Frenchman's shoulder but a lucky riposte dug a nasty trench on his sword arm. He staggered backwards as if stunned and might not survive another blow.

Dale drew his own hanger and made a mad dash at the petty officer, ramming the tip of his hanger between the man's floating ribs, and pushing until it had skewered the heart. He wrenched his blade free, and the man collapsed.

"Thanks, Sergeant!" said a grateful, white-faced Higgins. "That's two I owe you!"

"I couldn't let you break Miss Lydia's heart!" Dale yelled back.

The sailors on the poop deck had been delighted by the outcome of their handiwork, but its success had also made them the target of increased French attention. Two more succumbed to French musketry from *Aigle's* tops, one shot in the head and one in the stomach. The two remaining sailors had reloaded the carronade, but with the increasing accuracy of French musket fire both doubted either could remain long alive on the poop.

"Go, my friend, go. No reason for both of us to die."

"You sure? I hate abandoning a shipmate."

"You got a wife and young 'uns, and I ain't. I won't be missed, but some innocents will suffer if you ain't around. Just go!"

"I will never forget this." He squeezed his friend's hand hard.

"You damn well better not."

The two smiled unsentimentally at each other, then one ran while the other stayed. The one who ran reached his destination, but the one who stayed died at his post with a bullet to the chest.

The sailor's sacrifice did not go un-noted. Godwin had been preparing to advance with the second line of seamen, but seeing the sword battles he knew his blade skills were utterly inadequate to the task. He did not so much fear death as he did dying to no purpose. Then he had seen the exchange on the poop deck.

Though he could hear no sound, he could guess at the parting words of the two seamen. He saw the one who remained fall. The carronade now stood unattended and inert.

He would have to survive a barrage of heavy sharpshooter fire but remembered his friend's Overton's face and made his decision. His father had said he was just a bitter drunk who had tossed away his gifts.

Well, he was stone cold sober now, and all he could think was that it was better to die than let *Bellerophon* suffer the indignity of flying a French Tricolor. Fellowship mattered far more than his own hide. Heart in his throat, ducking low, he dashed over to the carronade.

Only to find when he arrived that there were no targets left to fire upon. God win stared after the retreating boarders, feeling oddly empty.

The sailors and marines had cut the French to ribbons.. The French boarders who still could do so turned, ran, and jumped onto the lowered spars, scurrying back like roaches suddenly exposed to sunlight.

Cumby came up to Pennywhistle, smiling delightedly and extending his hand in triumph. "A great day for British arms, sir! A great day indeed."

Pennywhistle shook Cumby's hand with considerably less enthusiasm than that with which it had been extended. He wanted to smile and return Cumby's compliments, but the hairs on the back of his neck stood up, and a discomfiting jolt of electricity shot along his nerves.

It was all too glorious, too perfect, too easy. His intuition screamed at him. He had missed something! What was it? His mind raced, considering a variety of factors, but could pinpoint nothing wrong. Then...

"L'abordage! L'abordage!" That and what followed, in exquisite French, translated roughly to, "Follow me, all those who can!" A commanding French voice rang out; it would have been at home in grand opera. It continued with a passionate appealed to patriotism, honor, and family, and reminded all that the *Empereur* would handsomely reward anyone involved in the capture of an English ship-of-the-line. The steel words and silken tones belonged to a tall and stately looking French officer who had leaped upon the distant edge of the boarding spar.

From the quality of his clothing and an accent that originated in Versailles, Pennywhistle guessed the booming voice belonged to Jean-Pierre La Tempie, the ship's First Officer. La Tempie was an aristocrat who had miraculously survived The Terror; a hardy veteran who did not give up easily. By the numbers he was beaten, and a prudent man would guide his ship away to fight another day—a traditional French naval officer would have done so.

But the passion on his face and in his voice proclaimed him a devotee of Bonaparte: a leader who believed that a victory less than total was hardly worth noting. It was hardly a first officer's duty to lead a boarding party, but British marines has accounted for a great many junior and warrant officers.

Frenchmen rallied, heeding the fire and patriotism of La Tempie's words. *Damn!* thought Pennywhistle. *Don't these people know when they are beaten?* Apparently not. La Tempie seemed to have Robespierre's gift for bewitching crowds. Probably thirty men had joined him on the spar, with more on the way. *My God, are they going to sacrifice every last sailor to take this ship?*

But one man was utterly immune to the French officer's words, and he was a man with a gun: a big gun. "Not so fast, you son of a bitch." Godwin muttered, and jerked the carronade's lanyard.

His aim was almost perfect. The blast turned most of the massing boarders into flying gristle and unattached body parts, but it missed the First Officer completely. La Tempie looked around him in utter confusion, an orator deprived of an audience. He glanced quickly back at his own ship, then scanned the deck of *Bellerophon.*

He smiled, removed his hat, and executed a long, gracious bow directed toward *Bellerophon.* Pennywhistle doffed his own hat in acknowledgment. La Tempie was accepting defeat and paying tribute to stalwart opponents. The man was clearly *ancien regime* to the core, with the same sense of honor that Pennywhistle's tutor du Motier had always displayed.

The Frenchman recovered himself and donned his hat. He then dashed off the spar with remarkable speed. He was honorable, not stupid.

A minute later, the boarding spars were retracted. The French had shot their bolt. Bellonna's verdict was in: sound training beat numbers.

CHAPTER 38

"What are you doing on deck, Mr. Whyte?" asked Cumby. "I thought you would have plenty to keep you busy below, since the day so far has been a bloody one."

"That's the problem, Mr. Cumby. We have run out of space. I have the men packed as closely as possible, and we cannot accommodate one more man. It is so full that I do not even have room to wield my saw. We must move the ones requiring amputation to some other place. The Captain's Cabin would provide sufficient space, and I am sure that our late Captain would have approved of his digs being used to help his men."

"I would normally approve without a second thought, Mr. Whyte, but the battle is far from over. We are still under distant fire, and I fear we will engage closely with more ships before the day is done. I do not want the men exposed to any danger. I will give you provisional approval with the understanding the men must be moved back to the cockpit if we again come under heavy fire. Is that understood?"

"Completely, Lieutenant. I could use some assistance transporting the wounded."

"I will detail the port boarders to assist you. But of course, they will have to be instantly recalled if..."

"If the needs of the Service require it." Whyte finished the thought with a standard Navy phrase useful in justifying almost any action. "I quite understand; the safety of the ship comes first.

Carrying twenty wounded up three decks was not a task for those with kind or faint hearts. It was brutal, sad work, and the men toting the wounded steeled themselves against the agonized cries, yelps, and moans of their passengers. The deck beams were low, and men carried over shoulders frequently bumped their heads on the heavy, unforgiving oak. It was considered manly for the wounded to bear their pain in silence, but collisions with deck beams pushed their capacity for stoicism beyond the breaking point.

The smoke from all the cannon discharges had not fully dissipated, making it hard to see much of anything, and necessitating the use of dim deck lanterns as waypoints on the journey. The reeking, thick atmosphere caused many of the injured to cough violently when they were not moaning or screaming.

The carriers stumbled frequently and sometimes dropped a passenger because the decks were slicked with blood and hazardous with splinters, which were hard on the sailors who were barefooted. Scattered oddments of bodies, guns, and misshapen fusions of the two made each deck a maze more intricate than anything designed by Capability Brown.

Pierson had been grazed on the left temple by a five-foot splinter that had knocked him senseless. There had been little blood, but he was dizzy and his eyesight cycled between reasonable clarity and double vision. The surgeon had diagnosed a concussion, but he was at least ambulatory.

He held on to the back of the checked shirt in front of him like a blind man and trusted that the carrier in front could detect obstacles better than his own uncertain sight. He recalled the morning that he had first reported aboard a King's Ship and decided that, except for today, it was the worst one of his life.

Pennywhistle heaved a long sigh of relief. Cumby walked over to him slowly, not quite willing to believe the fight was actually over. "What do you think, Mr. Pennywhistle? Have we seen their best effort?"

"I believe we have, sir. That last gesture of the First Lieutenant was not just chivalry; it was a signal to audiences on two ships that this particular play is over. The French on *Aigle* have neither the manpower nor the willpower to launch another effort. They are gallant and determined foes, but they know when it is time to cut their losses."

"Thank God for that. I am pleased at the way our men have behaved, but we have been very hard pressed and they need a respite. I am grateful other British ships have finally taken some of the pressure off us."

"I am grateful as well. I think—" Pennywhistle's ears perked up. "Do you hear that, Mr. Cumby?"

Cumby listened carefully. He cupped his chin and a moment later let out a sigh that was part relief and part satisfaction. He heard the sound of dozens of axes chopping fast and hard. It was coming from the point where the two ships had crashed together. He unfurled his glass and saw *matelots* furiously clearing away the huge, gnarled mass of wood and rope that bound the ships together.

A few seconds later, *Aigle* hoisted her jib and spanker. She was giving up and breaking off the engagement!

"I presume you are going to give them a proper send off," said Pennywhistle.

"I certainly am!" said Cumby with enthusiasm. "When she sheers off we should be able to rake her. I will send messengers to Mr. Douglas and Mr. Saunders to have their men ready. You and I may have done good work here, but it is their gunnery that has truly been our salvation."

Cumby looked over the weather decks, and his enthusiasm died. "Blast! Look at us. Jib boom shot away, three stumps for masts, and our spanker cut to ribbons. We are going to have to do a lot of jury rigging. Still, we have a good crew and will manage somehow." He sighed. "The main course is beyond hope, but if we risk the fore course we should be able to maintain some way. We are hurt and slow, but a long way from out of the fight. And we have one thing working in our favor that I fear most of the King's ships do not."

"What is that, sir?"

"Our boats are all intact. Our Captain was wise to have them towed astern. Some of the other captains have kept them on their skids and they are reduced to splinters. We will have the means to send prize crews to surrendered ships, while many other ships in our fleet will not."

"Agreed, sir! Now, if you will excuse me, I need to get my marines reorganized. We both have pressing duties requiring our immediate attention." Pennywhistle doffed his hat and executed a sweeping bow that was a product of true admiration rather than mere theatricality.

Cumby touched his hat in acknowledgment, then fingered the cross on his chest, silently thanking Jesus for his favor. He pivoted slowly on his heel and walked away with shoulders hunched slightly, finally understanding the burden of command. He now instinctively understood why Captain Cooke had smiled so little.

CHAPTER 39

Pennywhistle spent the next ten minutes doing a roll call and weapons check. Despite the intensity of the last engagement, only three Marines on the quarterdeck had been wounded: two privates and Mr. Higgins. When well trained men met indifferently trained ones, the result was often a great disparity in the casualty lists. His obsessive attention to training had paid exactly the reward he sought: clear victory with a low butcher's bill.

The marine wounds were painful but not severe, and all three men declined a visit to the cockpit. More action was likely soon, and none of them wanted to be absent. Dale scavenged some linen and jury-rigged bandages. He had seen enough action to perform creditably as a combat medical man, though he knew the wounds would require stitches in the next day or two.

The men looked with disgust at Wilson, sprawled unconscious on the deck. He was breathing heavily, still very much alive, and apparently unwounded. Nothing was said, but the expressions on his marines' faces told Pennywhistle exactly what they were thinking.

They saw the urine and the vomit; the large purple welt caused by the spent ball was hidden by his hair.

Pennywhistle also drew the wrong conclusion, but a generalized respect for officers had to be maintained whatever the defects of an individual specimen. He motioned to Warwick and Combs."You men, carry Mr. Wilson to the Great Cabin. He just needs to sleep this off."

Warwick and Combs were not pleased that rank cowardice was being treated like a hangover, but they saluted crisply and replied with a terse "Aye, aye, sir." Wilson soon disappeared, and the mood of the Marines visibly lightened.

"Three cheers for Mr. Pennywhistle!" shouted a very pleased Higgins, apparently oblivious to the pain of his wound.

The Marines responded with vigor. The three bandsmen still alive heard the cheers and struck up a bouncy rendition of "The Girl I left Behind Me." It was amazing that they could still manage any tune in the midst of so much blood and death; but then, some of the finest masterpieces had been created by artists suffering through great personal reverses.

Pennywhistle smiled in acknowledgment, but quickly waved his hands to restrain the start of a premature victory celebration."I am proud of all of you, but we are not out of this yet. The battle still rages, and we all have important parts to play. Those normally part of gun crews should now report as replacements to their respective stations. Casualties have likely been heavy and you will be sorely needed. The rest of you will stay with me. We will clear debris from the quarterdeck and then see what opportunities present themselves for useful service. Dis...miss." The marines snapped to attention for a brief instant, then dispersed.

Fifteen marines departed for the upper and lower gun decks. The remaining fifteen relaxed and conversed quietly among themselves. Higgins, Dale, and Pennywhistle talked animatedly, understanding that they would have to chart their own course, since Cumby was fully occupied with his new duties.

"I think we should spread the men around the ship in pairs to give the ship the widest possible defense," said Higgins.

Pennywhistle shook his head. "I think that might be unwise. Our firepower would be spread so thin as to be nearly useless. Fifteen muskets would be better employed in one spot to give us at least a local superiority of fire over an enemy. What do you think, Sarn't ?"

"I agree, sir. I think posting them along the starboard waist would be a good plan. They would be well placed to fire at any ships passing close, and in a central location so they could quickly move to any spot of the ship that was threatened."

"I concur, Sarn't. Mr. Higgins, your suggestion was not a bad one, but we just have too few men to make it effective."

Higgins chirped, "Just trying to help, but you two know a deal more than I do. I am happy to follow your instructions."

"I wish all newly commissioned officers had your attitude, Mr. Higgins. And now the necessary part of the job that sickens me and that I hate. We need to clear the quarterdeck. We need to get the men pitching these bodies overboard. I, you, and Sarn't Dale will each supervise five men. Let us all work as quickly as possible, so that men can take up muskets again."

The duty was awful, but the men did their jobs and made no complaint. The deck possessed a glossy sheen from blood, and some marines almost lost their balance. Men threw bodies and body parts over the side like they were sacks of old shoe leather. Everyone pretended that what they were handling was somehow not human.

Cleaning up the human detritus of battle was always a long, slow slide into melancholy and despair. Doing so in the course of a battle was a labor of Sisyphus since as soon as one body was disposed of a new one soon took its place. Bodies could be sliced, diced, ripple cut, and dissected in so many nasty ways that even the most fecund imagination could not begin to conceive of the results of well-directed cannon and musket fire. The images of smashed, broken bodies in fantastically grotesque states would curse many with nightmares for years to come.

Pennywhistle had witnessed dissections in Edinburgh, but they were measured, orderly, and served the cause of knowledge. This slaughter was profligate, chaotic, and offered no knowledge save that men were fools.

Twice in the next ten minutes, Pennywhistle felt vomit gurgle in his stomach, and it took every ounce of his self control to prevent it from heading for his throat. Several of his men voided their stomachs. No one said anything. A little vomit added to the bloody debris of battle was no more than a turd thrown on a pile of offal.

"By Jayzuz, I ain't dead." A man, an Irishman by his accent, about to be chucked overboard suddenly came wide awake and started struggling. "Ain't ready to quit life just yet." The startled marines holding his hands and feet dropped him hard on the deck.

"That hurt, damn your eyes."

The two marines looked at each other, then started laughing. When the man stood up they realized that the massive amount of blood staining his chest belonged to someone else and he had not a wound on him. The concussive force of a passing cannon ball had probably knocked him out.

Boom! Boom! The decks shook and men below cheered. Pennywhistle turned his head. An incredibly destructive raking broadside slammed into the retreating *Aigle*, now 150 yards from Bellerophon. 18- and 32-pound shot from *Bellerophon* plowed a vicious swath along the whole length of *Aigle's* decks unimpeded by anything except bodies.

Bits of men, timber, and metal flew high in the air, followed by a chorus of yelps, howls, and shrieks that seemed barely human. Men on fire jumped overboard, trailing columns of ash like dying comets. There was a huge hole in *Aigle's* stern, as if a giant had just punched his fist through it.

And then she was gone, swallowed up by a massive wall of smoke. A lone, defiant cry of *"Vive l' Empereur!"* marked her passing. *Aigle* was part of a pattern. Ships appeared like wraiths out of the massive bastions of smoke, sometimes fired a broadside and disappeared.

It was like going to a ball where all of the dancers had cloaks of invisibility that they whipped on and off at unpredictable intervals. Ships changed enemy partners, firing at whatever opponent appeared out of nowhere. The fog of war was not a figure of speech today.

The next hours passed slowly for Pennywhistle and his marines lining the bulwarks. The clouds of smoke grew in height and density, making the battle a deadly game of peek-a-boo. The marines fired at enemy ships when the opportunity presented itself, but those were few and fleeting. He was disappointed at the limited scope this afforded his men's extensive small arms training. The battle was chiefly a contest of great guns.

He checked his watch compulsively.

He and his men did not so much see the unfolding battle as hear it. The gigantic roaring of thousands of hidden cannons at close range left more than a few with a ringing in their ears that would remain permanently. He noticed that when he was talking to Higgins, he had to ask the young officer to speak up several times.

Over the next three hours, *Bellerophon* engaged six ships for brief periods, all at long range and with nothing like the intensity of her struggle with *Aigle*.

At 2:15 she poured two broadsides into a ship that they had first fired on when they broke the enemy line of battle. It turned out to be the Spanish ship *Monarcha*. She surrendered, displaying a large British ensign to show that she was open to possession. Midshipman Fairbrother and 25 sailors went over in a cutter. Fairbrother would never make lieutenant, but he would finally have a command.

At 4 in the afternoon, Cumby fired on a coterie of French ships fleeing the general engagement. He had no idea if *Bellerophon's* shots connected, but it was clear that only a small rump of the enemy fleet remained uncaptured.

By 5, most of the gunfire had died away and a steadily rising breeze cleared most of the smoke. Both fleets were reduced to sad assemblages of violently bobbing corks with stubs for masts; ugly parodies of what had once been exquisitely beautiful sailing ships. The British flag flew atop the mast stumps of all of the vessels. Nelson had won his great victory.

CHAPTER 40

Leaning heavily against the lone section of *Bellerophon's* taffrail that remained intact, Pennywhistle stared at the sun torpidly slipping beneath the horizon. He needed the wooden support; the battle had left him so deeply fatigued that he could barely stand. Even putting one foot in front of the other was an ordeal. He had expended huge amounts of energy today and the bill had come due.

He knew that he looked awful. His face was that of a chimney sweep and his hands those of a coal miner. His lower lip bled from his biting it, and two of the fingernails of his left hand had been chewed to nubs. He could not recall performing either action.

He guessed that he smelled like a cross between a rotten egg and a dog's fart. But then, so did the entire ship.

The battle had been a triumph and a tragedy, an epic and an obscenity. His survival was either a miracle or a joke; depending on whether you regarded God as a benevolent father or a macabre satirist. He finally concluded that God was both.

"Are you all right, sir?"

Dale's voice from behind startled him, and he jerked his hand from the rail as swiftly as if it had been on fire. At least his weary brain thought so; fatigue had actually rendered his movements as slow as an eighty year old getting out of bed.

He was embarrassed that Dale saw him grabbing the equivalent of a standing cat nap.

He turned slowly to face his sergeant, whose complexion was darkened to the hue of a blackamoor by powder residue.

"Not ready for a royal levee, but doing well enough, Sarn't." He was suddenly energized by an aroma that was as unexpected as it was welcome. Dale had a mug of coffee! How was that possible? He had used up the last of his beans.

"You have been pushing yourself hard since the battle ended, sir, and I thought perhaps you could back your sails for a bit and rendezvous with an old friend."

Dale handed him the steaming mug, and for the first time in many hours, Pennywhistle smiled.

"Your servant told me that he had set aside a secret cache of beans, figuring that you'd badly need them after the battle. He had no doubts about your survival. It's black and thick enough to stand a spoon, just the way he said you'd like it."

"My servant is a decent fellow but not over resourceful. I gather he acted at your suggestion, so thank you, Sarn't."

Pennywhistle sipped the nectar of the gods very slowly, savoring every sacred drop. He wanted to make this life-sustaining liquid last as long as possible. He felt energy returning to his limbs and hope to his thoughts. He wondered for the thousandth time why his countrymen were so in love with such an insipid drink as tea.

"I can handle things here, sir," said Dale. "Why don't you take a quarter hour stroll and enjoy your refreshment? You have earned it."

Pennywhistle took another sip before answering. "Thank you, Sarn't. I shall do just that."

He slowly pulled his watch out to mark the time and make sure that his stroll did not exceed fifteen minutes. He was glad that the expensive timepiece had come through the battle intact, although he had consulted it far too often.

His uniform was a complete loss: so shredded and saturated with blood, wafers of wood, and gobs of gore that it was better suited to a beggar clown at a county fair.

The Blancpain's engraving was a warning that, for now, he chose not to heed—*Procrastination is the thief of time*. He knew a respite from supervising the clean-up of human and ship debris would refresh him sufficiently that he might do his grisly job a little better. A brief perambulation about the weather decks would also give him a better idea of how repairs in general were proceeding.

It was 6:45. He had been awake since 2 am, but it seemed uncounted eons. It was almost as if time had run backwards today. Hands on clocks that ran down to their final remains of torque sometimes actually moved back a tic just before they died.

Pennywhistle walked slowly, allowing the coffee to press-gang into service the little that remained of his optimism. The scale of butchery was so vast that his emotions were mostly numbed, just as a wounded body shut down the pain receptors at the site of a wound so that it could fight on. He did at least feel saddened when informed of the death of the cat Screwloose. Men understood, but animals were innocents.

Pennywhistle had finally"met the lion" and was pleased with the outcome. Command had proven exhilarating, though he would never have guessed that the price tag for success was a lassitude of mind, body, and spirit so profound and shocking that he knew how Lucifer must have felt when he was cast out of Paradise. Directing men in battle did have certain similarities to ruling in Hell.

Cleaning up after a battle was the most macabre, exhausting duty imaginable and would have daunted fresh sailors under the best conditions. Instead, the gruesome task fell to battered, weary men whose physical and mental state closely matched that of their ship. Total casualties were 150 out of 540; one-third of the 72 Marines had fallen.

Twenty-five men had been detailed for a prize crew for *Bahama:* far fewer than were actually needed, but all that Cumby could spare. She had been so badly injured that she made *Bellerophon* look as if she had just left a shipyard.

The prize crew would have to guard, supervise, and assist Spanish prisoners cleaning up their ship: a truly Herculean task, considering that *Bahama* likely had casualties three times *Bellerophon's*. Only Carpenter's Mate Jacobs spoke any Spanish, which meant that there would be a lot of pointing and pantomiming.

Suddenly an enormous, blinding light flared on the horizon. A giant column of flame shot high into the atmosphere, followed by a great *Boom*. The column expanded into an immense red globe speckled with dark spots that represented, Pennywhistle realized with a shock of awe, bodies and timber. The whole hung suspended for a moment, like some morbid tableau.

A French warship had just vanished from existence. Likely, a fire had reached one of her powder magazines. It was a terrible thing to witness, and it reminded Pennywhistle that no matter how bad things were on his ship, the alternatives were far worse.

So much blood had cascaded down *Bellerophon's* sides that they displayed sickeningly large stripes of red, and the sea itself bore a sinister crimson taint.

Floating bodies bobbed against ship's hull at irregular intervals, their bloated, fish-belly-white faces fixed in pleading stares that would forever haunt any man who saw them. The faint knocking sound that the corpses made as they bumped against the ship's timbers made it seem as if they were demanding entrance. Most would eventually wash ashore on Spanish beaches, covering them as thickly as rotting seaweed and giving civilians an unpleasant education on the real costs of battle.

Bellerophon's weather decks were a jungle of tangled masts, sails, ropes, and fragments of wood that would take many hours to cut away and clear. Her scuppers still dribbled rivulets of blood, her deck planking was stained scarlet, and badly mangled body parts could still be found in in her ratlines. Jumbled layers of splinters, ranging from a few inches to six feet in length, littered her decks and made her seem a shipyard run by homicidal maniacs.

The ship drifted slowly. Her ruined masts hung over the sides, acting as giant anchors. The standing mast stumps were badly damaged, with large chunks missing and many of their supporting shrouds and stays severed. The ship's wheel was intact, but the accumulated damage made *Bellerophon* nearly impossible to control.

Her fore course was damaged but operable. She could eventually be sailed, if all of the debris were cut away.

Her hold contained four feet of water, because the ship was badly holed below the waterline. Manning the bilge pumps was exhausting work, but men understood that only by doing so could the ship stay afloat. Most of the other British ships were worse off in that respect, and several of the Spanish prizes were in danger of sinking in the next few hours.

The carpenter's mates worked feverishly to fashion new shot plugs. As soon as one was finished, it was slathered with tallow and hammered into a waiting hole.

Bodies so badly disfigured that their owners would remain forever unknown had already been cast into the sea. The ones intact leaked streams of bile and a few had bloated, reeking of the gases of decay. They had been stacked like cordwood and would later be identified and sewn into canvas shrouds made from their own hammocks. Those shrouds would be weighted with round shot. After a quick service, they would be given a burial at sea tomorrow morning.

The ship's general smell put him in mind of being inside a giant mouth filled with bleeding gums, running sores, and rotting teeth. The sickly sweet stink of incipient putrescence and stagnant water made him wish that he had a vial of perfume to inhale. The aroma of new lumber offered some slight mitigation.

Several sailors listlessly roamed the decks with buckets of vinegar. They cast ladles of it in various directions in an effort to disperse the blood, as well as mask its awful smell. It was like trying to clean the Augean stables with tea spoons.

Ooof! A very bewildered looking Scott collided with Pennywhistle. His eyes stared straight at the marine but there was no recognition in them. They normally glowed with life, but now were as dead as those of a shark. He appeared fine physically, so he had to be in some kind of waking trance.

"I say, Mr. Scott, are you all right? Mr. Scott. Mr. Scott!" Pennywhistle gripped his left arm and shook it smartly. Sometimes a human touch could break a spell that was every bit as nasty as one cast by witches.

Scott blinked as he if had just been roused from a deep sleep. "Ah, Mr. Pennywhistle, good to see you. You look rather the worse for wear." He looked down at his own uniform. "Come to think of it, so do I. How did that happen?"

"You don't remember?"

"The last thing I remember was eating supper last night and then retiring to my cabin. How did I end up here?"

Pennywhistle had heard of men so devastated by battle that they could not recall even a single detail, the mind simply pretending that awful events had never happened at all. Most sufferers recovered eventually, but a few spiraled deeper into a world of make believe and withdrew entirely from society.

Scott slowly surveyed the deck and his face became a mask of revulsion. "My God, what happened here? This place looks like a slaughterhouse after a hurricane."

Pennywhistle decided to give Scott a sanitized idea of what had happened but avoid any details that might send him back into a trance.

"A great battle was fought, and you stood side by side with me. Our fleet has won the day and *Bellerophon* has taken two Spanish ships as prizes."

"You don't say! What an extraordinary turn of events. It must have been a very hard-fought contest. I do wish I could recall a little, but my mind is absolutely blank."

"I dare say your memory will return in time, Mr. Scott. For now, I would suggest you not worry about the dead but instead focus on the living. *Bellerophon* is badly damaged and we are desperately short-handed. You are an expert in several key areas and Mr. Cumby would welcome your help. I believe you will find him in the sailing master's cabin checking charts."

"Cumby? What happened to the Captain?"

"He gave his life to save the ship."

"My God!" Scott gasped. He took a deep breath and recovered a little. "Well, yes, I do want to be of help. I'd like to have some memory of being useful. All these poor men...." His expression became profoundly sad. "I had no idea that a battle won could look so melancholy. You say I fought alongside you, Mr. Pennywhistle?"

"Your conduct inspired all of those around you. You have every reason to be proud."

"Thank God I recalled my duty, even if I do not remember performing it. Looks like there is much to be done." He shook Pennywhistle's hand with a lackluster grip. "Thanks for putting me in the picture. Now I best be off."

Scott turned slowly on his heel and walked away with the leaden tread of a man on his way to the foreclosure sale of his soul. Pennywhistle wondered how long he would stay tethered to reality once he realized how high the butcher's bill had actually been. Scott gave new meaning to the term "walking wounded."

The ship resounded with *whumps, bonks* and *bzzzzts* as men armed with axes, hammers, and saws went about the business of clearing decks and effecting repairs. There were also shouts and curses that were uncharacteristic of *Bellerophon's* crew. Men sometimes fell asleep as they went about their tasks, and petty officers had to rouse them with yells. Other sailors bellowed curses as hands, made clumsy by fatigue, cut themselves on sharp edges, and fingers lacking in deftness made the unexpected acquaintance of the business ends of hammers.

The low moaning of the wounded could be heard all too clearly, since the windows of the Great Cabin had all been shot out. Their thin, melancholy voices blended together in a chorus of misery that was as haunting as it was pitiable. The combined groans, sighs, and hoarse whispers seemed less that of men than the distress of the ship herself.

Pennywhistle had not realized how much he unconsciously considered the ship a living entity rather than an ingenious assemblage of wood and rope. It was illogical to think thus, but no more so than designating a ship a "she" rather than an "it". Every ship had quirks of construction and unique sailing characteristics that made it easy to believe that an actual personality existed.

There was a distant background chorus of sad shouts, anxious hails, and hopeful halloos as men in boats roamed the debris-choked waters searching for friends and survivors. Four of *Bellerophon's* six boats had survived, and three had joined the search.

Most sailors could not swim, but numbers had survived by clinging to fallen spars or large chunks of floating timber. It was important that they be picked up before nightfall, since many were injured and would not survive the night. Those sailors not found until the next day would suffer painful skin ulcerations from extended exposure to salt water. Others would kill themselves through ingesting sea water, since battle brought on an insane thirst.

At least sharks would not be a problem. So close to the Mediterranean, there were few man-eating species.

The iron law of the sea prevailed. Assistance was rendered to all in distress regardless of nationality. The battle was no longer men against each other, but men against the sea.

The ship's 34-foot barge containing her animals had been tethered to her stern. The animals were terribly agitated and it was felt unwise to bring them aboard until preliminary repairs were completed. No men could be spared for their care, but a ship's boy named Doolittle had volunteered to board and feed them. An extended survey through his Ramsden showed Pennywhistle that the boy had an affinity for animals.

A sad sight caught his eye that reassured him his capacity for pity was not dead. James Barron grasped the left hand of his dead brother Thomas, who lay sprawled at his side. He gently stroked his brother's hair and murmured the same phrase over and over again. "I promised Pa I'd bring you home safe and sound, Tommy. And I will. I will." No one had the heart to separate the two.

Godwin bent down and began speaking softly to the boy. Pennywhistle could not hear the words, but the expression on the schoolmaster's face was full of kindness.

Pennywhistle overheard another sad conversation. The Purser was weeping as he spoke to a young man whose back was propped against a nine-pounder. It was Jewell's 17-year-old son, James. The boy's left leg had been amputated two inches below the knee. Pennywhistle wondered why he was on deck, but guessed Jewell had helped him there because the air on the quarterdeck was so much better than in the fetid cockpit.

"Do not cry, Father. I am all right, and glad to be here. I have only lost my leg, and it was in a good cause. I do ask you to give it a proper Christian burial."

The Purser's dark expression lightened; the boy comforting the man.

Pennywhistle counted himself very lucky that he had survived the day unhurt, save for a half-dozen large purple bruises whose collective impact was of as little moment as a child's stubbed toe. Yet the wounding of his spirit was bad and deep. Had an artist painted his soul in its current state, he would have feared to look upon the canvas.

He was dismayed by how the overwhelming torrents of raw emotion had killed his innocence. Gone was his Enlightenment confidence that mankind was fundamentally good, if often misguided. Gone was his belief that nobility of character lay within the reach of every man, wanting only the right circumstances for it to blossom. Gone was his faith that reason could always prevail over caprice and blind chance.

He needed sleep but he feared that it might not come easily. He remembered his father's nightmares, and realized that the landscape in the realm of Morpheus tonight might not be pleasant. Remaining awake suddenly seemed a very fine idea. He pondered three lessons that he had learned.

There was no nobility in death, and civilians who prated about the great honor of dying gloriously in battle needed a smart horse-whipping.

Survival owed much to being in the right place at the right time.

And if God was a watchmaker, he built damn bad timepieces.

But at least two of his fellow marine officers had received exactly what they wanted. Wemyss' spectacular death would no doubt become the stuff of legend. Higgins' replacement of

Bellerophon's flag would be celebrated whenever British gentlemen gathered in their clubs, sipped hot toddies, and recalled the battle of Trafalgar in front of roaring fires.

He spied Wilson walking disconsolately along the port side of the ship's waist with the studied deliberation of a drunk trying to navigate a straight line, though Wilson was as abstemious as himself. The lieutenant stared at his feet as he moved, apparently unwilling to meet the disapproving looks that were occasionally cast in his direction. Pennywhistle had no idea if the man felt shame or just preferred to ignore the contemptuous expressions of mere sailors and marines.

Wilson's questionable conduct today could never be proven in a court martial as unbecoming; courts-martial were inclined to be forgiving of gentlemen who had fought in fleet battles. He had furnished no direct, actionable evidence of the cowardice that Pennywhistle believed lay at his core, though he had proved as adept at evading responsibility as he was at manipulating a deck of cards.

The Ancient Ones at the Admiralty considered it important for the Sea Service to always put the best face on questionable actions of officers. Sustaining the myth that timorous or cowardly behaviors were utterly unknown to British officers had great propaganda value; telling the unvarnished truth had none. When news of the victory reached home, there would be an outpouring of celebrations and joy such as Great Britain had never seen. The actions of a single officer would not be allowed to diminish that.

Pennywhistle's bitterness toward Wilson remained unabated, but he realized that Wilson faced an odd dilemma. He would forever be known as a "Trafalgar Man", but Wilson would never be able to boast of his role and would probably resign his commission quietly when the ship reached Gibraltar.

Then it hit him and he slapped his forehead at his misapprehension. His line of reasoning was entirely wrong. Wilson was as clever as he was devoid of heroic attributes. He would indeed resign his commission, but he would construct a narrative that served his interest.

Once *Bellerophon* and her crew departed Gibraltar, Wilson could make up any story that he liked. Ships and officers came and went with great frequency at "The Gib." Naval officers would only see a polished gentleman who had been present at the greatest naval battle of the current wars. He would be loath to talk about his experience, a reluctant hero, yet if pressed could supply any number of convincing details. Such an agreeable gentleman wishing a friendly game of cards would undoubtedly find many officers eager to accommodate him.

It was irony indeed that a battle that had ended the careers of so many good men would probably enhance that of a man who was as far from being a hero as a Mother Superior was from a streetwalker. Lady Justice was not only blind, but apparently deaf and dumb as well.

Or was she? He turned his head for few seconds as one of the ship's parrots in the barge squawked at Doolittle, and when he turned back, Wilson had disappeared from view. He had gone over the side at the point where the boarding nets and bulwarks had been blasted away by cannon fire.

"Man overboard! Man overboard!" Pennywhistle shouted reflexively. Men normally would have come running, but in their exhausted state they merely plodded.

"Get a boat hook! Get a boat hook!" The 40-foot-long pole with an iron head was Wilson's only chance, since all of the ship's boats were out searching for survivors.

"Who is it?" asked Jepson.

"Wilson," said another sailor.

"Oh," said a third sailor.

The other three men approaching to assist exchanged cynical glances.

The party of six headed toward the point of Wilson's departure with the speed of turtles lacking hind legs. The lower decks had their own way of judging an officer's worth.

Pennywhistle raced to the side, unfurled his Ramsden, and pointed it downward to see if Wilson had survived the fall. He had, but his face wore a look of sheer terror as his arms flailed in the crimson waters. "Help! Help!" he shouted, his voice that of a man knowing his death was mere moments away.

Pennywhistle looked down at the point where Wilson had fallen. The deck was badly slicked with blood, yet Wilson possessed good sea legs and a watchful eye. Wilson had not fallen; he had been pushed. That would have been unthinkable under ordinary circumstances, but today was anything but ordinary. Men were exhausted, tempers short, and patience thin. Good men had died, and a bad officer remaining alive might have caused a disgruntled man to take precipitate action.

Pennywhistle shook his head in astonishment. Wilson still possessed a gambler's luck. Or perhaps it was his magic ring. *Ha!* Pennywhistle smiled at the idea of magic playing any role in the affairs of men.

Wilson's shouts had attracted a passing cutter that was now gliding toward him with a short boat hook extended. A few seconds later, Wilson grasped the pole and was pulled aboard, half drowned and wholly terrified, but likely to make a full recovery.

That drama concluded, Pennywhistle walked slowly back to the quarterdeck, wondering who among the crew had been moved to murder. He disliked mysteries remaining unsolved, but right now his mind was too tired to begin considering suspects. Besides, in the interests of morale, this mystery might best be left without resolution.

"Ooooh! Ooooh! Ooooh!" Jobu proudly offered him Wilson's watch.

Pennywhistle smiled and accepted it. "Just isn't Wilson's day, is it?"

Saunders positively danced up to Pennywhistle and clapped him on the shoulder. "She is all right! By God, she is all right!"

"Who is, Mr. Saunders?"

"My mother! She had been gravely ill for some time. Mrs. Taffy ate my letters from home, but I just discovered that she missed one. My mother has made a full recovery."

"Congratulations, Mr. Saunders. It is wonderful to see someone receive good news.

Saunders raced off to tell others of his blessed fortune.

Cumby walked up to him with a grave look on his face. "A word if you please, Mr. Pennywhistle."

"What is it, sir?

"I bear sad tidings. I feel all of the officers should know, but I would keep it from the men until the basic repairs are complete. I had my glass out just now and noticed that the lights indicating the commander of the fleet's presence on *Victory* have not been lit. Those lights are, however, showing on *Eurylaus*. Ah! I see you understand."

"Nelson is dead?" said Pennywhistle quietly, the surprise in his voice nearly as great as the shock. "So, Collingwood is now in command and has transferred his flag to a frigate that is undamaged. I confess I have trouble believing Nelson is gone. He has always seemed curiously indestructible; losing an arm, an eye, and suffering several concussions, yet never failing to perform his duty in an exemplary way. Though I suppose his death should not surprise me. He was always in the thick of every battle and generally found at the point of greatest danger."

"True," said Cumby. "And he was very conspicuous to the enemy. I am sure French sharpshooters in the tops were gunning for him. With those glittering decorations on his coat, he would have been easy to spot. I know many asked him to dress drably and pay closer attention to his personal safety, but he would not hear of it. His sense of honor was a part of his makeup."

Cumby shook his head and sighed. "A hero like that comes along once in a thousand years. What will our Navy do without him?"

Pennywhistle thought carefully before replying. "I think, Mr. Cumby, that we may take heart that his spirit yet lives. He has infused every captain and officer in the fleet with his beliefs, confidence, and methods of success. He has, in effect, trained disciples to continue his work. The tradition of victory that he has established will continue well beyond the time when Bonaparte is toppled."

"There is much consolation in what you say, Mr. Pennywhistle. I have been told that it was his wish that his body be preserved and brought home for a proper burial. Where do you think that will be, the Abbey or St. Paul's?"

"St. Paul's, I would say, Mr. Cumby. The Abbey is already jammed with heroic dead, while there is room at the Cathedral to make his tomb large and inspiring. I am sure that he will also receive a grand funeral reflecting the gratitude of the nation. As I gaze upon the victorious fleet surrounding our *Bellerophon*, I am reminded of what is written on the tomb of the designer of St. Paul's. I believe that it would furnish a suitable epitaph for our immortal admiral. *Lector, si momumentum requiris circumspice.*" Pennywhistle smiled like a mathematician who had arrived at a correct equation.

Cumby returned a smile of embarrassment. "My Latin has suffered from years at sea. Could you translate?"

"Happily, sir. 'Reader, if you seek his monument, look around you.'"

Cumby hand squeezed his lower lip as he thought. "I like that! I like that very much! It is a fine way to look at things. Nelson forged this fleet into the superb fighting instrument that it showed itself to be today. Now I must depart and pass my sad news along to others. I shall, however, repeat your observation." Cumby nodded and departed, his step just a little lighter now.

Cumby would likely receive promotion to Post Captain for the brilliant way that he had met the challenge of command. Pennywhistle hoped that he, too, would receive advancement, since he had captured an Eagle.

For all of his revulsion at today's events, he was uniquely fitted to the brotherhood of arms. The irony reminded him of a reformed drunk of his acquaintance who had enjoyed a long and successful career as a tavern owner. It was odd that a profession that he been hastily thrust into might well be the one to best employ his unusual array of talents, almost as if the same Destiny that Bonaparte so firmly believed in had given him a smart push.

His battle savagery had shown him more a Hun than a gentleman; hard to accept. Yet Huns charged while gentlemen talked. The excitement of battle was a drug as heady as opium, and it carried similarly disagreeable side effects. His true nature was considerably darker than he had imagined, and only marginally consonant with the generous-spirited idealist that he believed himself to be. Battle slew illusions with the same ruthlessness that it slew men.

Yet, the satisfaction that he felt from leading stalwart men in a desperate fight, your commands granting the power of life or death, could never to be found in civilian life. Command conferred a unique fellowship only possible when men placed their trust in you because you earned that trust. Good leaders were desperately needed to bring down a gifted tyrant like Bonaparte. If men such as he did not rise to the challenge, it might fall to lesser lights with the character of Peter Wilson.

A groggy Thomas shambled up to him, rubbing his head with one hand but extending the other in gratitude. "Mr. Pennywhistle, I owe you thanks. You saved my life."

"I did? How?"

"That palm heel thing from *savate*. I used it and it worked! A Frenchman's blade caused my life to flash before me, and then the memory of how you laid me low in the wardroom popped into my head. That lieutenant suffered fatally from my demonstration of your art!"

He shook Pennywhistle's hand vigorously.

"Glad to be of service, Mr. Thomas."

Music swelled in intensity and delighted his ears. *Eine Kleine Nactmusik* was one of Mozart's most sprightly compositions, and the cheerful strains acted as a balm. He wondered why he had not heard the music earlier. Likely he had incurred some hearing loss.

The odd trio of a trumpet, a bassoon, and a tuba gave a new interpretation to Mozart, but music had made a genuine contribution to today's success, and now it was helping put heart into weary men.

He heard a feline yowl, followed by cheers and clapping. He turned toward the noise and and quickly deduced what had happened. Mild-mannered Mau had hidden in pile of splinters. Shredder had been prowling a deck rich in treasure for his kind and had no idea that he had walked into an ambush.

Mau was smaller than Screwloose, but faster. His jaws had clamped down on Shredder's neck and he'd shaken the rat violently, killing it like a crocodile killing an antelope. Man continued shaking the dead rat in triumph, announcing a new feline king of *Bellerophon*. *Cry havoc and let slip the cats of war,* thought Pennywhistle. Battle changed more than the affairs of men.

A powder monkey trudged by, looking bewildered and friendless. His face was covered in grime and dust, and he looked much older than his probable ten years. Pennywhistle moved to console him, but Mau acted first. He dropped Shredder and dashed over to the boy. He began rubbing himself energetically against his side and purring. The boy reached down to pet him and smiled. *God bless the beasts and the children.*

Mary Stevenson strolled close with her newborn. He tipped his hat to her and smiled. It was extraordinary that a new life had been brought into the world under the worst imaginable conditions. Even in the midst of carnage, life found a way to prevail. Word had quickly spread that the child was to be named Trafalgar, and even the weariest of sailors smiled as she passed by.

He marveled at the resiliency of women. To give birth in the macabre conditions of the cockpit, and a few hours later to have the mental and physical strength to walk decks strewn with the detritus of battle, showed him that women who braved the perils of the sea could bear any hardship.

A red-eyed Nancy Overton walked alongside Mary, her right arm round her friend's shoulder. Her face bore the look of a woman who was too exhausted to shed any more tears. Instead of succumbing to her grief, however, she had continued caring for the wounded and her friend's child. Mary's husband, at least, had come through the battle without a scratch.

He was surprised to see Whyte talking to Douglas. He would have expected Whyte to be extremely busy, but he was probably taking a much needed break, just as Pennywhistle was. Even with a cast iron stomach and a will of steel, there was probably a limit to how much blood and gore a man could take, penned up in a small, dark, noisome space for hours on end with scores of groaning, dying men clamoring for his attention.

Whyte's leather apron was stained a deep scarlet and flecked with tiny globs of flesh, appearing more fitted to a butcher who had just come from slaughtering an entire pasture of cows; not unexpected, considering *Bellerophon's* heavy casualty list, yet symbolic of what many sailor's believed about his skills with a knife.

Pennywhistle could not quite hear what Whyte was saying, but he was clearly upset, waving his bloody hands with considerable agitation. He finally managed to lip read the word that Whyte was saying over and over again. "Rum, rum, rum!" Douglas nodded patiently, as he absentmindedly fed cheese to Archer.

Pennywhistle gathered that the surgeon had run out of rum; unsurprising, considering the awful butcher's bill. Still, Whyte looked a little unsteady on his feet, and his color was more florid than usual. Pennywhistle wondered if some of the rum was for Whyte's own consumption. He also wondered if Whyte had washed his hands even once since his long ordeal began.

MacFarlane and Combs were pulling hard with the reverse ends of boarding axes to separate a mound of tangled rope into individual strands that could be chopped apart. Pennywhistle wondered where they found the energy to go about such a burdensome task as if they were just starting their day.

MacFarlane looked well pleased with himself. He deserved to, considering his fine performance with the cutlass. Pennywhistle had seen him kill at least six Frenchmen, and his towering strength had been a beacon of encouragement to his fellow sailors. Pennywhistle noticed that the French major's katana lay at MacFarlane's side: the tall Scot was a most appropriate new owner. "Gorilla" MacFarlane was exactly the sort of man who rated an appointment as a petty officer. He would speak to Mr. Cumby about that.

Combs had proven himself an exceptional marksmen and a good improviser, as had his friend, Warwick. He owed his life and his Eagle to both men, and they would receive the promised promotions. Combs would make a good corporal; he would jump the more experienced Warwick to sergeant.

He could not see the men he had lost as expendable ciphers. They would be sorely missed. He wondered if weeping would come later, and decided that it was possible. Sheer fatigue had rendered his tear ducts as dry as the Qattara Depression.

Higgins came walking slowly over, the fatigue in his step consistent with that in his sleepy green eyes. Yet the confident way in which he held his head and the firmness of his bearing made him seem considerably taller than his five-foot, four-inch stature. Bandages indicated that he had been twice wounded, once in the left arm and once in the right. He smiled wanly at Pennywhistle.

"Mr. Higgins, the wounded properly belong in sick berth, not strolling about the deck taking their evening's ease," said Pennywhistle with friendly sarcasm.

"I declined to have myself listed as wounded," said Higgins with quiet pride. "The bullet that hit my arm skimmed off only a small bit of skin, and the sword cut was not deep and missed the bone. I had no wish to take up space that properly belonged to the badly injured."

"Such behavior is certainly consistent with the hero that you told me you wanted to be. Do you feel changed, now that you have met the lion?"

Higgins tilted his head and brought his hands together in a steeple.. "No... and yes. No because I made mistakes which indicate that the schoolboy has not yet been replaced by the soldier. Fortunately, luck, sound men, and your training rescued me from the worst consequences of those follies. Yes because I feel that I have lived a lifetime in the space of a few hours.

"I cannot believe how badly I underestimated the enemy. They were... fine...even gallant men." He shook his head several times. "Those back home... are... well... misinformed. I am grateful that your plain talk disabused me of my more dangerous illusions.

"I killed a French Lieutenant with my sword; saw him die right in front of my eyes. He made a peculiar snorting, piggish noise as he fell. It was extraordinary. One second there was a man, a he, a something. In the blink of an eye there was a husk, an it, a nothing. You could kick, hit, even bite that husk and it would feel nothing.

"I felt sorry for the Lieutenant. He was just doing his duty. He was important in someone's life. I do not feel guilt, but I do feel regret. What I most certainly do not feel is hate."

Pennywhistle's eyes turned philosophical as he stroked his chin in thought. "I would say we both fought today not because we hated the people in front of us but because we loved the people behind us."

"Yes, yes that's it exactly," said Higgins with conviction. "And yet I would be hard pressed to put what I have seen and felt today in a manner that my father or Miss Lydia would understand. The lieutenant's death and battle itself are so... so..." His voice trailed off in exasperation.

"Ineffable is the word you seek, Mr Higgins. 'Too great, unusual or extreme to be described in speech or writing.'

"Yes, yes." Higgins looked skyward in thought. "That has the right ring to it. I confess to a certain measure of confusion about how God administers justice. Why am I still alive, while Captain Cooke, a genuine hero who performed flawlessly, lies stiff and cold, waiting to be sewn into a canvas shroud? I was at his side when he passed and looked directly into his eyes as the light departed them. They held no fear and spoke more eloquently than any heroic last words. I shall never forget that moment.

"I know I am different in one important respect. There came a desperate moment after Captain Cooke fell, when my feet frantically commanded me to flee below decks. Images of the greatest terror flooded my mind, and I came within a hair's breadth of yielding everything good in me to a moment of dishonorable insanity. At that instant, I saw Miss Lydia, my father, and you in my mind's eye. I knew I would rather die and have you all speak my name with honor than live and have you speak it with disgust.

"I then beheld the fear in the eyes of some of my men and knew they looked to me for reassurance. Had I deserted them, their faces would have haunted me for the rest of my days.

"Once that moment passed, a feeling of certitude came over me, and I knew that I would make it through the rest of the battle with honor. Still, I am far from a hero, and I appreciate the forbearance that you showed me when I rattled on about becoming one. You are the real hero, sir. Capturing an Eagle was a magnificent feat. If any justice remains in the world, you surely will be promoted to captain."

Pennywhistle's hand stroked his cheek, and his expression became that of a parent proud of a son. "You did a grand thing when you re-hoisted the flag, and I am guessing that it sprang from a concern for your men and the ship rather than yourself. You were simply doing what needed to be done. Am I right?"

"You are indeed, sir."

"So it was with me, Mr. Higgins. My chief motivation was tactical. I believed the standard's loss would undermine the French soldier's morale, since they regard those gilded raptors as nearly sacred things."

Higgins found his superior's remarks uncharacteristically disingenuous. "So you had no thoughts of fame and glory when you took the Eagle? None at all?"

Pennywhistle's leaned back and crossed his arms.. A half smile eased its way onto his face. "Well... maybe I was not entirely unmindful of the prospects for fame and distinction. And I will speculate that both might have made a brief appearance in your thoughts."

Both men laughed.

Higgins expression turned earnest.

"You acted brilliantly, sir, no matter what your motives. I also wish to thank you for the loan of your spare sword. It is indeed the weapon of a real fighting man."

"Please consider the sword not a loan, but a gift. You have wielded it with honor and earned the right to keep it."

Higgins blushed in embarrassment. "Mr. Pennywhistle, it is an extravagant present, and I do not wish to deprive you of —"

"Nonsense, Mr. Higgins," said Pennywhistle in a voice that brooked no argument. "I would say that the sword has found you, just as Excalibur's destiny was to belong to Arthur. I have merely served as a conduit."

"I don't know how to thank you, sir," said a pleased Higgins.

"Your performance today is thanks enough, and I ask only that you heed the inscription on its blade. 'Draw me only with honor and sheath me only with blood.'"

"I promise you, sir, this fine instrument will be used in the service of justice and virtue."

"Excellent! You spoke to me several times of wishing to be a hero, yet your discourse tells me that you believe that you have failed in that noble quest. Nothing could be farther from the truth. Realize that you are a hero, not because you felt no fear, but because you felt it yet refused its urgings. Dull men experience reduced impressions of everything, while perceptive men experience heightened ones. Most importantly, you taught your men courage by example, not words.

"I am honored that your regard of me may have helped guide your conduct. You may have made small tactical mistakes, everyone does, but Sergeant Dale has informed me that you never hesitated, nor left your men uncertain. Perhaps you flinched. That marks you as simply human. Your physical actions and the orders that you issued were sound.

"Feel no guilt about surviving battle. You bravery has earned you what I hope will be a long life; though, for better or worse, today has permanently branded you as a Royal Marine. The men that you meet from now on will always account you thus. It is said that a marine may leave the Service, but the marine never leaves the man."

"I confess that I feel closer to the people aboard than I ever have to any others," said Higgins with surprise in his voice. "That includes my father and my beloved. I feel the men aboard my brothers."

"The Brotherhood of Arms is small but real, Mr. Higgins, and your conduct has earned you a life long membership. When Henry the Fifth said, 'He who sheds his blood with me today shall be my brother,' he knew what he was talking about."

"I would be proud to call you a brother in arms, Mr. Pennywhistle."

"I consider that a high compliment, Mr. Higgins! I mourn the passing of Captain Cooke because he was a stellar member of our brethren. He will be buried at sea, but if he were interred in a churchyard near his home in Wiltshire, his tombstone might well bear the simple words: 'He died well and nobly.' It is what I would wish upon my own.

"Cooke died doing the thing he was best fitted for: commanding a fine ship with a brave crew in a great battle. He will be well remembered as a man who did much to safeguard the Realm. I cannot think of a better way to depart this life.

"We may not be able to choose the manner of our deaths, but we can certainly decide how we conduct our lives. Your manly comportment today tells me yours will be filled with honor and achievement. And I believe your suit with Miss Lydia can be... pressed with great advantage."

The prospect of his idealized love turning into something sexual was something that Higgins had been unwilling to consider before battle. His deliverance from extinction had not only given fire to his loins, it had dropped his voice a full octave. His freckled face flushed. He had met the lion and was ready to lie down with the lamb.

"Let us put aside this talk of war, Mr. Higgins, and look upon a sunset that is a lovely contrast to the mess that surrounds us. I think our troubled spirits require reminding that beauty still exists, even more than our bodies need the renewal of sleep. And yet, before we relax, one thing troubles me. I do not wish to embarrass you. but now seems a good time to speak out about it."

"What is that?"

"It's your uniform. Since it is badly cut up by the fight just past, you have the perfect excuse to purchase a new one. My own is so heavily soaked in blood and tattered by lead that it will have no further use save as laundry rags. A heroic man needs attire that matches his heroic conduct. *Vestus virum reddit,* as Seneca so aptly stated two millennia ago. Well tailored clothing inspires additional commitment in the men because they know that a gentleman commands them.

"Your uniform is a reasonably good fit made of fair material, but it could be much improved. This is likely the best product provincial tailoring could devise, but if you will accept my help you can do much better. When I visit my tailor to be fitted for a new uniform, why not accompany me?"

Higgins was crestfallen. "My father sent me to a good tailor, damn it!" He felt very bold adding in the curse; he really was a man now. "The best tailor in Belfast is my father's boon companion, and he serves only the most elite clientele! Everyone at home said I looked really splendid in my uniform."

Pennywhistle adopted the patient tone of an assayer informing a miner that a nugget of gold was actually only iron pyrite. "I am sure of that. I mean no disrespect to your father. I merely say that Gieve's of Savile Row will make you look like a Guardsman rather than a footslogger elevated to command: those melancholy chaps who never seem to quite belong in the mess and drink red wine with fish though they now sport a gorget. You should dress for the rank that you aspire to, rather than the one that you currently enjoy. You may think clothing a small thing, but it is from attention to such details that a man may exceed the sum of his parts."

Higgins considered his superior's words carefully and replied as if an important truth had just been pointed out to him. "I seem to recall that you once said that good clothing causes people to focus their attention on the man rather than his attire. A new uniform would be a fine use of my prize money. Even more importantly, it would make Miss Lydia proud!"

"It would indeed, Mr. Higgins. She could tell her woman friends how the original had been destroyed in heroic battle. It would be terrible to go through life resembling the scarlet scarecrows that we are now." Both men smiled.

Pennywhistle wiggled the big toe that protruded from the gap in his left boot. "A visit to Hoby my boot-maker is a must as well, though I suppose my exposed digit gives literal meaning to the saying, 'He stood toe to toe with the enemy.'"

Both men laughed like merry drunks, aware that the jest was lame. Laughter was the best anodyne of all, for both physical and psychic pain.

Pennywhistle pointed to the sunset and Higgins turned his gaze toward it, a look of quiet satisfaction on his face.

The blood-red sunset fading to the color of fireside embers was more beautiful than anything that even the great JMW Turner could have conveyed. Only Mother Nature could render such a brilliantly subtle blending of colors. Yet, though Higgins looked content, contemplation of the sky brought Pennywhistle unease rather than the repose that he expected.

Mother Nature had a fine sense of irony, often cloaking the dangerous with the beautiful. At the edge of the horizon lurked a creeping blob of dark clouds with the yellow-grey tint of bile. It was easy to miss if you were beguiled by the sunset. Overton's words came back to him. That ragged patch of sickening color was Nature's warning to those who understood the sea.

The wind was rising gradually and the wave peaks growing sharper as the troughs deepened. The change showed every sign of increasing in severity. By afternoon tomorrow, his battered ship would likely be facing formidable waves.

He recalled the terror of a hurricane off Antigua. Hour after hour, his ship had buried her bow in a wall of writhing water and then clawed her way upwards at a 45-degree angle to meet the wave crest 60 feet above. Before she took the next plunge down, she exposed her rudder and half of her bottom.

Mother Nature cared not at all about the petty quarrels of men. When such disputes blinded them to her incontestable supremacy, she refreshed their memories. The lesson she would administer on the morrow would be as harsh as it was cruel. There would be no rest for the weary.

Dale reported in and snapped to a parade attention so exact that it could have been a plate in a manual of arms. He then executed a palm down salute so crisp that his hand appeared a fusion of flesh and starch. How the man did that so well after such a grueling ordeal was a mystery solvable only by fellow NCOs.

Pennywhistle returned his salute tiredly and let out a distinctly unmilitary sigh. "I thank you for the short reprieve, Sarn't. Clearing this mess is like battling a Hydra: finish off one task and another rises to take its place."

He swallowed the last of his coffee, let out a final sigh of exasperation, squared his shoulders, and tried to decide which section of this wood and rope purgatory should be tackled first. It was going to be a very long night.

THE END

Tom Pennywhistle will return in:
A Rogue in the Mirror

Life is a trickster. It revels in head-butting you with new knowledge that shakes your confidence in shibboleths long taken for granted. One might well think that the details of the greatest battle of the Age of Fighting Sail would have been settled two centuries ago, but I found to my shock that it was not so. I discovered four discrepancies existing in the accounts of *Bellerophon's* role at Trafalgar, all written by respected modern authors. Trying to sort out those contradictions caused me considerable hair-pulling and numerous sleepless nights.

According to most accounts, *Bellerophon* fired her first raking broadside into the Spanish ship *Bahama,* yet one written by a reputable historian maintains it was the Spanish vessel *Monarcha*. Most historians say *Bellerophon* repulsed two boarding attempts, but one says three. The final position of *Bellerophon* at the end of the battle varies depending on the age of the diagram you consult. *Bellerophon's* crew count was either 540 or 590, depending on your choice of historian.

Historians do agree on one thing about *Bellerophon's* role: she suffered the second highest number of casualties of any ship in the battle.

The reader will have discovered the choices that I made, and I freely admit that I made them primarily on the basis of what best served the cause of drama. While I was trained as a historian, my main task as a novelist is to amuse and delight, not to play a historical Sherlock Holmes who belongs in a university lecturing rows of somnolent students.

Historical novels can be a fun way to learn history, but they are far more about creating impressions and conjuring moods than they are about providing a scrupulously accurate recounting of facts. Novels can speculate in ways that are impermissible to responsible historians; novels specialize in "what ifs" and "might have beens."

When JMW Turner created a large painting of the Battle of Trafalgar, he was roundly criticized for its inaccuracy, though he had carefully interviewed many of its participants. He replied that his intention was to summarize the battle in a single image and give viewers a general feeling for the event rather than an accurate rendering of its particulars.

I have followed Turner's course with this work, trying to give a general sense of the battle by focusing on a single ship and fleshing out details that are only hinted at in official accounts. No one participant is never granted the God's eye view that is favored by historians writing long after the fact. Add in gigantic thunderheads of thick smoke, and the average participant sees only a fragment of a fragment.

While this is a work of fiction, the technical details about ships, weapons, uniforms, medicine, and general procedures are accurate, as is the chronology of events. Most of the characters were real people. Tom Pennywhistle is fictional, but other marine, naval, and warrant officers are accurately named, though in many cases so little is known about them that I had to invent personalities based on a very few facts and deeds. In other cases, I have taken certain liberties with character outlooks and conduct in the interest of story-telling.

Tom Pennywhistle plays many of the roles that 1st Lieutenant Peter Connelly actually performed on *Bellerophon*. Pennywhistle's character is loosely based on the real life Royal Marine Captain Thomas Inch, who was an authentic hero. 2nd Lieutenant Luke Higgins was real, but little is known about him, so I borrowed the biography and experience of 16-year-old John Nicolas, who fought as a lieutenant of marines on another ship. Wilson existed, but unlike his fictional counterpart, he fought well and honorably.

The real Wilson did gamble, but he was not a professional like his counterpart in the book. Many of the observations about card playing were given me by a high stakes Las Vegas gambler whom I have come to know. I can only judge their accuracy by his success, which is considerable. Like Pennywhistle, I am a confirmed non-gambler.

I dislike blackening the memory of an honorable man like James Wemyss, but it was necessary to point out the dangers of an unfit commander. As far as I can tell, Wemyss was an exceptionally able officer not burdened with any dangerous affliction. He suffered eight wounds in the course of the battle and died of shock from the amputation of his arm.

Cooke, Cumby, Saunders, and Nelson are drawn as closely to life as I could make them. I was able to discover little about the remaining three naval officers aboard *Bellerophon*. Cumby is the most accurately rendered character, since he wrote about his experiences thirty years later. His writing was done at the request of his son and is considered one of the most accurate and detailed accounts of the fight. His gentle modesty comes through clearly. He was promoted to post captain at the end of 1805 for his gallant conduct at Trafalgar.

Nancy Overton and Mary Stevenson are fictional but based on the real life characters of two women aboard *The Royal Sovereign*. Their outlooks and philosophies are typical of women who followed their husbands to sea.

The final words of Edward Overton were actually those of Confederate general Thomas J. "Stonewall" Jackson.

Pennywhistle's quip about the convenience of a marine dying during drill rather than in battle is a direct quote from Field Marshal Sir Bernard Law Montgomery of World War Two fame.

Marines Combs and Warwick are fictional as well, but express the beliefs and attitudes of the ordinary marine. MacFarlane and Jepson perform the same function for the viewpoints of ordinary sailors.

Mrs. Taffy was the wardroom goat of another ship that fought at Trafalgar. The rum tippling goat actually did consume an officer's letters and was banished from the wardroom for a month. It took the officer in question eight months to obtain the information lost in the letters.

Screwloose was a cat that I grew up with and a great hunter. He killed mice, rats, lizards, squirrels, rabbits, hedgehogs, bats, and even several rattlesnakes. Cats were common aboard ships and were intended to keep the rat population to a minimum. Cats like Screwloose spread throughout the globe on 17th century English ships.

Dogs were not as common at sea but were still found with some frequency: Admiral Collingwood's constant companion was his rat terrier, Bounce, who was washed overboard five years after Trafalgar.

Parrots and monkeys were often brought back as souvenirs when ships visited the Tropics. 18th and 19th century newspapers of port towns and cities contain numerous ads offering them for sale.

I have sometimes transplanted events that took place on other ships to *Bellerophon's* decks. A baby actually was born during the course of the battle and was christened Trafalgar. A supposedly dead man about to be cast overboard did come back to life at the last second. A dying consumptive did render honorable service.

The episode of Punch and Judy cutting the ropes on the gun port lids is based on two oblique references I encountered. However, since I could find no mention of ship's names and battles associated with such daring action, I would assume it was a very rare occurrence.

The French 67th Regiment did serve onboard *Aigle*. They brought their Eagle into battle but it was never captured.

The heroic replacement of *Bellerophon's* flag did occur as described, but was carried out by a petty officer, not a commissioned one.

A grenade did almost vaporize *Bellerophon*. The explosion blew open the door to the Gunner's supply room but blew shut the one to the powder magazine.

Boarding helmets were a uniquely American invention and found only on their ships. The British were aware of them and thought them good ideas, but never adopted them for their own Naval Service.

The idea of a sailor strapping a Brown Bess bayonet to his arm may sound like something out of pulp fiction, but the always innovative Lord Cochrane sometimes had his sailors do so.

The Brown Bess used a . 685 ball in combat, though I have seen estimates ranging ranging up to .731. My figure is based on the rounds used by Sir William Congreve during official tests for the Board of Ordnance. Since .67 rounds are sometimes recovered on old battlefields, I have concluded that as fouling became a problem during an extended fight, men switched to a smaller size round.

It is also important to remember that Brown Bess barrels were manufactured in cottage industry conditions, not those of modern mass production with consistent standards. Though the bore was officially .75, the actual diameter might be somewhere between .73 and .79. I once owned an India Pattern Brown Bess with a bore of .77. Ball size likely varied as well to accommodate those differences.

Though I understand how some might be skeptical, death by flying head was not a freak occurrence. I have found shipboard examples of it from the Seven Years War up to World War 2.

The hurricane following Trafalgar was a deadly, five-day affair that caused more casualties than the battle itself. The British were hard pressed but did not lose a single vessel. Many of their prizes sank, however, and several were recaptured, significantly reducing the amount of prize money paid out. The British government somewhat made up for that by being generous in the granting of pensions and special financial awards. I thought about including the hurricane in this volume, but realized that story merited a book in itself with the theme of men against the sea rather than men against men.

I have used terms "larboard" and "port" interchangeably. Though "port" eventually triumphed simply because it sounded different from "starboard," both terms were in use at this time.

Pennywhistle's Ferguson Rifle was a real weapon. Only about 100 were ever made, and the few specimens that still exist fetch a very high price on the rare occasions when they are put up for sale.

Blancpain and *Breguet* still make fine watches. The top of the line *Blancpain* retails for $40,000, and the best of the *Breguet* line for $136,000.

A form of the duel described in the prologue actually took place. A British officer challenged a 16-year-old American midshipman to a duel in 1797. The British officer was an experienced duelist; the midshipman had never fought one. An American lieutenant suggested the midshipman might reduce the odds by reducing pistol distance to three feet. The duel was fought thus and the midshipman prevailed, killing his opponent.

Bellerophon was painted with large buff stripes along her gunports, just as Nelson's *Victory* was. Two centuries of maritime artists who rendered *Victory* with yellow stripes had things wrong. Microscopic fragments discovered by a laser scan during her last refit revealed the true color of her stripes.

Establishing exact times for particular actions was a problem, since there was no master atomic clock with which officers could synchronize their watches. The first shots of Trafalgar were fired between 11:30 and 12:00, depending on whose account you read. The Battle of Waterloo started about the same time of day with similar disagreements about the exact time of the opening shots.

The most surprising thing that I discovered in my research was the astonishing lack of training given sailors in edged weapon combat. Considering the careful attention paid to cannon drill, I had naturally assumed that the same care was given to instructing men in the use of hand held weapons. It made me look at all of the accounts that I had read of heroic boarding parties in a very new light. All were apparently assemblages of madly zealous amateurs who had to trust their success to the fire in their hearts because they had little skill with the blades in their hands.

The hardest part of writing this work was giving multiple characters a historically accurate mindset. Maslow's Hierarchy of Needs, ranging from basic physiological needs at the bottom to self actualization at the top, can be profitably applied to any period in history, but the way those needs are interpreted varies considerably depending on the place and century.

A very unusual book about the battle greatly assisted my understanding of the mindset of the Napoleonic Royal Navy. *Seize the Fire* by Adam Nicolson, the great grandson of Virginia Wolfe, is an intellectual history of Trafalgar focusing not on ships and events but on the thought processes of the officers who fought the battle. It is more a literary work than a historical one, but it covers a topic that is too often neglected or ignored entirely.

Most of the best works about Trafalgar have only been written in the last fifteen years. You would think everything there was to know about such an important battle would have been penned long ago, but that is far from the case. New materials have come to light with surprising frequency, and a new generation of nautical historians is examining old documents focused on history from the ground up rather than recounting battles chiefly from "The Great Man" point of view.

A case in point is the discovery of a coffin-sized cache of dispatches written by British commanding officers only hours after the end of a number of famous sea battles; some even contain bloodstains and penmanship made erratic by the writer just having lost several fingers. The documents were assembled in the 1820s with a view to publication, but the man in charge of the project died unexpectedly and the documents were stored away for a successor who never appeared, and so lost to history. They were rediscovered by historian Samuel Willis in 2010 and form the basis for his fascinating book, *In the Hour of Victory*.

If you enjoyed my book, I would encourage you to explore some non-fiction offerings about the battle. If you hated my book, you would have an even better reason to discover the real story of Trafalgar. Historical novels are great introductions to many periods and people, but they are just that: introductions. The truths on which good historical novels are based deserve to be explored in detail and you will be richly rewarded if you do so.

Suggestions for Further Reading:

The Billy Ruffian: Bellerophon and the Downfall of Napoleon by David Cordingly. *Bellerophon* saw more fleet actions than any other ship of the line and this easy-to-like work gives a detailed account of them. When Napoleon surrendered himself to the British, he did so to Captain Frederick Maitland of *Bellerophon*.

The Trafalgar Companion: the Complete Guide to History's Most Famous Sea Battle and the Life of Lord Nelson by Mark Adkins. It is a coffee table size work and expensive, but the best single resource on the battle. It is well written and beautifully illustrated with plenty of original art, as well as many classic images. In addition to giving a through account of the Trafalgar Campaign and its aftermath, it covers in detail officers and men, ships and seamanship, guns, gunnery and tactics, and command and control. It overflows with pictures and photos of uniforms, weapons, and ships as well as lots of maps, graphs, charts, tables, and cutaway views of ships. It tells you everything you need to know about the men who fought the battle, why and how it was fought, and the successes and mistakes made by both sides. For Nelson fans, there is plenty of information about their hero. Highly recommended.

Nelson's Trafalgar: the Battle that Changed the World by Mark Adkins. This much smaller volume focuses chiefly on Nelson and his crews. It gives you a general overview of weapons and tactics but it much more focused on the human side of the battle.

Trafalgar: The Men, the Battle, the Storm by Phil Craig and Tim Clayton. Well written and action oriented, it does a particularly good job of giving Spanish and French points of view and its descriptions of the post battle hurricane and the attendant human suffering are superb.

Trafalgar: An Eye Witness History by Tom Pocock. It delivers exactly what the title promises; plenty of gripping, gritty, riveting accounts, mostly British, by the men who fought the battle.

The Enemy at Trafalgar: The Battle from the Perspective of the French and Spanish Navies and Their Sailors by Edward Fraser. This is the story of "the other guys" and it is a compelling one. The French sought to bury the memory of Trafalgar until late in the 19th century, but the Spanish celebrated the gallant conduct of their men even in the immediate aftermath of the battle.

Seize the Fire: Heroism, Duty, and Nelson's Trafalgar by Adam Nicholson. An off-beat sort of book for those tired of reading the usual blood and guts accounts of sea battles. This is an intellectual and philosophical consideration of Trafalgar. It much less a recounting of events than a revelation of the thought processes which brought them about. This is a real breath of fresh salt air.

Nelson's Navy: The Ships, Men, and Organisation 1793-1815 by Brian Lavery. Probably the best single volume on the Royal Navy of the Napoleonic Wars. Lavery is plodding writer, but an excellent researcher. This work is packed with information, though sadly all of its illustrations are in black and white.

ABOUT THE AUTHOR

John Danielski worked his way through university as a living history interpreter at historic Fort Snelling, the birthplace of Minnesota. For four summers, he played a US soldier of 1827; he wore the uniform, performed the drills, demonstrated the volley fire with other interpreters, and even ate the food. A heavy blue wool tailcoat and black shako look smart and snappy, but are pure torture to wear on a boiling summer day.

He has a practical, rather than theoretical, perspective on the weapons of the time. He has fired either replicas or originals of all of the weapons mentioned in his works with live rounds, six- and twelve-pound cannon included. The effect of a 12-pound cannonball on an old Chevy four door must be seen to be believed.

He has a number of marginally useful University degrees, including a magna cum laude degree in history from the University of Minnesota. He is a Phi Beta Kappa and holds a black belt in Tae-Kwon-do. He has taught history at both the secondary and university levels and also worked as a newspaper editor.

His literary mentors were C. S. Forester, Bruce Catton, and Shelby Foote.

He lives quietly in the Twin Cities suburbs with his faithful companion: Sparkle, the wonder cat.

IF YOU ENJOYED THIS BOOK
Please write a review.
This is important to the author and helps to get the word out
to others
Visit

PENMORE PRESS
www.penmorepress.com

All Penmore Press books are available directly through our website, amazon.com, Barnes and Noble and Nook, Sony Reader, Apple iTunes, Kobo books and via leading bookshops across the United States, Canada, the UK, Australia and Europe.

More Books by John Danielski and others below.

BLUE WATER
SCARLET TIDE
BY
JOHN DANIELSKI

It's the summer of 1814, and Captain Thomas Pennywhistle of the Royal Marines is fighting in a New World war that should never have started, a war where the old rules of engagement do not apply. Here, runaway slaves are your best source of intelligence, treachery is commonplace, and rough justice is the best one can hope to meet—or mete out. The Americans are fiercely determined to defend their new nation and the Great Experiment of the Republic; British Admiral George Cockburn is resolved to exact revenge for the burning of York, and so the war drags on. Thanks to Pennywhistle's ingenuity, observant mind, and military discipline, a British strike force penetrates the critically strategic region of the Chesapeake Bay. But this fight isn't just being waged by soldiers, and the collateral damage to innocents tears at Pennywhistle's heart.

As his past catches up with him, Pennywhistle must decide what is worth fighting for, and what is worth refusing to kill for —especially when he meets his opposite number on the wrong side of a pistol.

PENMORE PRESS
www.penmorepress.com

Capital's Punishment
by
John Danielski

The White House is in flames, the Capitol a gutted shell. President Madison is in hiding. Organized resistance has collapsed, and British soldiers prowl the streets of Washington.

Two islands of fortitude rise above the sea of chaos—one scarlet, one blue. Royal Marine Captain Thomas Pennywhistle has no wish to see the young American republic destroyed; he must strike a balance between his humanity and his passion for absolute victory. Captain John Tracy of the United States Marines hazards his life on the battlefield, but he must also fight a powerful conspiracy that threatens the country from within.

Pennywhistle and Tracy are forced into an uneasy alliance that will try the resolve of both. Together, they will question the depth of their loyalties as heads and hearts argue for the fate of a nation

PENMORE PRESS
www.penmorepress.com

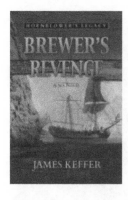

BREWER'S REVENGE
BY
JAMES KEFFER

Admiral Horatio Hornblower has given Commander William Brewer captaincy of the captured pirate sloop *El Dorado.* Now under sail as the HMS *Revenge,* its new name suits Brewer's frame of mind perfectly. He lost many of his best men in the engagement that seized the ship, and his new orders are to hunt down the pirates who have been ravaging the trade routes of the Caribbean sea.

But Brewer will face more than one challenge before he can confront the pirate known as El Diabolito. His best friend and ship's surgeon, Dr. Spinelli, is taking dangerous solace in alcohol as he wrestles with demons of his own. The new purser, Mr. Allen, may need a lesson in honest accounting. Worst of all, Hornblower has requested that Brewer take on a young ne'er-do-well, Noah Simmons, to remove him from a recent scandal at home. At twenty-three, Simmons is old to be a junior midshipman, and as a wealthy man's son he is unaccustomed to working, taking orders, or suffering privations.

William Brewer will need to muster all his resources to ready his crew for their confrontation with the Caribbean's most notorious pirate. In the process, he'll discover the true price of command.

PENMORE PRESS
www.penmorepress.com

Penmore Press
Challenging, Intriguing, Adventurous, Historical and Imaginative

www.penmorepress.com